TALES FROM RAMNON

JAE MAZER

FEATHERED

Copyright © 2025 by Feathered Tentacle Press

All rights reserved.

No part of this book may be reproduced in any form or by any electronic or mechanical means, including information storage and retrieval systems, without written permission from the author, except for the use of brief quotations in a book review.

Any references to names and places are fictional and are constructs of the author. Any offense the references produce is unintentional and in no way reflects the reality of any people or locations involved.

Interior graphics are original illustrated art by **Robert Elrod, LLC**. and may not be copied or duplicated without permission from the artist.

Exterior cover art by **Ruth Anna Evans**

I came up with the idea for Fort Ramnon during conversations with my dad while he was battling cancer. We talked about life, love, loss, and the possible fantastical worlds waiting for us on the other side of it all. This series is a direct result of this conversation that took place during the last month of his life.

Tales of Ramnon are for you, Dad. I look forward to seeing you on the other side.

Of Feather or Flesh

A Ramnon Tale

Jae Mazer

OF FEATHER OR FLESH

THE DAY OF

Layla imagined the pen pinched in the receptionist's chubby fingers would look quite pretty impaled in her cornea.

"Ms. Carsten, are you all right?" the receptionist asked, batting her mascara-heavy lashes in Layla's direction. "I mean, considering ..."

The gold and brass clock on the wall ticked louder than it should have, peck, peck, pecking a dent in Layla's final nerve. She wanted to drag her nails down that wallpaper, shred it like flesh, throw it in a pile to use as kindling, and burn the whole fucking place to the ground.

"I need you to sign here and here," the receptionist said, tapping the paper with her magenta nail, "and initial here. Okay, honey?"

Layla nodded. She didn't read what she was signing, or ask what it was all about, and the receptionist didn't offer an explanation. She finished inking the page and pushed it back to the other woman.

"Okay, that's all done. Now let me go grab your visit summary." She hesitated, her eyes nervous and sad. "And I'll call Dr. Schmidt for you, set you up with an appointment. It'll just take a moment."

Layla nodded, her head heavy and her heart weary. She should have sat, but didn't have the energy, instead opting to lean on the counter and shift her weight from foot to foot.

"Fuck the beast."

Layla startled. The waiting room had been empty. But suddenly, there was a woman crammed into one of those uncomfortable chairs with the stained green cushions. The woman was looking right at her with dark, twinkling eyes.

"Excuse me?" Layla said, glancing around the waiting room.

"Ain't nobody else I be talkin' to, my darlin'. Jus' you an' me."

Layla nodded, not sure what to say.

"Where is he?" the woman asked, her eyes searching Layla's body.

"Where is who?"

"The beast!" the woman screeched.

Bat. Shit. Insane.

Layla turned her back to the woman and drummed her fingers impatiently on the counter.

"No mind," the woman muttered. "Don't matter where it is. It's a beast, nonetheless."

It.

Layla faced the woman again. "You mean ..." The words caught in Layla's throat, forcing tears to swell in her eyes.

"Yes. The beast. The cancer."

"I—"

"Yer titties? Always gets the titties, doesn't he? Ah well, ye ain't be needin' them ol' bags of lard. Hack 'em off and be done with it."

At a loss for words, Layla stared at the old woman, willing her newfound secret to float through the air unspoken.

"Ah," the woman said, her lips pinching to a hard line. She nodded, and a strand of flaming red hair fell from her bun. "There's no bein' done with yours, I gather, judging by that look on yer face."

"Suppose not." Layla's voice was soft and weak.

Eyes locked and mouths shut, the women looked at each other for an uncomfortable moment before the receptionist returned.

"Here you go, honey," the receptionist said, setting more papers on the counter. "Appointment is booked for this Thursday. I figured we should rush it because, well ... I can't imagine how hard this must be for you."

The waiting room remained silent. Layla was drawn to the red-headed woman in the chair. Nothing else existed. The receptionist came around the counter and put her hand on Layla's shoulder.

"Dear? I know it's a lot to process, but are you going to be okay? Do you have family close by? Friends?"

Layla let the words settle for a minute before answering. "No. No one."

"Are you sure? I mean, an aunt, cousin, coworker ... anyone?"

Layla sucked in a deep, raspy breath. "I'm fine. I'm better off alone to gather my thoughts."

Doubt glowered on the receptionist's face; a scowl and wet eyes communicated her worry. With nothing left to say or do,

Layla took the papers and walked to the door. As her hand touched the brass handle, the room exploded with noise.

A blood-curdling scream rattled the pictures on the walls and the teeth in Layla's head. Her hands flew to her ears, and she found herself screaming too, from the shock and fear of the wretched noise. The sound was so loud she thought her head might explode; it felt like the only thing holding her skull together was her hands over her ears.

Then someone grasped her shoulders.

"Layla! My goodness, are you all right? What happened?"

The screaming had stopped, leaving only a faint trace of pain and sound in Layla's head. The receptionist was standing over her, hands on Layla's shoulders, trembling. The red-headed woman was still sitting in the chair, a wide smile across her face, lips sealed tight.

"I just ... did you hear that?"

"Hear what? You screamed and dropped to your knees. Is your head hurting? I think you should come back in and speak to the docto—"

With a gentle shove, Layla wriggled out of the receptionist's grasp and back to her feet. "No, I'm fine." She wiped away a tear that wasn't there, for effect. "Just overwhelmed. Upset."

"Of course you are."

There's no way she buys that.

Without another word, Layla pushed through the door and out into the street.

Glasses clinked together in a melody of merriment and inebriation. The aroma of hot wings and fried foods wafted this way and that, carried on the breeze of the passing servers. The mojitos were fresh, the beer cold, and laughter resonated from the pits of dozens of bellies.

Layla loved the Anchor and Crown, the pub just down the way from her office. She loved it even more tonight as she gorged herself on greasy fare and a multitude of colourfully named cocktails. Typically, she would have nibbled a salad and nursed a low-cal brew, fearful her thighs might become too thick or her face too round. She could never indulge in too much dressing on her romaine, lest the extra calories make her unappealing.

Life tastes so awful.
But not tonight.

Tonight, it tasted of potato skins and triple sec, buffalo wings and porter.

"You seem off," Wade said. His big, blue eyes studied Layla's face, clearly trying to focus through the haze of liquor sloshing over his vision.

"Off my rocker?" Layla joked, giving him a shot in the arm.

"Hungry?" he asked, tapping her massive platter with his finger.

"Yeah."

"Seriously." He touched her arm. Her body tingled.

Wade was beautiful. He was kind and smart and everything she could have hoped for in a partner. But then again, she had thought that about her ex-husband, too. His beauty faded fast, deteriorating with the slice of his words and the strike of his fists. Seemed so many moons ago her stomach had danced, full of butterflies at the sight of him. She fell for it then, and if she wasn't ill, she'd probably fall for whatever wolf hid behind Wade's mask as well.

Life is so ugly.

She pulled away and continued eating.

She watched her coworkers laughing, eating, pressing drinks to their lips, and stroking each other with sly fingers.

Hungry species, we are.

Propelled by liquid courage and her last fuck to give, Layla boarded the dance floor, arms raised and hair whirling. Wade joined her, taking every opportunity to brush against her, to feel her, to taste her. Normally, she would block his advances. It was a subtle game of covert refusal. A full on shut-down would result in icy demeanor from him at work, and if she indulged, she would be the subject of many a tale round the office cooler, each juicier and raunchier than the last. She was always wanting, but always on guard, ever seeking the correct course of action.

But no longer.

Between songs, when Wade went to refill her drink, Layla ducked out the back door, leaving her coat, purse, and the last remaining glimmer of human contact behind.

"Hello? Is anyone there?"

Hot tears ran down Layla's cheeks, soaking the receiver in her hand. Her mother's voice continued to seek the caller, but Layla couldn't respond. Anguish squeezed her throat in its calloused hands, crushing both her voice and her heart.

"If no one's there, I'm hanging up."

I'm here, Mom. I've always been here.

"This is unkind. Whoever this is, please quit calling."

I'm sorry, Mom. I'm sorry I haven't been around. I don't want to hurt you.

I am a weak person.

"Goodbye."

And with a click, her mother was gone. Layla set the pay

phone receiver back on its cradle and stood in the phone booth, thinking of her mom, of the life she had abandoned, of the family that had become a distant whisper. They were strangers, now.

She left the phone booth and shuffled out into the starless night.

Boxes packed with stemware and souvenir steins and glasses lined the wall by the door. Layla wasn't sure why she boxed them up, but she did. They seemed like something someone might want. The stemware was expensive, the steins sentimental. They came from all over the country, collected from various renaissance festivals, biergartens, and breweries she had come across in her travels. She travelled a great deal with her brother in their younger years, before he got married and started a brood.

He might want those. Then again, he has his own.

Her mother would love the stemware, but might also hate it. If someone had gifted it to her, she would have swooned over it, commenting on it every time she poured a merlot. But she might find it a touch unsavoury to drink from her dead daughter's glass.

Her brother would go on. He might shed a tear, feel genuinely sad while reminders of her are paraded before him at the funeral and each subsequent visit home, but those memories would pass as his life barreled forward. There were more important things to occupy his thoughts and emotions.

Mom would struggle. It had only been a few years since Layla's father had passed, and waves of guilt threatened to consume Layla every time she thought of leaving her mother more alone than she already was. But her mom had her bridge club, her volunteering at the garden center, her brother …

They will all be fine. Just fine. This, too, shall pass.

After the bulk of the cleaning had been taken care of, and the more important or expensive items divvied up, Layla flopped on the couch with a glass of red. One tap of a finger and the television sprang to life, a blaring distraction to drown out the screaming in her head.

It was still there, that horrible noise from the doctor's office, but after a few hours, it ceased to be a bother. It melded together with the voice of her doctor, telling her the tumor in her throat had spread to her lungs. And the voice of her employer, telling her to take an indefinite leave until she could sort it all out. A chorus of voices sang in her mind: the pity in the voice of the clerk at the market, the teller at the bank, the Uber driver, the delivery driver, and every other fucking miserable sap who now looked at her like the doomed poison-filled sack she was.

"So young," the pharmacist had said when she handed her a prescription for pain.

I'm thirty-eight. That's plenty old enough.

Layla hurled her wine through the air. The glass struck the television with a resounding crack. A spider web of crackling fissures spread across the screen.

It's time. I'm done.

Where panic should have been, calm emerged. Where sadness and loss should have reared their sorry heads, a calm euphoria blossomed. Layla had no regrets, no hesitation.

With a new glass of wine in hand, Layla changed into her favourite outfit: a pair of worn jeans with tears at the knees and ass cheek and a Fleetwood Mac hoodie she got when she saw them in concert a few years back. Life was simpler before she knew what a train wreck of an adult she would become.

No accomplishments, no legacy, just nothing.

The bed was a cloud as she sank into it and splayed out like a starfish. She breathed through her nose, drawing air deep into her belly, smelling the lavender infuser at her bedside and the dog shampoo she used on her retriever, Chuka, before dropping her at the shelter that morning.

With a twist of the cap and a swig of her wine, the entire bottle of narcotics was down Layla's gullet in two painful gulps. Another twist, and the bottle of sleeping pills joined the churning gruel in her stomach.

Layla was calm. Relieved.

At peace.

Plip plip plip.

An acrid smell, hot and stinging, burned the insides of Layla's nostrils.

Plip plip plip.

A nearby dripping sound roused Layla from her slumber. Her eyes were heavy and crusted with sleep. She gave them a few forceful rubs with the heels of her hands and pried them open. The room was silver, illuminated by the crescent moon glowing through the wide-open window of her fourth-story apartment.

Layla stretched her arms and legs, working out the kinks of a heavy slumber, and her hand brushed against an empty pill bottle. She grabbed it and froze. Letting that bottle go, her hand crawled over the sheets and found the second bottle. Also empty.

In one smooth move, Layla rose to her knees on the bed, pulling the cord of the bedside lamp. Warm, low light flooded the room. Layla's stomach flipped and threatened to crawl straight out of her throat.

The bed was drenched in blood. Layla scanned her body, lifting her hoodie, which was heavy with wet blood. Smearing her hands across her pale stomach, she painted a crimson swipe, but found no obvious injuries. Her arms, her legs, her neck and head and face—all intact, far as she could tell.

Plip plip plip.

Blood dripped onto the carpet, which was no longer a carpet, but a crimson lake. Layla stepped into the warm, gritty fluid, and it consumed her feet to the ankle. Layla waded through the bedroom, feeling all manner of terror brush against her legs. She dropped to her knees and slid her hands through the blood, bringing up globs of meat and chunks of bone with every swipe.

Everything was drenched. The open curtains did not billow in the breeze. They were soaked, fresh blood dripping on the windowsill. Layla crawled to the window and looked outside, down the fire escape to the alley below. It was as normal as it ever was—dumpster, newspapers littering urine-filled drains—with one oddity.

Feathers. So many feathers.

Iridescent black feathers made a path from the mouth of the alley to a mound at the bottom of the fire escape, leading up the stairs right to her window. She reached down and picked up a handful. They were wet, drips and plips pinging off the metal grate of the landing below as she squeezed, wringing out the blood.

A noise from the other room drew Layla's attention. She stood, feathers clenched in her fists, and waded through the blood towards the sound—a high but soft whine. Flickering light danced through her bedroom door from the flat beyond, reflecting off the liquid on the floor. Layla wiped her face, smearing blood into her tears, and her pulse threatened to split open her neck as she crossed the threshold into the main room.

Everything was red, splattered in blood, clumps and chunks of feathers stuck to the tacky crimson painted over every surface. Whispers and wheezing breath came from the television hanging on the wall, the lights flickering a manic show over the scene of carnage. Layla walked in front of the television, transfixed by the impossibility before her.

The screen was smashed, but displaying an image that should not have been. It was the woman from the doctor's office, naked and covered in blood, dancing around the screen, maneuvering around the cracks on a distorted, snowy picture. She cackled and whispered to herself, her smile wide and filled with sharp, rotten teeth.

She stopped when she saw Layla and pointed a jagged, broken finger out of the television. Her jaw dislocated, dropping her maw into a gaping black hole.

And she screamed, a heart-shattering, mournful wail that rattled every bone in Layla's body.

Layla covered her ears. She cried, called for help as she knelt in the blood and rocked back and forth. The woman kept screaming, laughter hidden within the horrible sound.

Hands clamped around Layla's shoulders, stopping her from rocking. Layla looked at the hands. The fingers were long and adorned with sharp, black talons, flesh pocked and covered in tufts of feathers and clots of blood and meat.

The wailing moved away until it was far in the distance. The blackness of the feathers dissolved into dark unconsciousness as Layla hit the floor.

THE MORNING AFTER

A gentle crackling roused Layla from her slumber. Once again inebriated by the deepness of sleep, she rubbed her eyes lazily and stretched out her arms to caress the bed. The sheets were smooth and soft, and the blanket heavy, encasing her like a protective cocoon. She bunched it up to her face and breathed deeply, expecting the scents of lavender and Chuka to fill her soul.

But there was no lavender, and there was no Chuka. The blanket reeked of smoke and rotting meat. Layla rubbed her hands over the sheets again, remembering the motion from the night before.

The pill bottles.

She sat straight up in bed.

The blood.

There was no blood. Her room wasn't there either, or her blanket, or anything she knew or had ever known.

Wood surrounded her: log walls and ceiling, and a well-worn hardwood floor. A wood stove crackled in the corner farthest from the bed, with an old burgundy and gold rocking chair sat nearby.

That's mom's old chair.

Images of her childhood flickered in her mind, her sitting criss-cross-applesauce beside that chair, listening to her mother's lessons.

"Be someone, Layla," her mother had said. "Be the someone you want to be. But above all, be strong."

How disappointed Mother would be.

Layla swung her feet out of bed and crept along the wall to

the nearest door. She entered a bathroom with an all-black claw bathtub and a pedestal sink. A yellowed, oak-framed mirror hung haphazardly on the wall, barely useful through the layers of grime.

My mirror was beautiful.

She had installed that mirror herself; brushed-gold frame, as long as the room, and lit by the most amazing antique bulbs, it was a little piece of Layla that gave her great joy every time she entered the bathroom.

But now it was gone.

Funny, in all of this, to miss a thing like that.

Layla returned to the main room—the only room in the cabin, save the bathroom.

The possibilities in her mind chattered like a thousand crickets.

I've been kidnapped.

I've shacked up with some random dude I picked up at the bar.

Someone took me in, to help me after I ...

Tears welled in her eyes.

I don't want to be here.

Without checking the place further, Layla went for the door, heaving it open with all her might. The hinges creaked as the heavy door swung open.

"Huh."

Dirty, thick snow blanketed the world outside. Layla looked down at her bare feet, then back into the cabin.

"Fuck it."

Determined to find someone, she stepped onto the porch and hopped down three steps to the yard below. She slipped her way down the front walk until her toes found the gravel of the road.

"Huh."

Slippery, but not cold. Snow cloaked the ground, but her feet stayed toasty warm. Layla dropped to her knees, scooped up a handful of powder, and smeared it between the pads of her fingers. She sniffed it. Dipped her tongue in it.

"Ash."

Everywhere, a thick coating of ash blanketed this—wherever this was.

And where is this?

Rows of cabins lined the lane, connected by gravel pathways, tidy cottages made of logs with identical porches bearing porch swings and a torch to light each entryway. There was nary a splotch of colour to be found; each building was made of greying wood and coated in ash. And if there was colour, it was too dim to notice. It was twilight or dawn, Layla couldn't tell; the sky was a dim purple emanating an eerie glow. No sun, no stars, no moon.

Layla walked gingerly down the gravel path, watching for signs of life. There were cabins, plenty of them, with footprints here and there, but everything was dormant. In the near distance she heard muted voices and some clinking and clanging. She followed the sound. Didn't take her long to reach the action.

The lane opened up to a courtyard with a large fountain in the center. A cracked pillar of stained marble reached up to the sky, topped by a great stone Goddess with snakes slithering from her ears, eyes, mouth, and vagina. The serpents wrapped around her like a royal robe. Blood spilled from the Goddess, pouring out from the places where snake met woman, cascading down the layers of the fountain to a pool below.

"Watchit!"

"Ouch!" Layla cried as a sharp pain exploded across her ankle.

"Outta my way, you lump!"

A tiny man, all of twenty centimeters tall, rolled by Layla with a wheelbarrow full of flowers and weeds, a thorny rose clasped in his fat, clubbed fingers. Layla looked at the little man, then down at her ankle. Blood trickled down from the thorn sticking out of her pale skin.

"The fuck—"

"Guessing you should move, lass, lest you be struck by the bigger folk along their way."

Layla stepped to the side. Folks hustled and bustled carrying all manner of wares, from food to clothing to trinkets. The food in their baskets was spoiled, stinking of rot and crawling with maggots. She could tell by the sight and smell that the clothes they were peddling were steaming in blood, feces, and urine, as were most of the vendors. And the trinkets? Bones, animal carcasses, fetuses of any number of species, all made into decorations, jewelry, or items for display.

Layla was mesmerized by the horror, the assault on her senses, and by her disbelief. Each person broke off and set up shop in a wooden stall or wagon lining the massive courtyard. Most of the market was mobile, but there were a few buildings in the back. Most notably, there was a large, two-story building with swinging doors on the front. Looked like a saloon. One foot in front of the other, Layla moved through the crowd. She had almost reached the saloon when a streak of red caught her eye.

Atop the saloon, balancing on her haunches, was a young woman with fiery red hair cascading over her emerald green robe. She rocked from foot to foot, fretting her hair through her fingers, and she sang to herself, a melody both haunting and lovely. Jaw agape, Layla stared at the woman, her glorious red and green a beacon in this world of grey. Layla took a step forward, and the woman stopped singing. She turned her face to Layla and parted the red hair from her face to reveal glowing green eyes. A single, pallid finger came out from beneath the robe and pointed at Layla.

Layla knew before it began. She knew when the woman's face contorted into a grimace and her mouth opened so wide, revealing the rawness of her throat. The woman wailed, a keening so loud and mournful it brought tears to Layla's eyes and a scream to her throat. The noise emanating from that little bit of a thing rattled the jars and bones on the nearby carts, but drew no attention from the vendors or customers.

"Oi, stop that nonsense, ye young skag."

The woman on the roof closed her mouth with a snap, and her brow furrowed into an angry caterpillar.

"You," Layla said, looking behind her.

"Me, yes. 'Tis I." The woman from the doctor's office sidled up beside Layla and rested a hand on her shoulder. "Surprised to see me 'ere, yes?" She opened her mouth wide, and for a second, Layla expected that horrible wail to escape. But the woman laughed, a deep, witchy chortle. "Can't say I'm surprised to see you 'ere, though. Damn shame, 'tis."

"Am I ... I'm dead, aren't I?"

"On yer way, yeah. Just not knowing which road to be choosin'."

"What?"

The woman rolled her eyes, then corrected herself with a firm slap across her own face. "Sorry, mah deary. Course you don't know. How could ya? It's just I tol' the tale too many a time for my likin'. But don't you worry. I'll take good care of ya 'til yer time arrives."

Layla's head was spinning. She wanted to scream, to cry, to wail like the woman on the roof. She wanted to punch the old woman in front of her and knock those yellowed teeth straight out of her head.

I want it over. This is a dream. A nightmare.
Why can't I just die?

"Not quite yet, you anxious young thing." The woman reached her hand out. When Layla didn't reciprocate, the woman grabbed Layla's hand from her side and shook it. "Me name is Saoirse. And that," she said, hooking her thumb at the scowling redhead on the roof, "is me sister Imogen. Bloody noisy fool. Hasn't learned to contain her song yet."

"How ... the scream?"

Saoirse's emerald eyes twinkled. "We be banshees, young miss. She be less experienced than I. Can't keep it bottled up like I can."

Before Layla could respond, the woman pulled her towards the swinging doors.

"Shall we?"

"Two virgin's bloods, Mauve."

Saoirse knocked on the bar with her knobby knuckles. A portly woman in a firm red corset swayed over to them, snatching a jug off the wall behind the bar on her way.

"Virgin's bloods?" Layla asked as Mauve filled two snifters with a thick, red liquid.

"Just a bit o' hooch, is all. Not the actual blood they serve the ghouls and vamps and lycans."

"The what, now?"

Saoirse sighed.

"It's gon' be a lot to take in, m'love. I'll tell ya what ya need ta know and skim the rest, 'kay?"

"Do I have a choice?"

"We ain't got time, so no. Now throw back a chug o' that, and let's get to it."

Saoirse tapped her jagged yellow fingernail against Layla's glass. Layla picked it up, sniffed it, and slammed it back. It was hot going down her throat, but the flavour was mild and sweet.

"Another!" Saoirse yelled at Mauve, rapping her knuckles off the counter again. "Okay, so let's start wit you havin' a look 'round."

"Town?"

"The saloon, ye idiot!"

"Jesus fucking Christ."

"Naw, he ain't here. That one ain't be nowhere but a fairytale book. But this lot …"

Layla followed Saoirse's hand as she swept it across the room. The saloon was full—people at every table, at the dart board, playing cards in the corner. But they weren't people. They were patrons of a different flavour: wee men with red beards and tall hats, tall gangly men and women with tongues hanging from elongated snouts, pale shadows with red eyes and blood-stained lips.

"We got 'em all, we do. Vampyres, lycans, leprechauns, fae … me and Imogen be the only banshees here at the moment, but some pass through from time to time."

"So … I'm dead? I'm dreaming this?"

"Naw, this all be real. All manner of hell beast congregate here, shuffling about this wee corner of purgatory. A resting place for the damned, if you will." Saoirse stood and bowed to Layla. "Welcome to Fort Ramnon, gateway to The After."

"The After?"

"What happens when life meets its end."

Layla rolled a finger around the edge of her refilled glass, then slugged that one back too. A blood-dipped cockroach skittered in front of her, leaving a trail of little red footprints. It continued on to the end of the bar, where a ghoul green with rot was resting his head on the wood, jellied brains seeping out of a cracked skull and puddling on the wood. The cockroach went to work, scarfing down the meat and soaking itself in the rot.

What I wouldn't give for an Old Fashioned right now. Layla longed for the warm kiss of bourbon on her lips, for the familiarity of the Anchor and Crown. She craved her normal.

"This is hell," Layla said.

"Not yet, nah. This is where ye catch yer connecting flight."

Layla looked around at the depraved departed, all in various states of decay, monsters of all sizes and shapes. A tentacle here, a talon there ...

"Not everybody comes to Ramnon, you know," Saoirse continued. "Those who come have a purpose. Or potential purpose. Dabbling in haunting, terrorizing, or hung up on other business."

Layla looked down at her hands and examined her soft pink flesh, wriggling her fingers and making a fist. "Why am I here? Hell ... suicide—"

"Naw, lass, no!" Saoirse banged her fist off the counter, making the glasses hop. Mauve took that as a sign to get pouring and waddled over with the bottle. "There's afterlife, but no heaven or hell. No god and whatnot, just lands beyond and between."

"Where do we go? And who decides—"

A bird cawed in the distance, and the air fell still. The patrons in the saloon froze for a heartbeat, then shifted, hiding their faces and busying themselves with tasks, eyes pointed down. Fear permeated the air.

"What's happening?" Layla asked, whispering without knowing why.

"'Tis them."

The swinging saloon door squealed long and slow. Layla watched as one, two, then three black talons wrapped around the edge of either door and pushed them open in unison.

"Don't be lookin'!" Saoirse said, pointing to the floor. But Layla couldn't look away. A long limb passed through the door, then another—black, thick legs with knees folded backwards like a bird. The creature was tall, much taller than the doorway, bending nearly in half to pass through. Once inside the saloon, it stood up straight, but still had to crouch so it didn't bang its head off the rafters.

Then another one followed.

And another.

Soon, a flock of the gargantuan creatures was inside, cackling and cawing amongst themselves, moving together towards the bar.

"Birds," Layla breathed.

"No, child. Not birds."

The creatures were shrouded in hooded robes made of thick fur and feathers caked in all manner of carnage: blood, bone fragments, fatty tissue. Though the robes obscured the main core of their bodies, Layla could see their arms were long and covered in feathers that sprouted out of their black skin. In place of hands were black bones tipped with crimson talons as sharp and long as machetes.

"Not birds," Saoirse repeated. And her next word, though hushed to near silence, turned every head in the saloon.

"Sluagh."

Everyone looked at Saoirse and Layla. *They* looked at Saoirse and Layla. The Sluagh started shaking, broad shoulders heaving beneath their heavy cloaks, and gasps and wheezing coughs exploded from inside their hoods.

They're ... laughing?

A couple of them doubled over in fits of laughter while the rest parted to the side and looked at the saloon doors. The doors swung open again, this time with enough force to take one straight off its hinges.

"Goddamnit. Do I gots ta keep replacin' that, you vile thing?" Mauve snapped from behind the bar, seemingly unfazed by her unsettling clientele.

This Sluagh was larger than the rest—a good foot taller than the others in the saloon. Its feathers were full and thick, and shone a midnight blue in the flame from the saloon torches. It sauntered over to the bar, dragging its talons across the floor as it went, leaving deep gouges to mark its path. When it reached the seat beside Layla, it stopped and tapped on the counter.

"I shouldn't serve ya, the destruction you cause," Mauve muttered, fetching a heavy stone bowl from beneath the bar. "Bloody cunts."

Mauve poured some grotesque concoction into the bowl—a steaming, glistening black fluid. The Sluagh leaned forward and the steam from the bowl wafted into its hood. It clucked and chittered. Feathers rained to the floor as its entire body trembled in apparent delight. Layla leaned away in fright. The Sluagh paused a moment before turning its hooded head in Layla's direction.

"The floor, you welp. Lookit the floor!" Saoirse hissed.

But there was nothing of interest on the floor. In front of Layla was the most interesting thing in the room, and the most terrifying thing she had seen in her life. She could not look away.

In slow, jerky movements, the Sluagh pulled back its hood, revealing its face.

A scream would have escaped Layla's throat had she not covered her mouth with both hands.

The Sluagh's face was a combination of wolf and bird; it had an elongated beak full of sharp, jagged teeth, a head that was no more than a skull of black bone with bits of rotting flesh hanging here and there, and a smattering of glistening feathers creating a huge mane atop its head and cascading down its back. And its eyes, jellied rubies jiggling around sunken craters in its head, focusing a silver slit of an iris at Layla.

"New meat," it warbled.

The Sluagh licked its beak with a meaty tongue covered in sores, each popping and oozing pus as it dragged across those razor-sharp teeth. It leaned into Layla, so close she could taste its rancid breath.

"Your name?"

Layla winced at the gravelly voice, a guttural expulsion of air from deep within the thing's belly. She didn't answer. Just stared. The sides of the beak curled into a smile that seemed to split the face in two. It heaved up its arm, and a massive wing spread out from beneath the black robe. It laid its hand on Layla's thigh, giving her one, two, three hard slaps before laughing like a pickled pirate.

"You Layla, I know." It sniffed, then dipped its beak hungrily into the stone bowl on the bar. It slurped and lapped with an infected tongue until the bowl was licked clean, then sat back up and looked at Layla again.

"Layla ..." The Sluagh paused, eyes searching Layla's body. "I Kantu. You mine. See you promptly."

The Sluagh stood and ruffled its feathers, shaking off the dust and debris it had picked up from the filthy bar. It spun, its mane and robe flowing behind it as it strutted out of the saloon and into the night. The remaining Sluagh sidled up to the bar, and Mauve poured more gruel into a long trough. They gorged themselves like swine until the last drop had been consumed, then swept out of the bar in a flock, creaking and cackling the whole way.

"What ... Sluagh?"

"Not jus' a myth, my love," Saoirse said, tapping the counter for another round. "Harbingers of death. On the living side, they swoop in and take ye before death gets ya. They're one step ahead, if they be lucky."

"What do they want?"

"Death. Pain. They desire to build a magnificent tribe. They need more, and can't keep up with the population, large and dyin' as it is. More Sluagh to do their bidding."

"So I ..."

Layla looked around at the patrons quietly milling after the invasion.

"They wanted you, yep. They gotcha. The Sluagh can git ya one of two ways: in the moment between the death blow and death itself, or if all hope of life has been lost. You's got both o' those covered."

Layla thought of the blood in her apartment, the pills, the feathers ...

"Sluagh are nightmares in the flesh. They consume souls simply to feed. They are gluttonous monsters, hungry for pain and death. So if you be still tickin'—as you be—they wantcha."

Layla's stomach lurched, the virgin's blood curdling on the top of her gut. "So they'll make me Sluagh?"

Saoirse swiveled her barstool and grabbed Layla by the hips, swirling her until they were face to face. "One of three things will happen. One—you become Sluagh. Feathers will sprout from yer flesh, yer body will contort, and you will fly with their flock for the rest of yer days, of which there is no end."

"Sounds awful."

"'Tis. Two—you ain't cut out for this mess, and they jus' eat ya anyways. You dead. Caput. The end."

"Okay ..."

"Three—you ain't ready for Sluaghing, and you ain't ready for death. Ain't yer time."

"You mean, like, go back ... come back to life?"

Saoirse snorted and chugged back the bloody fluid. "But you ain't be wanting that either, methinks. Regardless, time ain't on yer side. You gots four days here in Fort Ramnon to walk the life and contemplate the life ye left. On that fourth night, you will go to sleep in yer bed. When you wake up the next day, you wake up where you want, and where you're wanted."

What do I want?

A heaviness weighed on Layla's chest, a passenger that seized her lungs each time she drew breath. She scratched at her head, her hair thin and sparse between her fingers. Her hair had once been thick and lush and feminine. But the cancer had stolen that; it stole her energy, her hope, her routine. Every bite of food, every sip of wine, every conversation with friends or strangers was plagued by the knowledge that she was riddled with an evil eating away her very essence.

There was no life in her left to live.

"I don't know."

Saoirse nodded. "You will."

DAY ONE

"Come."

Layla opened her eyes. She was in the bed in the cabin. She didn't remember coming back from the saloon and was surprised she had been able to fall asleep. *Probably has something to do with virgin's bloods.* The light outside was the same, and she felt neither tired nor awake. Time was disorienting, as were her surroundings.

The fire crackled in the corner, the only beacon of life in the small space. Layla slid out of bed and went to the rocker. Fort Ramnon was small and odd, without an actual store or business other than peddlers of wares and disgusting edibles. Layla longed to see the golden glow of a fast-food chain anywhere along the broken and tainted streets, but all she saw when she gazed out the window was nothingness.

I'm fucking hungry. What do I do here when I'm hungry?

The rocking of the chair did little to soothe her. Her mind kept thinking, moving about her body, searching for signs of the sickness that had been riding her like a passenger the past year. She couldn't feel it anymore, the cancer. Her breathing was unencumbered, her throat loose and relaxed, and the fatigue had dissolved into an airy nothingness. She barely felt anything at all, and though that should have delighted her, it terrified her as well.

I've gone and lost my mind.
Is this limbo?
Is this death?

She didn't know what to believe. Her breathing quickened, looming panic rising inside her like a swell of lava threatening to erupt. She closed her eyes and covered her ears, willing this terrible, unfamiliar place to dissolve. Like nothing ever happened, she would fall right back into her bed, surrounded by her world and her life.

But I hated life, didn't I?

Failed marriage, dead-end career, friendless, hopeless existence ...

But the mirror. She loved that mirror. The food and drink at the Anchor and Crown. Wade, his thick chest and soft eyes.

Maybe there was no beast in him. Now I'll never know.

As a sob swelled in her throat, a voice whispered through the cracks of the cabin like puffs of dust.

"Come."

The voice beckoned from beyond the walls. With nothing to do and nowhere to go, Layla indulged the insanity. She looked out the window, wiping grime away with a steady hand. The street was empty, as far as Layla could tell, but the soot and dust on the window made it difficult to see.

"Come."

The urgency in the voice made Layla's stomach clench. She passed through the door and out into the street. Detecting no movement towards the courtyard other than flickering torches hung on cabins, she turned the other way and saw it. Kantu stood in the middle of the road, a black blotch in the surrounding sea of grey. The Sluagh lifted a wing and curled a talon as it turned and walked away.

Layla followed.

One step after another, Layla set her feet in the prints in the ash, following the Sluagh's trail without ever looking up. The prints were long—about a meter—and consisted of three toes, like a raptor. The tips of the toe prints deposited blood into the surrounding ash like oil on water.

The end of the lane was upon Layla before she realized it, and the footprints turned towards a black lake at the bottom of a rocky hill. She traversed the rocks, oblivious to the abuse inflicted on the soles of her feet. When she reached the water's edge, her feet were torn and bloodied, but she suffered no pain.

Imogen was perched on a boulder, washboard in hand, staring out at the lake. When Layla dipped her toes into the water, Imogen turned her head and her mouth opened into a great gaping chasm. Layla braced herself for the keening, but only a short burst of air squeaked out before Imogen's mouth shut with an audible snap. She looked so proud that she had been able to stop herself from wailing. Layla smiled, and the banshee blushed, her fair cheeks growing rosy beneath a mop of red hair.

Imogen was naked, her glistening white body glowing in the muted light. Her red curls cascaded down her body, pooling at her delicate feet. Layla tried not to look, but couldn't help but be enraptured by the young banshee's beauty and air of aloofness. Imogen, clearly sensing Layla's shame, arranged her hair over her breasts and between her legs to cover her more sensitive bits.

"Give."

Hot breath on the top of her head told Layla that Kantu was upon her. She turned her face up to the sky and met the Sluagh's red eyes.

"Give?"

Kantu scraped a talon down Layla's hoodie.

Oh God. I'm still wearing this.

Imogen held out her hands and waited.

"I'm ... I'm supposed to take it off? I have nothing underneath—"

"Woman beautiful," Kantu said. With a chitter and clatter of joints and bones, Kantu shrugged the huge robe off and set it on the ground. Layla couldn't help but stare, nor did she think to hide her shock. Under the massive robe hid an equally massive body. Kantu's skin was sheer like a sausage casing, showing the organs working and blood pumping beneath. The Sluagh had a long, lean core, and massive arms attached to gossamer wings like a giant, feathered bat.

"Have robe. Hide yourself, if need be so foolish."

The stench of old blood and vomit emanating from Layla's hoodie made her want to take it off, but the prospect of standing naked and exposed was terrifying. After hesitating a moment, she shoved her hands in the pockets of her jeans.

"No thanks," she said, her voice quavering.

Kantu bent down until they were nose to beak. "You do you. Whatever you need. Don't dismiss the liberation. This place? Conventions don't apply."

A loon cried out across the lake. Imogen let her arms float down and she crossed her hands in her lap.

"We go now," Kantu said, swiping the robe off the ground.

Layla couldn't help but notice.

"You are ... female?"

"Woman," Kantu said.

That didn't make Layla feel any more comfortable. She looked back at Imogen, who gave her a crooked, wavering smile before looking back out at the water.

Before Layla had a chance to wave goodbye to the beautiful banshee, a wing wrapped around her waist like a hook, swooping her into the sky.

The change in temperature was shocking.

Any temperature would be shocking after being immersed in the nothingness of Fort Ramnon.

But here, wherever they landed, her senses were back at full tilt. Her eyes were closed, and she was wrapped in a cocoon of fur and feather, but she could make out lights beyond her lids. Her feet touched the ground, gently puffing into white sand, and the wings unfurled, exposing her to the elements.

The sand was soft and wet, and the air hot and humid. A line of sweat had already formed at her hairline, trickling down her face and between her breasts. It was night. The moon glowed high in the sky, its reflection rippling in the distance, dancing in the mirror of the sleeping tide. Soft waves rolled over her feet, whispering sweet nothings in her ears. In the distance, the rapid pulse of a beach-side discotheque thumped and pumped into the night, its dazzling lights beckoning her.

Kantu was nowhere to be found. Layla looked around, up and down the beach, and towards what was likely a resort, but saw only a smattering of black feathers and tufts of fur littering the surrounding sand.

"Where do I go?"

Layla didn't expect an answer. There was no one as far as the eye could see. She debated going to the resort, but opted for some peace instead. She had always wanted to go back to the ocean. She was born on the island, in a town not far from the Pacific. Her parents would take her down to the coast to watch the orcas play, and she would scour the sand for treasures to add to her shell collection. She remembered those days with such crystal clarity, in more detail than any of the days in her adult life.

As she strolled along the water line, she dug her toes into the sand, unearthing tiny shells and treasures along the way. She bent to pick up a few here and there, stuffing them in the pockets of her jeans until she was sure they would rip at the seams. A ridge of rock and buildup of driftwood offered a convenient place to sit and drink in the respite from death.

The music of the night sang to her as she perched upon the rock—the lapping of the water, the wind rustling the sparse groves of palms, the chorus of insects.

The call of a bird.

Not a sea bird, though. A caw, sharp and distinct, almost a cackle ...

"Brian, stop!"

The voice was approaching, bouncing and panicked, almost breathless. It was very dark, the sliver of the moon giving off only a touch of light, but Layla saw movement. People, two of them, coming towards her at a fair clip.

"Sasha! You're being ridiculous." The second voice wasn't frantic, but irate. Angry.

Layla slid off the rock and crept back to a cluster of palms a few meters away. Crouching, she watched as the couple reached the debris.

Brian was all hands, and Sasha was having none of it. He stumbled into her, and they both came crashing down in the sand. She scrambled backwards like a crab, but he was on top of her, pressing into her, his hand seeking the flesh beneath her dress.

"Fuck off," Sasha growled. Her body heaved as she brought her knee up, driving his testicles inside his body. He screamed, then vomited the night's overindulgence of alcohol over the front of her dress.

"You goddamn wanker," she scolded, then rolled him off into

the sand. But she wasn't getting away that easily. He thrust his fist into her gut, knocking the wind and rum out of her as well. When she dropped to the ground beside him, he frantically clawed at her dress, snapping the straps and yanking it down below her waist and off her ankles. Sasha thrashed and screamed as she gouged pieces of him with nails and sank her teeth into any near and exposed body part. With every strike she landed, it seemed she might have bested him, but he managed to struggle his way back on top of her.

As his finger hooked the side of her panties, Layla could take no more. She jumped to her feet.

"Stop!"

But they didn't stop. They didn't even flinch.

"They can't hear ya, love."

Saoirse sat atop the driftwood, scowling at the rabid animal assaulting the woman in the sand.

"Why?" Layla was furious, panicked. She tried to get to them, to grab that fuck and claw his eyes out, but her legs refused to move.

"You ain't really be here," Saoirse said. "You's watchin', but you ain't be here. Not the physical here, that which let ya be grabbin' and savin' and stuff. Not until …"

Saoirse's head snapped to the side, and her eyes locked onto Brian's. He paused, confusion contorting his face.

He sees her. Suddenly, he sees her.

Saoirse smiled wide, then opened her mouth to the twinkling skies and released her blood-curdling wail.

Layla's anxiety washed away. She knew. The banshee was howling.

Sasha grabbed a chunk of driftwood, ripping it off the larger branch and brandishing it like a stake. She didn't hesitate.

Within a blink, the wood was pierced up through Brian's jaw and into his mouth.

Everything stopped. Sound, movement, even the pounding of Layla's heart stilled in her chest. The Banshee's wail trailed off to nothing, and her mouth closed into a soft smile. Sasha's lower lip trembled, and she backed away as Brian's blood spurted out of his neck and onto the front of his vomit-saturated sweater.

"Oh god, oh fuck, oh god," Sasha whimpered as she covered her face with bloody hands.

Saoirse slid off the driftwood and wobbled over to Sasha.

"Naw, dear, no need ta be seein' this." She slid her hands under Sasha's arms and hoisted her to her feet. Sasha flailed around, swiping and punching at the air around her.

"She can't see you?"

"That's what I said! You be daft, child?"

"But she ... you lifted her."

"Aye. Can do that. She don't know, though. Only know she be up." Saoirse looked towards the resort. "And now she be off and runnin'. That's good."

Sasha was running. Screams exploded from her throat—cries of shock, cries for help, cries of anger, shame, pain.

A wail echoed through the night. Layla jumped, then looked over at Saoirse, whose mouth was wide and sound was loud.

"Why? So goddamn loud!" Layla complained

Saoirse shrugged, but kept on keening, smiling even as the woeful wails bellowed out of her throat. Layla looked down at Brian, who was on his back in the sand, clasping at the stake in his head.

He's not dead. Not yet.

Saoirse nodded, knowing Layla's thoughts.

"You are announcing his imminent passing, so the Sluagh can get him before—"

Feathers rained down from above, and sand swirled up in a funnel, showering down on the three of them like a twinkling glass storm. Kantu landed at Brian's feet with a ground-quaking thud.

Saoirse fell silent.

Kantu shook herself, molting feathers over the sand, then crouched down at Saoirse's feet. He was frozen, watching Kantu's every odd, jerky movement as his life poured out of his wound.

"You want fucked?" Kantu said, her voice bitonal and hoarse. A long, leathery tongue licked out of her snout, seductively teasing the blades inside her beak. She leaned over him until her feathered, bony frame encased him in a quivering tent. Beak to his cheek, she pushed her meaty tongue right in his ear canal, whispering, "I'll fuck you."

Kantu crouched back until she was balanced at Brian's feet, then worked her way up, pecking and tearing at his calves and thighs, discarding bits of flesh and muscle to the side. Her talons came up and tore away his pants and boxers, and she paused to consider his flaccid cock.

Brian tried to scream, but only blood bubbled out around the stake. His pupils were waxing and waning, his head bobbing on and off the sand.

"He isn't long for this world," Saoirse whispered in Layla's ear, "but that's the thing with the Sluagh. You're done when they say you're done. Livin', breathin' nightmares, they are."

Brian's eyes stayed fixed on Kantu as she took him in her mouth, toying with him until he stiffened ever so slightly. She pulled, then pulled a little more, like a bird tugging a juicy, morning worm out of the dirt. She pulled and twisted and jerked her head until finally the flesh surrendered to the abuse and tore clean off. Kantu held Brian's severed manhood in her mouth like a trophy. Tears poured from his eyes, and muffled screams found their way through air pockets in the stream of blood as Kantu played with the penis, tossing it up in the air and catching it over and over again.

Layla wretched, her whole body convulsing as she tried to empty an already vacant stomach. She screamed along with Brian, giving him the air he was lacking to make the noise. Layla squeezed her eyes closed and covered her ears. She didn't want the blood, the pain, the dismemberment. She didn't want to hear the gargling, the squishing of the meat in Kantu's bite, Brian's limbs thrashing in the sand. It seemed to go on for hours before it came to a sudden end.

Kantu cocooned Layla in her wings again, but this time she had company. Kantu scooped Brian right up along with her, wrapping the two of them together and shooting towards the stars. Before Layla lost consciousness, she looked down past her feet at Saoirse sweeping the bloody sand into the sea.

DAY TWO

Nothing.

Not cold, not warm.

Layla felt nothing.

She was back in Fort Ramnon. She knew it. She felt the oddness of the place, the absence of temperature, heard the dampened, eerie noise of fae folk milling about outside. She could smell the ash and wood and blood, and hear the crackling of the fireplace. Still, she didn't open her eyes. Somehow, she thought if she didn't see it, it wouldn't be there.

She wished herself dead all over again.

Or alive.

Cancer would be a welcome reprieve from this.

She tried to rest in bed, eyes closed and mind elsewhere, but anxiety got the better of her. She felt like crying and screaming, like she was losing absolute control.

You've already lost control, Layla. It's gone. You have no power now.

"No."

The voice rattled the cabin walls. Layla yanked the blanket over her head and held her breath. She waited one moment, two, but no more voice. No sound other than the crackling of the fire.

She couldn't linger in bed any longer.

The bathroom was clean, so that was good. It brought a smile to her lips. She imagined a hellscape like this would have roadside rest stop bathrooms, with empty toilet paper rolls, shit and semen on the walls, and sticky urine coating the floor. This was the opposite of that.

A woman runs this show, for sure.

The mess in the mirror brought Layla's mood down again. She was disheveled, hair matted with blood and feathers, and her clothes were stained with vomit and sand. Her face was gaunt and yellow, her body a wisp of the woman she had once been.

She breathed in, and the smell of copper and rotting meat overwhelmed her. She heaved again, her muscles aching from the night before, but this time her stomach produced an offering. Thick, black blood mingled with wispy, wet feathers came pouring from her mouth, splashing over the white sink and counters. Layla couldn't catch her breath through the stream of gore, so just let it come until her body felt drained of every drop of fluid.

The bathroom looked like a murder scene, stark white splattered with black and crimson, smears of Layla's handprints on the edge of the counter. Once again, she dared to confront her reflection. A sheen of sweat glistened above her top lip, and bright red blood marred her colorless complexion. Her clothes were rotten, hanging off her in strips, caked with all manner of bodily fluid.

Am I ... what's happening to me?

The woman staring back at her was different, somehow. Her body felt foreign, her limbs longer and trunk thicker. *Am I imagining it? I mean, it's subtle ...*

Considering the not-quite-right Layla in the mirror, she decided the minute changes were products of her mind rather than reality.

She stumbled out of the bathroom and shuffled through the front door. As she expected, there was no one in the street. There was a low murmur of noise coming from the courtyard, but Layla turned the other way. She walked and walked, head hanging and feet shuffling through sepia ash, up the trail then over the rocks until she was at the edge of the water, standing over Imogen. The younger banshee was singing a macabre lullaby while she pushed bloody clothes across a washboard.

"She do yours, too, if ye like."

Saoirse waddled up and planted herself on a boulder behind Imogen.

Layla looked down at her body. "But I have nothing else."

Saoirse looked Layla up and down. "That really be a bother? More than the blood and puke?" When Layla didn't move, Saoirse continued. "Aye, ye be ridiculous. Free yourself, woman."

After a moment of hesitation, Layla slowly tugged down the zipper of her hoodie and let it slide off her shoulders. Imogen snatched it off the ground and set it in a pile beside the washboard. Layla continued, wriggling out of her jeans, then unclasping her bra and letting it slide off her arms as well. Finally, she slid down her panties, stepped out of them, and handed them to Imogen, who tossed them on the pile.

Though the air had no temperature, the water was cool and refreshing. Layla waded in until the water covered her breasts and her shame, and stood there, enjoying the wet, soothing embrace of the lake. She tilted her head up towards the sky, letting her hair fan out around her. There were no stars, no clouds, just nothing; a warm gold backdrop speckled with the occasional falling ash or feather. The more she watched, the heavier the feather fall was until a shape emerged from above, floating down in a gentle spiral.

Kantu landed on the rocks. She had BSaoirse's carcass in her arms, bloody and beaten, all its limbs missing and the eye sockets picked clean. Kantu looked out into the water, into Layla's eyes, then turned her back and walked into the trees. A flurry of Sluagh dove in, and Kantu walked out of the trees, leaving a crescendo of crunching and tearing behind.

The water rippled as Kantu submerged herself, diving head-first into the black lake and emerging a meter away from Layla.

"Not so terrible, yes?"

"Yes," Layla said, covering herself with her arms, despite the water being so dark.

"Acquired taste, nudity."

"Suppose so."

Kantu preened, pulling her feathers through her beak and mussing her fur with her talons. Layla admired the feathers glowing blue-black even in the dim light, an iridescent, glittering sheen.

"I can't do what you do," Layla said.

Silence filled the space between Sluagh and woman, Kantu prompting her to continue.

"Do I have to be Sluagh?"

Kantu's glowing red eyes met Layla's.

"You need to be you," Kantu cooed. Layla cocked her head, confused. Kantu floated forward and rested a hand on Layla's shoulder. "Let go, Layla. Be you. Be strong. Just be."

Kantu left the water and disappeared into the sky, a glitter of feathers marking her path. Layla stared up for a moment until she realized she was being watched. Imogen was washing clothes, but her eyes were fixed on Layla. Those beautiful emerald eyes, her pale, smooth skin glowing white, her dark nipples erect, and the fire between her legs glistening.

Layla felt a familiar, overwhelming want, one she had never indulged.

Imogen dropped the clothes and waded into the water.

Kantu's voice in her head was clear and loud. "You do what you want. Leave old Layla behind. She was nothing. Be you."

The water moving around Layla's body caused her cheeks to flush. Imogen's fingers glided over her nipples and toyed with her labia. Layla pushed herself into Imogen and forgot all about the things she would never do, never see, never feel. She forgot the feeling of loss when she received her diagnosis and the nothingness that came after. Her life had ended the day the waiting to die started.

Or maybe she had never really been born.

But she didn't feel that now, the cancer, the death. She had mourned her life while living, and now she was here. And here was good.

Kantu's voice hummed in her head. "You control. You are powerful."

A trick, Layla knew, to lull her into complacency. But she didn't care. She moved with Imogen, feeling the water, pleasure surging through her body, the strength growing inside her. Imogen wrapped around Layla, pulling their bodies close as Layla climaxed. As Layla's body surged, she lifted into the air, out of the water, and into unconsciousness again.

Layla's hand cupped her genitals, which were still throbbing with release. After a few finishing rubs, she became aware of the cold. Her nipples were erect, and her body still damp from the lake. A gentle breeze enticed gooseflesh to rise on her bare skin, and brought with it the scent of food. But good food; delicious street food.

Layla sat up.

She was sitting on a street, music all around her, lights

flashing and twinkling against the backdrop of the night sky. Raucous laughter erupted behind her, echoing against the tall buildings on either side of the street. Layla scrambled to her feet, arm across her bare breasts, hand still clasping her crotch. She ducked into the nearest sheltered nook—a closed storefront.

Wherever she was, it was night, and an active one at that. The moon was high in the sky, but the street was alive with energy. Pubs and discotheques lined either side of the cobblestone walkway, all lit with patio lights and blaring their own brand of music. The smells of pub fare filled the air, fried goodies from savory and spicy to sweet and creamy. Voices were loud and alcohol flowed freely; there was no sign of the party slowing down.

"They can't see ya, ma love," Saoirse said, patting Layla's arm. Saoirse's white, freckled skin glowed in the night. Layla gasped. Saoirse was completely naked too, her breasts drooping over her belly and a poof of bright orange hair between her legs. "Wha? Never seen a bare bitch before? We's amazing creatures, ain't we? 'Sides, I figured you'd feel more comfy if we both had our bits out."

Saoirse walked into the street, fluorescent white ass jiggling in the night and bright red curls cascading down her back. She walked past groups of men and women, lovers entwined in drunken groping, and bouncers standing sentry at the openings of classier establishments. Layla giggled and followed the bright woman through the crowd.

There would be death. Layla knew that. That's why she was there, to witness the Sluagh's work. But in that moment, she didn't care. The people moving about couldn't see her. They couldn't judge her or hate her or like her or expect anything from her. She was just there, enjoying the world, not having to pretend to be happy or healthy or anything she wasn't. The air passed the wetness between her legs, and she blushed. Even with her partners and her husband, she'd preferred sex in the dark, or only a modest portion of flesh exposed. But here she could walk around, exposed to the world, masses of people clothed and constricted around her.

It was amazing.

Everything. The smell of the food, the taste of the air, moving around unencumbered by worry or pain ... it was intoxicating.

Layla passed a patio table and lifted a mojito, drinking it back in three hefty gulps. The mint tingled in her mouth, the vodka sliding down and warming her belly. She stole another drink, and another, a nibble of a chicken wing and a chomp of pizza. It tasted amazing—every flavour, every texture.

Up ahead, the flowing red hair bobbed through the crowd. While Layla gorged herself, Saoirse kept going, ploughing forth to their goal.

Fuck it. I'll hear her.

Layla danced in the street, twirling and reeling around other people, dancing a frantic jig, her hair spinning around her bare shoulders. She laughed, deep in her belly, and brushed her limbs and breasts against bare hands and clothed legs, experiencing everyone and everything.

Her newfound euphoria dissolved when the wail took flight. She abandoned the revelry and made her way through the crowd toward the sound. It was so loud it pounded in her head, above the music, the laughing, the talking; but no one else took any notice.

Saoirse's wails led Layla into an alley at the end of the street. The old Banshee was squatting on a closed dumpster, looking into the dark corner of the alley. Though her steps slowed, Layla was not scared. She was invincible.

"What is it?" Layla asked. Saoirse couldn't answer, of course. Words would not form around her bellows.

A small camp was set up in the corner of the dead-end alley, obscured by the large dumpster. A sleeping bag was spread out under a makeshift tent made of two-by-fours and a blue tarp. Layla crouched down and peeled back the sleeping bag.

A young woman—early twenties, at most—was shivering from the cool night air. She had on a ratty set of lace pajama shorts and a black halter top stained with white splotches. Heavy makeup was smeared across her face, and a puddle of yellow-green drooldribbled lipstick down her chin. A half-pushed needle was sticking out of her arm.

Saoirse closed her mouth and rubbed her jaw, aching from the strain. "Bloody shame, this one."

"Can we call an ambulance?" Layla asked, noting the pulse in the woman's throat.

"Naw, can't even if we wanted to," Saoirse said, shaking her head. "Ambulance ain't no help to this one, anyways. She was gone long ago. Jus' waitin' for the body to call it quits. We're here fer mercy."

Kantu landed on the dumpster with a crash, sending Saoirse flying to the ground in a heap.

"You bloody ol' cock muncher, goddammit!" Saoirse flailed around like an upset turtle until Layla offered a hand, pulling her to her feet. Kantu cocked her head, smirking at the Banshee, then looked at the woman in the sleeping bag. She hopped off the dumpster and settled in beside the tent, nesting in a pile of soggy newspapers.

"Sometimes we take before death is apparent," Kantu said. "This one, dead already. Hope gone." Her red eyes moved from the body to Layla's face. "Like you."

The ground was littered with pill bottles, syringes, and a spoon and lighter. The woman was a slip of a thing—a hundred pounds, at most, grey and yellow skin stretched over a bag of bones.

"Suicide," Layla whispered.

"Tried," Kantu said.

"But if she isn't successful, do we let her be?"

"No. Hope is gone in her mind. We take then, too."

"That's horrible," Layla said, a lump forming in her throat. She remembered her despair, the calm hopelessness that led to her own demise. "But if there's no way out—"

"There is always a way out," Kantu scolded, rising to her feet. "Always hope. When you don't see it, you are damned. We leave you wishing for release, realizing the error; the hopelessness and defeat are not actually the worst."

Layla looked at the woman on the ground, a beauty hiding within her broken shell. "She could come back, yes? Like me?"

Kantu shook her head. "Only a select few are like you. This one, we relieve her of her pain. Show her the worst before she moves on. Does she remember us?" Kantu stroked a feather across the woman's face. "No. She remembers her life, but leaves in peace instead of despair. We are despair to remind of the beauty of life."

Kantu pointed her beak to the sky, and her body shook. She gargled and gulped, then tilted her head down and belched up chunks of her last meal, depositing them in the woman's mouth.

The woman started choking, then sat up and screamed. Kantu stepped away from the woman and put her wing on Layla's back.

"You."

"Me?"

The woman jumped to her feet and spit Kantu's regurgitated offering in Layla's face. Layla gasped and wiped the sludge off her eyes and mouth.

"You rancid cunt!" the woman screamed, lashing out and clawing at Layla's face. Layla grabbed her wrists and pushed her against the brick wall.

"Calm down," Layla pleaded. "It's not what you think."

"You whore!" the woman screeched. She wriggled her hands out of Layla's grasp, slapped at Layla's breasts, and strained to bite her face. With a strength she didn't know she had, Layla heaved up a leg and drove a knee into the woman's stomach, knocking the wind out of her and dropping her to the ground. After a quick perusal of the debris littered beneath the tent, the woman was on her feet again, syringe in hand. Leaving no time for a reaction, she drove the needle straight into Layla's retina. And Layla felt every bit of it: the cold penetration of the steel, the pop as her eyeball burst, the trickle of bloody tears running down her cheek. It hurt like fresh hell, but Layla didn't scream or cry out. She wasn't scared or upset or shocked.

Anger coursed through her veins.

She grabbed the woman's wrists again, this time with grinding strength, cracking and crushing her bones to dust.

"Down!" Layla commanded, her voice booming through the alley. The woman complied, mewling and curling up in the fetal position. A feral mania took over, and Layla went to work, breaking the woman's bones one by one, starting with her toes and working her way up to her ribcage. By the time Layla twisted the woman's head around backwards, she was nothing more than a wobbling, disjointed mess. A broken marionette.

Where Layla had found the strength, she did not know. She had snapped and shattered femur bones like twigs, worked feverishly through the woman's pleas for mercy. Bone tore through skin, and tendon caked up under Layla's fingernails, but she didn't hesitate, not even for a moment. Her heart remained steady, her work diligent, and she even caught herself whistling Imogen's ballad at one point.

When it was finished, the three stood side by side—Kantu, Layla, and Saoirse—looking down at what was left of the woman in the tent.

"Well, that's that, I suppose," Saoirse said, shrugging her shoulders. "Me work begins!"

There was nowhere to sweep the evidence this time. Saoirse let Kantu scoop up the body, then balled up the bottles, blankets, and other trinkets and piled them in a heap beneath the tarp. She collapsed the two-by-fours, and the makeshift tent joined the heap.

Kantu wrapped a wing around Layla, pressing her firm against the dead woman's body. Layla's eyes were fixed on Saoirse's hands, which were glowing white hot and spewing flame from her crooked fingertips. As they lifted off into the sky, Saoirse blew on her fingers, sending a burst of flame to light the pile of debris, reducing the addict's life to a pile of ash.

Sleep did not come yet. It would wait until the job was done this time. Layla was awake and aware through the whole flight, watching the stars fly by and the midnight blue of night dissolve into the warm glow of Fort Ramnon. The woman squirmed and moaned as Kantu landed on the rocks. Layla was freed from the winged cocoon first. After securing her footing on the rocks, she took a step back so Kantu could deposit the body on the ground. The flock of Sluagh swarmed in, eating, suckling, biting, picking flesh off bone and slurping organs. Frantic eyes rolled around the woman's head, open and watching until the pecking started, liberating her from the sight of her horror.

Layla went to the water's edge and stood ankle deep, allowing the cool ripples to sooth her raw, battered feet.

"How ya holding up?"

Saoirse was tits-deep, washing off the lice and ash she had acquired from the woman's belongings.

"I don't know." And she didn't know. It had been savage, horrible, violent in a way Layla didn't think she had in her. But there was no guilt, no regret, no terror. "That woman was already gone. Long gone."

"Were you?" Kantu's voice sliced through the air. She stood in the water, a few meters from Layla, red eyes boring into her soul.

"Was I gone?"

"When I came for you. Anything left?"

"I ..."

Was there? No friends, no family, no health. Death was imminent, anyways.

But absolutely nothing?

"I don't think so," Layla said.

"Weak!" Kantu shrieked, the noise shaking leaves from the trees. Layla cried out in shock and started weeping. "You had nothing left? Nothing in those moments to come? You left nothing behind? Be sure, human. Be confident in your loss of hope."

With a violent flap, Kantu took flight, drawing up a waterspout as she shot into the sky. Layla was left trembling on her knees in the water, tears pouring from her eyes, unable to breathe.

"Now, now," Saoirse said, pulling Layla to her feet and leading her out of the water. The women embraced, their skin warm and soft against one another. Layla cried and tremored, her face buried in Saoirse's chest, the beating of the banshee's heart providing a sense of calm. "There, there, child. Don't mind that beast. Let's get you some food and drink, shake off this night."

The pulse of Fort Ramnon was virile. Buskers were particularly exuberant, singing and dancing and juggling fire and bloody skulls. Vendors peddled their wares at top volume and low prices, hungry to move and sell. Faeries and ogres fornicated in the waters of the fountain, bodies heaving, gliding, and pulsating in rhythm with the leprechauns braying their ballads from a nearby stage. The energy of the place roared, bringing a smile to Layla's lips as she walked into the courtyard. What's more, the attention she drew puffed her chest and elated her.

Creatures stared, gawked, in fear and admiration. Saoirse had wrapped Layla in a cloak of feather and fur, not as grand as Kantu's, but regal, nonetheless. Somehow, Layla was taller, towering above everyone and everything, her muscles hard and bulky. She had never felt so powerful, so indestructible.

Dipping her head beneath the doorjamb, she followed Saoirse into the saloon and took a seat at the bar.

"Mauve," Saoirse said, banging a fist on the bar. Mauve wandered over, hips swaying, breast spilling over the top of her corset. Mauve considered Layla for a moment, then cocked a brow at Saoirse. Saoirse shrugged.

"One virgin's blood, coming up," Mauve said, her sing-song tones almost magical.

But she came back with two drinks. One virgin's bloods, and ...

"Yeah," Layla said without question. She grabbed the chalice of blood and sipped it, swishing the hot, gritty fluid around her mouth before finishing the rest in a single gulp. "Another."

One, two, ten drinks down her gullet, and Layla felt no pain. She felt nothing familiar, in fact. She was full of confidence, mania, pleasurable rage. She shed the cloak and danced naked on the bar, singing along to songs she had never heard, hugging and caressing friends she had never met. She was drunk, but not from drink. From her new self.

After slaying a game of cards against a crusty old Lycan, she stumbled to the head to relieve herself. She squatted over a hole in the dirt—the fanciest setup the saloon could concoct—then stood at the mirror, evaluating every centimeter of herself. She was still Layla, but stretched, at least eight feet tall. Her hair had grown and filled out, becoming a mass of a mane that cascaded down her back and over her breasts, curling up at the crease of her groin. Large patches of grey, rotting flesh sloughed off and peeled away in strips, revealing sparkling black bone beneath. *Gorgeous*, Layla thought, twirling, spinning her hair around, and watching bits of skin flutter to the ground like glitter.

When her eyes met their reflection, she stopped admiring. One eye belonged to her, icy blue and bloodshot; the other was foreign, glowing red, a sparkling ruby embedded in her skull. She looked at the jewel, into the black slit that was the pupil, and terror churned in her bowels. She pressed her nose to the mirror, and images flashed before her eyes.

Her apartment,

Her job.

Her brother. His family: kids, his lovely wife.

Her mother, howling in mourning.

Layla stepped back from the mirror and looked away from her new eye.

When she walked out of the bathroom, she vowed never to look herself in the eye again.

DAY THREE

Eagerness woke Layla from her slumber—a hunger to get to Kantu, to take the next soul.

Layla hurried to the toilet, dripping on the seat when she rose too quickly, and splashed some water on her face, a face she refused to look at in the mirror. She turned to dash out of the bathroom and ran straight into Kantu.

Kantu grabbed her by the throat and lifted her off the ground, then spun her around and slammed her on the counter on her belly. She pushed between Layla's legs, pinning her down with her hips.

"Why?" Layla shouted. A gleam from the mirror blinded her. Kantu was smiling, lifting a large scythe in the air. Layla squirmed, but it was futile. Kantu was stronger and larger, and her execution fast. The Sluagh hacked the blade down, connecting at the base of Layla's skull and slicing down her spine to her tailbone. Blood spilled down Layla's sides as Kantu eased the pressure, allowing Layla to stand and back away.

"What the fuck?" Layla screamed, grabbing at her back and spinning around to peek in the mirror. The pain was excruciating, skin tearing and bones cracking. Her body jerked and contorted, and she dropped to her knees as her shoulder blades and ribs shifted beneath her flesh.

When she thought she could take no more, relief washed over her, and the pain and pressure subsided. Feathers fluttered down to the floor as she drew breath, and she realized what had happened.

"Stretch," Kantu said, a wicked grin curving her fleshy beak.

Layla obeyed, maneuvering her new appendages until they

were fully extended. Despite her previous vow, she looked in the mirror.

They were glorious.

Wings, black and shining, protruded from her back and extended the entire length of the bathroom. She drew them in and flexed them out, testing and practicing the use of her new muscles. She swaddled herself in the soft down, caressing her naked body with the thick feathers.

"They're beautiful," Layla said.

"They're useful," Kantu said.

The Sluagh turned and clittered out the doorway. Layla ogled her appearance for another moment, then followed. When she got outside, she realized that she had been left behind. Feathers were twirling down from above, a scattered few remaining on her doorstep as evidence of Kantu's departure.

"Yer on your own, kiddo."

Saoirse rocked in the swing on Layla's porch, her eyes on the sky.

"Left behind?" Layla looked up, and all around the empty sky. "What do I do? Where do I go?"

"See where those motherfuckers take you," Saoirse said, pointing to Layla's back.

"That's ridiculous," Layla said. "Don't I get a flying lesson or something—"

"Whaddya think this is? The University of Hades? Git yer sorry ass in gear and figure it out."

Saoirse stared at Layla, rocking, waiting. Layla shrugged and moved her wings. She made it a few feet off the ground, but couldn't get any real height. Remembering back to her takeoff with Kantu, she closed her eyes and tried to emulate the sensation. She flapped her wings, slow and broad. Once in the air a few feet, she wrapped them around her body and spun.

That did it.

She shot into the air like a corkscrew, the force blowing straggling feathers off her wings and stinging like a plucked hair. The sky enveloped her, swallowing her into darkness.

The landing was bone-shattering. Literally. Not having Kantu's experience, or reverse-articulated legs, made for a sloppy landing. Layla hit the ground hard and heard the distinct snap of breaking bones. Pain shot up her thighs and burned in her knees and ankles.

"Fuck!"

"Wings, you fool." Kantu stood above her, shaking her head. "Spread them when you come down. Glide."

"Yeah. Would have been nice to know before I took off."

"Common sense." Kantu said, clucking her tongue.

Kantu hopped up on Layla's knees, clutched them in her talons, and bounced heavy with all her weight. Layla's knees snapped, and she wailed, more in shock than in pain. Her legs resembled Kantu's now, backwards at the knee. And it didn't hurt; it was a relief of an awkward pressure, somehow.

"Thanks, I guess."

They had landed in a cozy neighborhood, small bungalows lining the street, children's playthings scattered on front lawns, and sedans and minivans parked in driveways. Like any little sleeper town in the country.

But not just any town. This one Layla knew. It was Picton, the town where she grew up.

"Why are we—"

Kantu disappeared, her telltale trail of feathers spiraling

down from the sky. Layla looked around, hoping to spy Saoirse, but the night was still and quiet. Layla worked herself onto her feet and practiced balancing on her new legs. Some teetering and tottering later, she managed to walk about ten meters before she got the hang of it.

I must look ridiculous, my legs bent like this. Though the nakedness and the wings sprouted from my back might be an issue too, could anyone see me.

Thankfully, no one could. She walked up the street, peeking into windows at families having dinner, gathered around their favourite evening programming on the television, or visiting around tea and dessert. A towering figure such as Layla should certainly have drawn attention, especially with her wings extended to full span, but no one gave her the slightest glance as she passed by windows and across front yards.

A short jaunt brought her to the front steps of her childhood home. It was all the same—dark green paint on the outside, gold and black velvet wallpaper on the inside. Precisely as she remembered it.

But ...

"Wait!"

A child's voice sang through the night, calling up the street from the park at the end of the lane. High and sweet, it was a voice she recognized, even all these years later.

"Charlie?"

Her brother careened by her at full tilt, slamming into her feathers, loosening a few from her flesh. He took no notice, though. He just kept running, chasing someone ...

Layla saw her, the wee version of herself, red puffy coat and black toque stretched over her mousy brown curls, running towards the park ahead of Charlie. She had always been faster than him, even though he was older.

Layla followed the children to the park. Taking a seat on the old yellow park bench, she watched them play. They whirled and twirled on the merry-go-round, bobbed up and down on the teeter totters, and swung across the monkey bars, laughing and concocting games with complex scoring systems no adult would understand.

Before her eyes, the children aged to teenagers, left-handed cigarettes pinched between fingers as they sat on the small horses of the merry-go-round, talking about what college they would go to and who they were fucking and would fuck once they got there. In a blink they vanished, and the playground deteriorated into nothing more than a green space for the old folks to feed the pigeons. Most of the youth moved away from Picton to bigger centers to work, procreate, and build real lives, leaving the town to age with its permanent residents.

Wrapped in her wings, Layla made her way back to the house. Charlie was inside now, grey hair and receding widow's peak shining beneath the dining room light. His wife and children played outside on the porch while Charlie was inside with their mother, holding her hands at the table.

Layla passed through the door without opening it and stood above Charlie and her mother, casting a large shadow only she could see. The darkness made their faces contort and change into evil doppelgängers of the people she once knew.

"But I don't understand!" Her mom was hysterical, wailing, her foot tapping a frantic staccato on the hardwood floor. Charlie had been crying. A lot. His eyes were wet and swollen, and his nose red and peeling.

"She was sick, Mom," he said, a sob bubbling beneath in his voice. "We can't imagine. We weren't in her shoes."

"Because she shut us out!" Her mom sobbed and brought a shaking hand up to wipe her tears. "For years now, Charlie. We saw her so little, didn't know who she was anymore. Even if she had six months left, hell, three weeks! We could have said so much ..."

"We don't know," Charlie said. He didn't know what to say, and clearly didn't buy into his own condolences. He dropped his head in their mother's lap and sobbed, soaking her dress. They cried together, her mother stroking his head until they were exhausted and emotionally spent.

Charlie's wife strapped the kids in their car seats and gave them kisses on their rosy cheeks. Charlie didn't want to go, but his adulthood drew him away from his childhood, and back to reality. The grind. The life he had chosen to live. Layla watched him drive away, the taillights disappearing into the night.

The house was silent when Layla crouched back through the door. The lights in the dining room were on, but her mother wasn't at the table. Layla went room to room, running her finger over dust-covered furniture, breathing in the scent of the books on their old bookshelf. Layla grabbed a copy of *Ten Little Indians* off the top shelf and flipped it open. Her heart fluttered at the crinkling of the yellow pages. That sound had been so exciting when she was a child, hidden away in a blanket fort, sneaking book after book and reading into the wee hours of the morning.

Book tucked under her arm, Layla followed the hall back to the master bedroom. Her mother was there, rocking in her chair like she always did. She had a bottle of Merlot cradled in her arm like a baby.

Layla used to sit on the back porch with her mother,

drinking that wine and playing rummy while birds sang their night-song in the trees. Layla adored those moments, just her and her mother after her father had passed, taken by the same cancer that sunk its claws into her.

"Mom?" Layla said, barely able to force the words over her sobs.

Her mother didn't answer.

Of course not, you fool. She can't hear you. She has no idea you're here.

Her mother sobbed, stoking the wine against her cheek, shoulders convulsing. "Layla, my Layla. One more moment. Just one is all I want."

"I'm here, Mom."

"You were such a good girl, Layla. Kind, soft ..."

"I still am, Mom."

"But I should have given you strength."

Layla came to the side of the chair and crouched to the floor. She grasped her mother's arms. She wanted to feel her, to squeeze her skin and smell her L'air du Temps, but she felt nothing. Smelled nothing.

Layla held her mother's arm and swayed with her rocking, humming along with the song she was singing. It grew very quiet and still, so much so that Layla thought her mother had drifted off to sleep. Layla's eyes drooped heavier and heavier, almost drifting off, when a wail shattered the peace.

The yellow curtain on the window was billowing into the room. Saoirse was there, sitting on the window sill, keening from the pit of her gut, tears running down her face. Aside from the shock of the sound, Layla was disturbed by the rare show of emotion from Saoirse.

Then she realized.

"No."

Layla shook her head and stepped toward the window.

"NO!"

She grabbed Saoirse by the shoulders and shook her, warbling the wail bellowing from her throat. But Saoirse's volume only increased. She wailed, and Layla screamed, snot and tears rushing down her face as she frantically assaulted the banshee to cease her mournful song.

The sound of smashing glass stopped Layla's violent protest.

Layla braced herself and turned around.

The carpet was soaked with Merlot, the remnants of the green bottle shattered at her mother's feet.

"Mom, no."

The neck of the bottle was gripped firmly in her mother's hand, a hand that was now steady with determination.

"No, no, Kantu, no, stop ..."

It was almost ethereal, the blood pouring from her mother's throat as she opened herself from ear to ear with that wine bottle, a calm smile on her lips. The red flowed, swelling on the front of her blouse and pooling on the chair between her legs.

"Oh, Mom ..."

Layla pressed her hands against her mother's throat, but the blood poured straight through, bathing Layla's body in crimson gore. She barely noticed when Kantu slithered by Saoirse and hoisted her mother out of the chair.

"Stop, Kantu. Don't do this ... not her ..."

Kantu's eyes were dark, their red glow waning to a dull flicker. She wrapped her mother in her wings and took off, leaving Layla behind. Layla collapsed in the chair, her face resting in the wet of her mother's blood. Layla closed her eyes and wished herself dead for the umpteenth time. She screamed and cried as Saoirse slid in the chair beneath her, stroking her hair and holding her close.

The sponge hurt every follicle of hair on Layla's body, despite how gingerly Imogen rubbed it over her skin. Layla's mother's blood had dried in the hours she lay crying on the chair, Saoirse silently consoling her the whole time. It was horrible, beyond excruciating, knowing what her mother would face at the hands of the Sluagh. Layla's eyes stayed fixed on the spot just over the rocks where the Sluagh would pick the meat off her mother's bones.

"Ye can watch, child," Saoirse said from her spot on the boulder, "but I doubt ye'll see."

The lake was cold and black. It didn't ripple when Imogen dipped the sponge to rinse the blood. Layla wanted to be consumed by that darkness, sucked down to the deep, never to emerge again.

"Where are they?" Layla asked.

"Can't be sure," Saoirse said, "but I gots my doubts they be headin' this way."

"Why is that?"

"It's ye mum," Saoirse said. Imogen stopped scrubbing and let the sponge float in the water as she returned to the shore. "Kantu, old crusty cunt as she is, feels somethin' deep down in the well o' that dirty soul o' hers."

Does she? At a time when Layla should have felt more alone than ever, she didn't. Had she been navigating Fort Ramnon on her own, and this twisted fate she faced, she would have gone mad. She might have plunged herself into those dark waters, opened her wrists over and over again until she slowly and painfully reached whatever end she was damned to receive.

But she wasn't alone. Layla felt connection. Imogen enticed her in the most pleasant way. Saoirse guided her, caring for her with ridiculous turns of phrase and loving touch. And in an even more demented way, she had Kantu. How that creature supported her, she did not know, but with the Sluagh around, she felt somehow safe.

They lingered in the water, Layla and Saoirse, the Banshee combing boney fingers through Layla's hair to untangle the savage mane on her head. She smoothed Layla's wings, calming the feathers and restoring their sheen. Once her mother's blood had been cleansed from her body, Layla crawled out of the water and sat on the shore, contemplating the worlds.

DAY FOUR

It never ended, the day from hell. In hell. Whatever the fuck it was, wherever the fuck they were. It seemed like days had passed, but Layla had not slept in what felt like weeks, months even. It was impossible to tell how long she had been mulling about, what with Fort Ramnon's perpetual state of neither day nor night. Creatures scuttled past, talons and tails and tentacles swaying to and fro, the smell of blood and sex and death thick in the air.

Layla wandered through the streets on new legs, her wings and long mane flowing behind her. Everyone cowered in her wake, both in awe and terror. It was a feeling she had never experienced. Imogen was on her perch atop the saloon, scanning the streets, waiting for her call to wail. Saoirse's laugh echoed off the wagons and carts as she lent an ear to tales from vendors of all make and model: sleek Vampyres, shaggy Lycans, a portly old troll with a pixie on his shoulder. They were chummy, the whole lot of them, steadfast friendship born of an eternity of limbo.

The aroma from a particularly savory slab of meat garnered Layla's attention, drawing her to a vendor peddling culinary delights dripping in blood and gristle.

"Want a bite, my lovely?" he cooed, licking the thick layer of cold sores over his lips.

"No, thanks," she said, the pustulating sores overpowering the deliciousness of the fare.

With at least a dozen other food choices around the fountain, Layla didn't have the digestive fortitude to be able to consume something those diseased hands had fondled.

"Sure ya do," he said, swaying around the cart and sidling up beside her. "Me meat's the very best, I'm told. Thick, solid, delicious ..."

The touch of his hand between her wings, drawing a line down the middle of her back, was as sharp and painful as a blade. She felt this violation of her space right into the marrow of her bones.

"No," she said, a growl more than speech.

It didn't deter him. His oozing lips curled further into a smile as he hungrily eyed her bare body. "You don't mean that, sweet thing. Erryone's gotta eat. Might as well enjoy it. I's do you a favour, not even barter for it. You eat the meat, free of charge. No strings attached, only pleasure."

Her head was shaking no the entire time he spoke, but he was blind to it. Despite being significantly shorter than her, with clearly a snippet of her prowess and strength, he persisted. The finger on her back became a flat hand, pressing against her tailbone and curving over the arch of her buttocks until she was firmly grasped in his calloused hand.

Standing perfectly still, a deer in headlights, she watched his every movement: the hardening of his cock, the lick of his lips, the twitch of his brow.

"Ah, there ye be, my sweet. And sweet you are, I be thinking."

His tongue came out, growing long and high and forcing its way into her mouth. It pushed her tongue aside and groped around, his mouth sucking and cock hardening against her thigh.

The tongue was stretchier than she thought, but easier to bite off than a dick.

A few vendors laughed, and others looked away from the meat vendor rolling on the ground, blood pouring from his mouth. Layla took the tongue and examined it, the pocks and sores littering its surface.

"I believe this meat is spoiled," she said. His screams were silenced when she took the organ and shoved it down his throat, stopping when it reached the top of his stomach.

Even the bloody fountain seemed clean and inviting next to the diseased man. Layla submerged her head, inhaling and exhaling the water to cleanse the rot from her palette. She came up for air, then dipped down again, giving the filth a good, firm swish. Once satisfied all remnants of him were gone, she sat on the edge of the fountain, looking at the snake goddess with blood seeping out of every orifice.

"Beautiful," Layla said. "Powerful."

"She be, yes." Saoirse said, sitting on the stone beside Layla. "So be you."

For once in her life, Layla could believe it. With the life behind her dead, strong blood now pumped through her veins; she possessed a will and stature foreign to her in all her living days. There, back in the land of the living, she had been powerless, inconsequential. Here ...

"Ye like rippin off the bits, do ye?" Saoirse laughed, wagging a finger between her legs then poking out her tongue. "Atta woman. You show 'em what's what."

"Feels good."

"Supposin' it does."

"Really good."

A hard smack slapped the smile straight off Layla's lips. Saoirse smiled, pleased with herself.

"What the fuck did you do that for?" The feathers on Layla's head and back ruffled to attention.

"No need to posture, ye beast. Jus' makin sure you know the monster in ye is an actual cunting monster, long as you aware."

Saoirse didn't wait for a reply. She walked into the saloon, blowing Imogen a kiss on the way by.

A monster. Am I?

I don't want to be a monster.

I am a good person.

Layla looked up at the fountain, at the beautiful woman with tentacles for limbs and snakes for hair. She was larger than life, a powerful force, terrifying and gorgeous and everything Layla had always wanted to be, twisted as she was ...

So this is the choice, is it? Live as a monster or die human.

Layla followed Saoirse into the saloon. As she approached the swinging doors, Imogen smiled down at her, winking an emerald eye.

Lips closed. Silent.

Layla shuddered.

The way people shied away from her as she walked into the saloon both thrilled and upset Layla. She loved being noticed. After a lifetime of being invisible, she finally stole the breath of the room with her entry. On the other hand, it was out of fear, of horror at the creature she was becoming.

"Am I?" Layla said, taking her place at the bar next to Saoirse.

Mauve sauntered over and fetched the bowl from beneath the counter, setting it down in front of Layla with a resounding thud. Layla looked at the gruel and changed her question to a statement.

"I am."

"Not set in stone, ye know," Saoirse said, sipping her beverage.

Layla cupped her face in her hands.

Is my chin sunken? My nose longer? My teeth, are they ...

Layla wiggled her front teeth with her tongue. The taste of copper flooded her mouth as her front two teeth fell to the floor. The sound they made as they hit the wood went straight through Layla like nails on a chalkboard. Her tongue found the empty, bleeding gap, and sliced against the razor-sharp shelf hiding beneath her gums.

"I am Sluagh."

Saoirse clucked her tongue. "The night not be over, yet. You could still be a great many things."

Kantu walked through the door, her robe flowing behind her. She took her own place at the bar next to Layla and nodded her head in approval at the bowl of gruel.

"I'm not ... I'm not sure it's who I am ... what I—"

"It's food," Kantu said, a wheezing laugh forming beneath her words. "Just eat. It shall be over soon."

Layla swiped the bowl onto the floor, and it exploded with a crash almost as loud as her scream. The silence that followed was deafening—every mouth, foot, claw, and breath in the saloon as still as death itself.

"I want it all over now!" Layla screamed. "I can't do this anymore! I can't take anymore!"

Kantu stood. "Cannot do what?"

"This!"

"What?" Kantu hissed. Layla stood, and the two hovered mere millimeters from each other's face. "Can't do what, sweet Layla? Be Sluagh? Die? Go back to life?"

"I can't ..."

"YOU CAN!"

Layla crumbled. She took off towards the door of the saloon, but was blocked by the Sluagh coming in from a fresh feed.

Is that the meat of my mother hanging from their lips?

A sob wrenched in her belly, Layla grabbed her stomach, spun around and bolted for the back exit. Saoirse was saying something after her as she left, but all Layla heard was the pounding of her heart in her skull. She burst into the alley behind the saloon and crumpled to the dirt, sobs wracking her body.

"You slept long. So long."

Kantu's voice silenced the night. The ground shuddered beneath the Sluagh's weight as she trod down the alley. She stopped a few meters before reaching Layla. Layla appreciated the distance but craved Kantu's touch.

"Quit toying with me, beast!" Layla cried, a string of spittle hanging from her trembling lower lip.

Layla looked at the Sluagh. Kantu looked weary, worn. Her feathers were thin and tattered, the glow in her eyes a weak ember.

"I can't do what you do," Layla said. "You're a monster."

Kantu's head bobbed in a nod, a silent resignation. "You are good person."

I am. I am?

It felt so good, the power, the beauty, the fear from everyone …

"But also bad," Kantu said.

Layla's crying softened, and she watched the Sluagh pace between the walls of the alley.

"All people, good and bad. You've been plenty good," Kantu crouched down where Layla lay in a heap on the ground, brushing her beak against Layla's soft, pink nose. "All I ever wanted for you was happiness. Strength."

Those eyes.

"Here, in Fort Ramnon, you shall be Queen."

That voice.

"How long was I asleep?" Layla asked, a frantic reel playing in her mind. The pills, her suicide, waking in her cabin in Fort Ramnon.

"So long," Kantu said, wet, crimson tears falling from her eyes. "But you are here now. Now you begin."

Layla buried her face in Kantu's feathers and wrapped her arms around the old Sluagh's frame. Breathing deep, she salivated at the aroma of meat and feathers and L'air du Temps …

"Mom."

"My child."

They sat atop the fountain, legs braided around the goddess's snakes, wings entwined.

"I'm so sorry," Layla said.

"Nothing to be sorry for," Kantu replied, stroking the center of Layla's back with a single feather. "I'd have done it, too, had illness threatened to take the reins at the end. I go on my terms, and so did you."

"I should have said goodbye."

"No need. Things don't just end, now do they?"

No, they do not.

The carts, the vendors, the creepy crawlies and rotting monsters cajoling and cackling around the courtyard—they were all a reality Layla never thought possible.

"Magic is real," Kantu said, the ember flickering in her eye. "Magic is us."

"But it's so horrible."

"Horror is relative," Kantu said, a grin teasing the edge of her lips.

"But I'm not a bad person."

"What is bad?"

Layla considered the texture of human flesh tearing beneath her bite. How monumental she was, providing release, delivery to the next realm. Strong, beautiful, powerful.

And her new tribe. Saoirse and Imogen sat perched atop the saloon, holding hands, wailing a brogue tune into the night. Their red hair cascaded over their emerald gowns, dangling like bloody tendrils over the saloon sign.

And Kantu.

"What will come of you?" Layla asked, a lump swelling in her throat.

"If you accept your role, I am done. I move on."

The tears flowed, hot and heavy down Layla's cheeks. "But I just came back to you."

"Indeed," Kantu said.

"What happens if I don't? Do we move on together?"

Kantu's head bobbed. She looked so, so tired. "I do not know."

Layla's stomach compressed into a tight knot. Her body ached, every second the pain intensifying.

"Go, child. Sleep."

Kantu was shivering, a raspy wheeze brewing deep in her chest.

"Mom?"

Layla hugged Kantu, and noticed the frailty of her bones, the loss of control. The Sluagh wept, Layla wept, and the tears rained down into the fountain like droplets of blood.

"I love you," Kantu said.

"I love you."

"Goodnight, fair child."

Saoirse pulled the covers up to Layla's chin and gave her a firm, wet kiss on the forehead.

"'Tis been nice knowin' ye, whatever happens."

Imogen, who had been lurking in the corner of the cabin, avoiding eye contact, shuffled over to the bed and stood there without a word. Layla sat up and took Imogen's hands.

"Jesus, lass, ye be messin' the covers right after I tucked ya in! I ain't doin' that a dozen more times, you know."

Layla pulled Imogen down to her face. The young Banshee's lips were plump and peach, and her eyes the most ethereal green Layla had ever seen. Layla pressed her lips against Imogen's, tasting the inside of her mouth with her tongue. She tasted as delicious as she looked. When Imogen pulled away, her eyes were dark and her cheeks wet. She tried to say something, but only a cry squeaked out. She stumbled out the door before the wail escaped.

"Clumsy oaf," Saoirse scolded, chortling at her sister. "Very good then. Down you go."

They repeated the ritual, Saoirse pulling the covers up once again. Layla's heart beat harder, a steady increasing punch to her ribcage. Anxiety threatened to take hold.

"What's going to happen? What will I do?"

"You already know," Saoirse said, patting Layla's chest. "Always did."

"What does that mean?"

Saoirse smiled and turned towards the door.

"I don't have time for cryptic." Layla's tears streamed down her face, soaking the pillow beneath her head.

"Look, what happens will be right. Be it back to life, straight to the other side, or life here. What will be will be, and will be right for you."

Satisfied that's all Saoirse was going to give her, Layla nodded. Saoirse winked back and walked out the door.

The fire crackled in the corner.

Deliberation cackled in Layla's mind.

Be done. Be dead. No more pain, no more anguish. Move on. That's what I wanted to begin with, yes? But an eternity of nothing. Or worse ...

Or go home. When I get there, will the cancer come with me? Could I start from scratch, try to finally build a life? Or have a few extra moments to live my remaining life to the fullest.

Or stay here. As Queen. In a new world order, in a brand-new flesh. Rebirth, of the world. Of me.

Death.

The end.

Rebirth.

THE FIRST DAY OF THE REST OF HER LIFE

A fire crackled.

Morning birds sang their siren song, and the bustle of life clicked and chattered, waking in a nearby somewhere.

The smell of smoke and dirt and L'air du Temps hung in the air. It tasted of life lingering and life passed.

There was no pain, no anguish. Only peace.

A life anew.

Layla opened her eyes.

Consumption
A Ramnon Tale

Jae Mazer

1

With its tiny blue flowers and 24k gold trim, the small saucer upon which Brock's tea was balanced looked particularly pretty in the soft sun glowing through the window. That set of china, straight from Denmark, had been part of my mother's collection.

Be a shame if it broke, I thought as I sipped my own tea, the lavender hot and soft on my lips. *Bloody shame if someone broke it on purpose.*

But then, *oh how lovely it would look, that bone white china, peppered in blue with a tinge of gold, protruding from his shit-brown cornea.*

"Everything okay, Nell?" Brock asked, brow cocked.

I took another sip, a convenient avoidance of an answer, truthful or otherwise.

"Nell?"

I conceded. I wasn't getting off that easy today. "No, Brock."

"No? What's wrong, then?"

"No, I mean nothing's wrong. Yes, everything is okay."

With his eyes firmly fixed on my face, he set his cup and saucer on the table.

Oh shit.

"What is it?" Both a command and a question, his voice made me wince.

"It's nothing, like I said."

"Tell me." His fists clenched, knuckles blanching.

"Nothing. Like I said." I articulated each consonant, hard staccatos, driving the point home.

"*It's* nothing, you said. *It. It* is something. You might as well just tell me."

Why would I? To what end? A fight and series of insults. Brock had a knack for weaponizing self-doubt, insecurities, and every shortcoming and failure and flaw. *No, Brock. I don't care how you feel. Not anymore. I care how I feel, though.*

"I'm tired, is all." I tucked a sprig of loose hair back into the braid at the side of my face. To distract both myself and him.

"Unfuckingbelievable," he growled beneath his breath.

"What is?"

"You."

"What did I do now?" I set my saucer down harder than intended, but only half as hard as my mood dictated. Unbeknownst to me, I had already set foot on that slippery slope, and was careening down the hill.

"That's your go-to," he said, mocking. "You're tired. You're busy. Never a good time. Why don't you tell me what's bothering you? Naw, go ahead. Bottle it up. Let it fester, grow into a cancer that will destroy us."

If I let my thoughts loose, they would grasp your saucer, smash it off the table, and pierce your eyes with the shards. Maybe cut your balls off, too, just for good measure.

"Yeah, you're right. I'm sorry."

Brock huffed and puffed and picked up his tea. My chest tightened, both excitement and expectation swelling in my throat. *Is that it? Is it over before it begins?*

But it wasn't done. It never was. Never a quiet, happy ending. I laughed with relief when the doors started slamming and Brock's bellows rattled the pictures on the walls. I smiled when that saucer broke, flung at my head as I ducked casually to the side as his eyes bulged and voice crescendoed to a manic fury of accusations and insults full of hate and poison. As always, I could only nod, but even that infuriated him; it was condescending, that subtle bob of my thoughtless head. Remaining still was also infuriating, as it clearly communicated my apathy towards him, our life, our house, and the world at large.

There was no right answer. Hell, there was no answer at all. There was only waiting. Waiting for the end, whatever that might be.

2

Breakfast the next day was quiet, all coffee and half-assed smiles, the crinkling of newspapers and book pages as Brock and I carried out our routine, preparing for the peaceful daily separation.

"Busy day today?" I asked.

"Meetings."

"Same old same old." Immediately I regretted rolling my eyes.

Brock stopped chewing his bacon. My muscles tensed in anticipation.

Brock started chewing his bacon again.

"It's about the Peterson account," he said. "We can't seem to get our shit together. *They* can't, rather. Fucking house cats."

"House cats?"

"My partners. Not good for much, won't do what they're told. Lazy as fuck."

"Cats are rather smart, aren't they?"

A momentary pause in chewing.

"Not these ones. These ones are fucktards."

"Of course they are."

Non-chewing morphed into rapid and forceful gnashing. Brock's mouth had become a churning, violent Vitamix.

Mind that rage eating. You wouldn't want to spoil that new diet, with those chiseled abs and engorged ego, now would you?

"That place'll be the death of me," he said to his plate.

Hopefully.

My chair squealed when I stood to refill my coffee. I spoke as I poured, focusing on the cascading liquid to calm the words flowing from my mouth. "They have a long procedure today. Don't know if I'll be in on it, but I'll be on alert if they need—"

The clang his fork made as it hit his plate shot straight up my spine. I didn't turn, didn't want to see him stand, to view the back of his sport coat as he gathered his things and prepared for his day. A day leaving his house, going out into his world, in his car, in his life.

"I might not be home for dinner," he said.

I shrugged, quite sure he didn't see me. I didn't look as he picked up his briefcase and went about his business, business as usual, day after day, month after month, eternity after eternity. His eyes hadn't brushed me, I was certain, since we'd rolled out of bed that morning. Not even as my skin was wet and glistening when I stepped out of the shower, as he stood within centimeters of me, scraping his razor across his face. In that moment, bare and exposed, rejected and ignored, I imagined that razor, the beauty of its gleaming blade dragging, pressing across my flesh, splitting me open from palm to bicep or earlobe to earlobe.

But I craved less pain, not more. And death hurt, if only for the flesh wound.

The door clicked shut, waking me from my morbid fantasy. Beyond these walls, *his* walls, his whistle cut through the air, a shrill, clumsy joy and oblivion to my muted suffering.

Finally, I turned, but only after having a long, slow sip of my coffee. Taking inventory of the table, a lump swelled in my throat. A dirty plate, a half-empty coffee mug, a crumpled newspaper laid haphazardly on a chair, sections out of order, chaos and disregard. And the bacon, or lack thereof. I hadn't had a single piece. Not one. I hadn't even gotten to lick one goddamn strip of that maple-flavoured fatty swine, my favourite and he knew it. He fucking knew it.

Thank goodness I was able to set my coffee mug on the table before collapsing to the floor, my body wracking with sobs; more mess to clean was the last thing I needed on this very ordinary, typical, run-of-the-mill morning.

3

"Clamp."

I plucked the tool off the silver tray and placed it in the doctor's crimson-soiled glove.

"Suction."

Obeying, I rested the tube in the incision as the doctor clamped the artery. An eerie calm enveloped the room, the veil of professional detachment that often existed in the operating room, the calm eye in a hurricane of urgency. This patient would soon be dead, I was quite sure, but on we ploughed, flesh robots going through the motions.

My assumption proving correct, the monitors yelled and nagged, peppering the room with beeps and screams, rapid-fire digital nails in the patient's coffin. A flurry of movement erupted—medication, pumping, pressing. Futile.

My voice was distant, as if coming from down the hall or out the front sliding doors, somewhere far away—in the mountains, alone, isolated, peaceful. "Call it, Doctor."

His voice rang, a gong beside my head, drawing me back to reality. "Time of death, 4:28 p.m."

A slow loiter infected the operating room; gloves were peeled off and tossed to the floor, instruments set on trays, masks pulled off faces. No one said much, only shuffled and tidied, busywork to punctuate the completion of failure. I lingered, gathering gauze, tubes, and wrappers from the floor while everyone else filtered out.

Once I was the sole survivor in that room, I sat on a stool, evaluating the patient. He was a man in his mid-forties, hefty but not fat, average height, a mop of brown curls peeking from beneath his surgical cap. I rolled the stool next to the table and pulled off that cap, freeing those wild tresses. Taking care to use the most gentle touch, I brushed my fingers over his lids, opening his eyes. Soft brown and bloodshot, the eyes were vacant, wanting for nothing anymore.

Is that it, you poor sap? Did you want for too much?

With a gloved finger I poked his love handle.

Liked those burgers and chips, did you?

I stroked a finger down the bridge and over the tip of his bulbous nose.

Hit the drink, too, I see. Was it that which claimed your life?

Curling my finger, I peeled his lips away from the breathing tube and further still, revealing slightly yellowed teeth.

A smoker, too? You practically lured the reaper with hookers and pizza.

Bile bubbled in my throat. It wasn't that I had suddenly become aware of the copper smell permeating the room, or the chemical shit storm of sterilization and medication. It was all that emotion Brock accused me of bottling up. As if someone had shaken me, a can of pop, that hopeless desperation caught in my throat, a sob drowning in vomit. I ran to the bin and purged my anxiety over a pile of masks and gauze and wrappers.

After splashing my face with water, I left that final corpse of the day behind without so much as a second look. I had seen enough—of him, of all his kind.

4

The Anchor and Crown was a haunt my best friend Renee and I used to visit regularly. Until I married Brock. But I decided it had been a long day, and having a beer with her was worth suffering his wrath.

Renee tilted the pint to her lips, grinning. "Why are you being such a miserable cunt?"

"Mind your drink doesn't leak out the corners of that smug smirk, you bitch." I didn't mean that, of course. I loved Renee. We'd been friends since elementary school. Not that there'd been much choice in our tiny little corner of Northern Alberta, but of the handful of children, she was the one I gravitated to. And her to me.

"Seriously though, Nell. What's up with you lately?"

"Nothing in particular. Just the blues."

"Blues, eh? Goin' on about two years, pert near."

"Exaggeration."

"Fact."

I focused on the bubbles in my brew, floating, popping, floating, popping . . .

"It's him, yes?" Renee asked. She already knew the answer to that. "How long are you gonna let this go on?"

"I don't even know what this is."

"Sure you do. You aren't stupid. It's abuse."

"But is it?"

"Yes. It is."

But was it really? Seemed a dramatic diagnosis. Perhaps the years of marriage had just degraded into a half-assed effort on both sides, each feeling devalued, bored, lonely.

"He doesn't hit me," I said to my drink. I couldn't say it to her because I knew it was a weak explanation that couldn't hold the weight of a dandelion. No, he didn't hit me. I wish he did. If it was clearly defined abuse, my feelings of desperation, panic, and disdain would be justifiable.

"Are you happy?" Renee asked. Her drink was on the table, her hands folded in front of her. This was a serious discussion, now. I hated serious discussions. Felt like being cornered.

"Now that's a stupid question."

"No. It's not. Are you?"

No. I'm not happy.

"I'm fine."

"No. You aren't."

And I never will be.

I felt bad, lying to my friend. I loved her, so much. She was like a sister to me, and I know she'd support me, but . . . would she? When it came down to it, would she help? I'd never ask. I'd never put anyone out like that, even my most intimate friend.

Renee sighed and picked up her drink. "So what happened at work today? I heard your team lost one."

"He was lost before he came in. Some rich suburbanite with a heart condition."

"Huh. Pretty standard. Why did this one irk you?"

Because it was him. It was Brock laying on that table. Everyone was Brock, everywhere. The little things I can't stand about him that niggle at my brain . . . I see them, I find them in everyone, whether they're there or not.

"Renee . . . I . . . I think I . . ." Throat tightening, lip quivering. If my voice wavered on my next words I was done for. "Renee, I hate him."

That did it. The floodgates opened, and I cried. Heaving, breathless sobs that drew the attention of the other patrons. Renee put her arm around me, threw some cash on the table, and led me outside.

5

I took a long drag of my left-handed cigarette and leaned back on the rocks bordering the lake. Renee and I always holed up here when we needed to just get away. A good ten kilometers from the city limits, in the heart of coyote country, no one had any interest in being there after dusk.

The night air was crisp, swelling the gooseflesh on my arms. The smell of canola wafting off the fields lulled me into memories of my childhood, driving across the province to reach the National Park. There was nothing quite like spending the night with the screaming cliffs of the Rocky Mountains towering above, enclosing you in the safety and shelter of their shadow.

I tugged at a string on my scrubs. "He threw a dish at me this morning."

"Abuse!" Renee cried out, her voice echoing off the lake in front of us.

"It's a broken plate."

"Could have hit you."

"But it didn't." I drew another hit. "I'm tired." Renee said nothing. She could feel it, same as I could, that little bits of information might trickle out, that I might actually be able to get the poison off my chest. "He's joined a new gym. CrossFit or some bullshit. Lost a pile of weight."

"That's great," Renee said.

"Yes, but . . ." another drag, then, "now he's the authority on health. Comments on everyone else's weight and lifestyle, especially mine." I touched my face. Not sure when I'd started crying, but my cheeks were slick with tears. "He'll show me pictures of myself when I was younger, much younger. Tell me how I *used* to be beautiful. How I don't take care of myself. How if I get sick, there will be no one to blame but myself."

Renee reached out and placed her hand on mine. "That's cold."

"It's true. But it's more than that. He's spending money hand over fist—new vehicle, clothes, expensive liquor, and tech. If I spend a goddamn penny, he pitches a fit. But he's the one draining our account. He's gluttonous. Always more. Better car, better body, better wife."

I was standing now, the words pouring out as fast as the tears. Renee listened, tears of her own wetting her big brown eyes. "Seems like a midlife crisis. Catastrophe, rather."

Another draw and slow exhale. "That's it, though. I think that's precisely what it is, but it doesn't make it hurt any less. And I don't know if it'll change or improve."

Renee stood and wrapped her arms around me. I cried into her shoulder, dampening her hoodie. She stroked my hair. "You don't have to live this way. Leave him. Start over."

"I'm too old."

Renee pulled away from me. She pursed her lips in disapproval, the wrinkle between her furrowed brows a canyon. "Gurl, you ain't even forty yet."

"Pushing it, though. I can't start over. Not now."

She hesitated, then embraced me again. "What's the plan, then?"

Just wait for it to end.

6

By the time I pulled in our driveway it was well past one in the morning. The house was dark, which meant one of two things. Brock was asleep, which would be amazing, or he was awake and brooding. When I passed through the front door, I stopped. I listened. I heard less than nothing—no snoring, no movement.

Awake. Goddamnit.

I took my time. Not that it mattered; dick mode had already been activated by the lateness of the hour. I hung my purse on the chair and my coat in the closet, and poured a full glass of wine, drinking one slow sip at a time. After drawing it out longer than I dared, I ascended to my fate.

"Have fun?" His eyes were black as beetles, insects burrowing into my brain.

"It wasn't really about having fun. I needed to unwind. Had a hard shift."

His legs were stretched out in front of him, back pressed against the headboard, computer on his lap. I doubted very much he was actually doing anything on that laptop. It was a prop to make me think he wasn't perseverating on my every word and movement.

Going through the motions, I slinked into the ensuite, brushed my teeth, took out my contact lenses, and washed off my makeup. Before changing into my pajamas, I closed and locked the bathroom door. When I emerged, he was in the same position, but his eyes were focused on the screen. *Liar*. His hands were stiff, resting in the same spot, fingers unmoving.

He spoke first. "You can't keep going out after work. How much was dinner and drinks?"

"I had one drink and no food. I ate the lunch I took to work. Like I always do."

"No need to bite my head off."

"I . . ." *Breathe. Placate.* "I'm sorry. It helps, going out with Renee."

"What'd you guys do?"

"Went to the pub, had a yarn."

"That's all?"

There it was. The beginnings of the row.

"What else would I be doing?"

"I can't believe you don't talk to me."

"This has nothing to do with you, Brock."

"You'd rather spend time with her."

I had nothing to say. I couldn't even conjure up an excuse, a retort, a denial.

"Are you fucking her?" he asked, his words running together, muddy.

Drunk.

"Oh, for fuck's sake, Brock."

He mocked me. "Oh, for fuck's sake, Brock."

I ignored him, pulled back the sheets, and climbed into bed. There was a distance between us far wider than the California king, yet the space felt as small as a dorm room cot.

"I don't know what your goddamn problem is," he said. "You're always in such a mood."

Because, Brock. Because you're a cruel, heartless bastard. You're entitled, arrogant, and self-obsessed. And I've condemned myself to a lifetime with you.

But that's the thing. I'd made this bed I lay in. Either leave, or . . .

I had to say something, or the spark would turn into an explosion. "You know what I'd like?" I reached for his hand. It had been a long time since I'd made eye contact or even touched him. Judging by the look on his face, I'd say it startled him. "I'd like us to get away."

"Get away?"

"A little vacation. It's been so long since we've done that."

He paused—suspicious, no doubt. "What did you have in mind? I'm not made of money, you know."

I clenched my teeth, pushing my mind past the remark. "Nothing extravagant, just a quick mountain getaway. Go into Jasper, stay at that Ptarmigan campground. It'll be nice."

He watched me, searching my face. Was he trying to find motive? Thinking up an excuse so he didn't have to spend time with me?

"You know what?" he said. "That would be awesome. I could get in some hikes and climbs. Been a while since I've been into the mountains."

We. Since we've *been into the mountains.*

"I'll book it," he said as he opened his laptop.

While his fingers scrolled, and the screen flashed pictures of trails and maps, I turned away and let him plan his trip.

7

With my eyes closed and the moon roof open, I let my headrest back and breathed in the thick air of the prairies, the ripe aroma of canola, and the crisp pine of the approaching mountains. Jasper was a mere four-hour jaunt from where we lived, but we passed through a plethora of smells enough to cover an entire planet. It was peaceful and invigorating, calm and exhilarating.

"You know what you need?" Brock said, shattering the euphoria. "You need some nice clothes. Don't you care about your appearance?"

Sigh. "I thought you were worried about money?" I said.

"You'd feel so much better if you looked better. I've never felt so alive in my entire life."

I dare say. In this car alone you have a thousand dollars of new clothes, and another thousand in eclectic hiking and camping gear enough to get us up Mount Logan and back.

Despite my loathing disinterest, he continued. "All the girls at work are talking about how much weight I've lost and how fit I look." Brock flexed his bicep. "A hot chick asked if I was a triathlete."

"You've been doing great, Brock. I'm glad you feel good."

"Are you? Seems like you resent me for getting my shit together."

Can't we just enjoy the silence? "I don't resent you, Brock. I do, however, wish you didn't judge other people so harshly."

"I can't believe you're okay with being . . ." His eyes left the road and scanned me, evaluating me. "That's the problem with society. Greedy, gluttonous."

"Gluttony has many forms, the least of which is McDonald's, I think."

The vinyl on the steering wheel creaked as Brock squeezed it in a growing rage, his fists angry vices. "And what the hell is that supposed to—"

His heavy, over-priced hiking boot slammed on the brake in the nick of time. The car fishtailed, and we skidded onto the gravel shoulder, narrowly missing the hind end of a massive bull moose.

"Holy shit," he said, his white-knuckled grasp still planted on the wheel.

"Fuck me." I said it, but couldn't hear it with my heart pounding in my ears.

He was a big boy—had to be twenty-one hands at the withers, and almost as long as our car. His rack was thick and wide, and he had a massive dewlap swaying beneath his jaw. A healthy beast, with a generous layer of muscle and fat covering the entirety of his unblemished body, he chewed his cud as he stared at the car, evidently unfazed by our sudden presence.

Brock rolled down his window. "Jesus, motherfucker!"

"Seriously, Brock?"

His head snapped in my direction. "What? That goddamn asshole just about killed us! Can you imagine if we'd run into him?"

"Yes, Brock. If *we'd* run into *him*. It'd be our fault, now wouldn't it?"

"How about you shut your mouth!" Brock screamed. To punctuate his anger, which I knew was a byproduct of the near-moose experience, he punched the dash in front of me, buckling the composite foam. "You always have something to say, don't you, Miss Perfect."

Say nothing. Let him vent.

"What. Nothing to say?" He leaned over the arm rest, his attention focused entirely on me, the moose all but forgotten.

Let it pass.

"This. This is why I'm so stressed out all the time, why I almost hit a goddamn moose and totaled the car. Then where would we be? Can you afford a new car? It's like you have no concept of money."

Breathe in, breathe out.

And on he persisted. "Here we go again. Ignore it, like you always—"

It was almost magical, the sound of the glass breaking, a chain reaction of spiderwebs spreading across the windshield. The second blow was less beautiful, the crumpling of metal and crunching of plastic beneath a pair of pounding hooves.

"What the actual fuck?" Brock screeched, his focus back outside the car.

The moose was up on his hind legs, pummeling the driver's side of the car. The windshield was the first casualty, and now he was working on the hood. Brock fumbled for his seatbelt.

"Get out, Nell! Get the fuck out of my way!"

As my fingers found the release on my own belt, Brock's palms and heels drove into my thighs and stomach as he scrambled over me and out the passenger door. I watched him go, running into the ditch; I was shocked but not surprised. My fingers still rested upon the button of the seatbelt but had yet to depress it. I peered forward, out the gaping hole where the windshield once was, right into the eyes of the beast. He was huffing, sides puffing in and out, spittle dangling from his meaty lips. He was so close I could have reached out and touched him. One more trample and my skull would have been ground meat.

Please. Do it. Save me.

Nostrils flaring, it poked its massive maw into the car and nuzzled my chest. I wasn't scared. I wasn't panicked. My body flooded with warmth, with peace. I placed my hand atop its velvety muzzle and closed my eyes, welcoming the end.

But my end had not arrived. Not yet. The beast snorted, showering me in a layer of warm snot, then backed away and strolled up the road as if nothing had happened. My warmth drained, from the top of my head out the tips of my toes, leaving me shuddering, still belted into my seat.

"What the fuck is wrong with you?" Brock grabbed me by the shoulders and gave me a shake. "It could have killed you!"

But it didn't. It fucking didn't.

I cried, and Brock shook his head, looking at me in disgust. He walked away, fingers poking at his cellphone as I remained fastened in place, willing the beast to return.

8

This will do fine.

Beyond the sounds of Brock nailing stakes into the ground and the music blaring out of his portable speakers—Kanye West, even though he knows how much I hate him—was a chorus of nature. Once he was gone, off to his amazing hikes and adventures, I would hear it better, the music of the woods.

"You gonna help?" he shouted as he threw his hammer on the ground.

"Yeah, sorry. Lost in my own head."

Together we pitched the tent and unloaded the rental car, all but the food, which would stay locked safely in the truck, away from the hungry sniffers of grizzlies and black bears. Our insurance company had made quick work of the situation, bringing us a rental and towing the remains of my old sedan. Though he was initially shocked by the smash of Moose Banner, Brock's foul mood turned gleeful when he considered the ramifications of the four-legged attack.

"I've been texting Paul," he said as he set up the propane burners on the picnic table. "He says I could get a Corvette with a super charger for a steal this time of year."

But . . .

"But, Brock."

He looked up, his eyes daring me.

Grow a set, Nellie.

"Brock, the moose wrecked *my* car. Shouldn't I get a new one? I mean, doesn't really matter, but you just got your truck two years ago—"

"You can drive the truck. My drive to work is longer, and besides, I appreciate vehicles more than you do. And I've been itching for a car. Something sporty."

"I had that car for eight years. Might be nice to drive something new."

"Can't let me have something, can you?"

We finished setting up in social silence, with his music blaring and us muted. Once we were cocked and ready to survive, Brock disappeared into the tent, emerging moments later wearing head to toe North Face gear from his toque down to his thermal socks.

"Wow." I had nothing more to say. Nothing safe, anyways.

"I know, right? Cost a pretty penny, but worth it, for the work that I do."

"Work?"

He glared, right into my heart.

"You wouldn't understand," he said, shaking his head. Popping the trunk, he tossed in his freshly-filled hydration pack, a bundle of snacks, and his brand spankin' new galvanized steel hiking pole, which I guess he intended to use on the paved or grated-gravel walkways of his hardcore hiking trails.

"You sure you don't want to go see the falls with me?" I said. "Or Edith Cavell? We could have a picnic."

"When I'm done. We'll see how tired I am. It's a massive excursion."

I couldn't control it. My eyes welled with tears. I turned away. "You really want to go alone?" Not that I cared—but it still stung that he didn't care.

"I'm fast. Anyone else would just hold me back. I'll be up and back in no time."

I didn't look. Not as he finished loading the car—the only car we had. Not as he got in that car, fired it up, and backed out of the campsite. I didn't look down the road after him as the plume of dust rose from the gravel. When the dust settled, and the sounds of nature came to life, I looked. At a campsite with a tent, a cook stove, my clothes and hikers piled on the picnic table, and no car.

Panic struck, like Tyson himself had just nailed me in the guts. My chest heaved as I tried to draw a full breath, but I was choking, suffocating. My heart beat so loud, so hard I was certain the pressure of it would shoot geysers of blood from my pores, flooding the campsite and running into the river, tainting the pure, glacial water, poisoning it with my fear, my loathing, my emptiness.

No, Nellie. Stop.

I grabbed a folding chair and a bottle of wine and scrambled down the little trail leading from the back of our campsite to the river below. After finding a solid spot amongst the boulders, I plunked myself into the chair and opened the wine. Glass be damned, I took a long, slow, delicious swig straight from the bottle. I closed my eyes, listened to the water trickling, splashing. The thick, dry wine coated my tongue as I rolled it around my mouth. I breathed in the aroma of pine and campfires. Another swig, more senses. The sound of a distant loon, the aroma of citronella and dogwood.

The flowing of the wine ebbed the flowing of my tears. I sagged lower in the chair, the entire experience of the mountain wilderness overtaking my every sense, lulling me into a peaceful slumber.

9

I was roused by an aching cold. The chair offered no warmth, only a stiff neck, and an aching rib from the chair arm poking into my side. I couldn't be sure exactly how long I'd been out, but it had been a while, judging by the pitch-black night that had infected the woods. It gets dark early in the crevice of the Rockies, but this was blacker than black. I attributed this to the lateness of the hour, though the night was devoid of even the slightest hint of star or moon—the cloud cover from earlier in the day had decided to linger.

Rocks rolled down the bank, freed from the mud when I stretched my cramped legs. I pulled my hands from my hoodie and stretched them above my head; the empty wine bottle rolled off my lap and thudded to the ground. Reaching for it, my head protested, thumping and throbbing as I bent to retrieve my rubbish. I wrapped one hand around the neck of the bottle and pressed the other fingers against my temple, massaging away the pain. The thumping continued, louder, reverberating in my chest.

But...

It wasn't my pulse. My pulse was soft, rhythmic, growing more rapid as my fear swelled. The thumping, however, was steady, hypnotic. Distant.

I stood, my eyes squeezed shut to dull the spinning but also to listen—to the nature that would quell my looming anxiety, to the beating of my heart, to the odd thumping in the woods. I opened my eyes, and was greeted with darkness, so I felt my way between the birches and pines to the campsite. I'm not sure what I'd hoped for—Brock there, fire spewing heat, food cooking? Or did I hope for what I found: nothing. A dark, empty campsite. Though relieved that I was still alone, something was wrong. Brock hadn't returned. No fire had been lit, and the campsite was exactly how I'd left it when I made my panicked dash for the river.

Thump. Thump. Thump.

Nothing else. No crickets chirping, rodents scuffling, coyotes yipping. Only thumping, deep, rhythmic, close. One foot in front of the other, that thumping saved me from returning to my panic. Following that sound spared me the worry of what happened to Brock, what would happen to me, and what would become of life after the fact.

Finally remembering I had a cell phone, I pulled it out of the pouch of my hoodie and activated the flashlight, illuminating the gravel road down the line of campsites. Shadow demons flickered between the trees with every step I took, their tongues flicking and tails swooshing in time with the thumping.

Thump. Thump. Thump.

Not thumping. Beating. It was a beating sound that drew me

down the lane of this campsite where I knew no one and had no safe place to go. I couldn't even lock myself in my car. I had no car, not anymore. So I walked, one foot in front of the other, down the gravel lane, towards the noise. I had to focus to see a light through the trees. It wasn't the shaky glow from my meager phone lamp, but a warm glowing flicker of flame peeking through the heavy brush. I turned off my light and shoved the phone back into my pocket; stealth seemed as necessary as the thumping seemed ominous.

My footsteps matched each thump, the beats covering my approach as I moved towards the flames, a campfire too large to belong in the standard public sites this campground offered. I opted to stay on the gravel road rather than sneak through the trees for several reasons. One, if I was truly going to sneak up on whatever nefarious source was making the thumping, crackling though heavy brush full of snapping twigs and dried-out leaves would draw attention. Two, if there was nothing evil afoot, I would appear suspicious if caught lurking about the bushes, sneaking up on someone's campsite. My safest bet was to stick to the trail.

Calm the fuck down. What do you think is going on? Devil worship? Serial killer? Brock rotating on a spit?

My shoulders loosened and I let out a soft giggle, quickly stifling it with my hand. With my mood lighter, my step quickened, and I reached the edge of the offending campsite where the fire roared and the thumping boomed through the trees.

It wasn't devil worship, or Brock on a spit, but it was odd. Unsettling.

The campsite was large—at least three times the size of ours. The fire was made on what appeared to be a pyre of antlers, all shapes and sizes, tips and hooks poking out here and there.

People surrounded the fire in a circle, hands on each other's shoulders, connected, moving together in reverse. Beside the fire was a man, bent and broken, beating an old drum. The human circle danced backwards in rhythm with the drumming, steps pounding the ground, birthing plumes of dust. Their eyes were closed, mouths drawn in tight lines, almost like masks with the orifices sewn shut.

A flanker crackled up from the fire, startling me. Then another flanker, another crack—this one like a whip—and the old drummer's eyes snapped open. He stopped drumming. All feet stopped; all people were still. The fire burned, but even it was silent. The drummer turned his head in my direction and his lips parted, revealing teeth caked with rot and sharpened to the root. He laughed, a wheezing wet sound, and globs of black sludge dribbled from his lips, soiling his sagging chest.

"Ayaangwaamim." He tilted his head, recognizing my confusion. His next word was slow, precise. "Warn."

Another fit of laughter erupted from deep in his belly, and all heads in the circle turned in my direction with the audible crack and creak of bones. The drummer flexed his arms then resumed pounding, this time maniacally and at triple the speed. The circle danced again, falling backwards in clumsy, frantic motions, heads lolling around shoulders and limbs flailing. Claws sprouted from the dancers' fingertips and horns from their heads, the mottled bone protruding and growing into antlers that clanked together as the dance escalated into a violent fury. Those newly sprouted claws groped at exposed bellies, freeing entrails that splattered to the ground, leaving crimson filth over the dancing feet. Soon the dancers were on their knees, pawing at each other, devouring and chewing in sync with the rhythm of the drum.

The drumming continued as I ran away. The laughter

sounded just as loud if not louder as I rounded one corner then the next, growing ever nearer to our campsite and farther from that fire. The flame was bright, scorching the skin on my face worse with every step I ran. My feet moved, not clumsy and panicked, but graceful and purposeful, as if I, too, were dancing. I narrowed my eyes and covered my ears, intent on pushing forward until I reached the campsite which seemed oh so far away, too far away, farther than it should have been. I ran, and would have continued running had Brock not hit me with the car, sending me flying over the hood, breaking the second windshield of the day.

10

The music of the woods was replaced by beeps, whooshes, and muted footsteps, and the aroma of pine morphed into bleach, topical medicines, and bodily fluids. There was no mistaking the sounds, smells, and tastes of a hospital. Judging by the people shuffling up and down the hallways and laid out on stretchers, the Park Lodge Medical Center dealt mostly with climbing injuries, bike accidents, and exposure. Other than a few older folks clutching chests and holding heads, the clientele was a median age of mid-twenties and sporting the same pretentious trekking gear as my beloved husband.

"I can't fucking believe this," Brock complained. His elbows were on his knees, head in his hands. He was wearing the same thing as the day before, though now it was soiled with dirt and sweat.

"Should I be sorry?" I asked.

"What the fuck were you doing?"

What the fuck was I doing?

"I'm sorry you hit me, Brock." The rage in his eyes curdled my blood. Not with fear but with a rage of my own.

"This is one more goddamn problem we didn't need."

I got off lucky. Real lucky. Some fractured ribs, a broken arm, and general bruising and battering, but I wouldn't be off my feet for long. "Could be much worse."

"Yeah, well, it's not good. What are you gonna do? Be off work for a month?"

"I get sick leave—"

"Only partial pay."

"It's enough, Brock. We live excessively." You *live excessively*. "Other than me needing a little help around the house, we won't even notice this in a week's time."

"I have to work, Nell. What do you expect me to do? Take time off to help you around the house?"

I expect you to care. I expect you to hold my hand, to worry, to tell me you love me and we'll be just fine.

"I'll be fine," I lied.

The door creaked open, silencing any further conversation. Regina, the nurse in charge of the overnight shift, came moseying in, a warm smile across her plump face. "How are you doing, m'lovey?"

"Had better nights," I said, offering a wan smile.

"Well rumour has it the other guy's worse. You gave it to him real good, broke his glasses and all." Regina laughed, a pure, joyful sound. I watched as she worked, checking my vitals and refilling the Styrofoam cup on my bedside table. I looked up once to see the disgusted look on Brock's face as he evaluated her every lump and dimple, shaking his head.

"How long will we have to stay?" Brock said, his toe tapping an irate staccato.

Regina glared over her glasses, hand on her hip. "How long will the missus need our care? What would suit you, sir?"

It took everything I had to stifle the full-blown laughter brewing in my belly. She'd only met him just hours before but already knew what he was.

Brock's voice sweetened to sickly honey, his flirtatious eyes contributing to his ruse. "I just . . . this is so stressful for her, and I want her to be comfortable."

"Well, sir, the doctor wants to keep her for a day, just to be sure everything stays where it's suppose ta. That all right with you?"

Brock and Regina locked in a stare-down until his fists loosened and he exhaled. "You know, that's good, actually. Had a long trek yesterday, and no sleep after." He looked at me, a not-so-subtle glare. "I think I'll gather our things from the campsite, grab a room at the Jasper Park Lodge. I'll lounge tomorrow, have a round of golf, maybe go for a massage. Is that okay with you, my love?"

Regina's response was little more than a grunt. Despite Brock's performance, she appeared unconvinced. After jotting notes on my chart, she stroked my hair, gave my hand a squeeze, and headed for the door.

Turning back, she said, "Got anyone I can call for you?"

"No, but thank you for all your help," Brock said as he stroked my hand, feigning love and concern.

"Wasn't asking you."

Brock put his hand on my leg.

"No," I said to her shoes. "I'm fine."

Those shoes didn't move for several uncomfortable

moments, but eventually she walked away. Brock left too, after murmuring a see-you-later and grumbling about calling the insurance company.

I was alone again, but this time it felt wonderful. In that foreign room, in a building I didn't know, the world was locked out, and all the nastiness with it. I thought back to the accident, of sliding up that windshield in surreal impact, and imagined that the grill had snapped my legs clear in half, leaving me immobile. Even better, my back. My neck. How wonderful would it be, confined to a chair or a bed, in a facility where I didn't have to make the choice to get away, to start over, to have something different? Incapacitated was different, and it was a dream.

As I drifted to sleep, lulled by a cocktail of painkillers and anti-nausea medication, I dreamed of an eternity locked in medical purgatory.

11

After a long, deep rest, I woke, groggy but refreshed. The sun filtering through the drapes was blood red and low in the sky, which surprised me. Though staff must have come in the room repeatedly—checking vitals, dropping off meals, emptying garbage cans—I'd been none the wiser. I closed my eyes after Brock left in the middle of the night and opened them to the next evening's sun.

Antsy and stiff, I swung my legs over the bed and stood, careful not to tug the IV free from my arm. After killing the alarm and taking a few tedious test steps, I opened my door and headed for a stroll to lift the drug fog that shrouded my brain.

"Well hello there, sleepyhead!" Regina's voice was brimming with glee, more so now that I was solo, without my perpetual cloud by my side. "You really slept it off, didn't you?"

"Guess I needed it." I needed more. To never wake, at least not to this reality.

"Where you headed?" she asked.

"For a stroll. Is that okay?"

"Course it is! Good for ya. Blow off some of those spiderwebs, get you back on your feet quicker." Regina disconnected my IV and taped the tube to my arm. "Take your time. Building is small, but lots to see. Native art, a little cafe where you can grab a coffee with four names, and a courtyard on the main floor."

"Thanks, Regina."

"Anytime, m'lovey." She paused, wringing her hands. "Is there anything else you need? Anything at all?"

I shook my head. I wanted to say something, but what, I didn't know. There was so much to say, and so few words to properly articulate what I needed.

"Well, if you should need anything . . ." she paused again, then stuttered, "Your husband, well he's—"

"I know." I flashed her the warmest smile I could. She returned the favour, but her expression was coated in worry. Everyone knows but no one will say. No one will talk about it.

I walked away before the tears had a chance to escape. I boarded the elevator, on a mission for some decent coffee. Before the door slid closed, a hand jutted through, pushing it open.

I tried to speak. *Please, c'mon in*, I thought, but the words never formed. Shock stifled my breath and voice. The new passenger was pale and gaunt, hospital pajamas draped over his skeletal frame, and young—the poor boy couldn't have been more than fourteen. His hand tremored as he poked the button for the first floor. When the car started its descent, he looked at me. His eyes were bloodshot and sunken into his skull. I nodded, trying to feign casual indifference, and he seemed to buy it. His lips, tacky and dry, peeled back from yellowed teeth into a crooked smile.

The ding of arrival startled me, and I jumped away from the sickly boy as he exited the car backwards, his eyes fixed on mine, smile never wavering. I stepped out when he disappeared from view, and saw that he was still walking backwards, staring at me as he moved around the corner.

Addict, I thought as I went the opposite way.

The halls of the main floor were quiet, a staff member or two here and there but no visitors. Not surprising, seeing as visiting hours had long since ended and the professional staff had gone home for the day. The stillness and calm were unnerving. As I walked down the hall in search of caffeine, I imagined the emaciated teen around every corner, in every room, behind every curtain.

I reached the coffee shop without incident, practically flopping on the counter with relief. The barista handed over some diabetes-infused concoction that tasted like solid molasses, but I drank without complaint. It was hot, and it was distracting. I lingered at the counter where it was safe, where I knew what to expect.

"You need anything else, ma'am?" the barista asked, confusion raising his brows.

"No, I'm good, thanks."

He stared at me, and I at my drink.

"There are bistro tables in the hall, and full tables in the courtyard to your left."

"Thanks, but I'm good."

A dark form appeared in my peripheral, startling me, and I splashed my burning brew onto my lip. Reflexively, I closed my eyes, imagining the sunken cheeks of the boy, his rotting teeth, the sight of his collarbone protruding beneath his hospital-issued pajamas.

"I think the lad is trying to shoo you from his counter," the dark figure said. "You're giving him the creeps."

I opened my eyes to the pleasant discovery that it was, in fact, not the ghastly boy, but a gentle old man, puffy white hair tucked behind his ears, chocolate eyes and soft brown skin.

"My dear, you look as if you've seen a ghost," he said.

I had the strong and sudden urge to cry, to tell him everything. To ask for help. "I've been under the weather," I said, raising the cast.

"I see. On the mend?"

"I should taste sweet freedom in the morn'."

His laughter, like Regina's, was filled with warmth and joy. "Well then. Come. Let's sit you down and have a quick yarn, lest I never see you again."

He must have sensed my ambivalence, of which there was plenty. *Why does this stranger want to sit with me?*

"I understand," he said. "My apologies for being quite forward." Taking a step away, he offered me his hand. "The name's Basil. I volunteer here at nights, to keep myself busy."

"You know what?" I said, giving his hand a shake with my non-wounded wing. "I could use some company."

Looking positively gleeful, he led the way, carrying my cup of coffee for me. "Let's stroll. Sitting is formal and intimidating, especially since we aren't well acquainted. Besides, from the look of you, might be good for you to walk for a spell."

We walked and talked, about the Park, the mountains. He was a retired RCMP officer, and he regaled me with a few tales of patrolling the parks. I had little to speak of. Little I would speak of, anyway. There wasn't much to me or my life, not anymore. I'd had a career, two in fact, but Brock's work moved us every time I was rocketing towards management positions. Whether that was intentional or not, I'd never know. Didn't make it sting any less. So I'd remained in Brock's world, chugging along.

"I'm a nurse." I said. "Part time. Can't get on full time in this economy."

"You like it?"

"Pays the bills."

He didn't look at me, not directly, but I knew he was watching my every move.

"What would you rather?"

"What do you mean?" I asked, knowing full well what he meant.

His steps slowed, and he guided me into a small sitting room with armchairs, plants, and a table stacked with old magazines. I stopped. I didn't want to sit, to face my own thoughts.

"Sometimes, my dear," he said, stepping in front of me, "it's good to be uncomfortable." I didn't move. I looked into that room, claustrophobic as a coffin, and my chest tightened. "I am here. You don't know me, I don't know you. We'll likely never meet again. Take this chance to speak. Get it out."

The room opened, the coffin turning into an atrium as I gave in. I found a chair, and Basil lowered himself on the couch across from me, his hands bracing joints that acted tired and aching. Once settled in his chair, he shrugged.

"My apologies, child. It's what I do."

"I'm sorry?"

"I saw you there, wavering at that coffee bar, thighs pressed so hard against that counter I thought you might topple the whole works." Crossing his legs and folding his hands in his lap, it was clear I had his full attention. "As an RCMP member, I've seen my share of suffering. I know pain when I see it. And yours is great."

Against my better judgement, I started. "My marriage."

"Yes," he nodded, his eyes sad. "How bad?"

"Bad." And that's all I had to say. He knew. I could see it on his face. I didn't have to explain, or justify. He understood.

"Do you have a plan?"

"He doesn't hit me."

"Doesn't matter," he said, shooing the thought away with a wave of his hand. "Physical violence is easy. The rest is more painful, more complicated."

"He's not abusive."

"Mhmmm." He looked at me from beneath his furrowed brow.

I nodded. I couldn't speak, knowing with sound would come tears.

"So he didn't do this?" Basil asked, pointing to my arm.

"No, well, yes." I laughed. Basil did not. "Okay, so he did, but it was an accident." Basil frowned. "No, no. A literal accident. He hit me with our rental car. By accident. We were camping out at Ptarmigan, and it was dark . . . I was running down the lane, and he didn't see me."

His concern melted into relief, then to humour. "That's as good as a comedy."

I couldn't find a smile. "Basil, I . . ." He said nothing, just listened. Waited. "I saw . . . I have a problem."

"Your marriage."

"Yes, that too. I drink."

"Okay." It wasn't a judgement, or an accusation.

"I'm not an alcoholic, but I do drink to shut it all off, you know what I mean?"

"I know exactly what you mean."

"Is that a problem?"

"Yes, but at present, I'm thinking that's not what's pressing. Go on."

"Before he hit me, with the car, I'd been drinking. By the river. And I saw things that didn't make sense."

My face burned as he searched it, seeking, evaluating. "You were intoxicated."

A pause. A brief consideration of whether I would be honest or not. I rarely was, especially with myself. "Yes."

"Has this happened before, unbelievable things in the throes of inebriation?"

"Never. I drink, I sleep."

"Was it a nightmare, then?"

"Maybe. Seemed so real, though." I could still see their masks, feel the drum pounding through the ground and up into my chest, and taste the copper in the air from the flowing blood. "But yes, you're right. It's ridiculous."

"You've been under a lot of pressure."

"I have."

"You came out here for a vacation, to get away. To sort things out, I assume."

"Yes."

"But you were drinking. A lot. And your husband wasn't with you."

"No. He was out hiking."

"And what were you doing?"

"Relaxing at the campsite."

"Is that what you wanted?"

No.

"No."

He smiled. "Did you say that to him? Explicitly tell him what you wanted?"

The tears flowed. And it felt good. "No. I always hope that I don't have to. That'll he'll just want to be with me, without having to be asked."

Basil spoke. I knew what he was saying—I heard him tell me that the first step was clarity. Make my needs crystal clear, and eventually it would become natural. These are things I knew. But his voice faded into a muted hum as my gaze floated above his head to a series of framed art on the wall. Pictures of totem poles, of mountain huts. Of a drummer, masked figures dancing in a circle, hands on shoulders, a pyre made of antlers.

"Something else, isn't it? Quite beautiful and haunting." Basil was peering over his shoulder to the source of my focus.

"What is it?"

"Wiindigookaanzhimowin."

My eyes met his. "Um, what?"

"Ceremonial dance. Common among the Algonquian tribes, specifically the Ojibwe and Swampy Cree. Primarily performed in times of famine—of which there were plenty, especially on the central plains. It's meant to reinforce the idea of moderation."

Did I know that? Had I heard this before, and that's why I dreamed it?

"Indigenous art is displayed prominently around here. We believe strongly in our folklore and keep these stories alive through art and song."

I couldn't think of what to say, how to respond. "It's lovely."

He shook his head. "Lovely might not be the right word for

it. The tribes were subject to harsh conditions, brutal encounters, violent traditions."

"Such as?"

The warmth drained from his voice, replaced by sterile cold. "I come from Ojibwe ancestry. My family was subject to famine, death by freezing, and disease. The worst of it, though, was the displacement and environmental destruction at the hands of invaders." As if interrupted by his own thoughts, he shook his head and his smile returned. "Of course, those trials and tribulations are all but gone today. And we can certainly glean lessons from times passed."

"Stay indoors?"

His laugh boomed through the halls. "Oh, you have found a bit of spunk again! Good stuff." With a sniff, his demeanor darkened a touch. "The message to take away from the past is to be mindful of want. To control the greed that brews within."

Brock. All I could think of was Brock, always wanting more, always belly-aching about never having enough, of me never being enough. My eyes welled with tears, and I turned my face from Basil.

"No, no," he said, clicking his tongue. "Don't go back there. You were much more content focusing on legend than real-life horrors. Let's leave reality behind and get you to a comfortable space for a while. Give you a break."

I stood and walked over to the painting. "Why the antlers?"

Basil stood, too, with much effort and groaning, and took his place by my side, admiring the art. "The ones in the fire, or the ones on their heads?"

I hadn't noticed before. The dancers sported antlers that protruded from the sides of their masks.

When he spoke the word, it hit me like a punch in the gut. "Wendigo."

It sounded so far away, this word, foreign but familiar. "Is it a monster?"

"Very much so, yes. It is human."

The masked figures in the painting were skeletal, biped. Human.

"But they have antlers?" I whispered.

"Legend has it that men who consume the flesh of other men become the insatiable wendigo, gaunt, sickly beasts that are constantly on the hunt, ravenous for their next meal."

I stepped to the painting, my finger tracing the grooves of the antlers.

Basil continued, his voice hushed. "The wendigo symbolizes greed. What we're dealing with here is folklore with a purpose, as most folklore is. The myth of the wendigo, a beast cursed by the need for constant consumption, functioned as a warning to exercise caution and moderation in strained times. In simpler terms, when food is sparse, eat less. Don't eat yer neighbour."

This time, Basil's laugh was not comforting. Though genuine, it felt out of place. Unnerving.

"So serious," he said, patting me on the back. "The wendigo isn't real, of course. The legend coincided with the creation of wendigo psychosis, an actual psychiatric diagnosis often given to those who went mad after conditions forced them to resort to cannibalism for survival."

"That's horrible."

"It's false. The psychiatric community has long since dismissed it as bunk. But you can still read up on it. Incidents of cannibalism are few and far between in modern times. Not like back in the 1800s, especially on the prairies."

My stomach lurched at the thought of that fire, the drumming, the masked dancers gorging themselves on meat. I swooned, and Basil put his hand on my shoulder, bracing me. "Oh no, this won't do. Perhaps we should talk about the abusive hubby again."

I gave him a hard look. "It's not abuse."

"Course not."

Arm in arm, we walked back to the lift, Basil's voice in the distance, telling me about other, more palatable folktales like Banshees and Sluagh. Once we reached the lift, my stomach had settled, and I was walking under my own steam.

"Can you make it to your room okay?"

"Yeah. The nurses' station is right outside the lift, should I arrive in a pile on the floor."

"Good, good. Well, my dear . . . oh my word. I do believe I've neglected to ask your name."

"Nellie. But people call me Nell."

He bowed, miming a tip of his nonexistent hat. "A pleasure, my dear Nell."

"Basil?" I had so much to say, but no words. "Thank you."

It was enough. He nodded, his eyes wet, his face hopeful. "You will be just fine, Strong Nell. Give 'em hell, Strong Nell."

Basil shuffled away, warbling a tune that included "Strong Nell, give 'em Hell." I didn't know this man, but I already missed him. That caring interaction was precisely what I needed more of. Compassion. Permission to be myself.

I boarded the car and pressed the button for the fourth floor, then leaned back and rested my head against the wall. Despite all the sleep I'd had in the past day, I could have drifted off right there on my feet. Part of it was possibly the medication, and part injury and shock. Either way, I was glad to stock up on some much-needed rest. And time away from reality.

No sooner had the lift started moving, it jerked to a stop, bouncing my head off the wall. The car had stopped at the second floor. It seemed a long time before the doors slid open—too long—giving my anxiety the opportunity to work itself into a tizzy about who might be sharing my ride.

My anxiety was not disappointed.

The sickly boy boarded the car, followed by a man, a woman holding an infant, and four small children. Their skin was grey and waxy, but they were Indigenous people; they all had straight, raven-black hair, dark eyes, and pronounced features. They were all wearing hospital-issued pajamas but had traditional leather moccasin boots on their feet. Their fingers were black with what looked to be frostbite, and their lips were blue and bloodied.

What the fuck?

"What floor?" I asked, my hand hovering over the button panel.

They said nothing. Did nothing except for stand there, still as statues, eyes locked on me.

I pressed the close-elevator button—which didn't do a damn thing, of course. Those fucking things never do. As we ascended, I avoided looking at the deathly family, but saw in my peripheral they were staring at me, unblinking, unmoving.

When we came to a stop, the doors took an agonizingly long time to slide open. When they did, I scrambled out, tripping in my panic, and crashed to the floor.

"Help," I said, as calmly as my nerves would allow.

In a flash, Regina was around the counter, helping me to my feet. "Well good lord, child! What's happened?"

"They—"

It wasn't them. There was a family in the lift, but it was a scruffy hipster with a man bun and down-filled vest, a wife in Lululemon pants, and a toddler eating Cheerios off the floor. The man stepped out, offering his hand. "Miss, are you okay? Did we—"

I pulled away, too abruptly, and he stepped back, hands in the air. "No, I'm sorry," I stammered. "I'm just . . ." I held up my cast and conjured a goofy grin. Pretty sure it came across as inebriated and stunned. "Under the weather, is all."

Backing into the lift, Man Bun scooped his child off the floor and wrapped his arm around his wife, keeping an eye on me the entire time. When the door shut and the lift moved on, I looked over at Regina. Her eyes were squeezed into slits, her lips pursed in disapproval. "Somethin' you wanna tell me?"

I braced myself on the counter, unsteady on my feet. "Yeah. I chased my meds with some Screech from down at the coffee shop."

"Goddamn Newfies," Regina said with a shake of her head. "Spreadin' that poison rum to our parts. Rather drink me own piss." She wrapped her soft arms around me and walked me to my room. "Let's get you snuggled back in bed. Too much too soon, I think, 'specially with that cocktail of drugs we're givin' you. Let's not go gallivantin' around anymore tonight."

Though it was a crinkly plastic hospital mattress, that bed was exactly what I needed—a warm, safe cocoon I could melt into and drift away where husbands and monsters and ghosts would never find me.

"Will I be all right to go home tomorrow?" I asked as Regina hooked me back up to the monitors.

"Do you want to?"

Of course not.

But there was no more conversation, no more fiddling with tubes and beeping and fluids. Just a deep, silent slumber.

12

Regina was off shift when Brock came to pick me up. I was sad she wasn't there to see me off, but also relieved. She might have convinced me to stay, to get out of my life, to start something new.

But she wasn't there. And I knew better than to believe in such flights of fancy. Reality sucked, but it was necessary.

Brock didn't come inside. He texted impatiently as I signed form after form and gathered the plastic bag containing the few belongings I had arrived with. As I passed the front desk, I stopped to talk to the information clerk.

"Can I help you?" he asked.

"Yes, I was hoping to speak with, uh, Basil? He's a volunteer." I realized I didn't know his last name. "I just want to thank him. Maybe keep in touch."

"Mhmm," the clerk said, unconvinced. "He is a chatty old soul, that Basil." After a considerable amount of shuffling through drawers and files, the clerk handed over an RCMP member business card with Basil's name, number, and email on it.

I felt the need to explain. "We had a visit last night, and he . . . well, it was lovely to have someone to talk to."

The clerk tipped his chin towards the loading ramp outside. "That one yours?"

Brock blared the horn, and from the expression on the clerk's face, it wasn't the first time he had done it.

I shrugged and tucked the card into my jeans pocket. The clerk watched as I maneuvered around camping gear—with a broken arm, no less—loading my stuff into the trunk of yet another rental vehicle before sliding into the passenger seat. Panic swelled in my chest as we pulled away from the hospital, en route back to real life.

"You feeling okay?" Brock said, his eyes on the road.

"Yeah, much better. Got some good rest."

"Good. You can drive. I had a late night. Not feeling top notch this morning."

No surprise there. The weak scent of stale booze persevered beneath his toothpaste and Axe body spray. "I think you better drive. I'm still coming down off the medications."

He nodded, his white-knuckled grip on the steering wheel communicating his displeasure. I rolled towards my window and rested my face on the glass. Under his breath, but loud enough to hear, he gave his signature *'Unfuckingbelievable'*. I didn't respond. He didn't escalate. We continued the drive in silence. There was zero chance I would say anything, or turn and look at him, even though my neck was stiff and aching, cranked all the way to the side like that. Instead, I watched the mountains shrink into yellow fields, and the dim sky lighten to bright blue, not a cloud in sight. As nature zoomed by the window, the beauty of my province distracted me from the ugliness in the car. Cows, birch trees, wild roses blowing in the wind. But in the distance, a black smudge marred a field of bright canola.

I sat up in my seat. "Brock, slow down."

"What the fuck? I'm going the limit!"

"STOP!"

He hit the brakes, and the car screeched to a halt on the shoulder.

"The fuck are you—"

I silenced his shouts with a slam of the door. I walked off the shoulder into the field until I reached the wire fence barring me from the crop of gold. It was far away, almost too far away to be sure, but the black smudge looked like people, standing in the midst of the canola beside a tall, wooden pole.

I shouted, "Hey!"

A breeze riffled my hair, blowing it in my face. I swiped it away, tucking a sprig behind my ear only to discover that somehow, at some point, I had crossed the wire fence and was standing thigh-deep in the canola, mere meters away from the people.

It was them. The family from the elevator. Though the man was fully clothed, the woman and children were naked, covered in filth, moccasin boots up to their knees. Their heads drooped so I couldn't see their faces, and chunks of flesh were missing from their thighs, hips, buttocks, and abdomens. In contrast, the man held his head high, his mouth stretched unnaturally wide, revealing a predatory grin coated with fat and gristle. And the pole, that looming, menacing lodge pole . . . I looked, only for a minute, only to realize the infant was there, swaying in the breeze from a frayed noose, feet absent, legs punctuated by bloody stumps.

"Nellie! Jesus!"

Brock shook me. I wiped my hair from my face and the family disappeared. Instead of in the field, I was standing on the side of the road, trembling and sick. I vomited in the grass at Brock's feet and he cursed me, something about his new boots. As he went back to the car and wiped off his pants and boots, I glanced over the field—the empty field—and slid my hand in my jeans pocket, my fingers coming to rest on Basil's card.

13

While I fetched myself a cup of coffee, I wondered if Basil had been real. He seemed too good to be true. But I had his card—I ran my fingers over the embossed Mountie, verifying its reality. *I'm probably bothering him.* While I was stirring in coffee cream, a warm, deep voice came over the line.

"Hello?"

"Uh, hello, Basil? This is Nellie." Silence from the other end. "Nell? Give 'em Hell, Strong Nell?"

A laugh. "Ah yes, of course! Strong Nell! How've you been? Made it home safe and sound, I hope."

Maybe not sound. "Sure did. I had a little trouble on the drive back, though."

"Oh gracious! Not another accident, I hope!"

"No, nothing like that. Just me. I . . . saw things again."

A pause. "Nell, you've been through trauma. You were hit by a car, my dear girl! One your abusive husband was driving."

"It's not abuse."

A snort. "Fine. Point is, cut yourself some slack."

"I'm hallucinating."

Another pause. "Okay. I need more information. Give me a moment." I heard the pouring of a beverage, then the woosh of a chair cushion compressing. "Okay, dear. I'm ready. Hit me. What have you seen?"

I told him everything, including the emaciated kid in the elevator, the family that joined him on the ride back up, and the scene in the canola field. My story ended with my hands wrapped around the wire fence at the edge of the canola field.

I heard the scratch of pen on paper, breathing, then silence.

"Basil?"

A pause, then, "Nell, like I said, your mind is responding to trauma. To stress. After our discussion about them, it's not surprising, the state you were in."

What? "We talked about them?"

"Sure did. The whole wendigo mythology."

"Yes, I remember, but what do you mean, *them*?"

Basil guffawed. "See, this is what I'm talking about. Your mind was in and out, methinks."

Is it true? Did I omit part of our conversation? "Who are they?" I imagined their faces, dark and still.

"He's from your neck of the woods, I believe. You're central, outside Edmonton?"

"Around there."

"Uh huh. His name was Swift Runner. Used to be a guide for the North West Mounted Police. Killed his whole family."

"What?"

"Yep."

I hesitated. "Five children?"

"See, you do remember! Six, actually, but he didn't kill the eldest. That boy died of starvation."

Jesus.

"They were starving, he claimed. And one of them was. That eldest boy perished from starvation. They were a mere twenty klicks from the new Hudson Bay outpost—the Company was new to the parts, and sorely needed—but Swift Runner opted to, well, consume his departed son. For survival, he said."

"And the rest of the family?"

"Swift Runner showed up at the outpost, claiming his family fell behind on the journey. Succumbed to the elements. The Mounties reckoned they froze to death. Upon closer investigation, they discovered an uglier truth."

"I'm afraid to ask."

"I'm sure you can imagine. His North West Mounted Police troop found the bodies scattered, bones gnawed clean. The poor infant was intact, save her feet."

"Hanged from a lodge pole," I whispered.

"Indeed," he said, clucking his tongue. "See? You must have heard me tell the story, but glossed over it in all its brutality. Add a heaping spoonful of exhaustion and your mind decided to replay it for you."

Seemed so real.

"The eldest son."

"Yes?"

"I saw him first. On the lift. Before you found me at the coffee bar."

"You saw a sick kid, who you cast in the starring role of your waking nightmare."

Fear relinquished its firm grip on my heart, but it was still hiding there, breathing down my neck.

"Basil, am I insane?"

"I'm no expert, but I think not. You called me to work through your anguish. The insane would not do that, assume they are afflicted with conditions of the mind."

"It felt so real." The stench of the blood soiling that field lingered in my nostrils.

"Dare say it did."

I stayed silent, biting my nails. I wasn't convinced.

"Look," he said, "if you continue to have troubles, give me a ring. Never hesitate to call."

"Thanks, Basil. I owe you."

"My dear sweet thing, I believe us to be friends now, yes?"

Once off the phone I felt a tad better, but still unsettled. Those encounters were like nothing I'd experienced, and they were so, so vivid. But Basil was right. I was medicated, healing, stressed, and my routine was all out of whack. A bit more time and some semblance of normalcy was needed to settle my mind.

It occurred to me, then, that my regular anxiety was notably absent, my existential despair nowhere to be found. So focused on them—on Swift Runner and his family—that I hadn't been dwelling on my domestic . . . situation. During interactions with Brock, which had been few and far between, he'd been relatively quiet and distant. Though he wasn't picking at me, the anticipation of explosion was terrifying. It was glorious and horrible.

14

If I hadn't been insane before, a month at home isolated in my normal existence was enough to drive me stark raving mad. I couldn't work—not with my arm still in a cast—and Brock was unbearable. He spent late evenings at the office, coming home after midnight, stinking of booze and slinging insults from every direction. More often than not, I slept on the couch, happy for the peace and privacy it provided. When I dared to stay in the master bedroom, in our marital bed, he would launch into drunken tirades of how I wasn't enough, of what I needed to be doing, of what I did wrong.

One night, after Brock had been at a company function, he stumbled in at 3 a.m. reeking of smoke and scotch. I was on the couch feigning a deep sleep, drool and snores added for effect. He didn't buy it.

"What the fuck is your problem now?"

I didn't answer. Maybe there was still a chance he'd keep on walking, pass the couch, and leave me the fuck alone.

"We're married. Sleep in the bed." Grabbing a fistful of blanket, he yanked it, sending me rolling to the floor. "C'mon."

Too tired to fight, I followed. He stumbled into the ensuite, grumbling about the idiots at work, and I crawled under the covers. As he brushed his teeth and peed on the toilet seat, I grabbed the bottle of sleeping medication from the bedside table. I tapped one, two, three pills in my hand, swallowed them hard, chasing them with the swill of leftover wine beside the bed.

Brock stumbled into bed and got on his phone, scrolling through social media and muttering to himself. I wanted to turn over, away from him, but if I did that it would most likely spark a verbal attack I didn't have the strength to endure. I stayed on my back, staring at the ceiling, hoping he would pass out.

"Check this out," he said, thrusting the phone in front of my face. It was a picture on Instagram of a woman doing yoga—all muscles, perfect hair, impressive angles.

"That's incredible," I said. It was something I'd never be.

"Sure is," he said, pulling the phone back and flipping through more pictures. "I admire a woman who takes care of herself. That doesn't let herself go." His head turned, eyes narrowed at me, then he returned his attention to his phone. "Some girls are pretty, but only athletic women are hot. Ask any guy."

Agonizing minutes passed before he finally put his phone down and turned off the light. I held my breath, waiting for his to grow heavy, slow. But he moved, his hand on my stomach, grabbing, groping. It was no good to resist it. Better to endure it, the things he knew I didn't like, none of the things I did. It hurt, it dragged on and on; he smashed my cast against the headboard then cursed me for the inconvenience of a broken arm.

As soon as he passed out beside me, sticky and snoring, I slid out from under the blanket, dragging the pillow with me as I went, and headed out to enjoy the privacy and safety of the couch.

15

The Night Physician was a movie based on one of my favourite horror books, and I wanted to go see it. Brock disliked horror movies—because I enjoyed them—so I asked Renee. I'd seen very little of her since I'd returned from the mountains and was excited for a girls night out.

When Brock came through the door after work, I was hopeful. He was whistling; he set his keys gently on the counter, and the first words out of his mouth weren't a complaint or accusation. I was almost glad to see him. Almost.

"Dinner ready?" he asked.

"In five."

"What are we having?"

"Spaghetti."

"Again?"

"Uh, we haven't had spaghetti in weeks."

"I had it at work today. When was the last time you made pork chops?"

I hate pork chops. "Good idea. Maybe Friday?"

"Why not tomorrow?"

I went to the stove and stirred the pot. It did not need stirring. "I'm going to a movie with Renee."

"Oh really."

I nodded.

"What movie are you and Renee going to see?"

"*The Night Physician.*"

"Huh. I wanted to see that."

Oh, for fuck sake. "You don't like horror movies."

"Why do you say that? I do! What about that one with the clown?"

"*It?*"

"Yeah, that one."

"You hated that. Complained the whole time."

"Fuck, if you don't want to spend time with me, just say so."

"It's not that, it's . . ." *Breathe.* "Would you like to go?"

He took his tie off and threw it on the couch. "No. That's fine."

My stomach churned and tears welled in my eyes. I was standing on ground zero and bombs were falling from the sky. How did we go from him whistling to a war?

"You know how much money it costs you to go out like that?" he said, his voice a rising crescendo. "Tickets, drinks, an Uber home."

"I'm not going to drink. I just want to see the movie."

"I'm gone all day. Why don't you go during the daytime?"

"Because I want to go with Renee. Who also works during the day."

"So better to spend time with her, I guess."

The mere suggestion I might venture out on my own put him in a mood. Everything turned into a disaster, and he shot random rage at me like bullets. "I can't find my socks. What the fuck do you do with my stuff?" Then, "Is the laundry not done?" Later it's "This spaghetti is bland. Did you even use salt?" followed by "I'm so sick of never being able to find anything around here." And worst of all, "I can't believe you're wearing that. It makes you look old."

The final blow, the pièce de résistance, was when he spilled his drink on the floor. "For fuck sake, Nellie! You had to go and move the goddamn coaster! Glass stuck, and now it's spilled everywhere!"

My fault, is it? Like everything. I got a dishtowel to clean it up.

"Look, I'm working all day. And this house is a fucking disaster."

"You're exaggerating, Brock. It's not—"

"It's disgusting. I don't know why we live like this. Mariah down the street works all day and her house looks like a fucking show home."

"She has cleaners. And two working arms."

"Make whatever excuses you want."

As I mopped up the mess, Brock's voice faded into the distance. He was still in the room, not far from me, ranting and raving, but another sound overpowered his anger.

Thumping. Drums.

I stopped and stood. Brock was fighting with the remote, trying to log into something but having little success. His mouth was moving, but all I heard was the drums.

Thump. Thump. Thump.

I went to the window, looked outside at the neighbour who was mowing his lawn. No sign of drums or thumping.

Momentarily, Brock's voice raised above the drumming. "And another thing—" But the drumming crescendoed, explosive in my head. I hurried out of the room.

"The fuck are you going?" Brock yelled.

I held up the dirty dish towel. "Laundry."

Walking down the stairs, I hoped to get away from the noise of Brock and the drumming in my head, but the thumping got louder with each step into the dank, dark basement.

THUMP. THUMP. THUMP.

My feet hit the cold concrete, and I took four steps, hand extended until my fingers brushed a brass chain. I pulled, igniting the naked bulb, illuminating the room in a dirty glow.

Swift Runner's wife stood in the center of the room, naked and trembling, her body heaving with the pounding of the drum sounds. The children danced backwards around her, their faces stone and stoic like masks, their eyes solid black. Swift Runner edged through the circle, coming up behind his wife and wrapping an arm around her waist. She gasped, her face contorting in pain as her maw opened, exposing a cavernous obsidian hole. And from the tunnel of her throat came the drumming, pounding out of her frail body, rippling her flesh.

Swift Runner stooped over and whispered something to one of the dancing children, then the dancing stopped. The children turned to each other, expressionless, and exploded in a flurry of clawing and tearing, gnashing and biting, ripping each other to shreds. Swift Runner's wife dropped to her knees, grasping for her children. A gleam caught my eye; it was the reflection of the bulb on the blade of the axe Swift Runner lifted high above his head before burying it deep into his wife's skull. Her face lost all expression, her gaze fixed on my face. He knelt beside her, dragged his tongue through the creek of blood trickling down her forehead, then sank his teeth into her cheek. There wasn't a peep from her, not a hint of movement as he dined on her, ripping flesh from bone.

No. Not real.

I walked through the carnage, my bare feet squelching through entrails as the children devoured each other organ by organ. I tossed the beer-soaked dish cloth into the washing machine and poured in some detergent. After starting the machine, I closed my eyes and listened to the running water. I put my hands on the cold plastic and felt the vibration of the motor. After resting on these senses for a moment, I checked on my company.

They were gone. Nothing in my basement except me, a washer and dryer, a furnace and water heater, and a bare concrete floor. No entrails, no cannibals, no death.

16

My skin breathed a sigh of relief when the doctor cut the cast off. It was orgasmic, dragging my nails across the newly exposed flesh.

"Nell, don't scratch at that. Your skin will be sensitive for a while. I'll give you some cream, but after an hour, it'll feel normal again."

He bent my arm, gently contorting it this way and that. It was tender and sore, and stiff from lack of use, but it was good to be free of that stinky, confining contraption.

"Am I good to go back to work?"

"Yes. Modified duties, though. I don't want you lifting. And you're right-handed, yes?" I nodded. "Good. Even so, you shouldn't insert IV's or do stitches until your full dexterity returns. Just exercise common sense. You still up in the OR?"

"Yeah."

"Huh. Would you mind if I had you transferred, just until you're a hundred percent?"

"That'd be awesome."

One benefit of receiving care at the hospital where I worked was they would make accommodations based on comfort, not necessity. I'd stay in the OR if I had to, but it wasn't ideal. This was better; I could relax, get back into the groove where people's lives didn't depend on my fine motor skills.

I signed my papers and left the office, heading for the cafeteria. I figured that by the time I grabbed a bite to eat, they'd be ready to reassign me. My first shift wouldn't happen that very minute, but it would be good to get my bearings, transfer my coffee mug to the correct floor, all that. Besides, it was nice to be out of the house. To be anywhere but home.

The cafeteria line was a slow-moving snake, curling out the doors and down the hall. I looked at my watch. *Dammit. Lunchtime.* Again, no big deal. I had time I wanted to kill. I gazed over the tables; most were full, medical staff and visitors alike. I could tell them apart by the smiles, or lack thereof, and the disheveled clothing. Visitors didn't give a damn what they looked like, some having lived in the same clothes for days. The staff looked like props from a daytime soap opera, chiseled and made-up, preening and posturing for workplace mating.

The line moved quick; in no time I was at the counter, trying to choose which hot meal from the menu looked most palatable. I settled on the fried chicken, a selection Brock would have deemed "disgusting". At my last physical my doctor gave a thumbs up to all my levels—blood pressure, weight, cholesterol. But it wasn't about science to Brock. It was about appearance. That being said, fried chicken does no one any favours in the heart department.

"What'll it be, ma'am?" the lunch lady asked.

Sigh. "The spring salad with grilled chicken, please."

"Coming right up."

I dragged my feet to the register with my plate of limp greens and pale chicken. The cashier rang me through, then I took my place at a table by the window overlooking an outdoor green space. As I shoved a sprig of spinach in my mouth, I watched the people. Some wore green hospital gowns, shuffling along, IV poles in tow. One old fella had a cigarette dangling from his lower lip, his eyes barely open, skin sallow and sagging. But he was happy; he smiled and held hands with a woman who looked about his age but twice his health as they snuggled next to each other on a bench. When he coughed, she wiped the spittle off his lip, then grabbed his cigarette and stomped it out on the floor. He raised his palms in resignation, and she leaned in, hugging him while shaking her finger in his face. They were both smiling.

Brock would never love me like that. Love me no matter what, no matter my faults. If I got sick, ended up here, he would judge. Be angry. Even leave. And I'd die alone.

"Hey! Could you not?" A young gentleman sitting across the row from me motioned to my plate.

Suddenly registering the sound, I realized that I'd been tapping my fork on the table. Hard. A sharp thumping sound.

Thump. Thump. Thump.

"God, I'm sorry. Didn't even realize I was doing that."

He scowled at me, then dove back into his meal.

Fuck you then, asshole. Sorry we can't all be as perfect as you.

His meal looked delicious—meatloaf, with a side of mash and green beans. He pressed the edge of his fork into the meat, cutting it away, then thrust a chunk into his mouth. I could smell the sauce from where I sat, sweet and savoury, juicy. My mouth watered and stomach growled in want. I poked my fork through a brown-tinged leaf, stuffing that in my mouth and imagining it was ground beef, seasoned and garnished with sauce. Chewing the lettuce, I felt the warmth of his meal rolling over my tongue, squishing between my teeth, and my mouth filled with saliva. I swallowed, but I still had a mouthful of fluid. Breathing through my nose, I opened my mouth and liquid poured out, splashing on my plate.

Fingers to my lips, then in front of my face, I startled at the contrast of the thick, crimson fluid against my pale skin.

Blood.

Not real.

I dabbed at my mouth with a serviette, leaving deep red stains on the white paper. Wanting to know if this was real, if any of this was happening, I scanned the surrounding tables, seeing if any of my neighbours noticed. I made eye contact with the meatloaf man, and smiled. In my mind's eye, my teeth were coated in gore, black with blood, my lips wet with death. But my toothy, awkward smile must have been clean, save a few seeds and spinach tucked between my teeth—he smiled, nodded, and resumed eating.

Not. Real.

Another dab of my serviette, this time the white coming back clean. There wasn't a red spot anywhere on that paper, or on my plate.

I cleared my place, setting my tray in the bin on the way out of the cafeteria, and headed towards the lift. As I approached the cars, I hesitated, imagining the boy, Swift River's starving son, waiting for me. Perhaps he'd have his father in tow, and his siblings, and his poor, helpless mother. What was left of her, that is.

I opted for the stairs. Anyway, it was important for me to get a bit of exercise to aid the healing process. In my head I heard Brock say, *more importantly, good for your thighs.*

As the heavy stairwell door slammed behind me, I realized what a dumbass choice I'd made.

Gee, Nell, what's better? Elevator with lots of people heading back from lunch, or a quiet, empty stairwell. Man, the horror fans would love you.

I got my exercise, all right, sprinting up those stairs, imagining Swift Runner's hot breath on my neck and his cold axe in my skull. When I burst through the door to the fourth floor, my heart was slamming against my chest and beads of sweat had formed on my forehead.

You are being absolutely ridiculous, Nell. It's your mind. All you. No ghosts, no monsters . . . you.

Though the human resources receptionist looked puzzled by my abrupt arrival, she was more than pleased to help me out. Business was slow up in HR—the hospital was a great place to work. Minimal complaints or turnover. She gathered the requisite paperwork, and I signed for my temporary transfer.

"Rehab and long-term care," I said, reading the form.

"Yes, it's laid back. Wound dressing, vitals, chitchatting about symptoms and process. You'll find it a touch slow, though that's the point, yes?"

Thank fuck it's not pediatrics.

After everything was taken care of, I stood to leave, but my body wasn't having it. The stench of rotted meatloaf flooded my nose and mouth, and my stomach wrenched in a knot. The receptionist set her pen on the desk and looked at me. "Nell? Are you okay? You've gone ghostly pale."

I braced myself on her desk, sweaty palms pressed hard on the wood. "Little under the weath—"

I drowned out the end of my statement with a violent heave, vomit spewing over her paperwork. "Oh god," I sputtered, wiping my mouth with the back of my hand. "I'm so sor—" My stomach flipped again, but this time I managed to aim for the trash can, sparing the poor woman more splatter. Being the caring person she was, she didn't blink at the mess. Instead, she tended to me, easing me into a chair away from the smell of my own sick, and fetching me a towel and a glass of water. Within minutes, custodians flocked to the desk like locusts, cleaning, sterilizing, and disposing evidence of my defacement.

The receptionist rubbed my back. "You should go home."

"Agreed," I said, punctuating that with a gut-deep hiccup.

"Did you drive here? You probably shouldn't drive yourself."

"I didn't drive. I took an Uber."

"Can I call someone to get you?"

You wouldn't understand. Here you are, unconcerned about your desk, your work, your belongings. You rub my back, touch me, even though it might result in you getting a stomach bug. So you wouldn't understand that Brock would be angry about this. That he would be irritated about the inconvenience, mad that he might also get sick.

No. There is no one to come for me.

"I'm fine. Really. It's not far. A quick, cheap Uber ride rather than putting everyone out."

"If you're sure."

"I'm sure. Thank you for your kindness."

She looked at me as if I'd uttered an odd statement. As if there were any other way to act than to offer kindness in the face of need. I wanted to hug her, to melt into her arms. Instead, I slung my bag over my shoulder, stood slowly, and took a couple steps towards the lift. "Actually," I said, turning back around. "Would you ride downstairs with me? Walk me out?"

"Absolutely!"

Hooking her hand in my arm she led me to the lift and rode downstairs with me, warding off whatever images intended to join me for the journey.

17

Once home, I showered off the smell of vomit, swished some mouthwash, then downed three Gravol, chasing them with a few swigs of Canada Dry. I collapsed into bed and slept until the front door slammed, announcing Brock's arrival. Through my haze I heard keys tossed on the counter, shoes thrown in the closet, and a whole lot of muttering and griping. I didn't care. I didn't even bother to sit up in bed as his footsteps clomped up the stairs.

The bedroom door flew open with a slam. "What's wrong with you?"

"Sick. Threw up at work."

"You worked today?"

"Got my cast off this morning. They transferred me to another ward until I'm back to normal."

"So you didn't really work."

Hot anger gurgled in my guts. "I threw up on the HR lady's desk."

"Damn," he said. "Don't be givin' that to me. I'll sleep on the couch tonight."

Please do.

Brock's fingers worked the knot in his tie, tugging until it loosened from his neck and he tossed it on the floor. His pants and shirt followed, added to the same pile.

"Could you toss those in the laundry basket?"

He didn't answer. "I'm gonna need my red shirt tomorrow," he called from our walk-in closet. "Big meeting with management. Is it clean?"

"No, you just wore it yesterday."

"Well, I need it tomorrow. Can you do that tonight?"

He came out of the closet, red shirt in hand. But that's not all he came out of the closet with. The brood of little raven-haired children were there, moving with him like a hive, dancing their backward circle.

I tried to look at him, not at the children I knew weren't there.

He held the shirt out. "Where do you want me to leave this?"

"On the floor with the rest of your clothes is fine."

He threw the shirt on the pile of clothes and the children scattered, hissing like cats. As he went into the ensuite, they re-engaged, continuing their disjointed, silent circle.

"I'm flying to Calgary tomorrow," he said, oblivious to his swarm. "Meeting with the VP. I'll probably spend the night, hit Seventeenth Ave with the boys."

With every consonant he spoke the children jumped, startled, like kernels in a corn popper. It was almost comical.

"Maybe I could tag along." I forced my eyes to stay on him, to disregard the movement around his legs. "See some of my

University chums while you're working and we hit Seventeenth together."

"Nope. Work trip. Besides, I need some guy time." He opened the faucet to splash water over his face then shoved his toothbrush in his mouth. As he brushed, up and down, side to side, the toothpaste frothed, squirting out the sides of his lips, a crimson pink foam. The children crawled up on the counter, standing in front of him, gaping in marvel at the foam, which had darkened to a black crimson. One child, a little boy of maybe three, leaned in and licked the foam from Brock's lips. Brock spit into the sink, and the others pounced, lapping up the whipped blood and squealing with delight.

Brock rinsed the sink, and the children shrieked, crying and clawing at the drain.

"What's for dinner?" Brock asked, wiping his face with a towel.

"I've been in bed all day."

"So what's the plan, then?"

Anger boiled in my chest. I started sweating under the covers. "I'll get up, figure it out."

Brock nodded in approval and left the room. I threw the covers back, and the wind from the blankets blew the children away like scraps of tissue paper, sending them floating in the air and dissolving into nothing. After purging my stomach once more in the toilet, I freshened up, then headed downstairs so Brock wouldn't starve.

18

My first day on the rehab ward was short and sweet—I couldn't do anything without the training specific to the floor, so I sat through videos and PowerPoints before being dismissed for the day. With Brock away in Calgary, the city was my oyster. Pulling out my cellphone, I called Renee. She answered on the first ring.

"I was hoping you'd call," she said.

"Still on for the show?"

"Hells yes I am."

"Wanna go for dinner first?"

"Hells yes I do!" A hesitation. "Brock must be away, is he?"

I clenched my teeth, then "Yes. Calgary."

"Ah. You know that shouldn't matter. If he was home, we could go anyways, right?"

Wrong. "Of course."

A moment of silence, then, "Enough of that. No Brock talk tonight, okay? Meet at Dante's at seven?"

"Perfect. Movie's at nine."

It had been a long time since I'd gone to a movie with Renee, and a lot longer since we'd done both dinner and a show together. Brock was likely to shit himself when he found out; it was, after all, a hundred-dollar evening. No mind that his would be closer to five hundred.

After treating myself to a pedicure, I went window shopping and bought a new dress. It was bold and colourful, and hugged me in all the right places. I paired it with heels I hadn't worn in years and a hair clip I'd bought when I was overseas in my twenties. As I fastened the clip, stroking the mother-of-pearl inlets, I remembered my time traveling through Europe, a time when I was free, had all of my power, and the confidence to make mistakes. And the knowledge to know that not everything I did was a mistake.

But life is about choices, and I had made mine long ago. No one gets a do-over this late in the game.

I passed the full-length mirror in the front hall and stopped to admire my outfit: the new dress, the funky heels, the clip. It had been a long time since I'd felt so good.

It's all you, Nell. You can control how you feel.

I pranced out of that house feeling like the world was spinning for only me. Within half an hour, I was seated at Dante's Pub, sipping an Old Fashioned, with Renee regaling me with tales of her latest conquest.

"I mean, a beer can, Nell. Like a damn beer can—in circumference, but longer. It was otherworldly."

"Not sure that's a good thing."

We roared with laughter and the whole pub stared, our mood infectious, creating smiles on the sea of faces. The aroma of hot appetizers filled the air as the server set a tray of food in front of us, followed by another round of drinks. We dined, we drank, and we laughed; it was an evening long overdue. When the clock pushed nine, we cleared up the cheque and wobbled out of the pub towards the theater.

"Got the tickets?" I slurred, leaning on my friend, who was as reliable a support as a wet noodle.

"On my phone, grandma. 'Tis the digital age."

I gave her arm a smack. "Bitch."

Renee flashed her phone at the box office, then I sauntered off to pee. "Meet you at the seats. Want anything?"

"Cucumber martinis?"

I nodded. The pub—adjacent to the theater, though not part of the same establishment—allowed patrons to carry beverages into the theater. Doubled the traffic for both businesses. I wasted no time peeing and hurrying to the bar. There weren't a lot of people waiting, thankfully. Sometimes there was a lineup to get drinks when the movie was about to start. I leaned on the counter, my forearms sticking to the remnants of drinks gone by. The bartender gave me a wink and a nod.

"Two cucumber martinis, please."

As he walked away, twirling glasses in his hands, someone pushed up next to me. I spoke, my words garbled. "Excuse me, I—"

It was Swift Runner. He was wearing leather pants and shirt, and fur-rimmed gloves. With his body pressed to mine, he leaned in, his nose brushing my cheek. His breath was hot with the stench of meat, his teeth packed with pink fibers. He leaned even closer, his mouth opening and closing as if speaking, his tongue brushing my skin with each syllable. I tried not to react, to look away and pretend he wasn't there. When I turned my head from him, I saw a different flavour of horror.

Even though he was back on, sitting at a table across the pub, I knew it was Brock. We'd been together for two decades; I knew his shape, his hair, his movements . . . I'd packed those very clothes for him that morning. He was getting cozy with a long, lean brunette, breasts up to her chin, short dress exposing a jeweled panty line. She was gorgeous. Exotic. Everything I wasn't and would never be. I watched him in that booth, leaning over his brunette, brushing his lips against hers as his fingers toyed and fumbled with the fringe on the hem of her dress, working their way up her inner thigh as she looked around, face flushing red. They moved deeper into the booth, his arm thrusting further, her head tilted back and tongue running over her lips as they moved in a silent, subtle rhythm unbeknownst to everyone around them. Everyone but me.

I made it outside before throwing up. Though Brock's indiscretion was no surprise, it was devastating. I caught my reflection in the pub's window and felt sick again. I was too dumpy, too plain. He was right.

The bartender came out with martinis in hand. "Perhaps I should have cut you off before you started. You still want these?" I took the drinks, and he offered a serviette from his apron. "Take it easy, okay?"

I did not. I downed first mine then Renee's martini, tossing the glasses aside before finding my seat.

"Too long a line?" she asked, looking for the drinks.

"Something like that."

She grimaced. "What in the fresh hell? You look awful!"

"Feel it, too. Now can we just watch this movie?"

I watched two hours of ghostly twins, elevators of blood, and trains with faces, not really seeing what was on the screen or hearing a word they were saying. All I could imagine was Brock, driving himself into that brunette on our bed, while Swift Runner stood by, his mouth stretched into a blood-coated grin.

19

I stood over the pot of boiling water, stirring the tortellini, watching bubbles rise and pop, rise and pop. It's how I was making it through the days—watching the details, perseverating on the little things rather than addressing the overall picture. Brock was due home at his regular time. He claimed his flight landed mid-morning. Short of securing surveillance video, I'd never be able to challenge that. And why would I? He'd turn it around on me.

As expected, Brock sauntered in at half-past five, gym bag in hand.

"Hey," I said, giving the wooden spoon another pass through the pasta.

"Hey." He tossed his gym bag on the floor and flopped on the couch.

I sprinkled some olive oil into the water. "How was Calgary?"

"Hectic." He scrolled through his phone, the screen directly in front of his face. "What are we having?"

"Pasta. Tortellini."

"With that pesto sauce?"

"Yeah. Why?"

"That's so bad for you, Nell. From now on, I'm gonna need you to cook a lean protein and some vegetables for supper, okay?"

I white-knuckled the spoon, grinding it against the bottom of the pot. My stomach was sour, but not with anger. I wasn't angry with Brock. I couldn't be. This whole thing was my fault. I'd become cold to him over the years. I'd shut down. Granted, it hadn't come out of nowhere—he was an insatiable prick—but I wasn't helping matters by being a cunt. And expecting things would change by doing nothing was idiotic.

After straining the pasta and mixing it with the dreaded, fattening, gluttonous sauce, I set the bowl on the table and took my seat. Brock did too, making a big deal of tsking and sighing when he stabbed his fork into each offending tortellini. "So what did you do while I was gone?"

"Went and saw that movie."

"Which one?"

"The one we talked about. *The Night Physician*. With Renee."

He stabbed another piece of pasta, this time with more force, his fork chipping at his plate. "I thought we talked about that?"

"Talked about what?"

"I wanted to see that, Nell."

I raised my wine to my lips, giving myself enough time to formulate the correct answer. The careful one. "I'm sorry."

"I don't know how many times I have to drill it into your little head, Nellie. We aren't made of money. You know how much it costs to go out like that? I suppose you went for dinner, too. And drinks."

Another sip of wine, another moment of contemplation. "So, I'm confused." *No, Nell, don't. It's not worth it.* "Is the issue the money, or is the issue me going without you?"

Brock looked up from his dish, his teeth grinding rather than chewing. "You don't have to get so fucking defensive."

No, Nellie. Don't.

But I did.

"But I do, don't I Brock? I have to defend every little thing I do."

"And here we go," he said, dropping his fork on his plate and throwing his hands in the air. "Little miss perfect, can't do anything wrong."

This time, I slammed my fork down. I grasped the seat of my chair, readying myself to get up and leave. "What do you want from me, Brock? Seriously."

"You are so fucking high maintenance. Unfuckingbelievable."

"Yes, I know I am. I hear it all the time. So what do you want from me? How would you like me to act?"

"You don't have a goddamn clue, do you? No concept of money, no interest in pleasing me . . . you know, all the women who meet me, and even some men, would die to fuck me. To be with me. And you don't even give a shit."

"You want me to be jealous?"

"I want you to give a shit. To dress nice, and work on your body. I want my clothes clean and food made when I get home without all the dramatics. So many women would die for that chance."

A laugh escaped before I could suppress it, my hand arriving over my mouth a moment too late.

"You don't think so? I fucking work out three times a day. Everyone comments on how ripped I am. And I'm a manager, young, with the world in the palm of my hand. Who wouldn't want this?"

"This is beyond ridiculous."

"You're jealous. You're ridiculous, letting yourself go like you have."

Enough. "Then leave, Brock! If I'm so terrible, if you deserve the best of the best, then go!"

He softened. "Nell, you know I love you."

"No, you fucking don't! Your mission seems to be to make me feel as small and miserable as possible."

"What, you don't want me to care about you? About how you look and how you're living your life?"

A flicker in my peripheral drew my attention, but when I looked, nothing was there but the pictures on the wall. "I'm not unhealthy, Brock. I'd have to be absolutely perfect for you to be content. And even then—"

"I mean, I was disgusted when we went home for your grandfather's funeral, Nell. Your family. I couldn't get over how heavy everyone was. How *obese*. People can't live like that and expect not to get sick."

"Brock, Grandpa was eighty when he died."

"And how much longer could he have lived? And look at your brother and sister, their spouses. Disgusting."

I remembered vividly the funeral, how devastated and emotional we all were, but we had each other—hugs, love, and reminiscing warmed the mood and brought us closer together. Then there was Brock, making quiet digs about people's weight, the style of their clothing. On the day before the funeral, when we went out so he could get a new pair of jeans, he insisted I go wardrobe shopping to make myself look nice for once. 'Buy some stylish, sexy clothes', he'd said. He berated me when I said I wasn't in the mood.

The memories swiped away with a firm blink of my wet eyes. "Go fuck yourself," I mumbled.

Now he was standing, his fists pressed against the table. "You are a fucking nasty bitch, you know. You're a crazy, stupid bitch."

My eyes drifted from my posturing husband to movement on the wall. The pictures in the frames were no longer Brock running a marathon or Brock climbing a mountain, but Swift Runner, axe in hand, the remains of his family at his feet. He was holding his wife's head up by the hair, her detached cranium swaying in an apparent breeze, blood spurting on the inside of the glass and dribbling down in glossy streaks.

"Things are gonna change around here," he shouted. "If you think I'm gonna tolerate this shit—"

The blood was accumulating, filling the frames on the walls and the ones on the piano. I wondered how Brock didn't notice as the blood spilled over the top of the frames, cascading down the walls and pooling on the floor, deeper and deeper until my feet were submerged.

I stood. Brock yelled. "Sit your ass back down!"

I didn't. I walked upstairs, changed my clothes and brushed my teeth, then shoved a few meager belongings in a bag and marched out the front door.

Brock poked his head out as I walked away. "If you leave now, don't bother coming back!"

And that would be so very fine.

20

The glow from the green lamps at the public library reminded me of the forest. Warm light spilled down on dark oak tables, casting shadows over books and papers. After I wandered aimlessly for a few minutes, the ancient librarian helped with my search, locating books on Indigenous folk lore, monsters, and creatures of the prairies. I also took out a book about crimes in Alberta, which was much more terrifying than anything made of antlers and bones, talons and death.

I learned nothing Basil hadn't already told me. The wendigo was a gaunt, skeletal creature with an insatiable hunger for human flesh. Algonquians created the lore of the beast to warn of moderation, especially in times of deep freeze when resources were sparse. The consumption of human flesh would turn a human into a wendigo. The wendigo was also a commentary on colonialism and the displacement and destruction of Native culture.

Translation? Don't be a dick. Don't always want what you don't have, and put other people out while trying to glut your hunger for more and more and more, as the white traders had done.

"Sparked a fire, did I?" Basil's voice, though startling me from my studies, was a welcome interruption. I stood and wrapped my arms around him.

"Basil, thanks for meeting me. It's a long drive."

"Like I said when you called, I was coming anyways. Needed to pick up a few things I couldn't get in the Park. Besides, a change of scenery is good for the soul." He set two Tim Hortons cups down on the table. "Double double, if that pleases you."

"Basil, the librarian will chew you a new one if she catches you in here with those."

Chortling, he shrugged his coat off his shoulders and sat. "The old bat can try to chew me a new one, but I'm afraid she'd find me tough and gamey." When I didn't smile, his waned. "Ah. Inappropriate humour, all things considered."

With tender hands he flipped through the books, poring over images of creatures in the woods, sharp, jagged antlers protruding from skeletal heads. Now and then he would pause, tracing a finger over drawings of emaciated beasts and the bloody carnage they left on the floor of the woods and plains where they roamed.

"They are just a warning? Symbolic?"

"I assure you, my dear, monsters walk among us, but none as fantastical as these." He closed the book. "But you aren't really worried about these creatures, are you?"

I shook my head, loosening tears. "Basil, I'm unwell. I'm seeing things, and it's not because of the accident."

"How's your marriage?"

I didn't hold back. This man, this stranger, had been an ear, and a non-judgmental shoulder to cry on. He was kind and safe. At least I wanted him to be. "It's shit, Basil. Hot, steaming shit."

"I assume by hot you aren't referring to passions."

"He's brutal, Basil."

"I know. I could tell, even after only knowing you for just five minutes."

"Shows, eh?"

"Anyone who knows you sees it. Whether they acknowledge it or not, whether they can even admit it to themselves, they know. But people are weak and don't know how to address matters such as this."

He slid my coffee over to me, and I took a few sips. "You really know how to woo a girl."

"Ha! My wooing days are over, and my desire to woo has diminished to a mere flicker of a memory. That does not mean I care less. Much to the contrary. I find myself caring more." His warm brown eyes met mine. "It is not the beasts—neither Wendigo nor your husband—that cause you to question your sanity."

I shook my head. "Swift Runner."

Basil sat back in his chair and scratched the white scruff on his head. "Ah, that old bastard. Hard to get him out of your head once he's there."

"I'm seeing him, Basil. Everywhere."

"Your mind is."

"It's very real. And I've never seen a picture of him, but there he is, in my waking nightmares."

"Are you sure it's him?" Basil slid the Crimes in Alberta book over and opened it to the table of contents. After dragging his finger down the page, he flipped to the middle of the book, to a chapter titled *1878-9: Winters of Death: Starvation, Consumption, and Hanging.* "Swift Runner's son died early in winter 1878. By the end of the year, Swift Runner had butchered and consumed his family. After an exhaustive search, and some grisly discoveries by his partners at the North West Mounted Police, he confessed to the crimes. With no apparent guilt or remorse, and an odd, unsettling peace, he was hanged in December 1879. His was the first hanging in Alberta."

Basil turned the page, then slid the book over and put a hand on my shoulder.

My voice wavered. "Yeah, that's him."

The photograph, black and white but yellowed by age, showed an RCMP officer in a hat balanced on the side of his head, uniform buttoned to his chin. And his charge was a man dressed all in dark, shackled with iron, his hair soft and flipped to the side.

Basil's face darkened. "Swift Runner. That's him, the dodgy old codger. The face of evil incarnate."

Swift Runner's eyes were indeed black holes, nothingness, but they seemed to stare far off the page, right at me, deep into my soul.

"To play the devil's advocate, he's . . . um, how do I put this without being racist. Any number of men could represent this fellow, if that's what you had in your mind."

"They do not all look alike," I scolded Basil. "Look at him—distinct features, strong jaw."

"But indulge me. After hearing the story, would your mind not conjure an image based on assumption, which you could stretch to match the appearance of this man? Was what you saw so clear, so precise that it matches the monster in this photograph perfectly?"

It was. *But it can't be.*

Basil moved on, closing the book and drawing a mouthful of his own coffee. "What is our friend doing when you see him?"

"Nothing really. He just stands there, watching me, the carnage of his crimes littering my floor. Sometimes his mouth is moving, as if he's speaking, but there's never any sound. I see his wife, too, and she's filled with despair and panic."

"Charlotte," Basil said.

"That was her name?" My eyes fell to the book.

"You won't find it there, I'm afraid. Hard to get that bit of information, unfortunately. Not unlike modern day news, it's sensational to focus on the monster rather than his prey."

"She's tortured, Basil."

"Not anymore."

Like a punch in the gut, I realized I envied her. Her pain had ceased.

"Okay." Basil looked down at the bare oak table as if reviewing notes. "Swift Runner and his clan show you their pain, despair, and death. It's gruesome, horrifying, and intertwined with the reality of your own life."

"Yeah."

Basil looked up from his imaginary notes and took my hands. "Describe your husband for me."

I swallowed hard, terrified to carry out what should have been a relatively simple task. "He's average height, brown hair, works in commerce—"

"No. That's superficial. I want to know the husband *you* know. His personality, his demeanor, ideologies."

My eyes stung with tears, my throat bubbling with acid from my churning guts. "Entitled, judgmental, vain, cruel, egotistical . . ."

Basil waited. I think he would have stayed there a full day, letting me purge my anger.

My words continued, spewing forth like rapids. "Sometimes I feel like he's just a bad human. That I hate him, and I wish him the pain and suffering he inflicts on me and all the other people he judges and hurts."

"You want him to change."

"I . . . I don't want to feel this way anymore. I can't live like this."

"Yet you do."

Yes. I do.

"Why?" Basil asked.

No idea. It started as a barely noticeable drip, a pinpoint hole in a dam. Brock had been charming, fun, and seemed to genuinely care about me. Until he didn't. Until the mask wore off, and he did less and less of the things I liked, and criticized more and more of the things I did and said and was. The pinpoint hole cracked into a tiny fissure and more reality escaped: increasingly heated arguments, irritations. He pitched such a passive aggressive fit anytime I went out that I stopped going out as much; it wasn't worth the energy and subtle punishment. *Crack*—that fissure spread into a wider laceration, the snide insults and shade clouding every facet of me, so subtle that if I mentioned it, he had me questioning my sanity. I don't know when that fissure blew into a full-blown dam collapse, but it did. I was drowning before even realizing I was wet.

"No matter," Basil said. "You owe no one an explanation but yourself. When you are ready, you will take the necessary action to better your circumstances."

"But what if I'm never ready?"

"Well, it's all just waiting, isn't it? Waiting to be ready, or waiting for an end."

I see nothing but an end. The final end.

"Back to Swift Runner," he said, slapping his palm off the table to bring my attention back. "His appearance in your day-to-day affairs is an easy business to address."

"Easy? Basil, I saw him in my picture frames, moving. There was blood running down my walls, flooding my living room."

"Yes, well, hallucinations, of course."

"Thought you said I wasn't crazy."

"You are. We all are. But this isn't crazy like you think, but rather a situational occurrence."

"Meaning . . ."

"It's akin to PTSD. This is an overlooked product of emotional abuse that often proves more violent and severe than the effects of the battering, if I do say so myself. What was going on when your pictures started to bleed?"

The argument. The table. That damn fattening pesto sauce. "We were fighting. He was yelling, standing over me."

"You were under a great deal of stress."

"Yes, I was."

"And you wanted it to stop. You wanted Brock to stop."

I was quietly crying now, hot tears streaming down my face. "Yes."

"You wanted to scream at him, to show him how unacceptable his behaviour was, how gluttonous and selfish he was. You wanted to warn him."

It hit me like a sledgehammer. Swift Runner wasn't real. The wendigo was not real. It was me, grasping at straws, screaming for my end.

Basil smiled and ruffled my hair. "You were dancing backwards around a drum, if you will."

"Something needs to give. Brock's behaviour needs to stop."

Basil hesitated, his eyes growing dark. "It will not, I assure you.

I nodded. Brock would never not be Brock. I had no answers. "I don't know what to do."

"You will."

21

It wasn't a stomach bug. Or an intolerance to something new I was eating—I'd had nothing but crackers and broth for days, but I was still sick, throwing up at night and sporadically through the day. Thankfully, it wasn't so frequent that I was in danger of dehydration, and I could sip water and nibble food in small doses without purging every bite from my system.

Even though I wasn't at a hundred percent, I trudged into work. I'd had a few shifts—mostly just pushing papers and restocking supplies—but today marked my first time doing rounds since my return and I wasn't about to spend it offering my guts to the porcelain god in my home. I needed to get out and get some control back over my life.

When I arrived at the hospital, I swished some Gravol down with my peppermint tea and got to work, checking the patient board and starting my rounds. My patients were uplifting and hopeful, all rehabilitation cases on the upswing and preparing to go home. I helped with stretches, vitals, chatting, and snacks as I meandered my way from room to room, filling out charts and completing duties. With every patient, I felt better, more in control.

The morning flew by at light speed. Before I finished my second set of rounds, the smell of cafeteria fare and reheated leftovers wafted through the ward, sending my stomach into a lurch. I grabbed my sack lunch from the fridge and found a seat in the staff room.

"Not feelin' it?" the physical therapist, Simone, said as she took the seat next to me.

"What's that?"

"The cafeteria food." She pointed at my lunch, a pathetic collection of saltines and a banana.

"A little under the weather," I said, like a broken record. *That's my go-to. For everything. But I am, aren't I? Perpetually under the weather, in more ways than one.*

She inched away, crossing her arms in an exaggerated X. "Well stay away from me, honey. It's goin' around and I don't want no part of it!"

"I've had it a while," I said. "Not sure what it is, but I don't seem to be passing it around. My husband is fine."

With a squelching sound, Simone bit into her chicken leg and bloody juice dribbled down her chin, dripping onto the front of her blouse.

I pointed at the stain, unable to speak.

"What it is, sweetheart?"

The stain spread in bloody webs over the front of her shirt and across her skin until her whole body, clothing and all, looked like a cocoon of broken, bursting capillaries. When she spoke, blood splattered from her mouth into mine, hot and coppery, gritty and squirming. "You feelin' sick?"

Feeling the sick racing up my throat, I stood from my seat, frantically seeking the nearest trash can. I didn't find it, though, not before black explosions ruptured my vision and my head hit the floor.

22

Beep. Beep. Beep.

After not being a patient in a hospital for most of my adult life, there I was, for the second time in as many months, laid up in a narrow bed, hooked up to monitors and fluids meant for other people—sick people. My patients. Not me.

I'd woken up in the bed with a saline drip and monitors tracking my blood pressure and pulse rate. After a quick evaluation of my body, I determined I had no external injuries, and had only minor aches—sore spots on my hip, arm, and head.

"You hit that floor pretty hard." Johnathon, the charge nurse, came into the room with a Styrofoam cup of water filled with mostly ice. I welcomed it. I was hot and thirsty as hell.

"What happened?" I asked, trying to remember. "I was eating lunch, and Simone was eating with me . . ."

"She said the colour drained from you like someone had

pulled a plug, and you stood up before crumpling to the floor. Stood up too fast, I'm guessing."

I looked at the monitor. "Blood pressure?"

"Maybe a little low, but within an acceptable range."

"I haven't been eating much. I've been nauseated."

"Simone mentioned that. We ran a few quick screens to make sure it wasn't something more serious—hope that's okay. Your employee file said to go ahead if something like this happened on site. And you have no emergency contact on file—"

"It's fine," I said. Working in a hospital all my career, I could say with high certainty that medical professionals do not have nefarious intentions that involved using test results to implicate or frame unsuspecting patients for war crimes or government conspiracy. We're Northern Alberta, not Russia. "Find anything?"

Johnathon fiddled with the corner of my chart, and checked my IV drip, adjusting the flow.

"Johnathon. What's going on?"

"Would you like to speak to the doctor? I can go get her—"

"John, c'mon. You know me. We've worked together for years. Please."

With a sigh, shoulders slumped, he sat on the bed. The squeal of the frame startled me, but not as much as his words. "Nellie, you're pregnant."

What?

"No."

"Yeah, Nellie, you are. We did the blood work. Ran it twice. Explains the nausea, the fainting . . ."

I could still feel Brock moving in me, hurting me as I closed my eyes, willing it to stop.

Pregnant.

"Nellie, I know . . . well, I think we all wonder if things aren't great at home."

Infected.

"You have options, Nellie. And we can discuss them. We're all here to support you, quietly, whatever you need."

"It's fine, John. I'm just shocked. That's all. It's not the end of the world." *It's a burning, bloody, painful end.* "It's fine."

23

I didn't tell Brock right away. My plan was never to tell him. Not ever. I didn't want him to have that power over me—the child, *his* child, the strings to me, his marionette. Though Alberta was a conservative province, Canada was a liberal country. I would not be lynched, no matter what I chose for my body. People would agree or disagree, but they would move on. As would I.

But a *child*. Had I wanted to be a mother? The more I thought about it, the more I questioned my decisiveness. I lost myself so many years ago, my world becoming Brock's, my thoughts consumed by maintaining the peace. I never imagined wanting a child. Truth was, I never wanted *his* child.

But I'd become attached. I bonded with my passenger, envisioned him or her and our life together and my role as Mother. And I liked what I saw.

"What are you daydreaming about? Are you even listening to

me?" Brock said, slapping the newspaper on the table, rattling our breakfast plates.

"Sorry, no. I wasn't listening."

"As per usual."

I sighed. "What is it, Brock?"

"Do you even care what I have to say?"

Breathe. You're breathing for two, now. "You're absolutely right. I'd hate that if you did that to me. What were you saying?"

"I'm going to put those fucktards in their place."

As he droned on, telling me about how he had the worst job in the world and how everyone there was incompetent, I had my hand on my belly, fingers pressing my skin, feeling the warmth inside. I added nods and generic verbal acknowledgements at appropriate intervals, but didn't really hear a single word he said.

When he packed up and left for the day, my pulse was quiet, my mind at rest. I had made my decision. Tears of joy and fear rolled down my cheeks.

I can do this.

24

That night was not as peaceful as the morning. Brock had made good on his threats; he had gone into work guns-a-blazin' and put those fucktards in their place. Unfortunately, as it turned out, Brock was the one who had dropped the ball, and the fucktards above the lot of them—the management fucktards—had come down and put Brock in his place. Hard.

"I can't do it, Nell. I can't work there anymore. This company is run by a bunch of idiots. They make the stupidest decisions, treat their employees like shit, don't communicate at all. I gotta find something else."

I sipped my ginger ale and set my book in my lap. "Maybe you're just upset. If this is an isolated incident, perhaps it will blow over."

"Don't be an idiot, Nell. You don't understand. You know I hate work."

Don't I fucking know it. "But work is work. I mean, it's our livelihood, not a hobby. It's just a paycheck."

He glared at me, a thousand daggers piercing my heart. "*My* livelihood, Nell. Mine."

I drew a deep, painful breath, my anxiety rising. "Okay, be that as it may, there are bills to pay."

"So you get how much of a burden it is on me, being the meal ticket."

My tummy fluttered. I set my hand on it. "So you're gonna look for a new job?"

"You know how hard it is for me to just get a new job in this industry? You live in a fantasy world, Nell. Get a grip."

"But you just said you can't stay in your current job."

"You see the problem."

"So let me get this straight." I set my book on the table and leaned forward. "You want to quit your current job, but you won't apply for a new one."

"I didn't say I wouldn't Nell. Are you even listening? There's no point. No one is hiring right now."

"Okay." *Fucking goddamn circles.* "So you *are* applying?"

"Jesus, Nell, it's so difficult to talk to you."

Breathe. "I think you should look around, see what's available. Keep chugging at work—I know it's hard, but just put one foot in front of the other. You are smart and educated. You have options."

"Nell, you don't even know what you're talking about. Quit trying to pacify me—"

"Brock, I'm pregnant."

It was like I had slapped him across the face. He snapped back in his chair, his jaw slack, his fists bunched. "What?"

"Pregnant, Brock. Knocked up."

"I'm having a baby?"

We. "We're having a baby."

"How . . . that's awesome!"

Brock came to me, knelt beside my chair, and pushed my hand aside so he could rest his on my swelling belly. I cringed at his touch, wanting his greedy hands off me.

Perhaps this will have a happy ending. Maybe this is what he needed. What we both needed.

I willed my muscles to relax and wound my fingers through his as our hands rested on our child.

25

The sickness lingered another few weeks, but it wasn't as troubling, now that I knew why it was there. Brock was different, though only slightly, his overt anger softening to abrasive comments. But that didn't last. After a brief honeymoon, a break from his regular barrage of venomous insults, he came up with a new line of attack now. "Think of the baby, Nell. It's not all about you anymore." He commented on every bite I ate, the shampoo and lotion I used, where I went, and what I watched on television. You know, because of the baby.

A week after my first ultrasound, I was washing the dishes, and Brock was sitting at the table, finishing his dinner. I unbuttoned my jeans; though not showing, not just yet, the pressure of my clothes on my tummy was noticeable. Brock also noticed.

"Did you just unbutton your jeans?" he asked, watching my every move.

"Yeah." It was exciting, that little bit of growth, a foreshadow of days to come.

"Huh," he said as he shoved another bite in his mouth. By the tone of his voice and the look in his eyes I could tell nothing good was about to happen. My mood suddenly deflated. I focused on the sink, the bubbles, the dripping of the tap.

"You know," he said, a snake hidden beneath his tone, "Shawna at work has four kids. You'd never know. I bet you could bounce quarters off that body."

Don't respond. Don't encourage or participate in this.

"And Carrie," he continued. "When she was pregnant, you'd never know unless she turned to the side. That girl was all baby."

I bit my tongue, watching the bubbles pop, one by one.

He went on. "I hope you can stay healthy like that. Seems a bit early to have to loosen your pants."

"I'm pregnant."

He snorted. "Sure."

"What does that mean?" A twinge at first, then a cramp formed on the lower left side of my belly.

"I just don't understand why you don't care about your body. How you look."

The pain stronger, I placed my hand on my side, pushing in. "I care, Brock. But it's more than appearance, yes? I will never have Shawna's body, but that doesn't make me less healthy."

"No reason you couldn't have her body, if you tried. And speaking of trying, I think you need to do a little better with this house. The place is a pigsty."

The pain conjured nausea, which almost knocked me off my feet. Sweat formed beneath my arms and on my upper lip. I held the counter, bracing myself for the fall.

"Seriously, Nell, this place is unfit for a baby. Everything needs to be absolutely perfect. Lena and Paul's place looks like a damn show home. There's clutter everywhere in here."

"Your stuff." I waved a hand over his dirty laundry on the floor, his laptop and papers spread across the island.

"Nell, I work all day. What do you want from me?"

"A little help. Just pick up after yourself and it'd make a huge difference."

There it was. The red face and clenched fists. "Oh, perfect little Nelly, can't do anything wrong. It's all me, is it?"

He stood from his chair and walked towards me. For a moment I cowered, but then turned to face him. "All I'm saying is that it would make a huge difference if we both made an effort to clean up."

"I don't do enough, is that it?"

"I said nothing like that."

With a crash, he slammed his fist off the counter, rattling the dishes in the drying rack. The pain in my stomach surged, like someone reached in and twisted my insides. A wave of vertigo hit me, and I stumbled to the wall, sliding down to the floor. "Brock, I don't feel so good."

Saying nothing, he stood over me, watching as I controlled my breathing with deep, slow breaths, until the room stopped spinning and the pain dulled to a quiet roar.

"I'm okay," I said. "Just need to take it easier, I think."

"What you need is to take better care of yourself." And with that, he grabbed his coat, leaving me on the floor as he stormed out, slamming the front door behind him. As his engine grumbled to life, my eyes came to rest on his plate, dirty, still sitting on the table, mere feet from the dishwasher. Taking care to be cognizant of the dizziness, I stood and went to the table, to

Brock's fucking plate, and his cutlery, all dirty but not in the dishwasher. *His* fucking dishes.

It felt so good to throw that plate, the crash it made as it smashed against the wall, sending a shower of blue and bone china sprinkling to the floor. The fork and knife went next, careening off the fridge as I hurled them across the room. I released a wail that would put banshees to shame as I threw everything I could get my hands on.

Exhausted from my outburst, I sat down to catch my breath, putting a hand on my throbbing side. I closed my eyes. I was cold. Too cold. The world slowed, slowed, until it was still.

26

When I opened my eyes, the kitchen had changed. Everything was different. Wrong. I was still on the floor, my hand grasping my side, but the air had changed; a thin layer of frost coated every surface, and my breath came out in white, billowing clouds that lingered in the air before dissipating. All the lights were off, leaving the moonlight my only source of illumination, but even in that wan glow I could make out a figure standing in the mouth of the hallway, swaying ever so slightly from foot to foot.

"Brock?"

No answer.

Not Brock.

My legs aching as if I had been balled in the same position for hours, I got up on my haunches then struggled to a standing position.

Swift Runner.

I backed away from the figure who cocked its head at me as

my palms met the edge of the sink. And there we were at a standstill, me pinned against the sink and it wavering in the hallway, eyes glowing white. I gawked, examining the form in the darkness, noting size, shape, curves . . .

"Charlotte." I breathed her name without meaning to, and the word floated to her on a frozen plume of breath. When it reached her, she breathed it in in a great gulp. Hair billowing behind her as if she floated through water, she came to me, arms swinging gracefully and feet moving silently across the tile floor. Her skin was a silver sheen of frost, her raven-black hair and lashes stiff with glittering fractals of ice, her eyes glowing white in the darkness. A warmth rose in my frozen cheeks as my eyes moved down her body. She was naked, her body feminine and slender, skin smooth as glass, the hair between her legs was as stiff and frozen as her eyelashes but twice as sparkling with diamonds of frost. With every movement, frozen bits of her body crackled off, tinkling to the floor like glass.

Charlotte brought her hand up and cupped my face, sending a jolt of cold into my bones. I leaned into her. I trembled as her black lips parted, releasing the soft thumping of the drums from within her belly. With each thump, her long black hair shimmered, cascading over her bare breasts and shaking loose a snowfall of frost onto my feet.

I wanted to ask her what she wanted. I wanted to tell her to go away, to take her husband and children and move on, leave me the fuck alone.

But that's not what came out when I opened my mouth.

"Help me." Hot tears rolled down my cheeks as I said it, and I collapsed onto her, my head on her bosom. She wrapped her arms around me, stroking my hair and embracing me. It felt beyond amazing. She was the intimacy I needed, the care I so desperately craved. Though the thumping continued, a melody echoed from beneath her ribcage, haunting and melancholy.

'Cross the waves of the prairies, in a field of gold
Nights grow long and days grow cold
Crimson soaks the soil, death clouding my seas
'Twill end when no one left but only he.

The aching cold was sucked from the room like a vacuum, leaving a neutral climate in its wake. Not cold, not hot. Nothing. I pulled back from Charlotte, into another new reality. I was no longer standing in my kitchen, but in a vast wasteland of golds and sepias, a monotone canvas across a textured land. Dunes of sand glistened under a golden sky and trees of muted brown towered over us like skeletal beasts, twisted and in agony, reaching for us with mangled limbs. Totem poles stood sentry at a nearby village; the creatures stacked several stories high were intricately carved, feathers and scales and talons all cocked in my direction, reaching for me as I sunk lower and lower into the sand. Behind a nearby hoodoo lurked two shadows with glowing emerald eyes and cascading hair the colour of fire.

"Where am I?" I asked, entranced by the land and unfazed by my rapid descent into the dunes.

Charlotte stood over me, her skin the same colour as the golden sky, her hair a glistening black that stained the monochrome palette of my vision like a blotch of ink. Her eyes were hollow caverns, seeping thick ichor down her aged and weathered face. She opened that maw once again and released a frantic pounding of drums that heaved her body up and down, lifting her off the ground in manic hops.

I screamed. "Charlotte!" My voice went on forever, her name echoing across the land, unsettling large, black bird-people from the trees. "Where am I?"

She crouched down and the drumming softened enough for her to form a single word.

"Ramnon."

The drumming exploded once again, the volume deafening. The thumping quickened the sand's grasp, a million sharp talons pulling me below. I panicked, not because I was afraid to drown in the sand, but because I didn't want to go away. I wanted to stay there, in the golden land with the strange creatures. A land that was very much not my own. It was unrecognizable in every way, so far removed from my reality. It was magical.

With one last breath, I reached for Charlotte's outstretched hand, barely missing, our fingertips brushing as I was pulled beneath into the darkness.

27

A sharp inhale, then a cough, and my eyes flew open. My hand was still on my belly, though the pain had subsided, and I was still in my kitchen in the midst of my own destruction. My head snapped to the side as I sought the figure in the hallway, but the room was vacant, other than the hysterical, mentally broken woman on the floor.

I cried. This time the tears were cold and empty, and hurt right down to the pain in my gut. I wanted her back, that horrible dream. Charlotte, my golden angel. She knew what I was going through. She knew me, and I her. I wanted so desperately to be with someone who cared that I'd take even the whisper of a monster in my head as a kindred spirit.

I am unwell.

Fetching the dustpan and broom from the closet, I cleaned up my therapeutic vandalism one shard at a time.

28

Throughout the morning, the pain in my side waxed and waned, bothersome but not unbearable. Somewhere deep in the folds of my brain I knew something wasn't right, but in true Nell fashion, I ignored it, hoping it would go away on its own. To distract myself, I walked to the coffee shop to indulge in my favourite lavender latte—a treat to soothe my soul.

That's where it happened. I was sipping that beverage, one I could never again taste without thinking of that pivotal moment that changed my life forever. I took a mouthful of coffee, then felt the trickle. I knew then, though I think I had known all along. The fluid just solidified it for me. No more denial. After a quick trip to the restroom, and the discovery of a wet, crimson stain, I hauled my ass to the hospital for confirmation.

"I'm sorry, Nell." My obstetrician was a jovial woman, typically boisterous. But not today. Today, I dampened her flaming personality to a tiny ember. "You've lost the baby."

Over the next half hour, she explained the logistics—the bleeding, the discomfort, the duration of suffering. She presented me with options to expedite the process, none of which I wanted to entertain just yet. I donned a sanitary napkin—a thick harbinger between my legs—and sat in the waiting room, staring down the hallway. I wished for Charlotte to return, a golden angel that would bring me to that place in my dreams where I could drown in the sand and not have to taste, smell, or feel this life for one more agonizing moment. But she did not come.

I pulled my cellphone out of my pocket and poked at the screen with trembling fingers. Brock answered, his voice abrupt. Sharp. Like an axe. "What?"

I opened my mouth and tears poured from my eyes, wetting my lips with salty pain.

"Nell, I'm working. I don't have time for this."

"I lost the baby."

After a spell of silence, his voice came over the line, rapid-fire hate. "What did you do? See, I told you you needed to eat healthier. And it's probably that goddamn lotion you use. And you aren't young anymore, Nell. You waited too fucking long to have kids. This is my one regret, not doing this sooner. Now I won't have kids, and it's all your fault—"

I hung up the phone. It rang. I dropped it on the floor, pressed my heel against the screen, and stood, smiling at the crackle of the glass as it fissured under my weight. After giving it a few stomps for good measure, I tossed the corpse of communication in the bin and headed for the nurse's lounge. Sleeping in a chair was preferable to returning to that devil's lair.

29

It wasn't the first time I'd spent an overnight at the hospital in a professional capacity. We'd all hunkered in during a bad snowstorm a few years back, those of us on call not wanting to battle black ice and heavy drifting to make it in for a shift. But this time, spending the night on a cot in the staff room wasn't a fun sleepover. I was angry. Angry that I couldn't be at home in my own bed, or even on my own couch as the death inside me purged out in wet, embarrassing discomfort. Angry that I couldn't cry at my own table over a pail of ice cream for fear I would be subject to criticism and judgement.

I tossed and turned, as much as was possible on that tiny plastic bed. I tried to read, but my mind wandered, returning to the anger I tried to shove down to the pit of my belly. I played games on my phone, counted more sheep than roamed the hills of Scotland, and even tried to watch shitty syndicated sitcoms, but sleep would not come. Then it occurred to me.

I have no life inside me. I can do what I want. Like Brock would say, I can be my old selfish self again.

Throwing the covers off and piling them on the bed, I pulled my hoodie on and went out into the dimly lit hallway. I boarded the elevator, not giving a good goddamn if Swift Runner and his ghouls were holding a whole family hoedown in there. I wanted drugs, and I wanted them now.

The ride was uneventful—no consumed family tagging along—and the pharmacy floor was quiet; at the witching hour, the pharmacy was closed to the general public, and all inpatient medication had been dispensed to their respective floors during business hours. Andy the pharmacist manned the booth, and a lone security guard sat slumped in a chair in the hall, hat over his eyes, attempting to hide his obvious slumber.

"Hey, Nell," Andy said. He looked young, like he'd just unlatched from his mother's teat. "Need something?"

"Yeah, Andy. I need something for sleep. The good stuff." I flashed my pass at him and he scanned it, the computer beeping its approval.

"A benzo do? Clonazepam?"

"That'll work. Max dose, please."

"For how many days?"

"Just one. For tonight."

"Righto. Gimme a few minutes."

It's one pill, dude. You only need to count to one. How long do you need?

While Andy fiddled around behind the scenes, I strolled down the hall. If I stood still, my mind wouldn't, and it would take me places I didn't want to go. I walked past the security guard, soft snores flatulating off his plump lips, and to the gift shop. Through the windows I could see all sorts of swag, glittering and colourful, flowing and pastel. Balloons, cheap jewelry, teddy bears. They might bring cheer if they didn't remind people of the wares of a hospital gift shop.

The guard's snores sputtered, becoming erratic. I watched at a distance as his chest rose and fell, his breathing calm and measured, the snorts and gargles from his mouth exactly as they had been when I'd walked by before. But there was something else, another sound, something quieter and sharper coming from that direction.

With quiet steps I approached him, head cocked, trying to home in on the sound. It was a coo, a high-pitched snigger. Only once I was overtop of the man did I realize the sound was not coming from him, but beyond him, down the hall on the other side of the pharmacy.

"Andy?"

Andy didn't answer. Nor did I hear the rattle of pill bottles, the scribble of writing, or the clicking of computer keys.

He had to go to storage, is all.

I continued by the pharmacy window until I reached the corner. When I stepped into the adjacent hallway, I expected to see Swift Runner, axe in hand, a river of blood running between his feet.

Swift Runner was not there. But something was.

Oh fuck.

A soft brown form, plump and squishy, crawled across the white tile floor, leaving a trail of slimy gore. It gurgled and babbled, a happy sound, as its chubby legs pushed it forward. I gasped, drawing its attention. It turned to me.

It was Swift Runner's infant, in a cloth diaper, its smile punctuated by a single tooth. It reached for me, chubby fingers grasping the air, squeals of glee bursting from its tiny throat.

Like a necklace, the infant wore a tiny noose, strangled into its flesh like a wire on a growing oak. The blood smeared on the floor was from the stubs on the ends of its legs where feet used to be.

Another noise rang through the fold, loud and shrill. Jarring. Took me several moments to realize it was the sound of my own screams.

I ran, down the hallway, past the guard who had startled awake, past the gift shop and around the corner to the offices beyond. The lights came to life, presumedly motion activated.

The guard called out. "Miss?"

I need . . . help.

He came around the corner. Not the guard, but him. Swift Runner's child, my unborn fetus—who it was I'll never know. It was a gyrating, squelching conglomeration of flesh, bloody and ragged, standing on two stumps and walking towards me in spastic, frantic strides. Though my legs were twice as long as the entirety of its body, it reached me in two heartbeats, its wetness soaking up the leg of my pants, over my belly and chest until we were eye to eye.

When it spoke, a crimson mist wheezed out over my face and into my mouth. "Nimaamaa!"

Like warm liquid, it rolled down my front and onto the floor, reconstituting into a baby once again and thumping away from me on bloody stumps, its maniacal laughter filling my head so full I thought my skull might explode. I covered my ears and squeezed my eyes shut so hard it hurt.

A voice, muffled and close. Then a hand on my shoulder.

"Nellie?" Andy was there, white as the dead, security guard behind him with his hand on his radio. "Are you . . . what are you doing?"

I took the bottle. "Having a fucking breakdown."

I touched my face, my breasts, and stomach, searching for blood and baby flesh but my hands came back clean and dry.

"Okay, um, well, should I call someone?" He looked terrified.

I patted him on the arm. "No one to call. I'm just . . ."

A little under the weather.

30

The sleeping pill was magic. I slept like the dead; no dreams of Swift Runner and his half-eaten baby or consumed family plagued my slumber. When I woke, it was only because of the ruckus of the next shift arriving on the floor.

I used the employee facilities to shower and make myself half presentable for my shift. Though the patients wouldn't care, I did. Maintaining some semblance of professionalism was all I had left. As I pulled on my scrubs and tied my hair into a braid, the lounge phone rang.

"Hello?"

"Nell? It's Doctor Wainwright. You're on shift today up in rehab, yes?"

"Sure am."

"How soon will you be available?"

"Now."

A loud sigh of relief. "Thank God. Can I ask you a huge favour?"

"Of course."

"Can you assist in the OR? We've had a bad pileup on the QEII. We're overrun, and could use another set of hands."

"I wouldn't mind, but HR—"

"You let me worry about them. Do you feel okay to work?"

I flexed my hand, then bunched it into a tight fist. "Yeah, I'm fine."

"Great."

"When do you need me?"

"Now, if that's possible."

"On my way."

Whether I was ready or not, it would be a great distraction. Surgery always cemented me solidly in the moment, muting all other facets of my life. It was precisely what I needed.

31

The surgeon's voice was soft, barely above the Debussy playing in the background. "Clamp."

This time it wasn't a middle-aged, overindulgent white dude, but a young man with dark olive skin and a swath of thick, black hair. He reminded me nothing of my nightmares, though. He was gentle, young, and tragically mangled. They'd had to use the jaws of life to pry him from his Prius, which had fallen victim to a gas-guzzling pickup. The surgeon charged me with clamping and maintaining his femoral artery; his leg had been almost completely severed at the thigh.

"He's losing too much blood, even with the clamp," the surgeon said. I suctioned as the doctors worked, methodical but swift. "I'm not sure we can save it."

I was heartbroken for him, this young man in the prime of his life. My attention drifted to the tattoo on his leg, ripped and bloody, split open further by our blade. It was a shame his tattoo had been ruined. Such a beautiful design—a stag with a massive rack, rich browns and gold and meticulous detail on its thick hide. The crash had mangled the stag's hooves and legs, and we further defaced it by slicing across its antlers to reach the tissue and arteries beneath. Still, I could see one brown eye framed by golden wispy lashes, staring up at me, pleading.

The doctor's voice broke our staring contest. "Fuck it. This isn't viable."

The sound of the bone saw shivered right to my core. Like a robot, I cleaned and cauterized the amputation site. Once the surgery was complete, and the patient patched and bandaged, I spent a few minutes cleaning him up before they took him to recover in the ICU.

He was a mess. Broken limbs, some deep lacerations on his face. Before I'd arrived in the surgical suite they'd had a first amputation—a crush injury that had resulted in the removal of his penile shaft and one testicle. I stared at the site, a mass of thick, bulging bandages over a flat plain.

And that's what'll matter. Not his entire leg, but the removal of his power.

That stag. It was on the floor now, splayed in fragments, resting in pieces connected to the meaty thigh. I squatted down, peeled off my glove, and ran a finger over an antler, tracing each curve and groove.

"What are you doing?" the orderly asked as he stood overtop of me, shaking his head.

"It's a beautiful piece of art. It's a shame."

"Uh huh," he said. "And also, the man lost his dude parts. That's a bigger shame, if I do say."

I stood. "Of course."

"May I take that now, or would you like to play with it some more?"

I didn't dignify that with a response. Standing to the side, I watched as the stag was stuffed into a biohazard bag to be sealed away and destroyed. As the orderly left the room to continue his life, I thought of that stag, dead and detached, and wondered what would become of it.

32

Knowing I couldn't stay at the hospital forever, I packed my things and caught the bus. I got off a stop early to go the market and grab something nice for dinner. Something to help ease Brock's rage. Pork roast being his favourite, I selected a prime piece of meat, paying top price, which is something I never did. Baby potatoes, green beans, and fresh garlic bread in my bag, I trekked home, hoping Brock wasn't there waiting for me. I needed time to brace myself—a good hour or two of cooking and cleaning would be enough for me to get settled.

As luck would have it, Brock wasn't home. I gave the house a light cleaning, then got to work in the kitchen, peeling potatoes and seasoning the meat. By the time he walked through the door, the house smelled like warm memories of childhood, family gatherings, stories by the fire. Brock stood in the entryway, stunned, evaluating the shining surfaces and savoury smells.

I walked into the living room, scotch in hand, a smile plastered on my face.

"Hi, Brock."

"Hi."

He took the drink, watching me as I moved through the dining room, setting the table and fussing over the flowers I'd picked from the garden. I don't know what possessed me to do all of it, but I wanted to try. I had to save what little of my life I had left. And the truth of it was I had nothing besides this horrible, gluttonous human.

After everything that happened—me leaving, my outburst, the loss of our child—I expected something from Brock. Anything. A comment, a question, a loving touch. Any kind of touch. But I got nothing but apathy and indifference; it was a flawless slide back into our routine. He sat on the couch, drink in hand, playing on his phone as I finished dinner and brought it to the table. I had announced dinner was ready—five minutes before it was, because he never came when called.

While filling a pitcher with ice water, I stared out our kitchen window at the backyard and the green space behind. The first skiff of autumn snow kissed the yellow grass, a palate of leaves making their bed on the grey expanse with their rainbows of fire, oranges and reds and yellows. In the midst of the changing season, I spied movement. Not Swift Runner, as I'd become accustomed to, but a stag, stacked with a generous rack, grazing on the meager patches of green peeking through summer's death. Muscles rippled over his shoulder as he pawed the ground, unearthing fresh greens, chewing greedily on his mouthful of foliage. I put my hand on the glass, imagining how that hide felt, that rippling muscle and power. Seeing my movement, he lifted his head, his golden eyes assessing me, considering.

"You coming?" Brock called from the other room.

The stag bolted, galloping into the trees and out of sight.

I took my place at the table. I sliced the pork roast and set the slabs of meat on Brock's plate, then scooped up potatoes and beans, placing them artistically on the remaining space. To top it off, I tipped the gravy boat, drowning the lot of it in thick, rich gravy.

"Looks delicious," he said, drool dribbling from his lips.

I took potatoes and beans but did not douse them in gravy. He chewed his meat, the wet grinding of his molars like nails down a chalkboard. "Why aren't you eating?"

"I am eating. I'm just still a little under the . . . I only want the veg."

He nodded and stuffed another chunk of meat in his maw. "Good. You need to start eating better. Those potatoes aren't doing you any favours, though."

I set my fork down. "So what, Brock? Beans? Should I just eat the beans, and nothing more?"

I didn't give him a chance to respond. I pushed away from the table and went for the kitchen.

"Where are you going?" he called after me.

I tried to make my voice sound pleasant. Nonplussed. "I'll be right back. Just grabbing a drink."

I hovered over the sink, hands on the counter. I felt sick, but it was different from before. The stench of the pork roast was thick and stifling, the coppery roasted meat so heavy and sweet it overwhelmed me. I gagged, and when I opened my mouth, I tasted blood and meat coating my tongue and gurgling up my esophagus, despite the fact that not one bite of that pork had passed my lips.

After taking a shot of scotch to kill the taste, I dabbed my lips with a paper towel, and stepped on the pedal of the garbage can to lift the lid. The paper towel fluttered from my fingers, floating in slow motion, coming to a rest in the bin atop potato peelings, a brown meat wrapper, and a hunk of meat I hadn't known I disposed of—a thigh, complete with a defaced stag tattoo, its golden, bloody eye staring up at me.

I burst into the dining room. Brock was wolfing down the roast, juice dribbling down his chin, grunting as he ate. "This is delicious, Nellie. Best you've ever made."

There's no way . . .

I took my place at the table and ate my potatoes and beans. Brock sliced off seconds and then thirds, consuming the entire piece of meat in short order.

"Damn, baby. So good!"

It's pork. I bought it. I cooked it. I served it. It's pork.

"Glad you enjoyed it." My voice sounded far away, my mind in shattered pieces. On the gristle left on Brock's plate I could make out an image. The blurred outline of a hoof.

"This is fine," I said, sipping my drink. "Everything is fine."

33

I slept in the bed that night, next to my husband who reeked of flesh, his lips moist with fat from the meat. He was sweating, which he attributed to the sheer amount of food he'd consumed, but I knew different. I could hear Basil's voice in my head.

When a human consumes the flesh of another out of greed, of want, he becomes wendigo.

Wendigo.

Wendigo.

Wendigo.

The word played over and over in my brain, a scratching, broken record. I touched Brock's arms, feeling for the soft velvet of bovine hide.

You're crazy, Nell. Officially batshit insane.

It was a rough night. It was Brock's turn for restlessness, tossing and turning, moaning and contorting beneath the covers.

JAE MAZER

He sweat buckets, soaking the bed and emanating a stench of rotting decay. I moved to the couch, unable to bear the noise and odour any longer. And on that couch, I slept like a baby.

34

"Nellie." The fear in Brock's voice was palpable. I could have heard it a kilometre away. "There's something wrong. Very wrong."

I sat up on the couch and looked down the hall. Brock was there, grey, wavering like a drunk. Other than looking hungover, he was still Brock. No massive changes, only the general appearance of being unwell.

"You feeling sick?" I asked.

"I think there was something wrong with that roast."

"Shouldn't have been. Just picked it up from market yesterday on my way home."

To prove my point, I fetched the receipt from my purse, verifying that I had, in fact, not fed him spoiled meat.

"I dunno," he said, swiping the sweat from his brow.

"Well, just because I bought it yesterday doesn't mean it's not spoiled. Perhaps it was bad. Listeria and salmonella seem to make the news every week."

"Maybe."

"I'll tell you what. I'll pass by that market today after work, mention it to them. See if they've had any other complaints."

"I can't go to work."

He's never called in sick like this. For hangovers, yes, but not for actual illness.

"Rest. Sip water, small amounts. I'll call and check in."

"Thank you." He stumbled back down the hall.

Thank you? Don't believe he's said that in over a decade. Not to me.

A hand rested on my shoulder, and a shot of cold jolted my body. Charlotte sat next to me, her body stiff, blue ice. In her throat she hummed her melody, her eyes coated with thick, solid tears. I entwined my fingers with hers and we rocked, both humming the haunting folksong.

"Gibichiwebinan!" Swift Runner's voice was an axe, slicing at us across the void of the living room. He stood by the front door, naked and bloody, tatters of his uniform dripping off with his flesh.

Charlotte stuck out her chin and puffed her chest. "I will not stop."

His face contorted as if he'd been struck in the skull with his own axe. Charlotte turned back to me and placed a hand on my breast. "You strong."

I kept Swift Runner in my peripheral as I stared into her icy eyes. "I am not."

Swift Runner growled, his fists clenched, sweat forming on his brow. "Bagwanawizi."

Charlotte's frozen eyes sharpened to daggers, pointing in his direction. "Not dumb, love. Not stupid, not worthless." She swelled to her feet, dropping my hand in my lap as she moved in his direction, growing and contorting until she was towering over him, hunched over yet pressed against the ceiling. Her arms tore and bent, bone cracking and reforming until they were a pair of antlers protruding from her shoulders. When she spoke again, frost poured from her mouth, cascading down her breasts like a viscous mist. "I have *power*."

With a wail that shattered the glass in the picture frames, she swung her antler arm in an uppercut, goring his jaw and straight out the top of his head. Bit of brain and bone pelted the ceiling, raining down on the living room like hail. While smiling at me, her body decayed—first her flesh, then tendons and muscles, finally bone, all dissolving into a pile of sepia sand that sifted into the carpet and disappeared into the floorboards. In an instant she was gone, as was he and all evidence of their presence. No blood, bone, brain, or sand.

35

"You sound like you've been wound up, unraveled, and wound up again, my dear." Basil's voice on the other end of the line was a comfort beyond words. I had no idea what I'd say to him. Tell him what I'd done? What Brock had eaten, or at least, what I *thought* he ate?

"I'm tired."

"Not physically, though," Basil said, a statement rather than a question. "How can I help? Though that's the thing, isn't it? You aren't sure what you need, or you'd ask for it specifically, yes?"

Yes. If I knew, I'd ask. If I'd known, the thousand times I had wanted to escape my life, that I needed help, I would have sought it. But I was lost. Always had been.

I rubbed my fingers together, grains of phantom sand rolling between my fingertips. "Ramnon."

"Pardon me?" He sounded startled.

"Ramnon. Have you heard of it?" The line was quiet. I

couldn't hear even his breath for an uncomfortable moment. "Basil?"

He cleared his throat. "Ramnon. Yes. There are tales."

"So it's real?"

"'Course not! A mysterious place, concocted by many cultures. A melting pot of folklore, if you will."

"Where is it?"

"Everywhere and nowhere. It's not of this life."

"The afterlife?"

"In a way." I heard the familiar sound of him scratching that white mop of hair. "It is death. A place that all the creatures of folklore congregate when they have no business here. All manner of kooky things—vampires, lycans, Sluagh, banshees, vandheks . . ."

"Wendigo?"

"No, my dear. The wendigo is a creature of folklore, but also of curse. Ramnon is a place of comfort, a sanctuary for those who don't belong. The wendigo deserves no comfort, only suffering."

"How does one find this place?"

Basil laughed, but it was strained. Forced. "Oh, love, the same as you find the Loch Ness monster or the yeti. You don't! Because it's not real."

"I know." I was grasping, at anything and everything I thought might be in reach, like Charlotte's fingertips on the sands of Ramnon.

"But that's not it, is it?" Basil said. "You did not call to talk to me about a faraway folk land. You called because of how you learned of it, yes? Who told you?"

Charlotte showed me. "No one. It came up in my research."

Basil was quiet for a moment, only a throaty acknowledgment. "Mhmmm. And what prompted more research? Something has happened."

I didn't answer. So much had happened, yet nothing. It was all in my mind, placed there by some impossibility.

Basil's dulcet tones interrupted my thoughts. "How's Brock?"

Dying. Transforming. "Fine. I mean, he's Brock, but no different."

"So not fine. Still abusive."

I ignored the bait. "Actually, he was a touch better this morning. Thanked me."

"Huh." Basil did not sound satisfied. "Odd, yes?"

"I'm not questioning it."

"We need not discuss it now. Not until you're ready."

"Thank you for your time, Basil. I just needed to hear a friendly voice."

"Any time, strong Nell."

I wished I was strong. Strong enough to leave before I became the monster.

36

My shift crawled by. As promised, I called Brock every so often, but there was no answer. On the third call I felt a hint of panic—fear of what I might find when I got home. Fear of what I'd done.

But I did nothing. Right?

It was a slow day on the rehab floor, and I wasn't needed in the OR, so I took an extra- long break, and a little trip down to the hospital basement. It was a typical hospital basement—dark, old, and dead—and the morgue was there, which was where I was headed.

"Hey, Gabrielle," I said.

A slender woman with thick glasses and large hair popped up from behind the counter. "Nellie! How're you doing? Haven't seen you in ages, girl! I heard something about a car accident?"

"Wasn't bad. Few bruises, a broken arm."

"Damn. All better now?"

"Mostly." I hovered, leaning over the desk and looking past Gabrielle into the room beyond.

"Whatcha lookin for? Anything I can help you find?"

"Not sure." *Do I really want to do this? There's no way it was real.* "Tell me, what happens with . . . medical waste?"

"Needles and gloves?"

"No, like . . . biological waste."

"Someone shit the bed?"

I shook my head and dangled my arm. Realization spread across her face. "Ah, body parts. Spleens and appendixes and such."

"Limbs, specifically."

"Huh. Well, here's what we do. When a patient is scheduled for that kind of surgery—an amputation in your case, by the sounds of it—they sign away ownership of the surgical leavings to pathological labs. Their parts are used primarily in teaching hospitals."

"This was an unplanned surgery. Car accident."

"If there was no signed consent, we destroy the limb as medical waste. Here we use a rotary kiln."

"So nothing left of it?"

"Nothing but ash and memories."

Memories were something I had no shortage of. I remembered the details on that tattoo—the antlers, the golden eyes looking up at me from the floor of the surgical suite and then from the garbage can in my very own kitchen.

"Listen," Gabrielle said, rolling her chair over to the computer. "What's the name? We'll find out for sure where that limb went to."

"Don't know the name. They called me in last minute."

"Well, we ain't got lots of limbs passing through here. Tell me about it. When was it, and what was it?"

"Just yesterday. Male, Indigenous, entire left leg. The leg had a large tattoo on the thigh. A stag."

"Pretty specific," Gabrielle said. "No problem. Yep, here it is. And look at that. The poor fella signed an organ donor card. That leg was sent away, pathology request from another health authority."

"For sure?"

Gabrielle looked at me, examining my face.

"I mean, is it gone? I know it's weird, but I just want to be sure."

Her nails clacked the keyboard while she kept her eyes on me, then she looked away, brow furrowed, reading the glowing screen. "Yep. Left last night at midnight on our bio truck with a few transplant organs. I have a container number, packaging code, driver's signature—"

"Good." *Thank fuck.* "That's all I need. Look Gabrielle, I know this has been odd, but it's been a weird couple of months, and this was . . . I can't explain it."

Her smile blossomed again. "Nellie, no worries. It's not the oddest thing I've seen, let me tell you."

Before she could tell me, I bid my adieus and returned to work, relieved there would be no monster waiting for me at home. At least one I didn't know.

37

Though I rarely looked forward to seeing Brock at the end of the day, I was relieved when I found him sitting at the table when I got home, slurping a bowl of chicken noodle soup. I dropped my purse and coat over a chair and sat with him.

"How are you feeling?"

"Much better," he said.

He looked better; the colour had returned to his cheeks, and he was calm and relaxed.

"I checked, and no complaints at the market about that pork roast," I lied. "But maybe no one complained yet."

He waved a hand dismissively. "It's fine. I didn't throw up or anything, just felt like death. It passed really quick. Food poisoning is much more violent."

"True."

He slurped his bowl, cleaning up every bite. I put away my coat and purse, then opened the fridge. "I was gonna make some

BLTs for dinner, but if you've already eaten—"

"That sounds amazing. I'm famished."

The slightest pang niggled at my nerves. "Still hungry?"

"Ravenous."

My stomach flipped, but I shook my head, grounding myself with the sound of the breeze outside, the smell of chicken soup wafting through the kitchen. "Okay, I'll whip some up."

Instead of plunking himself in his divot on the couch, he stayed at the table, watching me cut tomatoes and slice open the package of bacon.

"So, what did you do today?" I asked, sating a nervous need to fill the silence.

His face reddened as he looked at his empty bowl. "Watched some movies."

"It's okay to take a day, just relax and kick back. I think you needed it."

A shrug, then he scraped his bowl with his spoon, licking droplets of broth with every swipe.

I needed to get out of that room, if only for a moment. I excused myself and went to the bathroom, locked the door, and sat on the edge of the bathtub, head in my hands.

It's okay. This is all normal. There's nothing different about him. It's all me. In my head.

I ran the water, focusing on the sound, and splashed my face. When I lifted my head and looked in the mirror, Charlotte was behind me, cradling her dead infant in her arms. He was black with frostbite, and stiff as solid ice, his eyes sparkling blue as she swayed back and forth. Bloody tears drained from her eyes, and in the reflection of each droplet was regret: images of her life, her children grown, having children of their own. Herself, knitting by a fire and singing songs in the woods with silver strands woven through her raven hair and deep smile lines framing her eyes and mouth.

A drop of blood plipped onto the floor. I looked down into it and saw myself, old and grey, rocking on a porch in Ramnon. I was smiling and playing a guitar, singing a lilting tune with a pair of banshee sisters by my side, Charlotte harmonizing with me, her voice drawing a flock of iridescent faeries with gossamer wings.

I punched the mirror and Charlotte shattered away with the glass, the shards of regret tinkling into the sink. I stood alone once more, my own blood dripping to the floor in great, heavy drops.

After wrapping my hand in gauze, I returned to the kitchen. Brock was at the counter, back on to me, his shoulders heaving.

"Brock?"

"Mmrrggmm."

I had no idea what he was trying to say. His words were muffled, but there was a panic in his tone I'd never heard before.

"Brock," I repeated as I walked to him. I placed my hand on his shoulder, but he wrenched away, pushing me back with his elbow. I moved to the counter beside him, peering around so I could see what he was doing.

The BLTs were gone. The tomatoes were not on the cutting board, the package of lettuce shredded, plastic and all. He was munching on the bacon, a handful still clenched in his fist, tendrils of white fat hanging from the corners of his mouth.

"Oh my god, Brock. That's raw! You really *will* get sick now." I reached for the clump of meat in his hand, and he raised his fist, pulling it away from me before retaliating and punching me square in the cheek. Those greasy knuckles landed with a crack, and stars fluttered across my vision as I stumbled to the floor.

He looked as shocked as I felt, tears streaming down his face as he crammed more bacon in his over-full cheeks.

Swallowing, gulping, sobbing, he devoured the bacon as I lay on the floor and watched, hot blood filling my eyes, coating the scene in crimson. When he was done, he fell quiet, all except his stomach, which was a roaring beast, gurgling and growling with displeasure.

"I'm going to bed," he said.

Without even wiping the grease off his face, which spanned from his forehead to his chin, he shuffled to the bedroom and slammed the door.

38

Renee sat beside me in the nurse's lounge, a scowl on her face and tears in her eyes.

"Not okay," Renee said as she added another stitch to the gash in my cheek, tugging tight to get her point across.

"You don't understand. It wasn't like that."

She stopped put her hands on her hips. "Not like what? Did he do this?"

"Well yes, but—"

"Was this from his knuckles on your face?"

"Yeah, but—"

"Don't you go and tell me you were asking for it, cuz then I'd have to flip my shit."

"He wasn't himself, Renee. And I know that sounds cliche, and it's a lame excuse, but it's true. There's something wrong with him. Really wrong."

"There's always been something wrong with that boy."

"Agreed. But this is something else entirely. I don't know how to explain it, Renee. He's . . . he's changing."

She finished the stitches in silence, allowing us both time for contemplation.

"What do you mean, changing?" she asked. "Escalating?"

I could still smell the raw meat on his breath, see the panic in his eyes. "He ate a pound of raw bacon in front of me, Renee. But he didn't want to. He was crying, forcing it in."

Her chest heaved as she drew a few breaths, same as I did when composing my thoughts. "That is disturbing."

"Yeah."

"So . . . damn," she said. "Mental illness, especially to this degree, or something like Pica . . . that shit doesn't happen overnight. And not at this late an onset in life. Have you ever seen this kind of behaviour before from him?"

Not before he consumed a human thigh. I pinched my leg, focusing on the pain to distract myself from that nonsense. *The leg was donated. Transported somewhere else, like Gabrielle said.*

"Nellie?"

Besides, there's no such thing as the wendigo.

"Nellie!" Renee squeezed my shoulder when she shouted in my face, startling me to attention. "Seems like you're having some issues of your own."

"Daydreaming, I guess."

Renee sat on the bed next to me, and held my hand, grip firm and pulsing. "Tell me."

"Tell you what?"

"Tell me what's really going on, Nellie. There's something you're hiding."

I was pregnant. Now I'm not. And my husband is a greedy, abusive motherfucker who is turning into some folklore hellbeast. "Nothing. Promise."

Though she looked unconvinced, Renee let it drop.

Once the stitches were complete, and my face cleaned up, I grabbed my coat and purse and headed for the door.

"That's it?" Renee said, holding out her hands. "Wham, bam, thank you ma'am?"

"Aren't you working?"

"I get off in 45. Wanna grab a bite?"

"I should get home."

Her eyes narrowed into slits—she was evaluating me and judging me, too. Just like Brock. I walked out the door and my purse vibrated. Brock's phone was a convenience I helped myself to after busting my own phone to silence his hate.

"Hey, Brock, are you okay?"

"Weird favour."

"Okay, shoot."

"Can you stop at C-C-Costco, pick up some g-g-groceries?" Judging by the tremor and stutter, he was either scared or in pain. Likely both.

"You okay?" *Dumb question.*

A pause. "N-no."

My turn to pause, then, "Yeah, okay. Email me a list."

The phone went dead without another word. Before I made it to the truck, my phone beeped. A message. Brock's list.

I sat behind the wheel, my hands shaking, reading the message over and over again. I started the truck and drove to Costco, tears of terror streaming down my face.

39

I got everything on Brock's list—two kilograms of ground beef, two whole chickens, two family-sized packages of pork chops, four lamb roasts—it was more meat than the two of us would consume in a whole year. But Brock was insistent, texting me several times while I wandered the aisles of Costco, wondering if I should diverge from the list and purchase something green and leafy.

When I arrived home, Brock was waiting. And he looked terrible—his skin was grey, his hair shaggy, his pants and shirt draped over him looking two sizes too big.

Since this morning?

I shook my head.

No, Nell. Not real.

I thought he was standing there to help me carry in the groceries. Not sure why I thought that. He'd never helped me carry in the groceries before.

"Just give me the beef," he snarled. "I'm hungry."

"Can you wait? It's in full kilogram packs, Brock. It's Costco. We need to break it down."

"Give it to me!"

I held out a Styrofoam tray, which he ripped from my grasp, running inside with it clutched to his chest like a newborn baby. The remaining meat was in two boxes, one of which I hoisted out of the truck. When I set it on the counter inside, the beef he'd carried in was sizzling, the entire pack in a skillet on the stove.

"Are you kidding me, Brock?"

He didn't answer. He just kept pushing the meat around with a spatula while he shifted from foot to foot and chewed his lower lip bloody.

By the time I brought in the second box—which couldn't have been more than a minute later—Brock was shoveling the beef into his mouth straight from the skillet.

"Is that cooked?"

"It's not," he grumbled, his voice a near growl.

I unpacked the groceries, keeping an eye on Brock the whole time I was separating the meat into freezer bags, labelling each with dates, amounts, and type. When everything was put away, and my hands washed, Brock was also done. He'd left the pan on the stove, spoon on the counter, and was sitting on the couch.

"Want me to turn the tv on?" I asked.

"Yes, please." He wasn't looking at me, or even paying attention. And it wasn't really Brock, as far as I was concerned. Brock hadn't said please to me in over a decade.

I sat on the coffee table in front of him and picked up the remote. "What's going on?"

He chewed his nails, his eyes wild. "Nothing. I just feel . . . weird. Off."

"Can you describe it?"

His head snapped towards me, his eyes dark with rage. "Can you go fuck yourself?"

He'd yelled at me many times before. Daily, for countless years, and most times worse than this. But something about this one made my bones cringe. I turned on the television, set the channel to a syndicated adult cartoon, and left Brock on the couch while I went to the bedroom to down a cocktail of sleeping pills and wine.

40

The witching hour was in full swing when I was woken by a ruckus from beyond the bedroom door. It was 3 a.m., the full moon illuminating the room like it was daytime. From the other side of the door—the kitchen, I presumed—came the sound of glass and plastic clanking and thumping together. And Brock, moaning, grunting, and crying.

Not sure what to expect, I grabbed the long metal flashlight we kept beside the bed. It was as good a weapon as any if I encountered something other than Brock in my house. Or if it wasn't quite Brock.

The noise was much louder when I swung open the door, and quite distinct—ripping plastic, wet splashes on the laminate floor, and chewing. Horrible, wet grinding, gulping swallowing, and stifled gagging. Though I didn't want to move, my feet carried me down the hall and into the kitchen. The room was lit by the same moon glow as the bedroom, with additional light from the fridge. Both fridge and freezer door were wide open, their contents spread across the kitchen floor. Brock was on his knees, tearing open packages with his nails and teeth and shoving great hunks of meat into his mouth. Before he'd even finished chewing, he was stuffing more meat in his gob, gasping for breath between every bite.

"Brock, stop!"

I fell to my knees and tried to get between him and the food, but he did the strangest thing. He dropped his head and charged me, butting me across the kitchen. He looked at me, and the chewing ceased for only a second before he scrambled back to the meat, clawing and eating.

"I'm sorry, babe," he cried through a mouthful of raw lamb. "I can't stop. I'm so hungry it hurts. Nell, it's excruciating. I can't seem to get enough!" Blood dribbled down his chin, squirting from his mouth as he screamed and clenched his stomach. "Help me!"

I ran to the bedroom. I got the bottle of sleeping pills—oh how I wished I'd gotten more of the good stuff from Andy at the hospital. When I returned, Brock was gnawing on a frozen pork chop, his teeth chipping against bone.

"Here," I said, shoving one, two, three pills between his gnashing teeth. "Take these." I shoved in a couple more. He did not protest. Every time I held up another pill, he took a break from chewing long enough for me to get it in his mouth.

"Will it hurt me?" he asked, his voice that of a child.

"No, sweetheart. It will help you stop."

The chewing slowed, his eyes grew heavy, and soon he slumped over, his chin on his chest, his back against the cupboard, and his legs stretched out in front of him. I surveyed the carnage. He'd gone through every bit of meat we had—everything I'd purchased from Costco, a pack of bacon we must have had hidden away in or behind a drawer, and random bits of deli meat from God knows when. He also polished off a full eighteen pack of eggs, shells and all.

Not real.

Not real.

But what, then?

41

After not enough sleep, I drove to work, dialing Basil at the first red light.

"Basil here."

"Hey Basil, it's Nell."

His voice brightened. "Strong Nell! Still givin' 'em hell?"

"More than you can imagine." Even after thinking about this call all night, after cleaning up my husband's buffet on the kitchen floor, I had no idea what to say. I was so sure I'd known how I would present this ludicrous conundrum, but the sound of Basil's voice wiped my thoughts clean. "I don't even know what to say."

He took a sip of a beverage I assumed was coffee. "Well first of all, you are driving, yes?"

"Uh huh."

"I can tell. So that's good. Not that you're driving and talking to me—I'd never condone such dangerous behaviour—but good that you have a car again."

"First of all," I said, as if addressing an irate parent, "I'm on hands-free. Second, it's not my car. I didn't get one yet. I'm driving Brock's truck."

"He has no need for it today?"

"He does not." My husband was suffering, but a part of me, hidden deep within the darkened nooks of my brain, was secretly thrilled to have a vehicle back. My ass cheeks were warm against the heated leather seats, my hands dry and clean, wrapped around a steering wheel rather than a bus pole covered in a plethora of germs and mysterious fluids. It was downright luxurious, being behind the wheel of my own ride, controlling the air, the music, the route.

"So one of several things has occurred," Basil said. "He is ill, and in no need of the truck. Or he has carpooled, or he's out of town. Or perhaps you have killed him, hacked him up into bite-sized bits, and stored him in your freezer."

Against any couth my mother had engrained in me, I cracked the joke before I could silence it. "Brock cutlets." I snorted, an explosive laugh, brief but jarring. Thankfully, Basil laughed too. How ludicrous and horrifying it was, given the circumstances, to be joking about meat and flesh. And cannibalism.

Brock hasn't resorted to that, thank fuck.

Yet.

"Basil, I'm sorry. That's terrible."

"It's releasing stress. Humour often comes at the most inappropriate of times, but it is a release, and mustn't be frowned upon."

"Brock is unwell."

"I am guessing this is more than the man flu, if it warrants a call to me."

"It's horrible, Basil. But I also want to make sure I'm not reading too much into it."

"I see. Because of the events as of late, I assume. You think you're imagining his illness?"

"No, it's real, whatever it is." That meat was cold and wet as I cleaned it off the floor. And as I helped him to bed, his breath was hot, rancid, and bloody against my face. It was all very real. "It's the strangest thing. He's ravenous, and I don't just mean snacking all the time. He acts like he's starving, but he only wants meat. He tries to cook it, but he can't wait. Basil, he downed raw meat in the middle of the night. A whole lot of it."

"Huh. Iron deficiency, perhaps. I haven't seen it manifest itself so aggressively, though. Does he look unwell?"

"A bit. His colour is grey, and he's really sweaty. But no fever, and no massive changes."

"Changes." Basil repeated my word, as if rolling it over his tongue to taste it. "My dear, has Swift Runner made an appearance through all of this?"

No. I hadn't realized, but even during this time of stress, the man had not graced my visions.

But was it that stressful, seeing my husband in such anguish?

"No. Nothing like that. This time it's all Brock."

"And changes, you say? What did you expect to change? My dear, did you expect him to sprout antlers?"

You know, maybe I did.

Basil laughed, his wheezy chortle, lightening the mood. "You could take him to the doctor. Though not as serious as a transition to a mythical beast, your husband is experiencing some sort of gastrointestinal trauma. A parasite, by the sounds of it. It is depriving his body of nutrients, and could also be working on his cranium. Time is of the essence with things like these."

"Of course. I mean, I probably should have taken him in the minute I found him bathing in meat on my kitchen floor."

"Definitely a sign of health gone awry. But that's not why you called. You know there's something wrong with Brock, but you wondered if it was you. It's likely that he's simply ill, but you imagined the wendigo in place of logical, scientific symptoms."

"How could I not?"

"Indeed. Take that man in, Nellie. Get him patched up. Then leave his sorry ass."

My turn to laugh. "If I wanted rid of him, would I not just leave him to perish?"

Basil didn't laugh. "You are all human, yes? Don't be the monster, Nell."

"Thank you, Basil."

"Anytime, my dear. And don't hesitate to call, should you need any more confirmation that you do not share your bed with the wendigo."

After disconnecting the call, I cranked up the stereo and heat. Throwing my blinker on as I rolled up to another red light, I started walking through the steps—go home, load Brock into the car, drive him to the hospital. Would I stay at his side while they ran a battery of tests? Would I fetch him ice water and new magazines from the gift shop? Would I subscribe to the television service and lie beside him in his uncomfortable hospital bed, watching shit television and holding his hand?

Had he done all those things for me? Or did he abandon me after putting me in my hospital bed? Did he go about his day, living in extravagance, pampering himself with expensive goods and services while I stayed alone, hurt and scared?

With a flick of a finger, I shut off my blinker. I turned up the radio. On the way to work, I went through a drive-thru and purchased a six-dollar coffee with as many monikers and a four-dollar pastry jam-packed with carbs and comfort. I took the truck to valet parking before strolling into work.

He's not dying.

He can wait, like I've spent a lifetime waiting for decency and humanity.

42

The Anchor and Crown beckoned me for a drink. That, and Renee had asked, though I think it surprised her when I agreed. Truth be told, I would have gone there even if she'd not asked. I wasn't too proud to drink alone.

We both clocked out at 1700 on the dot, and met each other in the pub, holing up in a corner booth away from the coming and going medical students and staff. Though nice to stay away from home, it was also good to get away from work. After ordering a platter of greasy fare and a round of craft beer, Renee got to grilling.

"So what's up?" she asked.

"Not much. Work, home, work again."

"Something's different."

"How so?"

"You're here."

"As are you."

She scrunched her nose in distaste. "Like pulling teeth, girl."

"I've nothing much to say."

"How are you feeling? The arm? Brock?"

"Those are three very different subjects."

She sighed and crossed her arms.

Fine. "I feel good—no more nausea. The arm is almost a hundred percent. Did you know I assisted in surgery the other day?"

That stag, his golden eye, staring up at me from the depths of my trash bin.

"I'd heard! How did that go?"

"Okay. Well . . . not sure I have it in me anymore, Renee."

"Have what in you?"

"The blood and guts. The loss. We took that poor young fellow's leg."

"Ugh. That accident on the QEII?"

"Yup."

"What a mess that pile-up was. Tied up imaging for half a day. We had over a dozen earfuls from people having to reschedule their scans and X-rays." She took a swig of beer, swishing it around her mouth before asking more. "What has you turned off? That messy business isn't for me, but you've done blood and guts your whole career."

It's the meat. I can't stomach the meat anymore. "Not sure. Just sensitive right now."

I could feel it, her eyes on me, trying to figure it all out. "And what of Brock?"

"What about him?"

"Still abusive?"

"Goddammit!" I slammed my fist on the table, rattling the pints. "It's not abuse!"

As always in restaurants, the food arrived at that inopportune moment. The waitress, looking sheepish, set our platter of wings and skins in front of us without saying a word. I didn't hesitate, stuffing a bacon and cheese-laden wedge in my mouth to cease my part of the conversation.

"Whatever it is," Renee said, selecting a wing, her eyes glued on me, "is he still at it?"

I chewed, swallowed, and took another bite. She waited as I finished the spud, which I took my sweet time doing. "He's still Brock. Though lately he's been a little under the weather."

She nodded as she tore a strip of meat away from the chicken bone. "It's going around. Have you been sick?"

All she'd need to do was snoop hospital records to find out I'd been seen as an outpatient. And had she known I spent a night at the hospital sleeping in the nurse's lounge, she would have been furious, after offering her couch multiple times when Brock had been particularly ornery.

"No, I'm okay so far," I said. "And I hope to stay that way."

We spent the rest of the meal filling the air with idle chitchat, though Renee watched me the whole time. She wasn't stupid, and we were far from strangers. If anyone could accurately assume something was going on, some unspoken secret, it was Renee. When the waitress brought the check, Renee pulled out her mental spade and did one last dig, hoping to unearth the truth.

"You said Brock's sick. Like the flu?"

"Something like that. Stomach bug, I guess."

"Vomiting?"

"No, just . . . unsettled."

"Fever?"

"He's fine, Renee."

"Something's not fine. I can tell. If you don't want to say, that's okay, but know that I'm here. You withdrawing like this makes me uncomfortable."

Usually, I'd find solace in that gentle confrontation. Renee had a knack for being blunt and direct without it seeming like a violation. Now, though, I felt poked and prodded. I sensed more suspicion from her than empathy, more morbid curiosity that caring. Probably that was all just in my head. Like everything, it was all me.

43

The halogens on Brock's truck danced on the garage door when I pulled into the driveway. Instead of getting out and going inside, I stayed put, sitting behind the wheel and contemplating whether I should turn the key and hit reverse, pull out of the driveway and go, never turn around, never come back. It felt right. It felt like my life, and my truck, and my journey. I was done with this life.

Brock's shadow passed the window, fast, blowing the curtains to the side. I pulled the key from the ignition and gathered my purse and the leftovers from the pub. *More meat for him*. I shuddered. My stomach lurched. The crying came in uncontrollable fits and I pounded my fists against the dash, ashamed of the horrible person residing in my mind. It wasn't until the appearance of the bedroom light at the end of the house and a looming silhouette in the window did I realize he was watching me.

He will think me insane and be right to do so.

I left the truck, *Brock's* truck, in the driveway, and finagled my keys, arming myself with the house key before reaching the porch. I ran my fingers over the deadbolt to find the keyhole, then slid the key in and pushed my way inside. The house was asleep, dark and stagnant in its slumber, no sign of Brock. My eyes fluttered to the billowing treatments over the bay window, conjuring up an image from only moments before when Brock passed by.

But he was so fast. Perhaps it wasn't him.

I didn't turn on the lights, as if it might draw attention to my arrival. For that same reason I dampened my footfalls, stepping lightly and setting my belongings down on the carpet so as not to make a noise. The kitchen was clean, just like I'd left it—no remnants of food to be found. I wanted to look in the fridge, to see if it was completely bare, but my desire for silence prevented me from reaching for the handle. Instead, I opted to move straight to the bedroom where I had seen Brock standing in the window.

Better to confront the beast straight off, rather than let him come for me.

The black gap at the bottom of the bedroom door told me the lights in the bedroom were off. I had clearly seen them on when I was pitching my fit in the truck. Either he wanted to surprise me, or he wanted me to think he was sleeping.

Or perhaps the light had never been on at all. Maybe my mind was playing the games of school children, driving me deeper into madness.

My stomach and heart could not tolerate any more tension. I wrapped my fingers around the cold brass knob and pushed the door open. The only electronics we had giving off any light were all in the living room or kitchen, so I could only make out vague shapes littering the room—the bed, the dresser, the door to the ensuite. I stepped closer to the bed and focused on the lump upon it, rising and falling, each movement accompanied by the strangled, wet hiss of lungs in distress.

"Brock?" My voice was so quiet I wasn't even sure I heard it, not that I could have over my pounding heart. Another step, more clarity—now I was able to see bones.

"Brock." My voice was a hard punch. Brock startled, swiping a weak limb in front of his face.

Should it be that long, his arm? Oh how the darkness plays tricks.

From blind memory my fingers found the chain on the bedside lamp. I pulled it, then wished I hadn't. I'd have rather kept the monsters in the dark—they were so much less terrifying in my imagination than in the flesh.

Brock was long and narrow. No other way to describe it. Like a victim of the rack, his arms and legs had elongated, all hanging to the floor even though his body lay prone on the bed. His back had contorted and his spine had curved, shaping him into an arc. His bones were most shocking, clearly visible beneath grey, decaying flesh stretched thin over his gangly, emaciated frame. With not an ounce of fat to be found, his organs were visible, working and churning beneath his flesh, black sludge pumped through his veins by a withered heart.

"Nellie," he said, his words a strained inhale. "I hungry."

His face was sallow, skeletal, his gums receding to his nose and chin, revealing gruesome plaque caked with several varieties of meat. His once blue eyes were now black and sunken into his skull, frantic, trying to scan the room beyond his protruding brow and cheekbones.

What made me an effective medical professional was my calm in moments of crisis. My body and brain went into autopilot, carrying out logical actions, problem solving. I fluffed a pillow and rested it against the headboard, then knelt on the bed and hooked my arms under Brock's, wriggling and heaving to prop him into a sitting position. Once he was seated upright, I steadied him by setting my hand on his chest. The heel of my palm sunk into his liquid, gangrenous flesh and came to rest directly on his ribs. I did not pull away.

Not real.

"It will be okay Brock," I heard myself say. "You ate something, is all. That pork was spoiled. No, a parasite. I talked to a friend who said it was probably a parasi—"

I saw them. Surprising, considering how shaggy and unkempt Brock's hair was, and how tiny they were beneath his grey, decomposing flesh. His head had bobbed forward while I was rationalizing the whole thing to him, to myself, and during that drunken bob his hair had flurped to the side, revealing them. Bumps. A bit more than mosquito bites, but not as prominent as goose eggs, protruding above his eyes at his patchy hairline. I ran a finger over one bump, pressing it with a nail, and the skin gave way, splitting, birthing the jagged, grooved bone beneath.

Antlers.

Someone spoke, from a land far away; it was a high-pitched whine like a machine in need of adjustment. It was me. "It's okay, Brock. Like I said, I've got a guy in my back pocket. Basil. He can help us both out. This will all go away, and things will go back to normal. It's fine. This will all be fine."

44

"Bring him here." Basil's voice was stern and direct, a far cry from the gentle man I thought I knew.

"There?" I said, the phone shaking in my hands. There was a chill in the air, and a slight frost on Brock's windshield, but that's not why my hands trembled. I shook at the thought of having to take the thing that was Brock out of the privacy of our home and drive him through the streets, announcing to all what I'd done. I'd poisoned my husband, intentionally or not, and now he was spoiled like the meat he consumed, racing towards a rotting, tortuous death.

"Yes," Basil repeated. "Come to me. I will have a look at him."

"It's not him, Basil." My voice was a whisper, snot and tears sputtering over the phone. "It's not Brock, not anymore."

"Of course it is, my dear. Who else would he be? A Brock twisted and turned by the violence your mind's endured, but Brock he remains, in flesh and bone."

"You'd have to see," I said. I would not close my eyes or I would see Brock, bones protruding through taut flesh, gristle stuck between his teeth.

"And I will. When you bring him here."

The background noise on the other end of the line fell silent.

"Basil?"

I looked at my phone, and the home screen glowed back. He'd hung up. I sat in the truck, engine running, parked in my own driveway and afraid to go into my own home. Not afraid of what Brock might do—over the years he'd escalated to the worst, and nothing short of killing me would be more painful. Also, welcomed.

Death is welcome here, for both of us now.

But something worse than death waited inside.

The truck rolled down the street, heading to an unknown destination. I wasn't sure if it was a round trip or one-way journey, but I had to think. Or to not think anymore. I just needed some time to cool off, calm myself, and rest. I just needed some damn rest.

The liquor store glowed in the night as if adorned with a halo, the sign flashing at the night sky. Inside, the bottles looked like gems—rubies, sapphires, golden amber. I selected Cold Lake Honey Shine, a vodka kissed by the area's very own honey bees. I even bought an expensive mule forged with copper art—a stag with golden eyes. With my vodka and mule in a bag and ice under my arm, I headed out to the truck and out of the city until the lights were a faint glow in my rearview mirror. Turning off my headlights, I picked a canola field with a farmhouse that was but a speck of light in the distance and pulled in, nudging the truck forward until I was far enough in that anyone passing by on the highway wouldn't notice me in the field of gold.

Ice in the mule, then the vodka, cascading overtop like Athabasca Falls. I sipped, then glugged, greedy, wanting sleep and peace and death. What I got was a headache and a churning stomach.

Pass out. Make it all go away.

I didn't want to die. At least I think I didn't. What I didn't want was to keep living like this.

The pain in my head intensified, and my stomach gurgled, making me question both my choice of beverage and the speed at which I drank it. It didn't take me long to recognize the familiar rhythm of my throbbing pulse. It was pounding inside my head, drumming a steady beat . . .

I stepped out of the truck, quickly closing the door to dampen the interior light. It was the middle of the night, but the field was aglow with yellow, the soft flowering canola swaying in the breeze. I followed the sound of the drum, my head lolling back and forth with the dance of the field until I reached an inky mass standing sentry in the crops.

"Swift Runner."

With his large fist wrapped around what looked to be a human femur, he banged his drum, his children and wife wincing each time the makeshift mallet struck the hide. The children were chanting, something dark and melancholy in a language I didn't recognize.

"Why are you doing this?" I asked. "Why won't you stop? Leave me alone?"

Mid-swing, Swift Runner ceased his banging. Fear is what I saw in Charlotte's eyes, but not fear for herself. It was for me, same as the pity in her children's eyes.

"Why are you doing this?" Swift Runner mimicked. "Why

won't you stop?" But the voice was not his. It came from his throat out his black, moving maw, but the voice was mine. His face lit with delight at the sight of my horror. His fingers went slack and the drum and the bone mallet fell to the dirt. A child gathered the instrument and resumed pounding, same tempo, same dynamic.

I wanted to run, but Swift Runner moved forwards and I stood still. He reached me, wrapped his hand around the small of my back and pulled me in, my breasts pushing against him as he tilted my chin up and kissed me. His tongue rolled around my mouth, thick and coppery. When he pulled back, we remained connected by a rope of bloody, gleaming saliva.

"Iskwêyâc," he said, his voice a deep, bitonal growl. "Nitawêýihcikâtêw."

My head cocked, my mind breaking down the words but nor understanding. Swift Runner's head tilted to the side, too, possibly confused by my confusion. His brow furrowed into a solid line, his mouth moving as he formed silent words, as if tasting them, feeling them out, creating a new language. He met my eyes again, and with what seemed like a great deal of pain and discomfort, conjured a new voice and semantics. As he spoke, he jabbed his thick, index finger in the centre of my chest in rhythm with the drum and my heart.

"End. You. Desired."

Though the breeze was gentle, it blew my hair in a whirlwind, much like my emotions. The canola, once delicate and yellow, was now speckled with blood and globs of tissue and whipped violently against my calves.

"What end?" I asked, already knowing. The end to life as I knew it—my life with Brock, my life of being forgotten, ignored, overruled.

"Nuppuk." He considered for a moment, then generated a word I could understand. "Death."

One final jab to my chest and his finger cracked off and fell to the ground. His children scrambled for it, teeth gnashing, raking at each other's hair in the fight to get the meager piece of meat. Swift Runner hunched over and patted their heads, a proud papa. When he stood tall again, he stood very tall; he hovered above me—a good three meters tall or more with a rack that added another meter. His eyes were black caverns, his face elongated into a snout. His arms were long and skeletal, knuckles dragging on the ground as he swayed back and forth. With those long knuckles and bloody fingers, he picked up the mallet and drum and resumed beating, this time the tempo a heavy, loping allegro. He closed his eyes and sang as he pounded, a melody in a minor key, lilting, haunting.

When his eyes snapped open with the final beat, they were not his. They were soft, familiar, green.

Renee.

Her voice bellowed from his throat in a mixture of laughter and screams, full of maniacal pain.

I sprinted through the canola until I slammed into the truck, ripped the door open, and piled in. I sped off into the night, dirt flying up from beneath the spinning wheels. When I looked in my rearview mirror as I entered the highway, Swift Runner was standing at the lodgepole, his infant hanging from a noose, its left foot and ankle lodged down his throat as he gobbled and chewed, gnawing at his offspring. Charlotte and the other children were a burning pyre, skulls glowing in the night, her long tresses draped over the embers. Even when I looked away, trying to focus on the glowing lines on the asphalt, I could still see the flames, and their shadows dancing as demons in the night.

45

I didn't care that my neighbours might hear when I peeled into my driveway, Brock's truck fishtailing and striking our recycling bin as I slammed the brakes a mere centimetre before it struck the garage door. I ran for the front porch, ignoring the red car parked on the street. Renee's car.

The voicemail from Renee waiting for me on my cell phone when I returned from the field made my heart clench.

Hey Nell, what the hell? I've called you an assload of times. Been texting you for hours. Why aren't you picking up? I'm worried, Nell. Enough is enough. I'm coming over. You can't live like that anymore. I'm on my way.

Poor Renee. Ignorant of the horrors that awaited her. In all the long years we'd been friends, she'd only been over to my house a handful of times. I didn't want her to see how I lived. How Brock treated me. Our routine was appalling; his behaviour could be construed as abusive.

Which it is.

"It's not abuse," I said to the truck.

I fumbled for my house key.

She's in there, checking on us. On me. She already said she was worried, and she called so many times. I was drunk. I didn't answer. Of course she came.

She probably thought he'd finally killed me.

I slid the key in the lock and opened the door, expecting to find Renee and Brock arguing at the table. He'd probably thrown my mother's favourite Chinese vase at her. And Renee was probably screaming at him, possibly throwing something back—a pot or a pan, maybe an entire appliance.

But they weren't arguing. And I didn't have to wonder. They were there in plain sight, sprawled out on the couch, more of Renee's body exposed than I'd ever cared to see. Her legs were long and thick, her arms muscular. The curve of her breast was sensual as it heaved, up and down as Brock buried his face into her abdomen, pulling out her entrails clenched in his grinding jaws. Her face was a mask of frozen fear, her neck a gaping chasm framed by marks I could only assume were made by Brock's teeth. He was naked, his belly bloated, his skin tarnished with streaks of crimson. Her black hair stuck to his tacky cheek, and every few bites he would swipe it away like a pesky blowfly.

"Renee?" The word sounded more like a squeak from an oboe, but it got Brock's attention. "Brock?"

"This helps," he said, a giggle tangled in a sob. "The hunger is there, pulling from inside me. It consumes me, babe, but I can slow it."

How? I didn't really want to know.

"It's people," he said, laughing as he demonstrated his Charlton Heston impersonation. "It's people!"

Against my will, my feet carried me into the kitchen. My

laminate flooring, the beautiful grey wood, wide slats and chestnut shading, was swimming in blood. And in the center of the pool, spread out like bloody snow angels, was a stack of three people. Their hair was oily and patchy, threadbare clothes piled in a heap on the floor. An overpowering stench of urine and blood and other waste permeated the air. Brock had flayed them down the middle; their organs were gone along with all the meat on their thighs, biceps, and cheeks. The top member of the pile must have had plump lips, because they were missing, too.

"Homeless," Brock said as he licked his fingers. "Took nothing to convince them to come here. They were cold as fuck."

Well then. That's good. They were warm for a minute. At least they had that.

"Brock, we need to go."

"Get more?" His voice perked and his eyes brightened.

I stood tall and steadied my nerves. "Yes. Give me a moment."

In three long strides I burst into our bedroom. If I was going to the mountains, I was packing a suitcase. Would I ever be able to come back? Unlikely. Would I be implicated in these murders? I knew what my husband was, and I left him alone anyways.

The voice in my head was Basil's. *But what is he, my dear? A murderer? A monster? Wendigo?*

My hand found the light switch, and I flicked it on. The bed, Brock's bed, was occupied by the brunette I'd seen that night I was out with Renee. The one who'd felt my husband's fingers inside her. The one who'd allowed it. She was a starfish on the bed, naked, wide gashes over her thighs, abdomen, and face. The consumption of this one was not complete; she had plenty of voluptuous meat left on her bones.

"Didn't eat her, yet," Brock said, coming up behind me. He was as tall as the ceiling—taller, even. He had to crouch to fit, his spine an awkward arc, his horns now ten centimetres high. "She wasn't for eating. Tasting, maybe, but I needed her car. To pick up the rest." He hooked his thumb, now split and solid as a hoof, towards the kitchen. "And also, for this." He pressed his manhood against the small of my back; it was throbbing, hungry. "She's dead but not cold."

I pulled away and went to the closet, blindly grabbing clothes and stuffing them into a suitcase. I ignored Brock's brays and grunts as he mounted the meat on the bed, driving his mangled shaft inside her, pumping and thrashing his head as blood splattered over the walls, his antlers further goring the woman I once hated but now pitied.

"I have more meat for you," I heard myself say as I rolled the suitcase out of the room, down the hall, through the kitchen. I dragged bloody wheels across my pale carpet as I took the suitcase out to the truck. When Brock emerged from the front door —face dripping blood and cock drizzling come—I'd already laid out a foam mattress topper in the box of the truck.

"Here," I directed, pointing.

He didn't argue. He crawled in, circled three times like a dog, and laid down. I wasn't sure he was completely concealed below the walls of the box. I didn't care. As I drove into the night, all I cared about was leaving everything behind.

46

I texted Basil, telling him we'd just left, then drove, focusing on the rumbling of the road and the stars overhead. I loved those stars. Had driven beneath them so many times as a child. This time I'd stay close, familiar, and secluded. Most of the campsites would be vacant this time of year, with frost crumpling the leaves and the night frost chilling the bones.

Shadows grabbed for me as I turned the wheel, steering the truck into the campsite. Sure enough, all the campsites were empty. I drove the path, around one curve then another until we were all the way in the back corner, a few steps from the lake. I killed the engine but not the headlights. With the campground vacant, and the ranger's trailer at the head of the road, the only people that might see the lights were on the opposite side of the lake, or on the lake, but no one would be rowing the frigid waters this time of year.

I had nothing—no tent, no supplies, no chair. No plan. As Brock stumbled out of the box, I fished through the glove box, finding the vehicle manual, a stack of service records, and a knife. I tossed all that aside and struck gold: a pack of matches. I got out of the truck and spoke to Brock, regardless of whether or not he was paying attention. Whether or not his animal brain understood me. "I'm starting a fire. It's colder than a witch's tit out here."

His head bobbed—a nod or a droop in consciousness, I wasn't sure. I went to work, using the knife to shave bark from a nearby birch tree into curls of thin wood perfect for kindling. A rustling from the trees behind me gave me pause, so I stopped. Brock was scraping his antlers against the trunk of a thick oak, his sinewy muscles tensing and flexing with every push and pull.

"Feels good," he moaned.

The velvet on the antlers peeled away, exposing shiny, fresh bone. They were growing, those antlers, and so was he.

With the flesh off his antlers came shards of the tree, falling to the ground in perfect splinters. He already had a pile that put mine to shame. As he continued shedding, I grabbed handfuls of his wood pieces and laid them in the circle of rocks in the centre of the campground. After criss-crossing them and constructing a mini pyre, I walked into the brush and scraped the fuzz of foliage growing on the tree trunks, collecting it in the pockets of my hoodie. I lit the last piece of moss on fire on the end of a stick, sheltered it with my hand until it birthed a strong flame, then poked it into my pyre. With soft, coaxing breaths, the fire was soon roaring.

"Come, Brock. It's warm over here." I patted the seat of the picnic table beside the fire. Not sure why I did that. He'd never fit, not in his state. If he sat beside me, his knees would be up to his ears and his head between his legs.

No matter. He was too nervous, anyway. He paced the perimeter, huffing and puffing, head swaying to and fro.

Really does look like a rabid deer on two legs, doesn't he?

He did, but a sickly deer, starving, its flesh and muscle concave and decaying, hide hanging off his crooked body in strips.

"I'm hungry," he mewled.

"You can't be. Renee, those vagabonds . . ."

With a braying scream he sunk his teeth into his own arms, ripping away a chunk of hide and muscle, tugging until it was free from his limb and down his gullet. Next chomp landed on the other arm, blood spurting as his teeth pulled out veins, slurping them up like spaghetti.

"Brock, stop that!" I jumped to my feet and ran to him, forgetting his stature. He towered over me, his long snout pointing down at me, dripping gore onto my shirt. His grey tongue licked my cheek. It was sticky, abrasive, cold.

Does he mean to eat me?

Crying, he turned away, pawing at his face with jagged hooves. "No, no, no . . ."

"It's okay, Brock. I'll stay away."

"I can't . . . help myself."

"I know."

The grumble of an engine and a pair of bobbing lights appeared on the path. Brock startled and backed into the woods.

"It's okay, Brock. It's Basil."

He cocked his head, his antlers scraping the surrounding trees.

"A friend, Brock. A friend."

"I can't," he whimpered. "He has to stay away. I can't control myself."

"You can, and you will."

Brock backed out of sight as Basil rounded the last turn. Instead of pulling into the campsite, Basil parked in the neighbouring site and wandered over, flashlight in hand.

"Good fire," Basil said. "Quite adept at outdoorsmanship, aren't you?"

"I grew up camping in these parts." When he was within range, I wrapped my arms around him and collapsed into his embrace, nearly knocking him off his feet. He held me—no questions, no condolences. Just a hug, warm and tight, his weathered hands stroking my hair. After my sobs were managed and his jacket thoroughly saturated with my tears, I pulled away.

"Where is he?" Basil asked, cool and calm.

Weaving my fingers with his, I led Basil through the woods to the lake beyond. Brock was kneeling on the shore, his head and antlers bobbing in the water as he lapped up the drink, his concave abdomen shuddering with every swallow.

Basil's eyes were dark. Knowing. "Yes. He is far gone."

"What does that mean?" I said, my voice a squeaking rat. "What is it he has?"

"No, child." Basil's voice was smooth and thick, deeper than I remembered. "Not what he has. What he *is*."

No. Not real.

The trees rustled and a dark figure emerged, bringing with it a hot stench of decay that summoned a gag from my belly. Swift Runner stood by my side, leaning over and offering Basil a curt nod.

"Long time," Basil said, his lips tight and eyes narrowed. "You look plump and healthy, Swift Runner, unlike this young man."

Brock gargled and sputtered. He'd gone from delicate sips to panicked gulps, drinking water so fast it purged out, pouring from his lips and nostrils in blood-tinged vomit. Basil reached in his pack and drew out a plastic grocery bag. He turned the bag inside out, dropping a large meaty limb on the ground. A thigh. Human.

"The fuck?!?" I shrieked.

"That'll keep him busy while we talk," Basil said. Brock, upon hearing the thud of the limb on the loam, came loping over, drool swinging as he dove into the meat, slurping, tearing, and swallowing with audible delight.

I looked at the meat, fresh, with little sign of decay. "Where did you—"

"No matter," Basil said, waving a dismissive hand.

I met Basil's eyes, those dark mysterious windows with blinds drawn. In them I saw the stag with the golden eyes. "Was it you? That pork roast?"

He leaned over and whispered in my ear. "No, dear. Not pork."

They were so close, the men on either side of me. I could feel heat radiating off their bodies, their musk thick in my nose and mouth. With careful steps, I backed away from them, to the shore of the lake. They closed the gap I'd left, shifting together until there was a small space between them. That's when I saw it.

"Who are you?" I knew Swift Runner. I'd researched him, his dark expression seared into my mind. But Basil . . . "Who are *you*?"

He bore a pin on his left breast pocket—a pin bearing the emblem of the North West Mounted Police.

I searched his face, the same face that had been beside Swift Runner in that black-and-white photograph. The face of a man who had just put a cannibal in shackles.

"You're him," I whispered.

"Who, my dear?"

"That man. The arresting officer. But how?"

"How indeed." Basil sighed, a sound fat with pain, and the fire flared. Brock sprung to his feet, twice as tall as either man, and bared his rotting black teeth. After pawing the ground with both feet, Brock charged, but Basil simply stepped to the side as my husband thundered past. Swift Runner advanced, drawing his axe and burying it in my husband's chest. Brock ducked the next swing, the blade finding the tip of an antler and slicing it off, the bone thudding into the dirt. The blade found a resting place in Brock's head, embedded in his skull with a crack that rippled the lake.

That did not stop Brock, only slowed him down. He shook his head, black blood oozing into his eyes, then charged Swift Runner. The two sparred, melee between axe and antler, each strike ringing through the night. As they battled, they pushed deeper into the woods, until the sound was as quiet and distant as a memory.

I picked up the severed tip of Brock's antler, squeezing it, caressing it in an attempt to believe its reality. Though I wanted to, I did not cry. I couldn't find a single tear anywhere in my soul.

❧ 47 ❧

"Come," Basil said, walking back through the trees to the campsite. I followed, in a daze. We sat on the ground in the dirt, legs crossed, fire warming our flesh and light flickering in our eyes. I dropped the thick shard of antler on the ground in front of the fire.

I thought of my home, the stacks of bodies.

"What will I do, Basil? Where will I go?"

"Where do you want to go?"

A deep sadness flooded my soul. "What I want and what's feasible are very different things, I'm afraid."

"Miracle question," Basil said, taking my hand. "In a perfect world, your perfect world, what would you do?"

What would I do? How would I want things to be, where would I like to go?

"I would like a fresh start. To make different choices, live a different life."

"Hmmm." Basil's eyebrows were scrunched together—a

thoughtful, white caterpillar. "That's time travel, my dear. Wishes being fishes, and all that. But moving forward..."

The sadness I was swimming in turned sour, a bitter bile sitting at the top of my stomach, stinging as I spoke. "There is no forward."

"No?"

"At one time, maybe. But that time is long gone. My choices have landed me here—no friends, no home. And I'm far past my prime, as Brock would say. There's no starting over for me."

"As Brock would say." Basil shook his head. "Therein lies the problem. What does it matter, what Brock would say?"

I shrugged, unsure of how to answer. How to defend my weakness and the life I'd chosen. So many years I had wasted, so many paths I could have walked. But I chose to follow instead of forging a trail of my own. And now here I was, unable to live any kind of life. Even without Brock, I'd be merely surviving, waiting for an end.

My end.

My toe teased the piece of Brock's antler on the ground. I picked it up, rolling it between my fingers, aware of every groove caked with dirt and death.

"I don't understand," I said.

"There are a great many things people do not understand about life. And that is fine. Understanding is too much."

"How are you him?" I asked, changing my focus from myself. Brock's voice echoed in my head, *always avoiding, Nellie. Always shifting the focus.*

"How am I who, my dear?"

"That man? That officer in the photograph? It's impossible. That was over a hundred years ago."

"It is impossible. It cannot be, yes? And yet it is. Almost like a wendigo and a dead man fencing through the woods."

He laughed, but quickly stifled himself. "I am sorry. I'm much more used to this than you are."

Real. "So . . . the wendigo folklore is true?"

"'Fraid so."

My eyes found Swift Runner, his axe gleaming in the moonlight as he took a swipe at Brock. "But Swift Runner is just a man."

"Always was," Basil said, his narrowed eyes following Swift Runner through the trees. "He was never wendigo. Claimed he was, then tried to claim wendigo psychosis, too, right up until I wrapped a noose around his neck."

"But didn't he murder and eat his family?"

"Sure did." Basil swiped a tear from his eye, his lower lip trembling. "But he was no magical monster. Only a vile, deplorable man."

I looked out at the fight, antler meeting blade. Both wendigo and man were crazed, desperate, and violent.

Basil continued. "It was horrible, Nellie. Just awful. I was first on the scene. I saw what he did to that lovely woman, and that sweet, sweet babe . . . the lodgepole . . ."

A sob escaped before Basil covered his face. As his shoulders heaved, I put a hand on his shoulder. On his other shoulder, another hand appeared, slender silver fingers. Charlotte's long hair cascaded over Basil's chest as she embraced him, humming her melody.

As Swift Runner moved through the trees, it was fluid, smooth, liquid. "He's a ghost," I said.

"Indeed. Caught in his purgatory."

I took Basil's hand. "And you, too."

He nodded, shaking free tears onto his trousers. "I joined that infant, not long after I hanged his daddy. Couldn't bear to see them anymore, in my dreams or my waking nightmares."

"You hanged yourself."

"Not uncommon among officers, especially those who see the likes of what my eyes saw."

Basil turned to me, his tears clearing and smile blooming across his face. "And now I walk this earth with newfound purpose. To bring comfort. Warms my soul."

Charlotte smiled, her black lips glistening with her own frozen tears.

A clang caught my attention. Swift Runner's axe had once again buried deep into Brock's bone, but without consequence. Brock kept on fighting. "Why does he want to kill Brock?"

Basil shook his head. "He thinks he has purpose, too, old bastard. He would like to ease Brock's pain and suffering. The wendigo is a tortured beast, always in want, always aching for more. A hollow pain, pervasive and excruciating."

Again and again Swift Runner struck, hacking the axe into Brock's belly, his face, his back. Blood and meat spurted, but Brock did not fall, only rose again to gore Swift Runner, dispelling him into mist before he reconstituted again to swing his axe over and over.

Basil laughed. "They're both buggered! Wendigo lives! He's of this world. A ghost, though he can be felt," Basil squeezed my hand, a loving touch, "can inflict no physical change. Swift Runner can chop that beast to his heart's content, but a ghost cannot kill the living."

Swift Runner, tilting his head towards our conversation, smiled. Basil's smile dissolved.

"You bastard," Basil muttered.

Swift Runner entered the campsite. He stood beside me, dripping ghostly blood on me.

Brock sniffed the air, and I knew. I knew how it would all end.

Brock charged me, with a hunger in his eyes, one that had been there for all our years.

A hunger for my pain.

48

Brock leapt through the fire, flames licking the strips of hide dangling from his carcass. I rolled out of the way just in time, avoiding his antlers by mere centimeters.

"No, foul beast!" Basil shouted, struggling to his feet and tossing rocks at Brock's head.

Swift Runner, a grotesque smile still plastered across his face, stood by the fire, pounding his drum with the back of his axe. Charlotte's mouth was wide and black, caught in a silent scream, and crimson tears poured down her glacial blue face.

Brock charged again, this time his antlers crashing through the stones around the fire, flicking flankers onto my face. I screamed, swiping away the burning embers as I stumbled away. My foot caught on a tree root, and I fell on my back, the wind knocked out of me in a dull huff. He was grunting, his chest heaving with each wheezing breath, drool pouring from his jowls as if the thought of my meat had opened a faucet.

You motherfucker.

He charged one last time, this time hitting his mark, his hooves landing on either side of my head. He lowered himself onto my body, the stench of death and lust and greed thick between us.

"Nellie," he groaned, a wicked smile stretched across his elongated face. "Unfuckingbelievable."

He laughed, the meat in his belly sloshing as he dragged his thick, grey tongue between my breasts.

"Motherfucker!" Never once, in all our years, had I let Brock have it. Every bit of frustration, desperation, and hate came spewing out of me like a rabid volcano. "You are an entitled, selfish piece of shit! You've *ruined* me! You destroyed everything I had, murdered everything I was." One deep breath, and I screamed, spittle flying from my own mouth. "I hate you!"

Like an elephant stepped off my chest, relief allowed me to suck in a deep breath. I cried, a release I'd needed for a lifetime. My fingers came to rest in the dirt on top of something pocked. Thick. Sharp.

Brock's teeth sunk into my face, tearing away my cheek with a ripping squelch.

I wrapped my fingers around his severed antler buried in the dust beside the fire. *This, Brock, is where you meet your end.*

The woods slowed, muddying like molasses, the sounds and movement grinding to a snail's pace. Everything was in slow motion, every sound muted and muffled. Basil was yelling—I could see his mouth moving, open and closed, lips forming words, but none I could decipher. Brock was chomping, slow, steady, coming in for another bite. Swift Runner was cheering, pounding his drum, a smile ear to ear.

Then everything went from slow to still. Muffled to silent. There was no movement, no sound. Brock was hovering above my bicep, posturing to take his next bite. Basil's mouth was frozen open, his hand in front of him, reaching for me. Swift Runner's axe was in the air, halted right before pounding the drum. But his smile was gone, replaced by a grimace. And his eyes were no longer focused on me, but on someone else.

Like a dancer, Charlotte glided in, her blue flesh now glimmering gold. Her black tresses were once again floating as if suspended in water, gently rippling in the air around her head. She approached her husband, reached out her slender fingers, and peeled the axe from his hands as he stood helpless, motionless, his eyes filled with screams. She raised the axe, bringing the gleaming blade down through the skin of the drum, severing it in two.

After tossing the remains of the drum in the fire, she knelt by the flame, red flickering in her golden eyes as she sang.

'Cross the waves of the prairies, in a field of gold
Nights grow long, and days grow cold
Crimson soaks the soil, death clouding my seas
'Twill end when no one left but only he.

She continued singing, swaying with the flame, her black eyes focused on me. Right into me.

Basil's voice echoed in my mind. *Swift Runner would like to ease Brock's pain and suffering. The wendigo is a tortured beast, always in want, always aching for more. A hollow pain, pervasive and excruciating.*

The campsite animated, but everyone did not pick up where they left off. They watched me, quiet, anticipating my next move.

I held the shard of antler to Brock's throat.

Swift Runner smiled.

I spoke, with a certainty I'd never known before. "No, Brock. This is not your end. You will suffer."

I'd like to say it didn't hurt, but it did. Every millimetre of movement pained as I plunged the tip of that antler beneath my ear and dragged it, tugging it across my throat until it reached the lobe of my other ear. I rolled the bone in my hand, slick, warm blood squishing through my fingers. It was hot, the waterfall of life spilling from my throat, down my chest, and it hurt like hell, my organs struggling, screaming for intervention.

"My end," I said, sputtering droplets of crimson over my husband's face.

The forest changed, dark greens and browns morphing to gold, the textures of the trees and bushes dissolving to sand. Swift Runner was on his knees, fists clenched, screaming in defeat. Brock brayed to the stars—a mournful, pained wail that bellowed from his throat.

Though small and distant, I could hear Basil's voice and see his smiling face as he looked down upon me. "Strong Nell. Always givin' 'em hell."

Charlotte knelt by my side and kissed my cheek, her lips and my flesh dissolving to gold.

49

Charlotte and I sat on the edge of a golden lake, fingers entwined.

"Am I dead?" I asked.

"Yes."

I pondered for a moment. "Am I alive?"

"Yes."

In the distance a banshee wailed, a sorrowful keening that echoed across the land. In a storm of feathers, a Sluagh descended, a carrion with its fare clutched in massive talons. It landed on a pile of bones at the side of the lake and began stripping its victim of its flesh, tossing hunks to the flock of Sluagh waiting hungrily by.

I had a vision of Brock, rambling through the woods, mewling and crying. "He will remain there. Suffering."

Charlotte's voice was liquid calm. "He is not your concern anymore."

I walked to the edge of the water. Like unrolling a lifetime of tightly coiled anxiety and depression, I stood tall and looked at the red stars that peppered the rusty sky. A banshee ceased her wail to look at me. She curtsied, her flaming hair dipping into the black lake. A swarm of crystal fae the size of mosquitoes flittered over the water like glitter, their song the sound of tinkling bells.

Charlotte stood beside me, her head held as high as mine. "Your new life. Your new start."

I cried, but it felt good. I smiled as salty tears wet my lips.

I'm free.

"This isn't real," I said, completely content. "I am dead."

Charlotte spoke, her voice a chorus of harps:

"*Welcome to Ramnon.*"

AFTERWORD

Though this story is fictional, not all of the characters are. Swift Runner did exist. He was a notorious killer in Fort Saskatchewan, Alberta. He did kill and consume his wife and children in the winter of 1878-79, including hanging his infant from a lodgepole and consuming his feet. Swift Runner was indeed hanged for his crimes in 1879. It was the first legal hanging in the province of Alberta, known then as the Canadian North West Territories. The arresting officer, though I've included a picture, was not our sweet Basil. Basil is entirely fictional, though the man in the arresting photograph of Swift Running is quite real.

Whether Swift Runner, Charlotte, or any of the children have appeared in elevators, homes, or hospital hallways, we may never know for sure...

SWIFT RUNNER

THE REMAINS OF SWIFT RUNNER'S FAMILY

Blood Wail

A Ramnon Tale

Jae Mazer

I
ONCE UPON A TIME

Nuair a thiocas an bás ní imeoidh sé folamh.
When death will come, he won't go away empty.

Old Irish Proverb

I

Finn adored the smell of books. Old books, new books—even ones that'd resided within the walls of a smoker's abode; the sweet odour of parchment and ink was still evident beneath the taint of tobacco. But he loved the smell of the old tome grasped in his hands the best. It was a large volume containing a plethora of folktales, its cover a leather canvas of eyes and wings, talons and tails.

"Tell us another, Dadaí," Imogen pleaded, her bright eyes like shimmering emeralds.

"Nah, lass," Finn said, ruffling his daughter's fiery curls. "'Tis well past your bed. Ye need sleep, or ye will only grow the size of the leprechauns in these here stories."

"That's some fookin bollocks," his eldest daughter, Saoirse said, punctuating the sentiment with a roll of her eyes. At thirteen, she was much too old for nonsense such as fairytales. But Imogen was only six and eager to be amazed.

"Oi! Mind yer language, miss! If Ma be hearin' that bullshit . . ."

Both girls' eyes widened at the expletive, then their smiles spread to laughter.

"Dadaí said a bad word!" Imogen giggled.

Finn furrowed his brow and pointed a finger at Saoirse. "But . . . but . . . so did she! Imma tellin Ma!"

All three doubled over in laughter, the bed clothes bunching and wrangling as they squirmed. Once the raucous laughter waned to gasping giggles, Finn snuggled his children back in their beds and smooched each on the forehead. He lifted the book from the bedside table and tucked it under his arm.

"Where did they come from?" Saoirse asked, her eyes on the book.

"This?" Finn asked, tapping his finger against the spine. "I got it from yer Nana. My Ma."

"No," Saoirse said. "The stories. Where did they come from? Who wrote them?"

Finn paused. He was tempted to look at the book, to open its cover and search the inside for authors, publishers, editors—anyone who had a hand in its creation. But he knew better. He had thumbed that book front to back more times than he or anyone could count. He sat on the edge of Saoirse's bed and gazed out the window to the rolling hills beyond the farm.

"A great number of people made this book, I suppose. Ole folklore, dates back many-a-year."

"But why are there no names?" she asked, sitting up.

"There *are* names. The characters."

"No, the names of who done wrote the tales."

"Well, the Bible hasn't authors, either. Only characters."

"Well," Saoirse argued, "the Bible is real. Them characters *are* the authors."

Finn chuffed. "Oh, spirited one. Methinks ya think too much."

From the other bed came a meek, trembling voice. "Dadaí?"

"Yes, Imogen?"

"Are those stories real too? Like in tha Good Book?"

Finn placed the book on his lap, his fingers tracing the gold-embossed title.

Tales from Ramnon

"No, love. These be fairytales. Nonsense."

"Is Ramnon a real place?"

Finn remembered back to his childhood, huddled under the stairs, reading stories about all manner of creatures that roamed Fort Ramnon. He could almost feel the golden sand beneath his feet, the gnarled, naked tree branches reaching for him like arthritic fingers. There was no light or dark in Ramnon, no colours. And there were creatures everywhere, mewling and slithering, consuming and cackling . . .

Perhaps he'd introduced Ramnon too soon.

"No, 'tis not real," Finn said, tucking the tales of horror beneath his arm once again. Though he'd censored and altered the stories to read aloud, perhaps the ideas were still a touch too dark for young minds. "Ramnon is fiction, like Hogwarts or Narnia."

A splash of horror crossed Imogen's face. "Hogwarts ain't real?"

This time, Saoirse's eye roll was audible. "Ya wee idiot."

"Am not!"

"Are too!"

"Meany!"

"Girls." Finn's voice was firm enough to stun the room to silence. "That is plenty for one night. For many nights, the way ye be carryin' on."

"Dadaí!" The girls whined in unison, a chorus of disapproval.

Finn responded with a smile and another pair of smooches before he turned off the light and closed the door. Roison met him in the hall, her orange hair draped over her pale nightdress.

"Allo, beautiful," he said, kissing the ivory skin on the side of her neck.

She moved her mouth against his ear, her breath warm and moist. "We need a bag o' milk."

He pulled back to find her smirking. "Ah. Right then. I'll head out."

"Ye need to quit fillin' their heads with those gawd-awful tales, Finn," she said, snatching the book away from him.

As he passed her in the hall, he gave her round bottom a pat. "What can I say? They prefer blood o'er glitter and creatures o'er princesses."

Roison tried to look angry, but he knew she wasn't. She confirmed this by striding down the hall, her long legs peeking from beneath the billowing gown. When she reached him, she wrapped her arms around him and kissed him, pushing her tongue through his lips and lingering.

"I adore ye," she said into his mouth.

"And I, ye."

"Come home quick," she said, grazing the front of his trousers with her palm.

"The quickest." And with that, he jumped behind the wheel of his car and barreled down to Byrne's market.

※

Byrne's Market was pert near empty, not surprising, seeing the hour. It's not like they lived in the heart of the city. The farm was smack in the middle of a rural community, flanked by a thin smattering of businesses, including Byrne's. Finn was thankful he'd made it there before the old man closed for the night.

"Heya, Finn! How's ye been?"

"Nothin to complain for." Finn had been coming to Byrne's since he'd been old enough to venture out and buy bottle caps and gummy cokes. Byrne—William Byrne, though everyone called him by his last name— had been a close friend of his Pa. Ole Byrne had no qualms sending lil Finn home with a brown bag full of fags and whiskey, even before he reached double digits. But that was no mind. Byrne helped them when times were tough, and they helped him, too. He was as good as family.

"I gots a haul o' cod fish, if you have a hankering," Byrne said.

"Just a bag o' milk tonight."

"Shoulda guessed it," Byrne said. "At this hour, all the ladies be sending the men for milk or rubbers, depending on the life stage."

"You assume I's too old for the latter?"

"Naw." Byrne paused. "You fixin' for 'nother?"

Finn hesitated, though his face burned, which he was quite sure was all the answer the old man needed. He was still elated, the news still fresh. Roison's belly had barely yet begun to pudge.

Byrne's mouth stretched into a gaping smile. "Atta boy! Now let us go gets some milk for yer ladies!"

Byrne shuffled away, his cane tap-tapping on the tile floor as he went down the aisle and into the cooler to fetch the milk. Shame, Finn thought, that the old man had to mosey to and fro like that, but it was his own doing. He liked the milk cold—really cold—and it wasn't likely to be that way with every single body opening the cooler all day long. People browsed, people lingered, and the milk warmed as if in the udder again, he'd always say.

The market fell silent, the tapping of Byrne's cane muffled by the heavy cooler door. Finn winced at the whining of the fluorescent light overhead, bright and abrasive. Suddenly uncomfortable, Finn shifted from foot to foot and hummed an old Irish lullaby to fill the suffocating, vacant air.

Finnegan.

His heart stilled and crawled into his throat. The voice was a scratchy breath, nails on limestone. In his peripheral, a black mass swelled in the centre of the canned goods aisle until it almost brushed the light fixture overhead.

Finnegan.

He didn't want to look, but he was confused and curious. His mind needed to see it to rationalize. So, he gave in and faced the figure in the aisle.

It was a woman, rail thin, bones protruding through sickly white skin. Her breasts swayed over her torso and her too-long arms dangled at her sides, her fingernails scraping the tile as she shifted from foot to foot. She was indeed as tall as the ceiling—hunched over, even—and it appeared she had been stretched out that way, like taffy.

But though her body was terrifying and unnatural, her face

roiled Finn's guts with horror. She had wide, solid black eyes set like stones in her face, and a gaping maw that seemed to lead to a bottomless cavern. Her lower jaw unhinged, swaying as she moved and dangling between her clavicles.

"Hello?" It was ridiculous, Finn knew, but he didn't know what to do—say something, or run, or maybe he was dreaming this whole thing. Perhaps he was at home in bed with Roison, their bodies sticky with sex.

"You all right, lad? Looks like you swallowed a spirit whole!" Byrne appeared from the cooler, milk bag in hand. He stood in the aisle, mere centimetres from the woman, seemingly unaware of her presence, and her of his.

Before Finn could answer, she opened her mouth, and what came out shook Finn's very soul. A wail bellowed from the pit of her belly, rumbling the goods on the shelves and rippling the skin on her body like a boulder had struck a pond. She raised a gangly arm and pointed in Finn's direction, her elongated finger nearly touching his forehead.

New voices emerged from the entrance. The room fell into slow motion. The bag of milk slipped from Byrne's hands and crashed to the floor, bursting over the aisle.

"Fuck it! Get the register!" one of the voices yelled.

Finn spun to find two young men in balaclavas, IRA patches sewn onto denim jackets, brandishing guns. One hopped the counter and busted open the cash register with the butt of his pistol. The other kept his gun trained on Finn.

"Don't move, buddy!"

Instinctively, Finn raised his hands. Too fast, though. Too sudden. The thief startled.

It's warm. Finn mused that he had plenty of time to consider the sensation as he crumpled to the floor, the motion slow and thick as if he was falling through molasses. *It doesn't hurt*, he thought. *Must mean I'm okay*, he rationalized. His head hit the floor with a dull thud. He looked down and found that his legs and one arm were twitching, dancing, like marionette strings tugged and pulled them. Raising his good arm, his fingers disappeared into what had, at one time, been his face. His head. Only half of it was there; his fingers sunk into hot, mushy brain matter.

Finnegan.

Byrne was overtop of him, his mouth moving, but Finn did not hear his words. The only thing he heard as his wick burnt to ash was the word that floated out of the woman standing over him, black tears streaking down her pallid cheeks.

Bás.

"Bás!"

At the same moment her father took his last breath, Saoirse sat straight up in bed, the word fresh off her tongue. Imogen woke and started to cry. Saoirse shushed her, but was flustered herself, so had no words of calm to offer. Instead, she stood and walked to the window to crack it for some air. She always did that when the terrors woke her. The cool breeze dampened her nerves.

Not this night, though. When she opened the shutters and breathed in the midnight air, movement in the field caught her eye.

"S-Saoirse, what is it?" Imogen whimpered.

"Shhh, ye brat! So I's can see!"

"It need not be quiet for yer eyes to work."

"Fook off!"

Imogen swung her feet out of bed. "I'm tellin' Ma!"

Though she knew she was in for a tongue lashing, Saoirse did not convince her sister to stay and make amends. She needed to focus on what was in the field. It looked like a person, bright white against the rippling blacks of the wind-whipped grass. The person was toiling furiously over something . . .

Saoirse opened the shutters and crawled out into the yard. It was a frigid night, made worse by tramping barefoot across the grass and mud in their yard.

"Oi!" Saoirse shouted. "Who goes there! This be our land, ye know!"

It didn't take long to reach the stranger. *Odd*, Saoirse thought. She felt she'd only taken a few strides from the house, but there she was, in the middle of the field, the stranger an arm's length away. It was a naked woman, raven hair rippling down her back as her shoulders heaved.

"What's all this, then?" Saoirse asked, bravery fueled by the knowledge that Imogen went to tattle, which meant Ma was on her way.

The woman responded to Saoirse's voice by moving faster, harder, feral grunts escaping her skeletal core. Giving her a wide berth, Saoirse circled to see what she was doing.

The woman was washing clothes in a wooden bucket with a steel washing board. Faint suds glistened in the moonlight as she ground the clothes across the board, crimson-tinged foam frothing up onto her pale arms. The true horror came when Saoirse looked closer, recognizing the *Hurling Champion* logo on the shirt in the woman's hands.

"That's my Dadaí's," Saoirse said, her voice quavering, crescendoing to a scream. "Where's my Dadaí!"

The woman kept scrubbing, but locked eyes with Saoirse. They wailed in unison, their screams radiating over the fields. Saoirse dropped to her knees and covered her ears, but she was infected with the racket coming from that horrible woman. She was still screaming when Ma arrived at her side, a shell-shocked Imogen in tow. While Ma comforted them, whisking the three of them towards the house, Saoirse looked back at the silence and the empty field.

2

The keener was a lovely woman, a third cousin on Finn's side. She stood at the headstone overlooking the bluff, her voice ringing across the ocean waves like the strumming of a harp.

My mind's too full of memories
Too old to hear new chimes
I'm part of what was Dublin
in the rare ould times.

As the coffin was lowered into the ground, Saoirse held Imogen, who wept violently into the ivory frill of her dress. Their mother stood stoic and silent, though fat tears dribbled down her face, soiling the front of her jumper. Saoirse stared at Ma's eyes, which did not leave the coffin until it settled at the bottom of the hole, and even then, she did not peel her gaze away until she had tossed in her ceremonial fistful of dirt. Then she directed her attention to her daughters, who each returned their own little bits of earth back into the ground.

Bagpipes blared in the distance, and people filed towards their vehicles. A handful who couldn't attend the wake stayed to offer condolences, each giving love and hugs to the mourning trio. Soon, only the girls and their mother remained, three silhouettes in a field of green, orange sunset blazing on the horizon.

Saoirse dragged her toe through the fresh earth from the hole that contained her father. "Don't seem real."

"'Tis not fair," Imogen said, her expression contorting until sobs erupted from her body.

"'Tis real, and no, it isn't fair." Roison knelt and embraced her daughters. She opened her mouth to say more, something comforting, but a choked sob escaped instead. She drew the girls close, and they swayed and cried with the wind.

Once the sun dipped below the waves and the evening chill saturated their bones, Roison coaxed the girls to their feet. "Come on, now. They'll be waitin' on us back home."

Imogen pouted, her face glistening with sorrow. "I don't want them in our home. I only want Dadaí!" Her screech released a fresh batch of tears.

A quavering sigh passed Roison's lips. "Ay, me too. But this is what people do. Let's go be done with it."

She scooped Imogen up in her arms, and Saoirse pressed against her other side, glancing back only once at a nearby headstone, and the lanky creature perched atop, its scraggly hair blowing in the Irish breeze.

SAOIRSE FELT AS IF SHE WAS CRAMMED BETWEEN CRAGS, ROCKY walls pressing in on her each time she moved, ocean thrashing beneath her. The house was packed to the brim with well-wishers—relatives she'd never met and acquaintances who made an appearance for the food and drink. Every movement, slurp, chew, and sniffle grated her nerves.

"Saoirse, love?" Roison stroked her daughter's hair.

"Ma, dunnae ask me how I'm doing. Everyone be askin' me how's I'm doin'. Like, gee, fookers, I'm jolly good this fine evenin', if you please."

Roison's head turned to her eldest.

Saoirse rolled her eyes. "I know. Watch me language."

Despite the pain on her face, Roison smiled, and something close to a giggle came out with her whispered speech. "No, love, I was gonna say these *fuckers* are drivin' me batshit as well."

With a wink, Roison disappeared into the crowd, guided by a series of back-pats and cheek kisses. Old Marnie Brick reached up and cupped Roison's face. Saoirse couldn't help but smile, remembering Ma and Dadaí talking about how the Bricks reeked of whiskey and cheese from sunup to sundown. But Saoirse's humour waned as a black ripple cascaded over the arm of her ma's jumper.

The woman from the washtub the night her Dadaí died now clung to the ceiling like a bat by dirt-caked feet. Her hands uncoiled, revealing fingers tipped with sharp talons. Bloody spittle swung from her split lips, pooling on the carpet between Ma's feet. Black sludge dribbled from empty eye sockets, but despite the absence of actual eyes, Saoirse knew the creature was looking right at her.

Squeezing her eyes closed, Saoirse pushed through the crowd, down the hall, and disappeared into the master bedroom. With the door closed behind her, she flopped down on the bed and cried, loud and hard, for the first time that day. She was a great many things—devastated, angry, panicked. What would happen now? How would their life ever be the same?

She stretched out and her fingers brushed something hard tucked beneath her Dadaí's pillow.

Tales from Ramnon.

Ma must have shoved it there when he left for the store that night.

Flipping through the book, she uncovered colourful illustrations breaking up tangles of black and white. Dadaí had never let the girls handle Ramnon. She knew damn well he'd been leaving out all the good bits—the sex and violence and such. The artwork was phenomenal and terrible: great towering bird women with severed penises swinging from beaks lined with sharp rows of teeth. A huge skeletal beast—a man-deer—lurking in the woods, massive antlers thrashing through the trees and globs of meat hanging from its jaw. The taboo of her eyes finally seeing these pages almost stole the horror of her Dadaí's death until she flipped one page too many.

Saoirse blinked hard. Twice. But the image remained, hollow eyes staring at her from the page. It was a woman, naked, her long, dark hair swirled over her breasts. She crouched at the side of a great black lake washing a set of bloody clothes on a washboard.

It can't be.

Saoirse brushed away the thought. Her Dadaí must have told them the story, and in her anguish, she imagined it.

That must be it. But...

The pictures moved. Subtle at first, then obvious. The woman stood, slowly, her wet washing dropping to the rocks at her feet. She lingered for a moment before her head creaked towards Saoirse, her shoulders squared with the page. Saoirse pulled the book closer, studying the picture, the delicate lines of ink and pencil, the intricate details on the woman's skin.

In an explosion of movement and sound, the woman on the page came to life, flying at Saoirse and coming to a thundering halt once her face was the size of the entire page. Her black maw opened, swallowing any bit of yellow parchment, offering a tunnel down to her very soul. The pages rumbled as the back of the woman's tongue undulated, and a sound like no other exploded from the book, blowing Saoirse's hair back from her face. A wail, mournful and wicked, filled every centimeter of air in and out of Saoirse's body. She covered her ears and wriggled under her Dadaí's pillow to stifle the noise.

The sound faded to nothing beneath the shelter of hands and pillow, until it was a weak echo in Saoirse's brain. She crawled out from under the pillow and looked at the book, still open to the page, but the woman was back where she belonged: washing clothes on the lakeside.

But the sound was still there. Not there in the book, but somewhere else. In the house.

Ma.

Off the bed, through the door, Saoirse ran until she reached the lavatory where a cluster of people were gathered, faces white and hands wringing. Saoirse wriggled her way through, beneath the arms of outsiders, until she was standing next to her Ma.

"Saoirse." Ma was out of breath, beads of sweat coating her grey skin. Her hands trembled, one clutching her belly. Between her legs, on those light trousers Dadaí liked so much because of how they made her bum look, was a spreading slick of crimson. "It's okay, Saoirse. It's all goin' to be fine."

"What's the matter with ye?" Saoirse practically screamed. "Ye get shot too?"

Roison laughed, a sputtering, strained sound. "Naw, child. Nothin' so excitin'. Jus' losin' the baby. All the stress, I suppose."

Her ma gasped and winced, and with trembling hands, clawed at her belly. Saoirse gasped when Ma collapsed.

Edwin, the family physician, fell to his knees with her. "Ay, Roison. Tis fine. We need to be gettin you to the hospital, though. Get this taken care of."

"The girls," Roison. "We've no one now."

A wave of panic threatened to suffocate Saoirse as her Ma's eyes rolled back in her head, her face losing what little colour it had. When she crumpled to the floor, the sound of wails filled the room again, but the noise was coming from Saoirse's own throat. But too much sound for her alone. Her eyes left her ma and moved to the woman perched in the corner of the ceiling of the shower, her black tresses streaming down the white tile like thick blood. Her mouth was wide open, chin down to her navel, matching Saoirse's pain and fear.

❧

THE BEEPS AND WHIRS OF THE HOSPITAL WERE UNNERVING, but oddly comforting. Saoirse and Imogen were cuddled up on the pull-out couch beside Roison's bed, Imogen snoring softly into Saoirse's lap. It was late—much later than Ma and Dadaí would have ever let them stay up—but the doctor said it would be fine if they wanted to stay. Their Auntie Alice was in the waiting room, ready to take them home if the need arose. Ma had some procedure no one would talk about, then returned to the room to recover. Beneath the sadness and fear, Saoirse was a bit relieved to have a sleepover at the hospital.

Better than their home where the death woman waited.

"Love." Roison's voice was raspy but calm. "Come."

Saoirse wriggled out from beneath her sister and went to her ma, snuggling in beside her on the narrow bed. Roison held her and wept quietly into her hair.

"Are we gonna be okay, Ma?"

"We are."

"I didn't know ya was pregnant."

"'Twas barely," Roison said with a shuddering sigh. "We were waitin' to tell ya until I started showing."

"Growin' a belly?"

"Yeah."

Roison was quiet, her breathing heavy. Saoirse watched her sister, face scrunched in a grimace, eyes flickering under a restless slumber.

"Is we cursed, Ma?"

"What you be meanin' by that?"

"Well, Dadaí, he . . . he wasn't even sick. Not a thing wrong, and he off and dies. Then the baby—"

Roison tilted Saoirse's chin until they were looking at each other. "The baby was because of stress. Of course I lost it. 'Twas early in the pregnancy, when it's tricky business anyhow. And your Dadaí . . . well, sometimes that's what life gives ya. Not much to be done about it but keep livin' for all the other good stuff."

"What other good stuff?"

"The stuff you don't know 'bout yet. Who knows what's to come if you don't let it?"

Saoirse glanced around the room, imagining hair sprouting from corners and beasts crouching in shadows. But there was nothing. Only sea foam green hospital walls and paintings of sheep and valleys.

"There's something more," Roison said. "What aren't you tellin' me?"

Saoirse wanted to tell her about the woman and the wash basin, the same woman from the Ramnon book and hanging from the ceiling as the baby died. But her mother would think her a nut, or at least a child. She had to be the other grown-up now that Dadaí was gone. "I's jus' thinks we be cursed, that's all."

"Well, that's foolishness," Roison said, ruffling Saoirse's hair. "That's all those silly stories yer Dadaí read to you."

"Is there ... you think there's any truth in them pages?"

Roison and Saoirse locked eyes, but Roison looked away.

There's something.

"You are the eldest, Saoirse. You are my chil', and I will care and provide, but you need ta look out for your sister. She is young and soft, and we need to give her all the love's been stole from her. We all need to give that to each other. We are family."

Saoirse couldn't hold it back any longer. "Family," she said, her voice releasing tears that had been aching in her soul. She and her ma cried together until Saoirse fell asleep and dreamed of black hair growing over the lands and swallowing the world.

II
SOMETHING IN BETWEEN

Looks like freedom but it feels like death. It's something in-between, I guess.
　　Leonard Cohen

3

The lot across the street from Our Lady's was practically empty, save a burned-out truck and a handful of rusty cars. Few people came around the area after the fire of 2017 halted the conversion of the old asylum to residential apartments. Since then, the rooms had decayed to a shanty town for the dark and dank in both body and spirit.

Saoirse parked the car and crossed the road. No one had bothered to erect fencing or security, despite the heavy traffic of vandals and squatters. Saoirse was surprised there was anything left to the building. There was a smattering of graffiti, and many of the windows in the lower two stories were cracked and smashed, but it could have been in much worse shape. As with most derelict hospitals and asylums, there were tales of violence and hauntings, but Saoirse doubted that was the reason people avoided this place. Things more terrifying than ghouls and spectres resided here now.

On the side of the building, a heavy door was propped open

with an old leather boot. Saoirse shimmied inside, taking care not to tear her wool coat on the metal frame. She covered her mouth, trying not to taste the stench of urine and bile, sex and burnt hair.

"Bloody fucks."

The footfalls from her blocky heels echoed through the halls like a gavel issuing judgment on anyone within earshot. She didn't care. Sneaking around was unnecessary. If there were ghosts here, sound was the least of her worries. As for what she knew was here, they wouldn't know footsteps if they clomped directly on their faces.

In the middle of a long hallway, a faded turquoise door waited for Saoirse, its paint flaking a greeting as she pushed her way through. With a single purpose in mind, and the desire for her visit to be brief, Saoirse side-stepped old rockers and overturned tables, then over half a dozen threadbare blankets and charred sleeping bags until she reached one with lavender filigree. She drove the toe of her boot into this one.

"Up ye get."

The sleeping bag moaned. Saoirse stepped on the lump and rolled it back and forth.

"Up an' at it." Saoirse chuffed, igniting a chorus of groans, whines, and complaints from around the room. Saoirse scolded back, her voice fat and booming. "I ain't talkin' to the lot of ye. Just 'er."

One more shove with her foot, and the sleeping bag answered.

"Bugger off," Imogen growled from beneath her pile of bedding.

"Naw."

"Eat a goddamn fuck."

Saoirse sighed. "I shan't, stubborn lass. I shan't eat a fuck."

Imogen peeled back the sleeping bag and recoiled at the dusty ray of sun reaching for her through the yellowed windows. Saoirse tried not to gasp, swallowing her shock like a lump of porridge. Imogen's face was gaunt and pale, not the fresh warm ivory of her usual pallor; her freckles were gone, as was her porcelain skin, replaced by grey droopy flesh and clusters of freshly picked pocks. She was clothed, but barely—a stained pair of men's briefs around her protruding hip bones and a cutoff *Sunday Bloody Sunday* jumper barely covering the bottom of her breasts.

"Huh. A right sight ye are," Saoirse said.

Imogen grumbled something in response but rolled to her knees. Saoirse offered her hand and Imogen took it, allowing herself to be hauled to her feet. Saoirse took the brunt of her sister's meager weight as they zigged and zagged through the cluster of addicts and abandoned asylum furniture. When they stumbled out into the hall, Saoirse let Imogen fall to the floor.

"'Tis too bright." Imogen's voice was gravel, her breathing strained.

"Ay. 'Tis daytime. You should give it a try once in a while, lest ye turn into a bat."

Imogen rolled her eyes.

"'Ere, lemme help you up. Can ye walk at all?"

Imogen nodded but struggled to her feet. She held tight to the wall, wavering in place. With a gulp, air caught in her throat, and she looked over her shoulder down the barren hallway. Saoirse's eyes followed her sister's gaze, but she saw nothing but split doors and crumbling walls. Something had her sister rattled, though. Gooseflesh had swollen on her gangly arms, and her bloodshot eyes widened in terror. For a moment, Saoirse examined Imogen's face, then shifted her attention to the still and vacant expanse of the hallway. Her senses lingered on every colour and sound, but she could not experience what troubled her sister so.

Tears filled Saoirse's eyes. "Aye. The sight of ye." Without giving the waterworks a chance to fall, Saoirse hooked her arm around Imogen's waist. "No matter, I suppose. That's why I nicked you a day ahead of time, so I's can getcha half presentable."

"A day ahead of time?" Imogen parroted, her brow crumpled in confusion.

"Yeah, you wouldn't know, would ye. 'Tis Ma's birthday tomorrow." Before Imogen could refuse her attendance, Saoirse silenced her with a yank. "We's goin to tha farm, and we's gonna have a delightful time. She our Ma, we love her, and she us. We's family. End of story."

Imogen didn't put up a fight, not that she could have. They fumbled and stumbled their way out the door and to the rental car. Saoirse nodded at a passing Garda, musing how it must look, her dragging a half-conscious, scantily clad young woman and dumping her in the car. But in true fashion, the Garda kept going. They avoided anything to do with the addicts. The heroin in Munster was an epidemic, specifically in east Cork; addiction was a dangerous beast, not massive and powerful like a bear or a werewolf but small and wily, like rats or hornets. If the Garda tried to deal with every little hornet, they'd risk getting swarmed. Overwhelmed. A single wee addict wasn't worth the effort.

"Come on, love." Saoirse buckled Imogen's belt and covered her with a blanket she'd brought for this very occasion. She also tossed an airsick bag in Imogen's lap, though she doubted Imogen would have the foresight to use it should the purge arise.

Imogen was asleep by the time Saoirse had rounded the car and buckled herself into her own seat. They began the drive, and Saoirse turned on the radio to muffle the pained din of her sister's shallow breaths.

4

Even from inside their room, the spastic neon sign looming over the roadside motel caused Imogen's eyelids to twitch and flutter. She didn't hurt, not just yet, but it was coming—the aches and pains, the chills. Vomiting, anxiety, agitation. And all those horrible things she'd hear and see.

"I'm not gettin' clean overnight," Imogen said to the closed bathroom door.

"Feckin well know that," Saoirse muttered.

"Then why's we here?"

The bathroom door opened, and Saoirse came out, drying her hands on a stiff, over-bleached motel towel. "For a sisterly yarn, yeah?"

Imogen narrowed her eyes and crossed her arms.

"Nah," Saoirse said. "I likes ya, but I mean to clean you up, is all. Not the black tar in yer veins, but, just . . ." Saoirse tilted her head, encouraging Imogen to look at the mirror, "you."

Imogen refused to look. She knew what would be looking back—bones and sallow skin, tangles of thin, stringy hair hanging over emaciated shoulders. *And whose clothes are these?* Her yellowed fingers fumbled loose threads hanging from her outfit.

"Dunnae worry," Saoirse said. "Some sleep an' new clothes—which I scooped up from Paco's, I'll 'ave you know—and you'll be half-presentable."

"It'll take more than that," Imogen said to her lap. "And without the . . ." her voice trailed off, stifled by shame.

"Don't fret." Saoirse sat on the bed, and Imogen leaned on her. "I know how it is. And you know Ma worries, but with nary a judgement."

Imogen squirmed but couldn't find words.

Saoirse smiled and put her hand over her sister's heart. Imogen recoiled at the touch, but Saoirse's warm, familiar love thawed her.

"C'mon now, lovey," Saoirse said softly. "Let's get you properly showered, then chow down on some take away."

There was no shame and all the shame in being bathed by her sister. When Saoirse lifted Imogen's shirt over her head, exposing her, Imogen felt awash with embarrassment—not because her sister saw her, but because of her own body. A prematurely decaying shell, filthy and broken. The fact that she was exposed to Saoirse didn't bother her in the least. Even when Saoirse leaned over to peel off the stained underwear that Imogen had plucked from fuck-knows-where, she didn't bat an eye. Because Saoirse never batted an eye.

The bathtub was hard and cruel, the water both too cold and too hot, searing her rice paper flesh. Saoirse guided Imogen's hand over her own body, encouraging her to cleanse herself, to save any pinch of humiliation she could. What Saoirse did do, however, was shampoo Imogen's hair. Head lolling to the side, eyes disappearing behind heavy lids, Imogen let Saoirse's fingers take her back to their younger years, after Dadaí's death, when Saoirse had assumed her role as co-parent.

※

Imogen loved it when her big sister bathed her. When her big sister did anything with her, really.

"Hold still, ye wee eejit!" Saoirse scolded as Imogen slid her bum around the tub, giggling and crashing her toy dory against the side. Saoirse was knuckle-deep in Imogen's deep auburn mane, fingers tangled in the mess of curls, dirt, and food. "How the bloody hell you get yourself such a mess?"

Imogen squealed, part out of delight, part out of humour at the sopping front of her big sis's jumper. "Jus' from playin, I 'ppose."

Saoirse tried to look cross, but she wasn't, Imogen knew. There was a laugh jiggling at the sides of her frown, daring those lips to turn to a smile. Which they did. Saoirse reached into the tub and squeezed Imogen in a bear hug, which Imogen promptly squirmed out of like an eel.

"I loves ye," Saoirse said, sneaking a quick final lather of Imogen's hair.

That funny feeling swelled in Imogen's stomach again. The playing ceased, the waves stilled, and the boat came to rest after tapping the side of the tub a few times. These feelings of melancholy and rage were still frequent, striking her like a truck travelling full tilt.

"Love?" Saoirse said, and her hand came to rest on Imogen's shoulder.

"You suppose it hurt?"

"What hurt?"

"Dadaí. When he . . ."

Saoirse was quiet, then answered, "Naw, don't believe so. Too quick to register, I'd think."

Imogen thought about that as she teased the bubbles with her finger. "Was he scared?"

"I hope he didn't realize."

"Didn't realize?"

"That death was there for him."

Imogen fell quiet again. Soft and quiet, Saoirse rinsed her hair with the pitcher.

"There's so many nevers," Imogen said, her voice louder than she intended.

Saoirse stopped. "So many what?"

"Nevers." Imogen stood suddenly, splashing water onto the floor. Saoirse held an arm out so Imogen didn't slip as she stepped out of the tub and into her fuzzy bear robe. "So many nevers. Dadaí will never read to us 'bout Ramnon again. No more smoochies, no more singin' on the cliffs. Never gonna see me inna big weddin gown and dance my first married waltz with me."

Imogen felt like a cork had been popped, releasing weeks' worth of ramblings. She screamed and yelled, threw the soap and kicked the waste bin on her way into the hall. When she reached their bedroom, she continued her ranting and raving, throwing around her plushies and bedding before collapsing on the floor.

Saoirse said nothing. She just sat beside her and started brushing her hair, humming a lullaby until Imogen calmed.

"'Tis okay, wee lass. We will be okay."

Imogen tipped over and rested her head on her sister's budding breast. Ma appeared in the doorway, wringing her hands, watching silently, waiting for the right moment to come in.

"'Tis okay," Saoirse said.

Imogen hated that, being talked to like she was the only child in the house.

Imogen folded in on herself, crying into her bare knees.

They shifted places, Ma and Saoirse, so effortlessly that Imogen didn't realize Saoirse had gone. Ma resumed the brushing Saoirse had started.

"She means well, Imogen."

"She ain't replacing Dadaí."

"She's not meant to. But she is your big sister, and she cares for you."

"She ain't better than me."

"Nope. Just older."

"That means nothin'."

"Means she has experience. Not enough, but more than you. Besides, caring for you helps her cope too."

Imogen let her tears flow free. "I miss him, Ma. Should I still miss him?"

"Ay, Lass," Ma said. "'Tis only been a year. Hell, if it'd been twenty and ye didn't miss him, I'd wonder if yer brain broke. Now ye be way more sensitive to everything than yer big sis. Always have been. And she's got skin as thick as Aunt Alice's thighs, so lean on her when 'tis all too much."

Imogen couldn't help but giggle, and it was then she noticed Saoirse sitting on her bed.

"I's sorry, Saoirse."

"No need," Saoirse said, sliding to the floor and cuddling in with her and Ma. "Let it out, whenever you needs to. Nothing you can say will drive me away."

"I love ye," Imogen said, and nuzzled into her ma and sister, twirling her fingers around Saoirse's thick plait and worrying it between her fingers. But the hair was coarse and hard, a far cry from her sister's billowy fluff. Imogen pulled back and looked at her hands, which were coated in clumps of manky black hair that bound her fingers together.

Breathless, she held her hands up, but was greeted by confused expressions and exchanged glances.

"Kiddo, what's wrong?" Ma said.

Imogen tried to scream, but her mouth was stuck shut with tangles of sticky hair, gumming up her mouth and sealing off her throat. The room darkened as black strands trickled down, falling like a curtain over her eyes.

Saoirse parroted Ma. "What's wrong?"

Nothing. A breath, and the hair was gone; Imogen's hands were white and wrinkled, her air freely flowing from an unhindered throat. And Saoirse's plait was in place, tidy and soft.

"Nothing," Imogen stammered. "Never mind."

She crawled off the floor and into bed, ignoring the raised brows and whispered conversation behind her. So she wouldn't have to say more, she closed her eyes and faked sudden sleep.

IMOGEN OPENED HER EYES. SAOIRSE WAS MASSAGING conditioner into her hair. When Saoirse reached over to get another squeeze from the bottle, Imogen noticed the black strands, clumped on Saoirse's hands like thick spiderwebs. It was everywhere, that black hair—floating in the tub, stuck on the walls, balled up in the corners of the motel bathroom. Imogen closed her eyes, but she could still feel the hair on her body, on the roof of her mouth.

"Ye okay?" Saoirse stopped pouring and closed the faucet.

Imogen didn't answer. Saoirse didn't press. They fumbled and stumbled their way out of the tub and to the bed. Thankfully, Saoirse had brought a pair of fleece pajamas, the kind with no buttons or ribbons. Any embellishment was an infuriating assault on her hypersensitive skin. After she was dressed and her hair tied back in a plait, Imogen slithered under the covers and exposed her arm, turning her palm to the ceiling.

"Naw," Saoirse said, tucking Imogen's arm back under the covers. "I'll only use the needle if it gets real bad."

The sound of a spoon tinking the side of the drinking glass crackled through Imogen's brain like lightning. Despite being down this road before, she appreciated Saoirse walking her through each step.

"Methadone, full dose to get ya through the night. 'Nother dose in the mornin'. I've mixed it with pineapple juice. Fuck knows why ye like that horrid swill, but there it is."

The straw was small, making the sips manageable, but it took an agonizing amount of time to finish the dose. Once she finished the last suck of liquid, Imogen let sleep take her, comforted by Saoirse's soft singing as the soundtrack to her slumber.

5

The land was the same as it had been when they were small children—vibrant and full of life. Even teetering on the edge of the bluffs, the yard was thick and green, hedges of dogwood dotting the fertile soil. Though few trees grew there—only a sturdy few could withstand the onslaught of wind gales and salt—the scattered Threave's Seedling and Silver Sheen stood sentry, guarding the smaller flora. Ma had made quite the hobby of gardening after Dadaí was killed, creating a lush environment protected by boulders and rocks and the shade of the hardier trees.

As she navigated the car up the narrow drive, Saoirse scanned the cliffs, seeking their Ma. Ma hadn't been warned ahead of time about Imogen's state, though she wouldn't be surprised. Imogen had been deteriorating for a good half decade now. And their visits home were frequent. Saoirse made sure to keep them all connected. She fretted that Ma would be lonely or depressed since they'd moved out. Ma never remarried and had always been a tad of a homebody. Didn't seem to trouble her, though; she claimed her books, plants, and daughters were all she needed. That being said, life without Dadaí couldn't have been something she'd anticipated.

Imogen squirmed, sliding lower in her seat. Though her little sister didn't say much, Saoirse knew Imogen was horribly embarrassed each time they visited Ma. But that was Imogen's demon, not Ma's. They would continue to visit. Ma was always happy to see them. Both of them.

As the tires rolled to a stop, crunching to quiet, a white moon of a face popped up from behind a hedge of dogwood. Ma looked lovely as ever, her pastel lips blushing against the fairness of her skin. Coils of thin white snakes threaded through her hair like tinsel, the only evidence of Father Time lurking in her footsteps.

"Girls!" Ma stood and brushed her hands on her smock, leaving smudges of soil over the embroidered flowers.

Saoirse left Imogen to struggle with the dented buckle of her seatbelt; she hoped to reach Ma first, give her a heads up about her youngest, who looked a mere poke away from the finger of death. But in classic Ma fashion, she reached the car before Saoirse had even shut the driver's side door.

"My beautiful lass," Ma said as she grabbed Saoirse's face and kissed her cheeks.

"Ma—"

But Ma had already rounded the car. Imogen opened her own door and slid out, her movements slow and pained. Ma didn't even hesitate; she wrapped her arms gently around Imogen and gave her the same kisses she'd given Saoirse, though slower and softer.

"My love," Ma said. "I'm so very happy to see you."

Imogen's lip trembled. Saoirse was sure that if the girl had any tears in her ducts, they would be spilling over those sickly grey cheeks. When she spoke, her voice was raspy and brittle. "Happy birthday, Ma."

"Yes, happy day to you," Saoirse said, her smile wide and eyes wet.

Saoirse gave Ma and Imogen a moment to embrace, then joined the huddle, wrapping her arms around them both. When they finally peeled apart, Ma's face was wet with tears and flushed with joy. "My girls," she said, ruffling their hair. "Come. I've prepared a savage mug up inside."

"Ma!" Saoirse scolded. "'Tis yer day! We's the ones should be cooking!"

"Gives me joy," Ma said. "Besides, you bein' here is gift enough."

Imogen feigned a smile, and Ma threaded her fingers through their hands, guiding them to the house.

Oh, what yer missin', Saoirse thought as she watched her sister, hunched over and frail, and listened to the sounds of her feet dragging across the gravel. *Yer sickness be worse than death, I fear.*

DINNERTIME WAS LOVELY AS ALWAYS, AND IMOGEN WAS SAD she could not enjoy it. Though the linens were neither linen nor lace, and the silverware stainless steel instead of precious metal, the whole affair felt fancy, nonetheless. It was not formality that elevated the meal, but rather the camaraderie of family that warmed bellies, brains, and souls. Ma's dishes of Shepard's Pie and boxty were better than any five-star meal at a stuffy restaurant, not that Imogen could enjoy the flavours.

Though the food was savoury, and the air fresh with love and laughter, Imogen's mood was dark and dank, as if kept too long in the cellar with the whiskey. She pushed her peas and mash around her plate with her fork, her belly roiling from the medley of aromas. A sour belch gurgled in the back of her throat. She put her fist to her mouth to quell the looming nausea.

"You gonna be fine, Imogen?" Saoirse and Ma were both looking at her, their cutlery rested on their plates.

Imogen didn't dare speak for fear her words would emerge with a coating of vomit. She nodded, hoping that would be sufficient.

"'Tis okay," Ma said as she picked her fork back up. "You don't have to hide it from me, Imogen. I know you're still using."

"Gave her methadone last night, and a pinch this morn'. To tide her."

"Ay, good," Ma said.

"Don't talk about me like I'm not here," Imogen snapped. Her tongue soured, foul liquid spilling into her mouth. She swallowed the food down, refusing to unveil her weakness, though she knew it shone like a lighthouse over still waters.

"Does it help?" Ma asked. "The methadone?"

"Guess so." Despite the nausea, Imogen determined the conversation to be worse, so she stuffed her cheeks full of boxty, attempting to chew without inhaling the smell.

Matter-of-factly, Ma spoke, loving and direct. "It's a sickness. A disease like diabetes or cancer, nothing more. Needs dealt with. 'Tis not your fault, and it sucks, but there it is."

Unable to stomach the warm mush on her tongue any longer, Imogen spit her food into her serviette. "'Tis my fault, Ma."

"Nope. But if it be, so what? Who cares of fault? What's done is done. There's nothin' to gain by assigning fault."

"I ain't weak," Imogen said. The tears were flowing now.

Saoirse inserted herself into the discussion. "No, you ain't, and no one thinks it."

"You do."

"I don't!"

"Girls." Ma's voice was firm but full of love. "Loaded issue, this. Saoirse, we can't pretend ta know what Imogen goes through. We jus' gotta let her be. But Imogen, we's scared. Because of all tha love we has for ye. We want to protect you and love you and help. We're doin' the best, same as you."

Saoirse kept going, her tone high and impassioned. "So what's the plan, then? Let 'er die?"

"I ain't dying," Imogen said.

"Like hell. Look at ye, all bones and greys. Ain't much left but the black beast in yer blood."

"Fuck you," Imogen hissed.

Ma struck a serving platter with her fork, ringing the girls to attention. "Enough. 'Tis my birthday, and I tire of this nonsense. Saoirse, lay off for now. And Imogen, we'll never lay off. Because we loves you. And know this: I will never stop loving you. You are always welcome here, death in yer veins an' all."

"Ay," Saoirse said, nodding, her curls bouncing around her face. "I loves you as well. But seriously, I cannot watch ye die. Let's get yer shit together."

"But we loves you even if you don't," Ma said, raising a brow at Saoirse.

The conversation dissolved; the only sound that remained was the chewing of food and sipping of drink. Guilt swirled with need, with nausea, with panic, creating a cyclone in Imogen's mind, setting her off balance. She wanted to leap up and flip the table, to scream at her Ma and her sister. She wanted them to know how much she loved them, so much she thought her heart might explode against her ribs. She wanted to beg, to submit and ask for their help, to tell them she wanted to be healthy and happy. But she also wanted to scream at them, to blame them for her pain. For everything they didn't do. For exposing her weakness, confronting her, and making her feel like vermin.

It was too much. Their eyes were on her, boring into her, judging and evaluating.

Imogen's gaze flitted to the ceiling, and the black claws of terror pierced her lungs.

So many eyes. Always watching.

She dropped her head, her hair dangling in her food.

Ma looked at her, but Saoirse examined the ceiling.

Imogen set her fork on her plate. "I'm sorry, I just …"

"I know." Roison continued eating. "Take a break from us and this food, but come back and finish. You need some meat on yer bones."

Imogen stood and pushed her chair into the table, leaving all the eyes behind as she went to hide in her old room at the back of the house.

Saoirse found Imogen sitting on the windowsill of their old bedroom, staring out over field and sea. To not startle her, or make her suspicious of sneaking, Saoirse announced her presence with the clomp of her boots.

"Dunnah prefer the festivities?" Saoirse asked.

"I dinnah prefer much these days," Imogen said.

"And what be it precisely that ain't to yer likin'? The food be too tasty, the company too engaging?"

Imogen sighed. "Nothing. Nothin's to my liking anymore."

"There's no fault in that, chil'. We've no more control over our hearts than we do the blood pumpin' through our veins. But try choosing to be happy, and ye may trick that ole ticker of yers to follow suit. But lemme tell ya, regardless of if ye be blue, red, or purple, I'll love you just the same, pouts and all."

With her plump rose lips, Saoirse kissed Imogen on the forehead, lingering. Imogen leaned into the moist pressure of her sister's mouth, her eyes fluttering closed.

"I love you, Saoirse."

"And I, you."

Saoirse took a perch on the windowsill beside Imogen, and the two entwined their fingers.

"Truth be tol'," Imogen said, her face flushing a bouquet of roses, "I'm jealous of ye."

Saoirse's braying laughter startled the room. "Don't ye be so foolish! You've youth and spunk enough to fill all of County Cork, if you cleaned yourself up."

"You are not a weathered boot, Saoirse. You be only seven years my senior."

"Like a mutt's years, seven years in a woman's span makes me an old crone to yer sproutin' bud."

"Dunno 'bout that." Imogen's eyes found the floor. "And cleanin up ain't that easy."

Saoirse shared Imogen's pain as she gazed at the remnants of her little sister. Though it paled in comparison to the pain Imogen felt, she imagined. Saoirse watched Imogen's eyes flutter to and fro, scanning the landscape. She said nothing, and Saoirse didn't prod. They sat there, quiet, letting the sounds and sights of the cliffs wash over them. Saoirse's eyes came to rest on the lawn, halfway to the cliffs.

Saoirse spoke, but did not turn her head to her sister. "What happened to ye?"

"When?"

"Don't be coy, ye skag. When did your brain turn so troubled?"

Imogen's eyes did not move from the yard.

Is she looking at that spot too? Saoirse wondered.

Imogen's voice was small. Far away. "When Dadaí died, I suppose."

"'Tis a lie. Know how I know? My Dadaí also died."

"You want a fucking medal for holding it together?"

"I want ta understand. I want to help."

"We shan't be discussing this anymore."

"Oh, we shall. Every time I see ya. I's not gonna pester ye, but I'm gonna ask, each and every damn time I sees ya."

The grass shivered, an undulating glisten of blues and greens as the ocean breeze ruffled up its skirts. The sun had grown fat consuming the day, its weight sagging below the horizon and making way for the starving moon. The night brought with it a quiet dread, unseen terrors able to move around unfettered, the unknown trying to claw their way into knowledge. Saoirse recalled seeing her, the nightmare on the lawn, an impossibility that struck twice like forbidden lightning, alighting both Dadaí's graveside and her Ma's bathroom.

But those were times of stress and childhood. These were times of reality.

Saoirse had to ask. If she didn't, it would gnaw her from the inside out. "Did you see her, too?"

Imogen's gaze lingered out the window a moment before shifting to Saoirse. "See who?"

"That night. When Dadaí . . ."

Puzzled. There was no better word to describe the look on Imogen's face.

Saoirse watched her sister's expression as she disclosed her story, hoping for disclosure in return. "'Twas a woman in the yard the night Dadaí died. A haggard ol' wench, washing clothes out yonder."

Imogen cocked a brow, the corner of her mouth tugging into a half grin. "What? That's ... what?"

"When you and Ma came out to get me, ye was scared."

"Hells yeah, I was! You was screechin' to wake the dead!"

No lie flickered on Imogen's face. And this addict, Saoirse knew, could no better contain a lie than a colander holds whiskey.

"Nightmare, then. Just thought maybe ..."

Imogen's eyes glistened with tears. "I have nightmares. Bad ones."

Here it is. "Wanna talk about it?"

"They're gone." Imogen tapped her head with a skeletal finger. "Not much stays in the attic these days."

"Call me when they happen." Saoirse wrapped her arm around Imogen and handed her a new green cellphone. "I got you another phone."

"You shouldn't have."

"Fuck no, I shouldn't have, but hope lives eternal. I want you to 'ave something in case you need to call. Try not to sell this one or trade it for fuck knows what. Though better to sell this hunk o' plastic than your pussy."

Shock widened Imogen's eyes, which darted to the bedroom door.

"Oh, Ma knows. Lord knows she's thought about where yer money's comin' from, seein' as you won't take ours. No matter, though. Just use the phone. Call me when the nightmares come. Or when you need help. Or if a rat with a fancy hairstyle runs by and you gots to tell me 'bout it. Anything at all."

Imogen tried to speak, but a gulp came instead. Saoirse could tell she wanted to speak, but couldn't.

"I love you too, wee lass."

❦ 6 ❧

Saoirse was impressed when Imogen remembered to use the carsick bag on the drive home, rather than puking over the dash as she'd been known to do.

It had been a good visit. Ma was happy; they talked and laughed and hugged, and Imogen had been alive one more day. But as they returned to reality, the illusion of joy faded.

Crumpled like a body bag in the passenger seat, Imogen looked a fright, nothing more than taut flesh over crooked bone. Once beautiful, bouncy, and lush, she was now greasy ash, a smear of her old self. Worse than that was the powerlessness Saoirse felt deep in her soul.

Ma had asked her to take care of Imogen. Saoirse royally fucked that up.

As she did on most drives from Ma's, Saoirse pondered the plague that infected her baby sister. It had happened so fast. Imogen went from outgoing, boisterous, emotional to completely withdrawn in the blink of an eye. Ma had told

Saoirse that it was menstruation, and all the joys that go with it, that changed Imogen into a quiet, skulking recluse. *That isn't it*, Saoirse thought. *The whole lot o' us spill blood from our cunnies, but only she turned to the needle. No sheddin' uterus be that much of an asshole.*

At the risk of questioning her own sanity, Saoirse dared to think of the nightmares of her younger years. That which visited her only briefly as a child, too horrific and unbelievable to consider.

No mind. 'Twasn't real, anyhow.

"No need to walk me inside," Imogen said, startling Saoirse to attention as they rolled up alongside the asylum.

"You won't make it more than a couple o' metres before you drop like a sack o'—"

"No." Imogen's voice was firm, surprising Saoirse.

"You're goin in. Why can't I?"

Imogen didn't answer, but she didn't have to. Saoirse knew why she shouldn't go in. Imogen wanted to be alone with her fix.

"Fine then," Saoirse said. "Ta hell with ya." She leaned over and hugged Imogen, then planted a slow kiss on her cheek. "I love you, all the same."

"And I, you," Imogen said, her voice barely the volume of a breath.

After the briefest hesitation, Imogen hauled herself out of the car and stumbled toward the building, shimmying her waifish frame through the door. Saoirse's eyes remained on the dark insides of the asylum that peeked through the open door.

What wanders your nightmares, little sister?

Saoirse was fed up with her brat of a sister. A six-year-old in a thirteen-year-old's body.

"I won't," Imogen sulked.

Saoirse gritted her teeth. "I suppose ye be stompin yer damn feet next, will ya?"

Saoirse and Imogen stood in the kitchen, Imogen with her fists clenched at her sides and Saoirse with her arms folded across her chest.

"What's the fuss?" Imogen said. "Go get 'em yourself!"

"The fuss is I asked ye. Ma asked ye. You ain't a wee thing anymore, Imogen. Go get a few logs for the wood stove; do your share. Won't take ya but a moment."

Imogen looked out the window at the yard and shed beyond. There was something in her eyes that gave Saoirse pause.

"Is ye scared?"

"I's not scared!" Imogen snapped. "I jus' don't see why it's gotta be me."

"Okay, well ye tend to the coddle, and I'll go get tha wood."

Imogen shrugged. "Not much ta tend to. Just stirring a pot o' shit all mashed together."

Saoirse rolled her eyes as she slipped on her Wellies. "Jus' stir the pot."

The ground was mushy, saturated with a week's worth of coastal drizzle. Ma praised the way the wet made the gardens grow and the air fresh. Mostly it just made Saoirse's hair frizz and her Wellies gunk up with mud. She supposed that's why Imogen always balked at having to fetch wood or pluck veg from the garden.

It wasn't until Saoirse opened the shed door to utter blackness that she realized she'd forgotten the torch.

"No mind," she said to herself. "I could do this with my eyes sewn shut."

And she could. It had been several years since Imogen would go out back to help with chores. Irritation swelled in Saoirse's chest; she had a mind to go back empty handed, scold her sister, and make her come out to carry a few goddamn pieces of wood. But that would upset Ma, and the fire in the stove would go out, and the coddle would burn ... no, she'd just haul it in herself. Save all the fuss.

Saoirse emerged from the shed with an armload of wood, then lifted her foot and kicked the door shut. The latch clicked, echoing across the yard louder than it should have. Saoirse took two steps, and a new sound arose—a rhythmic clicking, clear and sharp in the still night. When she glanced at the shed, she found precisely what she thought she would: nothing but a closed and latched door. But beyond the shed, there was something.

Along the cliffs, in the riffling long grass, were shimmers not belonging to the blades. Though dark, they gleamed, stars fallen from the sky, their charred remains littering the cliffs.

Eyes.

Without hesitation, Saoirse dropped the wood at her feet and stomped towards the cliff, waving her arms. "Away with ya, vermin! Ye gets away from the veg, you scoundrels!"

Upon reaching the cliff, she discovered no stars, no eyes, no tiny footprints in the dirt. The moon was full, pouring down a plentiful glow, but Saoirse wasn't convinced there was enough light to expose the leavings of small game. Or large, for that matter. Besides, they were gone now, skittered over the cliff or in some hidey hole on the crag.

Saoirse kept her gaze locked on the grass as she returned to the dropped wood. When she bent to retrieve it, her eyes drifting from the cliff's edge back to the yard, the sound ignited again—muffled chuffs and chitters. It was a repressed sound, vocal but restrained, accentuated by the chattering and grinding of teeth.

No. 'Tis not teeth. 'Tis only the song of the ocean.

Regardless, Saoirse quickened her steps, anxious to put distance between her and the cliff. The chitters and chatters got louder, the teeth *gnashing and chomping. She envisioned those obsidian eyes, gleaming, watching, chasing.*

Probably the grass is wet. Droplets of water shining, is all.

But the night was dry and cool. By the time Saoirse reached the house, she was not. Arriving at practically a run, her face was flushed, and dampness formed beneath her arms and breasts. She tumbled inside, locked the door behind her, and thrust the wood at Imogen.

"See? Nothin' to it. All done."

Imogen's eyes searched the yard over Saoirse's shoulder. Saoirse watched as her sister placed the wood beside the stove—the way her hands trembled, the hollow, sleepless dark beneath her eyes.

What wanders your nightmares, little sister?

❧ 7 ❧

The furry taste of Ma's boxty rested thick and dry on Imogen's tongue, enticing gags as she slipped through the turquoise door into the common room. Imogen had her own room—they all did, the more seasoned residents—but often she haunted the common room. She couldn't be alone, not until her brain was swimming, floating, dark with heroin.

As Imogen passed a rubbish bin, she tossed in the green phone Saoirse had given her. Not only did she not want to disrespect her by selling it for drugs, she also didn't want to phone for help if she got in a pinch. She didn't want her family involved in her mess, no matter how deep she dug her grave. Besides, Saoirse or Roison could get in trouble coming to her aid. Hurt, or worse.

There was a smattering of junkies spread over the floor of the common room—some seated, some flat on their faces or backs, most only semi-conscious. Imogen ruffled her feet through blankets and rubbish until she found a patchy head with sprouts of black hair poking out like beans.

No matter the drug of choice, addicts did not like it loud, so Imogen kept her voice low and level. "Cait. Cait, wake up."

Cait was not asleep. Not really. Imogen dug a toe beneath her arm, poking into her armpit.

"Cait."

"Fucking Christadilly." Cait rolled over on her back, a dribble of thick, yellow drool staining her cheek. "The fuck you want?"

Imogen held her palm out.

"Oh ya, right. You's been gone a spell. How was merriment at the ole manor?"

"'Twas lovely," Imogen said. "I don't deserve them."

Cait rolled to her knees, then wrenched herself to a standing position, bracing herself on Imogen as she cracked her back and scratched her face. "Naw, you don't. But you 'ave them. Be fucking grateful."

Imogen followed Cait to the second floor where most of the bedrooms were located. Some bedrooms even had mattresses, stained and flattened as they were. Better than tile floor, though. Most of the locks were broken, and some doors torn completely off. Regardless, regular squatters each claimed a room of their own. Outsiders who stopped in for a hit or a squabble took camp in the common area on the main floor, a room formerly reserved for patients and their families when the hospital was operational. The third and top floor was occupied by former doctor's offices, treatment areas, and a recreational room for patients. After the syringes and drugs had been stripped from that floor, no one had cause to visit it again.

Imogen entered Cait's room ahead of her, earning herself a tongue lashing.

"This ain't your room, princess, and ye shan't be stompin' in here as you please."

Imogen motioned to the jamb, and the space a door had once occupied. "Would ye prefer I knock?"

Cait narrowed her eyes. "I'd prefer you wait on me. 'Tis my room."

Cait's room was one of the better ones, furnished with a thicker mattress and a chest of drawers. Cait used only the bed, though, as keeping her product organized in drawers was easy access for anything prowling in the night. She knelt on the bed, prying at a thumbtack holding up a Cranberries poster on the wall, her yellowed fingernails bending and flaking as the poster came loose. Beneath the poster was a hole punched in the gyprock, and in the hole, a dirty brass urn.

"How much you want?" Cait asked, pulling out baggies and vials.

Imogen hesitated.

Cait raised a brow. "How much cash you got?"

Imogen tried to contain her emotions, but her face deceived her, her lower lip giving way to trembles and her eyes swelling with tears. Cait set the urn back in the hole and pinned the poster back up.

"I don't get it." Cait slid off the bed and wriggled out of her acid wash jeans. "Your ma has money, yeah? And that sister o' yours looks well off enough. Lift from them so ye don't gotta whore yerself like this."

"I can't. I can't do that. Not to them." A sob ached in Imogen's throat, but she would not free it. She'd never be able to contain it once it found wings. All the pain and suffering over the years, all the torment, Imogen had considered ending it all. But in her darkest moments, suicidal highs and lows, she clung to thoughts of her family. They kept her alive. *I'd rather die than hurt them. And dying would hurt them, too, so here I am.*

The odour wafting off Cait was that of sour milk and rancid trout, made worse when she lifted her arms over her head to peel off her shirt. Imogen looked away as Cait removed her panties; they were torn and a stained shade that may once have been pink, or perhaps white spoiled by menstrual blood. Cait licked her fingers, teasing those yellow, dirt encrusted cuticles with her tongue before burying them inside herself.

"I'll prime myself, but ye gotta finish the job." Cait's mouth stretched into a sour grin, exposing brown chunks of dangling teeth. "You could earn a double shot, depending on how ya perform."

Cait lay on the bed and drew her knees to her ears, spreading herself. Imogen dropped to her knees, closed her eyes, and willed her mind to fly far away, off the cliffs and over the sea.

IMOGEN WOULDN'T LAY ON CAIT'S MATTRESS, WITH ITS STAINS and wet spots and cigarette burns. After a few minutes of Cait rubbing away the coital aftershocks, she untacked the poster and retrieved the urn.

"No complaints," Cait said with a smirk as she handed Imogen two baggies.

Imogen closed her fingers into a fist and hurried into the hall, desperate to be far away from that room, and from her own mind. Cait's voice rang out, an offer of a towel for Imogen to clean her face with, but Imogen didn't care. She wanted her room and her hit.

By the time Imogen reached the opposite end of the ward—

her room was at the end of the adjacent hallway, far away from Cait's lair—she was at a sprint, her weak legs stumbling as fast as they could carry her. She had a door, but it hung haphazard on rusted hinges, and at best, closed only partway. *Better than nothing*, Imogen thought as she wedged through and collapsed on her bed. Sliding her hands between mattress and floor, she retrieved her tools and got to work—heating, boiling, drawing. The drugs burned like hate violating her veins, but cooled to aloe, a slick comfort coating her every nerve and sense. She no longer tasted Cait and her rot, or saw the death that resided in these walls. But a sound wormed its way through her part-open door, refusing to be silenced.

"No." Imogen's voice was forceful, a directed bullet of sound. But it didn't stall the noise, only prompted it to swell.

It was a hum, a melancholy ballad reverberating deep within an unseen throat.

Imogen covered her ears, but the song grew ever louder, only softening when she dropped her hands and listened. As she homed in on the tune, trying to decide if it was structural noises or human voice, the voice grew smaller, more distant, until it was little more than air from a faerie's wing.

Coy, Imogen thought.

I won't wander far, just poke my head in the hall, see where it's coming from.

Though the poison was running its course, clouding her veins and mind, her panic rose, threatening to sear through her chest.

It's only Cait.

A lie she'd told herself many times.

And there are others here likely be makin' tha racket.

Imogen stepped outside her door, confident the sound's owner was not awaiting her in the hall. The keening was coming from both ends of the ward and from above and below all at once.

Pipes. Settling limestone. The drone of junkie chatter.

Her feet carried her, the sludge of euphoria calming her nerves and inflating her bravado, until she reached the stairwell leading to the third floor. All at once, the melody swirled as if in a tunnel, swooping by her like wind and coming to rest at the top of the stairs. Imogen covered her ears, her nails digging into her face and scalp. Despite her fear, her feet found the first step, lifting her body closer to the top floor. The sound crescendoed as Imogen progressed up the steps, until she reached the top landing. There, it was like a gurgling aquarium, noise everywhere, deeper and louder, pulsing through her bones. She screamed, but her voice was drowned out by the din of the throaty ballad. She drew her own blood, her nails leaving crimson crescents on her white cheeks, and she swooned. To prevent herself from falling on the concrete and cracking her skull, she braced herself on the steel bar of the third-floor doorway.

Silence flooded both her mind and the stairwell. Her hand lingered on the bar as she regained her composure. The metal was cool and silent, a ball gag on the horrible noise. Slow and tentative, she lifted her hand, cringing in anticipation of an audible assault. There was nothing.

A moment passed, then two, until finally, she decided the onslaught had ceased and she could return to her room. Or the common room, where the presence of others repelled fear.

When she reached the second-floor landing, the sound ignited again. This time it was subtle, gentle.

Taunting.

It wasn't a song, or a scream; it was crackling chitter like ticking teeth that pelted the stairwell like hail. Imogen listened only briefly before passing into the second-floor hallway, destined for the extra hit Cait gave her. After that, she would hunker down in the common room to wait out the night under the protection and distraction of a room full of witnesses.

8

The town of Ballinspittle was long asleep by the time Saoirse pulled into her carport and trudged into her tiny bungalow. She'd had the place since college, and it suited her just fine—near both the city and the country. Keeping Ma and Imogen close was a necessity. There was no life without family.

After dumping her keys and purse on the kitchen table, Saoirse clicked on the kettle and grabbed a biscuit from the cupboard. As she gnawed on the lemon sweetie, she thought of Imogen. Of the way she looked in corners and out over the land, as both a child and an adult. Looking for something.

Or *at* something.

May be time to have a chat 'bout the elephant in the room.

As a child, Saoirse had told herself none of it was real. And the same as an adult. She had seen nothing wildly unusual since her Dadaí's wake—no shouting pictures or women hanging in corners like spiders—but there was still sound that did not belong. Quiet, hiding in nooks and crannies, in the pages of books, and down the dark of drains. Barely more than white noise now, though; the years had dampened Saoirse's notice.

The kettle squealed, demanding attention. Saoirse poured up a tea and sat by the window to watch the sleepy town—the sprays of flowers, the flickering streetlights. Both Saoirse's mind and body were heavy with sleep. Her eyelids fluttered with the lights, her mind calming with each sip of hot liquid. All was settling into peace until the kettle screeched a second time, startling Saoirse off her stoop.

"Gawdamn fecking thing!"

Saoirse stormed to the kitchen, scolding herself for leaving the stove on, but when she reached it, the flame was off.

She looked at her perch by the window.

Dreamin.

But the sound was so real and fresh it still bristled the tiny hairs on her body. Convinced she would never settle to sleep, Saoirse decided to crawl into bed and read, rest her body to trick her mind. After topping up her tea, she snuck to the bedroom and sat on the bed. The wail of the kettle still rang in her brain, bringing her back to her childhood, to all the things she'd pushed aside in her mind and her memory. All the things she'd refused to acknowledge.

Mayhap time to address yer demons if ye expect Imogen to address hers. Methinks they be the same.

From the kitchen, all hell broke loose. There were sounds of screaming and laughing all at once, from voices both high and low, near and far. Not knowing what else to do, Saoirse ran for the kitchen to scold the kettle once more. When she arrived, the phone on the counter was jostling, shaking from its own emanating noise.

"Tha feckin hell?"

Saoirse placed her hand on the receiver, and the voices ceased their barrage. There was noise, but it was just the phone ringing beneath her fingers.

When Saoirse raised the receiver, she expected a demon at the other end to chant and screech, his tongue licking out, down her throat, to rip out and consume her bowels and her soul. "Um ... Hello?"

It was only Ma. "M'love, you made it home okay. How was Imogen?"

Saoirse sighed. "Oh, she's Imogen, Ma. I mean, she isn't fine, but she's still kickin'."

"I worry," Ma said. Saoirse swore she could hear Ma wringing those weathered hands.

"I know, Ma. Me too. But we worry 'cause we love. Part and parcel, but that's it."

Ma usually called after their weekly visits to see if they both made it home in one piece—ever the Ma, she was—but this time an unspoken conversation lingered.

"Ma, is there somethin—"

Before Saoirse could ask, Ma offered, "Saoirse, we need to talk."

Like a soft breeze through a distant wood, a noise swelled over the line. Voices, melodic, both speaking and keening.

"Ma, you got the tele on?"

"What? No."

"Ay, sorry, I thought I heard—"

Louder now, more than one voice, garbled nonsense from anxious throats.

"Saoirse, I was hoping ... it's a lot to ask."

Ma's voice faded away, drowning beneath the racket of other

voices, the chittering and gnashing of teeth, the tearing of flesh. Saoirse wanted to drop the receiver, to run to her room and hide her head beneath her pillow like she'd done at Dadai's wake.

And just like that, the line went quiet. All but Ma's voice. "Saoirse? Are ye okay? You listenin'?"

"Yeah, I's sorry. Head's got tired moss growin' over it."

"Could you come by?"

"Now?"

"Naw, no. Not an emergency. Tomorrow, if ye aren't busy."

"That should work," Saoirse said.

"Best let you get to bed, now. Ye need your sleep. Can't have two zombies shamblin' round my family."

"Naw, sleep is a coy fooker in my world, Ma. I needs very little of it to function."

"Always that way with ya, Saoirse. You've always been the resilient one. Tough as nails and stubborn as an arse. But it's my job to care for ye."

"And I, for ye."

They exchanged love, then Saoirse hung up the phone with a slam.

"Now listen here," she snarked at both phone and kettle. "That'll be enough nonsense for this night."

But despite the scolding, as she settled into bed, she swore she could hear chitters and mutters from the kitchen.

9

There was zero chance Imogen would return to Cait for a top up. She just simply couldn't face the method of payment that awaited between those legs, not so soon after the last encounter. But she needed another hit and had no money, so her only option was the streets. It was late—well after eleven, judging by the darkness spilling through Our Lady's filthy windows—so the stags would be on the prowl.

The roads and green spaces speckled along the River Lee were no strangers to stealthy pros. Problem was that Imogen was no pro. This was a move of desperation, one she'd made only a handful of times before. She had a part-time job at the Horse and Cradle, slinging brews and wiping tables, until the tar took hold. After that, she suffered a constant state of inebriation, and, therefore, unemployment.

Some walkers had big shiny hair to match their holographic clothes and bedazzled platforms. Most had Imogen's regular sense of style—addict couture: acid-wash jeans stained with the ghosts of meals, matted hair dumped on top of heads in knotted buns, and bare feet, crooked and mangled from hours of walking without shoes or in shoes that didn't fit. But tonight, Imogen felt clean. The outfit Saoirse had bought her made her feel like royalty amongst commoners.

None of that mattered, though. The tricks never much cared about the clothes.

A job rolled up as his window rolled down, his lips wet.

"Get in."

He didn't ask how much. Didn't matter. She'd take whatever they'd give her and give whatever they wanted. Her need was greater than theirs. Still, her urge to bolt was nearing greater than her need for a hit when this one pulled his car into a dark corner of Fitzgerald Park.

"Get out." There was nothing sexual in his voice. There would be sex—he'd ejaculate, one way or another—but that's not what this was about.

Imogen did not speak. She was quite certain her voice wasn't what interested him.

It took him very little time to undress her. It was as if her own flesh tore as he ripped off the new outfit Saoirse had bought her and threw it in the mud and shit of the sewers. She didn't even need to position herself; what a gentleman he was, doing all the work, slamming her chest on the bonnet of his car and stabbing himself inside her.

It's not sex, she told herself, though he was inside her, bruising her, tearing her. He had her hair wrapped in his fists, yanking so hard with every thrust she thought her bones might crack and her head pop off.

It's power. When he relinquished his grip on her hair, he grabbed her by the hips, his claws digging into her flesh as he pulled, slamming himself into her until he came. He grunted like a swine, and a line of drool dribbled from his mouth onto the small of her back. He slapped at that puddle with his now flaccid cock, then zipped up his pants.

"Done." That was all he said. He reached into his glove box, pulled out 20 euros, and threw it on the ground. Pain radiated from Imogen's ribs as she peeled herself off the car. Avoiding eye contact, she knelt to the money. After picking it up, she drew her torn shirt into her lap, stroking the ruined fabric and mourning this gift of love and dignity. She barely heard the engine start, or the gravel crunching beneath the tires as he drove off, leaving her to the night.

Imogen brought the shirt to her face, smelling the aromas of Ma and Saoirse that lingered in its fabric. Her tears came in violent heaves, pouring down her face and soaking the shirt. It felt like tattered ribbons of flesh, that once-pristine garment clutched in her pathetic hands. Imogen bunched it tight, covering her mouth to muffle the sobs. But her emotions had boiled to steam, blasting out of her in a wail that sliced the night like a hatchet. Birds, disturbed from their trees and power lines, fluttered above in a frenzy, and the water in the river rippled, as though recoiling from the sound.

Much as she tried, Imogen couldn't contain a second onslaught. The sound erupted from her throat like the bray of an obese donkey, punching the air with warbles and wails from deep in her guts.

After the longest of moments, the sound withered until it was little more than a wheeze. Imogen gulped in air, trying to catch her breath but tasting only desperation and sorrow.

A GLOW OF FIRE RADIATED FROM A NEARBY GREEN SPACE, THE calling card of a shantytown. Imogen figured she might find a blanket there to cover herself until she made it back to Our Lady's Asylum. She clutched the shredded, tear-soaked blouse in her fist, refusing to let it go as if it contained her last breath. Thankfully, her suitor had left her with the new boots Saoirse had given her, making traversing the gravel and broken glass a less excruciating journey.

The shantytown was an outdoor version of her own squatting grounds, but louder with the soundtrack of traffic roaring nearby. And the stench was less with the wind carrying away the aroma of urine, vomit, and yeast that coated the people and their belongings. No one turned to see the naked woman in their midst. She was exposed, all her shameful bits free for all to ogle, but no one batted an eye.

I'm repulsive.

A thin trickle of blood dribbled down her inner thighs, remnants of her encounter. She stumbled, her ribs bruised and hurting, her face stained with tears that spilled over her swollen, split lip. No one saw, and if they did, no one cared.

They feel nothing for me.

She stepped around an old man on a tattered blanket, a solitary yellow tooth hanging from his blackened gums, pus caked in both the corners of his mouth and his milky eyes. The smell of shit and bile was thick around this one. Despite her disgust, Imogen wanted him to hold her, to wrap his needle-marked arm around her and tell her it was all going to be okay.

On she went, until she found a pile of fabric—stained and rotted blankets, sleeping bags, and abandoned jackets. Sifting through, she laid her hands on a long green coat with minimal stains and most of its buttons. She tugged on it, but it would not come free from beneath the mass of discarded clothes, so Imogen toppled the pile to unveil her prize.

She uncovered the coat, but also its owner.

Do the dead still own their clothing? I don't want to be a thief.

And dead he was. Creatures had made a meal of his eyeballs, leaving crusted empty sockets in their place. Imogen grabbed a nearby metal pole and lifted the jacket open and the stench nearly knocked her off her feet. This one had been dead a while. Resident rodents and insects had consumed great chunks of meat from his arms, abdomen, and thighs, and what was left was no more than saggy jelly. One diner remained—a bloated rat, lazily gnawing on a gangrenous testicle. It was loud, so loud, that squelching and gnawing coming from that rat as its chompers pierced the skin, tearing and churning and gulping. It groaned, too full to keep eating but too intoxicated by the indulgent meat to cease its feast.

Imogen lifted the metal bar to shoo it away, and the rat winced, looking up at her with sad eyes.

"I won't hurtcha," Imogen said. "I jus' need ya to move so I can take his coat." She motioned to her bare body. "To cover m'self."

The rat moved to the side. That small gesture of kindness gave Imogen the strength to wrestle the corpse onto its stomach so she could retrieve her prize. After slipping the jacket over her shoulders, she took the time to turn the body over for her new friend.

"There ya go, little buddy. Bon appetite."

With a new confidence, Imogen scrambled up the overpass onto the road and set off towards the asylum. The night was quiet, but there were still vehicles about, people coming and going from their tidy, beautiful lives. Her confidence deflated, a balloon pricked by all the eyes upon her, judging her hair, her face, the manky coat hanging from her bones. Imogen focused on her feet, trying to straighten up, to walk like a normal person, but the aches whispered to her, pulling her into a hunch. She would need a hit soon, because with the aches came lucidity, and with lucidity came . . .

Mere blocks from the asylum, Imogen was forced to a halt by a red hand warning her to stop. She would have kept going if it wasn't for the traffic, spaced just enough apart that there wasn't time for her to dash across. She looked up, into the windows of passing vehicles.

So many eyes were watching her. Hollow, black sockets, some red and bloody, others writhing with worms and millipedes. Imogen wanted to look away, to unsee what had been seen, but her attention was drawn to each and every car, their occupants similar and equally horrifying.

They were all women, long hair draped over naked shoulders, mouths contorted in silent screams. And in those mouths were rows of sharpened teeth dripping with gristle, rotten and black as the lips that framed them. One woman had only half a face, with a shattered cheekbone protruding from her vacant eye socket. There were dozens of cars, each stopped in the intersection and surrounding roads, all faces turned in her direction with maws wide open.

Imogen ran against the red light—all the traffic was stopped, anyway—weaving between vehicles. Heads creaked, gazes following as she passed. Sound crawled from those cars, following her as she ran, ticking behind her like skeletal fingers on a typewriter. Cars were motionless all down the road, piloted by the same blank stares and gaping mouths, long hair shrouding naked bodies. And that littering of sound got louder, closer, chasing her until she rounded the corner where the asylum lay in wait. There, the sound stopped. Imogen proceeded slowly, glancing over her shoulder, but nothing followed her.

The entrance to the asylum was about forty metres away, and there were no lights on this street, but Imogen could make out the figure just the same. A woman, tall—unnaturally so, a good three metres. She was pale and wearing a wispy ivory gown, a beacon in the night, fluorescent against the dark ivy climbing the brick wall of the asylum. Her nails were long like claws, gleaming in the moonlight, as were her eyes, though Imogen knew if she were closer, she would find only empty sockets. Her mouth was closed, a tight black line slashed across a white canvas.

There was nowhere to go. Back towards the line of cars and an entire horde of these things, or forward and sneak past only one. The woman standing there seemed to take no notice of Imogen; her head was facing the lot across the street.

Imogen continued, her boots hitting the pavement as softly as she could manage. She hugged the wall, trying to stay out of the line of sight. The closer she got, the more details she saw. Scraggly black hair, sagging, translucent skin, and yes, hollow sockets like endless night. Imogen inched forward, watching for any sign that she might have been noticed, but the woman was a statue. Thankfully, the woman was on the other side of the door, so Imogen didn't have to cross in front of her.

Now just a few metres away, Imogen held her breath, focusing on the entrance maintained by that crumpled leather boot. She'd almost reached it when the smallest of sounds caught her attention. A bubbling, like boiling water. Imogen dared look up, and her chest seized in fear. The woman's head had turned to face Imogen, and her mouth was open, her unhinged jaw hanging on stretched skin in front of her throat. That gurgle was coming from that cavernous throat, a sound lodged somewhere deep down in that horrible belly.

Imogen took another step. The woman didn't move, but a symphony of gentle noise rained down from above. Imogen craned her neck to look skyward. A whole line of ghoulish women was perched atop the asylum, poised on their haunches like gargoyles, hair streaming down the brick wall and braiding itself in the ivy. There wasn't much movement, save the breeze tousling their hair, and their bellies clenched with the minute sounds coming from within. Chatters and coos spilled from their mouths to Imogen's ears, musical but threatening. Hitchcock's *The Birds* came to mind as she crept forward, wrapping her hand over the door jamb and slipping inside.

Once both feet were on the tile floor inside, Imogen exploded into a run, sprinting down the hall and up the stairs, determined to reach Cait's room and buy a hit to murder these hallucinations.

Please be there, Cait.

But when she reached Cait's hallway, Imogen stopped dead. The tall woman was there, standing in front of Cait's door, a black grin tearing her face from ear to ear.

Both Imogen and the woman were still for a moment, then the woman held her belly, her fingers sinking into the soft marshmallow of her flesh. Brays of wet laughter belched from her throat, loud enough to rattle dust from the gyprock and stipple from the ceiling. Imogen wanted to run, but the noise was debilitating, driving her to the ground where she curled into a ball and covered her ears.

In a blink, the woman had crouched over Imogen, rolled her on her back, and pressed her shoulders to the floor. Her dangling breasts brushed Imogen's cheek as she laughed. She drove one of those elongated, taloned fingers into Imogen's panties and drew out the 20 euro note.

"No," Imogen said through a breathless sob. "I need that."

The woman laughed deeper, harder, as she crumpled the note and tossed it in her mouth like popcorn, gnashing it with blood-covered teeth and swallowing it with a great gulp.

Imogen screamed, wishing the woman would eat her heart as well.

10

Ma stirred the tea, the sharp clinking of the spoon against the ceramic owl mug stabbing Saoirse's mind. Why she was so on edge, she couldn't say, but every little sound stabbed at her like a woodpecker.

"How was she?" Ma asked as she squeezed a drop of honey first into Saoirse's cup, then her own. "I mean, other than a bleedin' mess."

"Well, she be Imogen."

Ma stirred her tea again.

"Ma, that's plenty mixed. Out with whatever ya needs to say."

One more stir. "Saoirse, the time for doin' nothing has come to an end. We got ta help her."

This conversation was not unexpected, but still Saoirse felt like it rushed up on her, leaping like a werewolf. "Ay. Yeah, it's high time."

"It won't be easy."

"I know."

"Ugly, in fact."

"I'm plenty prepared."

"It's gonna hurt all of us, but we'll come out better on the other side."

"Like *The Exorcist*. We's gonna get covered in green vomit, but we'll come out squeaky clean in the end."

Ma's eyes were stern, scolding. "With none of us broken at the end of a staircase."

Never suggest harm to a cub in front of the mama bear. "So, what are ya thinking?"

Ma answered straight away. She'd obviously been thinking plenty. "Rehab, of course. We aren't equipped or knowledgeable enough to handle this ourselves."

"Steep price."

"No mind. Finn left us well off, and what would put a bigger smile across his face than to use that money for somethin' so important. 'Sides, without health, there's nothin' that money's good for."

"She'll resist."

"No good for her to. Choices are gone until she can make better ones."

Saoirse nodded in agreement but scrunched her brow in worry. "She'll be mad."

"Sure will. Mad's better than dead, or even what she is now. And mad fades."

Ma's mind was made up. It showed in her face and in the certainty of her plan; she had taken a while to come to this point. But she looked tired, both in body and soul. Her eyes were a little darker, her hair a tad unkempt. As she lifted the tea to her lips, Saoirse noted the definition of her wrist bones beneath dwindling fat.

"You okay, Ma?"

"My daughter's sick. Makes me sick too."

"'Tis not your fault."

"Sure as hell know that, but I did miss somethin' along the way. Where did she go wrong, Saoirse?"

A good question indeed. Saoirse thought back to the time after Dadaí's death. There was grief—tears, yelling, outbursts. All normal, healthy stuff. But after that, it got darker, quieter. Imogen had withdrawn, her energy withered away. She seemed to just be living each day to have it end.

"Is it mental illness, Saoirse? She seems disjointed. Disconnected, somehow. You two are close. What have you seen?"

"We were close, Ma. But she's pulled away."

"You are still close, even if she's not all there."

"Yeah."

Avoidance. That's what it seemed like to Saoirse. Imogen had withdrawn, hiding in dark corners of her mind, lost in thought, eyes on empty corners and blank spaces.

Ma spoke, the tremble in her voice conveying her guilt. "Where did I go wrong?"

At ten, Imogen was a thief.

Saoirse stood in the corner of the living room, watching Imogen squirm as Ma stood over her, arms folded over her chest.

"What were ye thinkin'?" *Ma said, firm but not angry.* "Ye aren't a bad one, Imogen. What made ye do this? Yer friends put ya up to this?"

She ain't got friends, Ma.

With her hair over her face, hiding her shame, Imogen would not look at Ma.

"No one put me up to it, Ma." Imogen's meek tone was not that of a snotty teenager.

Rebellious, no. Scared, yes.

"What drove ye to it, then?"

Imogen's eyes were fixed on the package in Ma's hand—a set of hundred-dollar, noise cancelling headphones. "I jus' wanted 'em is all."

"I don't get it." Ma held up the package, examining it. "Ye never stole so much as a single goodie when you didn't know better, and now that you do, you take something the likes of this."

"You'd have never got them for me," Imogen argued.

"Dare say I wouldn't! You know how expensive these are?"

Imogen nodded, more hair cascading over her face. "They're the best."

"And why you be needin' the best?" Ma knelt next to Imogen's chair and put a hand on her bouncing leg. "Imogen, talk to me. What's goin' on? I'd have got ye headphones. These are a wee bit excessive, but we coulda found something good—"

"Not good enough!" Imogen's screech filled the room like shattering glass. Ma winced and stood, backing a step away as if Imogen was a bomb. Imogen's hands went to her ears, tears streaming down her face. "Please. May I keep them?"

Ma looked at the stolen swag in her hand, then back at her distraught daughter. "No, ye may not. We do not steal. I will find you another solution once I understand the problem."

With her fists curled into balls, Imogen flew up from the chair. "Never mind," she said as she stormed off to her room and slammed the door.

"Sweet thunderin' Jesus," Ma said as she tossed the headphones on the table. "Where did I go wrong?"

Saoirse scootched her chair beside Ma's and put an arm around her shoulder.

"Ye didn't go wrong, Ma."

The hallway was dark, beckoning Saoirse's thoughts and memories.

"There be somethin' plaguing Imogen, Ma. For a long time, methinks."

Ma sniffed, rubbing her eyes with the back of her hand. "Mental illness, then."

"Not so sure 'bout that." Saoirse's mind went down the hall, seeking her Ma's room and the memories within.

Ma slapped her hand down on the table, drawing Saoirse's attention back to the kitchen. "Well, no good gonna come from speculatin'. Let's get shit done. If it's mental illness, we'll find treatment. But we gotta slay the first beast before stormin' that castle. I'll find a rehab centre, and we'll make a plan."

"Sounds good." And it did, though Saoirse had a side quest in mind. "Ma, you mind if I grab somethin' from yer room while you make the calls?"

"'Course not. Whatever ya need. Jus' not me jewels or liquor."

Ma laughed, and a few tears leaked out of her eyes.

The best heart, Ma has. Saoirse watched Ma pour another cup of tea and sit down with her laptop, no doubt scrolling through to find the most comfortable, effective centre for Imogen to recover. No matter what, Ma was always on their side. Always had been, always would be. No fuck ups would ever change that.

"I love ye, Ma."

Ma looked up, her eyes great emerald pools of love and wisdom. "And I, ye."

Ma cursed at the tears dripping on her keyboard while

Saoirse set her tea aside and made for the bedroom. It was surreal, her footsteps pattering down the hall. She felt like a small child again, creeping into forbidden territory. By the time she had entered the master bedroom, she was wee again, sea birds flapping in her stomach as she crossed the threshold. The bookshelf loomed above all else, towering, almost leaning into her when she approached. She ran her finger across the dusty spines as she had many times as a girl. This time, she could reach the volumes on the top shelf, those filled with murder and mayhem, sex and drugs. She didn't have to use her eyes to find the book she was looking for. As her hand neared the tome, sound rose like a tremble, churning quakes from deep within brittle pages. The noise was deep, but soon it surfaced, a guttural growl moaning from unseen guts.

Tales from Ramnon. The book her Dadaí had read them oh so many times. The last time she'd held this book, a beast within had wailed at her, and she had slammed shut the cover, never to touch it again. Until now. She pulled the book off the shelf, and the sound fell silent.

The bed complained when Saoirse sat and opened the cover, flipping through pages until she reached the washer woman.

Banshee, the title read. *The wailing woman, forewarner and prophesier of death.*

As am I, so you shall be.

Flipping the page with sweaty fingers, Saoirse read about wretched, crooked hags and beautiful young waifs, the many manifestations of the fae spectres. She thought of the woman in the yard, washing clothes. The very wench from these pages, and the one stuck like a spider in the corner of the bathroom.

The night of Ma's miscarriage had been the last sighting Saoirse had, though every so often, a sound would niggle at her brain—the uneven ticking of a clock, a melodic dripping of a faucet, a voice braided in the song of insects or the birds.

Tales from Ramnon contained a fictional account of banshees living in Ramnon, a land where all things unbelievable end up. Saoirse flipped another page to gorgeous artwork. An aerial depiction of a town, ancient and rustic, built of weathered wood and golden dust. She ran her fingers over the page, lingering over a black lake rippling, dancing the light from a red moon. When she pulled her hand away, liquid dripped on the page, fat, thick droplets that landed with heavy plops.

"What the fuck?"

It couldn't be, but it was. She tilted the book, and the golden sand sloughed off like glitter, falling to her feet and coagulating with the thick mucus of the lake.

And somewhere in the distance, a voice keened in polyphonic overtones, riffling the pages with each rise and fall in pitch.

"Nah. Nope." Saoirse slammed the cover closed. "Not doin' this right now."

Tucking the book under her arm, very much the way Dadaí had on that last night, she marched out of the bedroom, leaving the mess of Ramnon behind. When she stole a final glance through the door before returning to Ma, it was as she suspected —a clean floor, no sign of sand or squelches of blood lake.

"Find what you need?" Ma asked when Saoirse appeared in the kitchen.

"Did you make the calls?"

Ma paused, looking at the book held tight to Saoirse's side. "Aye. We have an interview there in two days' time. Can ye join me?"

"Of course." Saoirse slid the book into her bag, then washed her hands at the sink. "You gonna be okay, Ma? 'Til then?"

"Oh hell, child. Don't worry 'bout me. I'll keep on until I don't. But I worry for not just Imogen. What will you do, Saoirse?"

"I'll worry, too. But I got ta look into somethin'." Ma raised a brow, one hand finding her hip. *Ah shit, if that other hand lands on the other hip, Ma's gonna put me in my place.* "Nothing extra ta fret over. Just a bit o' research is all. See if I can get ta the bottom o' what's brewing in Imogen's brain."

Ma's eyes flitted to the floor where Saoirse had laid her bag. When she looked up, those greens were dark and damp. "Saoirse?"

There's something. What is it? What do you know? "Yes, Ma?"

Ma pressed her tongue against her upper teeth, something she did when she was trying to form careful words for little girls. Saoirse waited, but nothing was said. Ma hugged her, wished her well, then gathered her tools for gardening. As she puttered around, she sang a lullaby Saoirse had heard many times as a child.

"*Over in Killarney,*
Many years ago,
Me mither sang a song to me
In tones so sweet and low..."

There's something yer not sayin, Ma. Something I've been missin' all along...

11

When Imogen woke, the walls were closing in on her, the confined space threatening to compress her until her organs burst and squeezed out every orifice in her body in a bloody sludge. Once she gained some composure, she realized she was in her room. In her bed. The walls were not closing in on her. After spending most of her sleeping hours in the common room with high ceilings and wide-open space, her room swallowed her like a dungeon.

Hands jittering, body aching, she rolled off the mattress and shed the coarse woolen blanket to the floor as she stood. Cold air fondled her nakedness, hardening her nipples and stiffening the thin hair on her arms and torso.

How did I get here?

Memories of the beastly, laughing woman wafted over her flesh, silent air caressing her skin like breath.

Did I ... Imogen looked for her clothing. *Where's my money?*

Chewing, slobbering.

She ate it.

Imogen hadn't gotten her hit. She wondered what time it was, how long she'd been asleep. Surprised she had slept at all, she wondered if perhaps she had scored a dose or two and dreamed the whole thing.

You know you didn't, stupid girl.

A quick inventory of the room told Imogen nothing. Her newly acquired green coat was there, balled up in the corner. Her boots were set by the door, and the bed made with old bedclothes. It was as if someone had undressed her and tucked her in.

Imogen slipped the coat over her shoulders, pulled the door open, and stepped into the hall. Whether it was still night, or night again, she couldn't be sure. Perhaps she had slept a day away, or had been asleep only five minutes, but darkness lingered in the halls, barely disturbed by weak lights from the windows on each end of the hallway. Without electricity or a torch, she had only shadowy shapes and weak recall to guide her to the stairwell leading to the main floor. Before she could open the door, music ignited behind her, a lullaby at the opposite end of the ward.

She started moving toward the sound. It terrified her, but experience told her that if she went the other way, the sound would follow, become both persuasive then aggressive until she acknowledged it.

I need a hit.

Imogen knew what would happen. She'd round the corner, go to the other end of the hall, and up the stairs to the third floor where a touch of the handle would mute the music. She'd been down this road many times before. Perhaps it was because every other time, she'd been incoherently high, but this time, it was different. The sound was different—clear, close, intimate.

The adjacent hallway was not empty. At the end of the hall stood a woman, naked, save a tattered rabbit mask over her face. Her hair coiled in tendrils down her pale body, reaching her fingertips, where she twirled it. There was a white cardboard box at her feet, long and narrow, crisp and clean against the yellowed filth of the asylum decor.

The sound was coming from this woman; her belly flexed and shuddered with each note, a hum speckled with giggles. Her breast rose and fell as she breathed and hummed, hummed and breathed, a rhythmic dance.

Imogen couldn't help herself. She didn't want to. She walked to the woman, intrigue outweighing fear, until they stood a metre apart, separated only by the box on the floor. The woman cocked her head, her face tilted towards it. Imogen tried hard to see behind the mask, to look into the eyes of the songstress, but there was only black.

The mysterious woman was gorgeous, ethereal. Her song, seductive. Imogen's attention shifted from the eyeholes of the mask to the woman's breasts, and lower to the bare, velvety split between her legs.

Sensing she was being examined, the woman stood straight, her lullaby echoing louder through the hall as she pointed at the box. Imogen knelt until her fingers found the cardboard. She fumbled with the flaps, picking at them with her nails until the tape peeled away. Imogen gasped when she opened the lid.

It was a dress, emerald green, detailed with opalescent beads and embroidered leaves of silver and gold. Imogen lifted the dress as she stood, unveiling shimmering fabric that billowed down like a waterfall, the silk resting atop Imogen's feet. In sharp contrast to Imogen's borrowed coat, the dress smelled like utopia—fragrant lily of the valley and creamy spice. Imogen brought it to her face, breathing in the beauty, tasting it. When she lowered the dress, the woman was still there, observing her every move.

Imogen spoke, unsure if she would get an answer. Unsure if any of it was real. "What is this?"

The woman motioned a hand over Imogen's body, then pointed at the dress.

"For me? But why? What for?"

The woman pointed to the ceiling.

Imogen scrunched her brow to communicate her confusion. The woman reached out, causing Imogen to jump, but her hand didn't touch Imogen, only the dress. With great care, the woman settled the dress back in the box, pushed it aside with her foot, then took a step forward. Fear clenched Imogen's throat, but the sensation loosened into something else as the woman tucked her hands into Imogen's borrowed jacket and slid it off her shoulders.

Imogen felt no shame in standing exposed in the middle of the hall. Her body responded with want as the woman bent to retrieve the dress, her hair brushing Imogen's thighs. The woman grazed her fingers between Imogen's legs as she stood. Imogen leaned in, wanting more, but the woman lifted the dress and dropped it over Imogen's head. The fabric slid over Imogen's body like liquid.

"This feels ..." She couldn't finish the sentence. Right? Perfect? Blissful? All of it. But something troubled her, clouding the pleasure of the experience.

"What is all this? And who are you?"

The masked woman giggled, a wet, gargling sound, before

the humming started again. She turned and walked away from Imogen, towards the stairwell. When Imogen didn't follow, the woman looked over her shoulder and held out her hand.

I must be high.

Imogen placed her hand in the woman's and allowed herself to be led up the stairs.

This is a terrible idea.

Once they reached the door to the third floor, the woman stopped and motioned for Imogen to enter.

Imogen put her hand on the steel handle, and sound exploded down the stairwell. Chitters, ticks, growls, the flapping of wings. The clinking of glasses and the braying of raucous song.

Imogen pushed the door open and, hand in hand with the masked woman, walked inside.

12

The library was bustling with activity. Saoirse wasn't surprised—it was the middle of the week, and the public library was quite close to the university's north campus, with its hoity toity English programs and flaky philosophy paths. The people bothered her, though she wasn't sure why. It's not like it was overcrowded; there were plenty of empty seats, and it was relatively quiet, even with the flipping of pages and scribbling of notes. But Saoirse felt like what she was doing was scandalous, dangerous. Insane, even.

Banshees. Plenty of them in pop culture, but vague and inconsistent. Saoirse wanted the actual scoop on these things, the tales of folklore passed down by crones rocking by fires, smoking, and drinking whiskey and cackling.

But it's all naff. Stupid bullshite, it is. No more real than Mr. Krueger with his burnt face and blade claws.

Regardless, Saoirse's mind wouldn't let it alone until she'd researched it, dug a little deeper into the mythology that lingered as background noise in her life.

The librarian had directed her to the history section, back to Irish beliefs and mythologies. Saoirse was pleased to find such rich folklore in her culture, well beyond leprechauns and shamrocks. There were a great many creatures that roamed fables of the emerald isle, including Sluagh, the Pooka, the Merrow, and, of course, the banshee.

After selecting an armful of heavy volumes, Saoirse found a seat in the corner and got to work flipping pages. As she'd understood from childhood ghost stories, banshees were scary old women screeching on rooftops, scaring children half to death. But as it turned out, there were many manifestations of the banshee, some specific to regions, some variations of the same iteration.

There was the old hag on the rooftop, as Saoirse remembered as a child. But also, there was a youthful version, beautiful and sensual, hair cascading over eaves as she keened into the night. Then there were the more ominous versions, women screaming in the woods, clawing their faces off as they experienced premonitions of death. Some were beautiful, some were ugly; all existed as a warning or precursor to death.

Saoirse licked her finger and flipped the page. The image that waited there grabbed her by the throat, her long-repressed childhood fear rearing its head. It was artwork of a woman, bent and contorted, washing bloody clothes in a basin in the middle of a field. Not just any field. The field where Saoirse had spent her childhood, frolicking through the long grass and hollering out over the cliffs.

"It can't be."

Saoirse's exclamation was answered by a chorus of shushes

from the surrounding library tables. She glared up at the other patrons. "Dinnah take much to piss you off, ye snoopers."

Another shush, and a couple of tsks. Saoirse shook her head and looked back at the page. The washer woman was still there, but now she was standing, a soiled shirt clenched in her claws, blood and ichor dripping onto the dirt and splashing over her bare feet.

"Great," Saoirse said, ignoring the shushes, then read out loud to herself in a cautious whisper. "The *Bean-nighe*, or laundress, a creature who appears at bodies of water, washing the clothes of those who are about to die. Though the Scots claim the folklore, she appears in Irish mythology, as well as others. The French call her *Les Lavandieres*, and the English know her as little washer of sorrow."

Another shush. Saoirse didn't look up, just flipped the bird in the direction of the scolder.

Saoirse shifted her attention from the black print to the art again, looking into the banshee's eyes. "Ye was washin' me Dadaí's shirt, wasn't you, ye wench?"

The art on the page flickered, the Banshee's black slit of a mouth curling into a smile. Saoirse did not look away this time, nor did she slam the cover as her panic demanded she do. Instead, she maintained eye contact as the banshee walked towards her, that wet shirt slapping against her thigh, soaking her sheer nightdress so it clung to her body. When the banshee's head filled the page and her nose pressed against the parchment as if it were glass, her mouth opened, freeing her sound. Coos, gurgles, and quiet cackles came from the wide black expanse of her maw, which widened further and further until the entire page was black. The sound inhaled, as if the entire library had drawn a breath deep into the book at Saoirse's fingertips.

Saoirse slammed the cover closed. "I ain't gonna hear no wailin' from you today, ya crazed lass.'

Silence. The fine hairs on Saoirse's body rose to attention at the absence of sound. She had spoken aloud, and no one had shushed her. Not a single cluck of a tongue or an irate complaint. Saoirse raised her head and peered around the room.

"Ah fuck."

The library was still full of patrons, but not the same patrons as when Saoirse had taken her seat. They were all women, some naked, some dressed in tattered gowns. They all had long hair, blonde or red or black, cascading over bent, contorted bodies. Their eyes were solid black, spilling crimson tears onto table-tops, notepads, and book covers. The drips splashed and spread across the surfaces, leaving everything coated in a slick, red sludge.

All heads were turned in Saoirse's direction. Every mouth was closed—thin, jagged black lines sliced across pale faces.

Saoirse stood, quietly, so as not to disturb this horde and ruffle them from their perches like timid sparrows. Tiptoeing around chairs and tables, Saoirse kept her eyes focused on the exit, ignoring heads turning as she passed. She had almost reached her goal when jaws started snapping open with audible clacks. Then she couldn't help but look back over her shoulder.

The banshees were all on their feet, lower jaws swinging loose, mouths open wide. Saoirse braced herself, but jumped and screamed, regardless. They all wailed at once, an unearthly bellow that shook the dust off the books on the upper shelves. They wailed and howled, growling and singing and crying until Saoirse thought her head might explode.

But there was another sound. A tinkling, like ice in a glass.

My phone.

The wailing stopped.

They'd gone silent. Saoirse opened her eyes. The banshees were gone. Saoirse was now looking into the faces of a room full of library customers, as they should be, normal people sitting and reading at tables or scanning the aisles for books.

The librarian approached Saoirse and touched her arm. "Listen, Mum, ye need to silence yer ringer, if you'd be so kind."

"How's that kind?" Saoirse snapped. "Listen, I'm goin', all right?"

The librarian's mouth was a tight pucker, no doubt from reaching the threshold of her tolerance for Saoirse's noise.

"Look, I'm sorry—"

The phone rang again. The librarian's ears turned red, so Saoirse offered a sheepish shrug, then walked out the door before the woman could release a wailing scold of her own.

Saoirse lifted the phone to her ear. "Hello?"

People passed Saoirse on the sidewalk, stepping around her as she listened to the voice on the other end of the line, her stomach gurgling and her muscles turning to jelly. She braced herself on the brick wall to keep herself from crumbling to the ground as black spots floated over her vision.

"Yes. Yes, I heard ya. I'll be there straight away."

Saoirse dropped the phone in her purse and sprinted for her car.

13

When they stepped through the door to the mysterious third floor of the asylum, Imogen's feet thudded on planks of weathered wood dusted with golden sand. It was a bar, no, a *saloon*, dark wood from ceiling to floor and antique chandeliers adorned with drooling red candles hanging from the ceiling. There were tables scattered around the room, and a bar along one wall tended by a portly woman in a dusty lavender corset. The patrons were all female, old and young, dressed in flowing sheer clothes that exposed their long, contorted frames. A player piano in the corner tinkled out a distorted version of the lullaby the woman had been singing, but here, it was jovial and upbeat, a jigging tune.

The woman sauntered forward, blocking Imogen's view of the saloon. She had changed. Now she was wearing a silver dress made of fringe and gossamer that shimmied with her every movement. Her mask was no longer that broken one-eared rabbit, but feathers and lace, framing her deep brown eyes. And she'd found more than just her clothing. She'd also found her voice.

"*Aisling*," she said, touching her chest.

The sound was all wrong. Muffled. Imogen thought of how the world used to sound when she was young, submerged in the bathtub. All the sounds in the saloon were like that—the conversations, the shuffling of chairs across the wooden floor. Dampened, traveling to Imogen's ears as if through thick ocean.

"Sounds are funny, eh?"

This voice was crystal clear. It was the barkeep, who had set a whiskey glass on the counter and filled it with a yellow liquid the consistency and colour of mustard. Aisling picked up the drink, gave the barkeep a wink, and flitted off to join a gaggle of women huddled in the corner.

"Don't mind them," the barkeep said. "They only get together once in a harvest moon, so I can't much blame them for breakin' loose. 'Sides, there's much worse walks through my doors."

As if in acknowledgement, the saloon doors swung open, and a pair of old women came in, their ghastly white faces blotted with rouge and gloss. Before they reached the bar, the barkeep had two martini glasses set out, full to the brim with viscous red fluid. They drank greedily as Imogen gawked, congealed red dribbling from the sides of their wrinkled mouths.

"Listen 'ere, ye old hags, bugger off," the barkeep scolded. "Yer makin' a right mess o' me bar!"

One of the crones gurgled something under her breath, then punctuated that thought with an articulated 'fuck'. The other tapped her glass for a refill, then turned to Imogen and smiled, revealing blood-coated teeth and a pus-riddled tongue. She spoke, but Imogen couldn't make out the words.

"Naw," the barkeep said, waving her hand at the decrepit pair. "Imogen can't understand ya yet."

They looked at Imogen as if observing an animal in a zoo—amazed, examining her up and down. Self-conscious, Imogen fiddled with the beading on her dress, remembering the luxury that covered her flesh. The rise and fall of voices behind her drew her attention. More woman gathered, pointing at her, squawking their noises as they poked at Imogen, pushing sharp nails into her arms and sproinging the curls of her hair.

"Be gone, ye skags!" the barkeep yelled, and the women scattered like pigeons, cooing and bobbing to their respective tables and corners. That's when Imogen noticed it—the red iron embellishments on the wood fixtures, the ornate bar carved with totems of Sluagh and wendigo, selkies and vandheks.

"Where . . . where am I?"

Imogen had heard the description of this place many, many times.

A smirk curled at the corner of the barkeep's mouth, exposing a wide grin interrupted by a single golden tooth.

Imogen asked, unbelieving. "Mauve?"

The barkeep curtsied and mimed a tip of an invisible hat. "Ay, nice to meet ye, young Imogen."

It can't be.

Seemingly reading her thoughts, Mauve said, "Oh, it can be. And it is."

The dings in the floor from hooves, the scrapes on the ceiling from claws, the decanters on shelves behind the bar filled with red fluid, enough to feed entire flocks of vampyres and pods of chupacabra.

Imogen's voice sounded oh so far away as she spoke, removed from her body, lingering somewhere in a reality that was no longer hers. "Ramnon."

"Welcome, dear lass."

Impossible.

"Am I dead?"

Mauve smiled.

Imogen remembered fondly all the nights Dadaí sat in their room at dusk reading stories from *Tales of Ramnon*, each one detailing a unique folklore and fantastical creature. Though all beasts were different, and they hailed from other places and times, their paths came together in this little village removed from everything. Ramnon had no place, no time—it just was. A land of beautiful horrors.

Humans could end up in Ramnon. Ghosts. Those possessed by demons. Tortured folks who had lived in hell so much they became beasts themselves.

"But if I'm not dead, then why am I here? What am I?"

Imogen touched her head, then her face.

Mauve laughed. "Looking for horns or wings, are ye? Ye ain't got none, m'love."

"Why am I here?" Imogen repeated, her voice rising with her anxiety.

"Perhaps you're not here."

The drugs.

None of this is real.

I'm not here.

Again, in answer to an unspoken question, Mauve spoke. "Not yet."

Imogen looked at the crowd. They were women, but not quite. They were too long, stretched out like taffy, their skin grey and pale but not sickly. Long hair swayed over gangly bodies, dark eyes and wide mouths dotting the landscape of faces like hellholes waiting to swallow her alive, digest her, and shit her to eternal decay.

"Yer Dadaí didn't read you this tale, eh?"

"Which one?"

Mauve leaned across the bar, her face hovering at Imogen's ear. When she spoke, her breath stank of hot meat and bourbon.

"They be banshees."

Twitters and shrieks erupted around the room, and the eavesdropping banshees shifted in their seats and from foot to foot. The music from the player piano increased in tempo, banging out a manic jig that brought everyone to their feet. The banshees wailed and clapped, stomping their feet and hooking arms to swing each other around in a frantic waltz. Masses of hair swirled around the room, a storm of tresses that caused the candles to flicker.

"They meet here at harvest moon for a grand ole banshee ball. A family reunion of sorts."

"Family?"

Though alike in their ghoulish, frail qualities, each woman was distinct. All hair colours, different shapes, old and young. Some had high cheekbones, others button noses. And the occasional scar or birthmark.

"Banshees come from many cultures, in many forms."

Mauve motioned to the window where a tall woman stood. She was naked from the waist up and headless, the severed meat of her throat dangling over her pale chest. In her arms she carried a porcelain bowl filled with blood that splashed onto her dress as she moved with the music. There were banshees with red eyes and silver hair, some with black hair and solid white eyes. Some carried wet clothes and laundry boards; others stroked their locks with silver combs.

"Though from different families, they all be the same creature."

Imogen watched a skeletal banshee by the window chewing the head off a crow, the bird's mewls reaching Imogen's ears like pinging sonar.

Imogen looked back at Mauve. There was something in the barkeep's eyes that had softened.

"Family?" Imogen asked.

"Ay. Inherited."

A disease.

"More like royalty."

The pair of old banshees laughed, a blood curling bellow that rocked the dust from the rafters and swung the chandeliers.

"That wail be in their blood."

The jig from the player piano tinkled to an end and a new song fired up, an old favourite of Dadaí's, "The Irish Washerwoman." Squeals of glee chirped from the crowd, and the dancing intensified, feet stomping and hands waving in the air. Imogen couldn't help but smile, remembering her own feet pounding their floor as Dadaí strummed his guitar and Ma stroked her fiddle.

"Go on, then," Mauve prompted. "Let yourself go."

Imogen floated onto the dance floor, the melody creeping into her bones. Aisling found her, greeting her with a firm kiss, parting Imogen's lips with her tongue and breathing sweet breath inside her. When they pulled apart, both were smiling. Aisling wrapped her arms around Imogen, and they danced, moving with the crowd. Imogen let her head fall as Aisling spun her around, feeling the caress of fingers over her hair, her face, and her dress. The music was louder, the song belting from every throat in the room, full of joy.

When I was at home, I was merry and frisky,
My dad kept a pig and my mother sold whisky,
My uncle was rich, but never would by aisey
Till I was enlisted by Corporal Casey.

A sharp tug on the bodice of her dress caused Imogen to open her eyes. Aisling had stopped spinning. She pressed her palms against the small of Imogen's back and pulled her in, pressing their bodies together. Her tongue traced Imogen's collarbone as her hand worked its way up, twirling Imogen's hair. Imogen tilted her head to the side, giving Aisling access to her neck.

Och! rub a dub, row de dow, Corporal Casey,
My dear little Shelah, I thought would run crazy,
When I trudged away with tough Corporal Casey.

Aisling's lips were moist, exploring Imogen's neck and jaw, working their way to her mouth. Before their lips pressed together, Aisling pulled away. Imogen opened her eyes as Aisling led her through the dancing, gyrating crowd. In the midst of the ghastly women were more earthly figures, red curls bouncing, pink cheeks flushed with ecstasy.

It was a handful of doppelgängers, versions of Imogen in various life stages, peppered amongst the banshees. There were at least half a dozen Imogens, dancing and squealing with glee. One wore a crisp business suit and a ruby smile. Another few steps, and there was an older version of herself, crow's feet sketching a story of experience around her twinkling eyes. One was holding hands with a beautiful brunette, another in a graduation gown and cap. A lifetime of Imogens.

One Imogen approached, a bouquet of black roses in her

hands. The real Imogen leaned down and smelled the flowers, the sweet aroma a reminder of Ma's garden. As she exhaled, the player piano slowed into a dissonant mess, wrong notes stabbing out into the saloon. The banshees were no longer singing and laughing, but sobbing and squalling, their faces contorted in pain. Behind the black roses in front of Imogen's face, a crimson stain bloomed across the Imogen's abdomen. All the Imogens had a similar patch of blood pouring from their bodies and gushing to the floor.

"No!" Imogen grabbed her side, damming the flow of her own blood. "Help me!"

The Imogen with the roses smiled, and blood poured from her mouth, gargling out with gags and belches. She clenched her fists, snapping the rose stems with a sound like broken bones. As the petals floated to the floor, she took the thorny remnants and dragged them across her corneas, splitting her eyes and releasing a flow of golden sand. The gold poured to the floor from all the Imogens until they were piles of sand, leaving only the real one standing.

In a nearby distance, a door slammed. All heads in the room snapped toward Imogen, and everything fell silent. The banshees stared, mouths open, faces expressionless. They were all standing, stretching taller, looming over her. Imogen teetered on the edge of the anticipated blast of noise, but all that broke the silence was a solid voice—not muffled, not underwater. Clear and direct.

"Imogen."

Saoirse had Imogen by the shoulders, shaking her. Imogen looked back to the bar. But there was no bar, only a counter, abandoned medical equipment and crinkled files strewn over its dust-encrusted surface.

Ramnon was gone.

"Imogen, ye all right?"

"Yeah, I just ..." Imogen swirled her thumb over her fingertips, feeling the grit of Ramnon sand beneath her nails. "High, I guess."

"Would expect no different," Saoirse said, "but other than that?"

Imogen looked down. Her beautiful gown had been replaced by the rancid green coat.

"I'm fine," Imogen said, wrapping the coat tight around her body.

"Blech," Saoirse said, wrinkling her nose. "Ye ain't be wearing that to the hospital. Where's the clothes I bought ye?"

Imogen thought of the car, of the man inside her, the clothes torn and left in a pile in the mud.

"Never mind that," Saoirse said, waving a hand. "Not important. I got new ones in the car. No time to scrub ye up, though, but I got some wipes. Ye'll have to do the best you can on tha drive over—"

"Hospital?" Imogen said, the word finally registering.

This is it. They're committing me.

For the first time since Saoirse had shaken her, Imogen looked at her sister. Her face was pale, her eyes blood shot.

The pain in Saoirse voice was heavy, a swinging axe that imbedded in Imogen's heart. "M'love. 'Tis ma. She's had a stroke."

14

Saoirse was used to seeing her sister in an absolute and utter mess. She had seen Imogen in quite a state before, bloodied and reeking of God knows what from God knows where. But sitting in that hospital room with a background of crisp white bed clothes and pale green walls, Imogen looked like the right testicle of death. The haunting in her eyes was heavy, the pain on her face more defined. And it was impossible not to notice, as Imogen cleaned herself in the car on the way over, the bruises and blood marring the insides of her thighs.

Monitors beeped and machines whooshed, narrating a tale more horrific than any between the covers of *Tales of Ramnon*. The sterile, mechanical sounds of the hospital told the end chapter of Ma's life, the final dandelion seed clinging on in an autumn breeze.

"Girls." Ma's voice was smooth silk, gently floating away.

Both sisters jumped to their feet, each taking a place on either side of Ma's hospital bed.

Saoirse spoke, knowing Imogen couldn't, but she could not hide her emotions. "We're here, Ma." Her voice wavered, and she gulped down a sob.

"Where's Finn? We're supposed to catch the ferry at noon."

Though Ma's eyes were open, searching the room, she saw nothing. The stroke had taken her vision, and most of her mind. Now her organs were playing their final tune, coming to that final fermata with no hope of an encore.

"Finn's waiting for you, Ma. We'll get ya there safe and sound."

Imogen sniffled and stroked the side of Ma's face. "Ma, I'm so sorry."

"No sorries," Ma said.

"All the sorries," Imogen argued. "I just ... I couldn't handle it, Ma."

Saoirse had a powerful urge to reach across the bed and slap Imogen. Part of that, she realized, was the devastation of Ma slipping away. But she was angry at Imogen. Angry at her for not speaking up and asking for help before it got out of control. Angry for making Ma worry.

"Saoirse?" Ma's voice was waning, but lilting and peaceful. She brought a calm to the room, as she always did. "My trunk."

"Ma, we're at the hospital. Yer trunk is at home."

"No," Ma said, her head rolling back and forth. "My trunk, at the foot of the bed."

Imogen covered her face and stood, her body trembling as she ran from the room.

I's got bigger fish to fry at tha moment, little sister.

Ma turned her head to the sound of the shutting door. "Did

Imogen go? It's just in my bedroom, at the foot of the bed. I'll stay here and brew up a pot o' tea."

Saoirse held Ma's arm. She couldn't hold Ma's hands; they were wrapped in bandage mitts to prevent her from tearing out her IV tubes and messing with the monitors. "Okay, Ma. I'll go fetch it."

"Yer Dadaí meant for ye to have it. To understand once you were old enough. Suppose you should have had it sooner."

"It's okay, Ma. You didn't know …"

That he'd be dead so soon. And now you, too.

"Saoirse, come to me." Ma's voice was so small. Saoirse leaned in until Ma's warm breath dampened her cheek. Her mitted hand came up and tapped Saoirse's chest. "Fuil Olagón."

Ma grimaced, her eyes twitching. The beeps of the heart rate monitor intensified, a rapid staccato, and her limbs went stiff as she convulsed on the bed. Saoirse froze until she saw froth at the corners of Ma's mouth, then she launched into action, slamming her fist on the call button.

"Imogen!" Saoirse wailed, not knowing or caring if her sister could hear.

The next moments were a flurry of activity, doctors and nurses flooding the room. Imogen came, her shoulders heaving with sobs at the sight of Ma. Saoirse held Imogen as they stood to the side, watching all sorts of interventions meant to prolong Ma's life another few minutes, at most.

But in that panicked bustle of purpose, a quiet calm shrouded Saoirse; the movement slowed, the lights rose to a near-blinding glow, washing the room in white. Ma remained in full technicolor, her auburn hair coiled around her face, her golden-brown eyes gleaming. The seizure had stopped, and Ma was quiet. Still but not gone. Her chest rose and fell, her breath one of the only sounds Saoirse could hear, despite the activity in the room. The other sound was coming from the doorway.

A banshee, tall and naked, hunched beneath the door frame so she did not strike her head as she entered the room. Her long black hair shimmied and rustled against her body as she sang, her voice coarse and smoky.

Too-ra-loo-ra-loo-ral,
Too-ra-loo-ra-li,
Too-ra-loo-ra-loo-ral,
Hush, now don't you cry . . .

It was a song Dadaí had sung to them every night as they cuddled under their covers. He'd sing and play his guitar, his voice sweet and low. This stretched woman who now hovered above Ma's bed had a glint of Dadaí's dulcet tones in her pitch.

Too-ra-loo-ra-loo-ral,
Too-ra-loo-ra-li,
Too-ra-loo-ra-loo-ral,
That's an Irish lullaby.

No one else seemed to hear the song or see the woman lingering above the precipice of death. Imogen seemed oblivious, which struck Saoirse as odd.

Mayhaps she doesn't see them after all.

Or they be gentle on her, fragile as she is right now. She could snap like a twig at this.

Verse after verse the banshee sang as the staff fussed like worker bees over their queen. Once the verse was done, the woman inhaled, sucking every bit of air from the room. Silence, stillness, then that explosion of sound, bellowing from deep in the woman's gut. It blew the hair off Ma's and Saoirse's faces and rattled the medical instruments on the tray.

But nobody noticed. Nobody but Saoirse. The staff were

fixated on the monitor, which went from beeping to a solid whine, the final note in Ma's symphony.

Imogen struggled away from Saoirse's grasp, screaming and sobbing as she collapsed over Ma. The staff tried to pull her away, but Saoirse stopped them, shooing them until only family remained in the room.

Saoirse draped herself over Imogen and Ma and had a good cry, soaking the bedding and her little sister.

After a solid bathing of tears, the sisters sat up, holding hands and looking over their ma.

"She's grey, Saoirse."

"Ay. No blood flows."

"It's odd. She looks fake. Wax."

"So do ye."

Imogen glared at Saoirse. "Leave me alone."

"Nah." An anger rose in Saoirse, one so hot she dared not stop it or it would melt her insides. "This is it, Imogen. Yer wake-up call. Stop killin' yerself. Do Ma proud."

Imogen waved a hand over Ma. "Really? It's too fecking late, Saoirse."

Imogen collapsed on the bed again, her body trembling, wet, garbled apologies spilling from her lips. Saoirse took a slow breath to contain her sorrow, her rage and frustration, then rubbed her sister's back. Her gaze moved to the silent banshee in the corner, her black eyes wide and focused on Saoirse, her mouth a tight line.

"Come home with me, Imogen. To Ma's. At least for tonight."

Imogen didn't look up, but she nodded.

Saoirse sat on the bed and unraveled the bandages on Ma's hands. The girls each took a hand, squeezing as Saoirse sang.

"Over in Killarney,
Many years ago,
Me mither sang a song to me
In tones so sweet and low..."

The banshee swayed with the melody. She opened her mouth and growled out a dissonant, wordless harmony that tangled with Saoirse's voice.

"Just a simple little ditty,
In her good ould Irish way,
And I'd give the world if she could sing
That song to me this day."

15

The darkness of the car was a welcome relief from the intense lights of the hospital. Imogen was used to zero electricity, her path illuminated by sun or moon alone, so full immersion in a tank of fluorescent lighting was enough to drive her raving mad.

And that's how people had looked at her as Saoirse led her down the elevator, through the lobby, and past the emergency room where looky-loos gawked and judged. Imogen wanted to sprint, to race away from all those eyes, from Ma and her dead expression and yellow-grey flesh.

Once seated in the car, Imogen's panic settled, and she realized how quiet it was. It had been quiet in Ma's room. There'd been the rush of blue code—the whirring of equipment and medical professionals barking orders at each other—but it was as good as silence to Imogen.

No humming. No singing. No wailing.

Only the normal din of life.

"Are ye okay?" Saoirse asked, startling Imogen.

Before Imogen could answer, Saoirse waved a hand. "Fuck no, ye aren't. Course not."

They drove through the city, neither speaking until Our Lady's appeared over the rooftops.

"Ye need me to stop for anything?" Saoirse asked.

Imogen searched the dark windows. There were faces in each one, black mouths smeared across each.

"I've nothing," Imogen said.

"Ye have me."

The sisters held hands the rest of the way home. Imogen was grateful that Saoirse said nothing more. The white noise of the road was soothing, and the absence of all other sounds was something Imogen hadn't heard in years.

Once out of the city, light pollution faded like smoke, giving way to the purple twilight of the countryside. A handful of kilometres after that, Ma's house appeared on the cliffs, its amber porch light beckoning them home. Saoirse parked the car and killed the engine, but neither woman moved. They just sat, staring at the house. Imogen half expected Ma to pop out from the bushes or mosey out the front door with food and hugs.

"I cannot believe it," Imogen said.

"Nor I."

"Was she ill?"

Saoirse shrugged. "Suppose she was. She'd never tell us, though, for worry we'd fret."

That was true. Ma would have figured Imogen had plenty of her own to worry about and would not burden her further. Always the protector.

I'm a stupid, selfish girl.

"Come on, then," Saoirse said, unbuckling.

Imogen couldn't move. The fog of her life and choices had crawled into that car and rested on her chest, pressing her into the seat and forbidding her from moving—Dadaí's death, Ma's body, still fresh in her mind. The addiction, the sex, the pain, the toxic highs. All those years wasted, all the happiness she pushed away.

Her door opened and Saoirse reached in, unbuckled her, and pulled her out. "C'mon, now. No good lingerin' out here. I knows how you hate the night outside."

I do, Imogen realized, *but 'tis not the night. 'Tis what waits there, using the night as a blessing to unveil its horrors.*

Saoirse had the key in the door and one foot inside when Imogen stopped, her eyes coming to rest on the rocking chairs on the porch. Clicking. Gliding. Moving without a bit of wind. Saoirse turned to her with a scold in her eye, but immediately softened when she saw the chairs. They watched, mesmerized by the movement, the creaking of the wood strained by an impossible weight. When Saoirse broke her gaze, Imogen stole it, the sisters looking at each other for a pregnant moment before Saoirse spoke.

"Them wailin' bitches be in yer mind too, eh?"

❧

Fresh off the school bus, Imogen hadn't the energy for a *fight, but Saoirse was going for one, regardless.*

"*Them wailing bitches be in yer mind too,*" *Saoirse said accusingly.*

Imogen studied Saoirse's face, trying to decide if she was baiting her, or if she genuinely saw something as well.

"*I've no idea what yer on about,*" *Imogen said, furrowing her brow in anger. In defense.*

"Bollocks! I sees the way ye cower. The way ye jump when nothin's barking out to make ye do so."

"And jus' what might I be cowerin' from, ye know-it-all?"

Imogen wondered what was going on in her sister's mind as she took her sweet time formulating an answer.

"Some boogeyman, I suppose."

"I'm not crazy!" Imogen snapped.

"You acts it!"

"Well you tell me, all-knowing one, how I'm supposed to act." Imogen's red hot embarrassment had been poked with a stick, turning it to rage. "Ye understand nothing."

Saoirse's hands lowered from her hips, dangling in front of her, very much like Ma always stood when she worried. "D'ya see them?"

Imogen snapped back. "Do you?"

A standoff, neither girl uttering an admission, nor revealing an emotion that might tell a story. The whole story, and nothing but the truth. The words lingered in Imogen's throat, begging to be spoken, practically clawing at the back of her tongue with their talons. But there were other words there, too.

They'll think I'm weak.

Insane.

They'll lock me up.

A foolish girl.

Always the baby.

Imogen swallowed her admission, talons and all, and they dragged and scratched to the pit of her stomach to roil and fester. "No."

Saoirse shook her head, her eyes wet with tears. "All right, then."

Imogen stormed past her, into the house, and retreated to their bedroom where she slammed the door and hid under the covers, ignoring the clicking of teeth and warbling of voices from the rafters, the windows, and beneath the bed.

Would life have been different had Imogen made a different choice so many years ago? If she'd just admitted her fears and nonsense to her sister? Realization hit her like a hammer.

Saoirse was on her side. She'd always been on her side.

"Yeah." The word spilled from Imogen along with a lifetime of tears. "I see them. Hear them."

Saoirse gathered Imogen in her arms, holding her so she didn't crumple to the ground.

"Ay," Saoirse said. "They're with me, too. Not like you, I suppose, but we aren't tha same person."

"I've always been the weak one."

"Not weak. Sensitive. And I, the ole boot, tough and gritty. Neither of us a bad thing, we's just who we are."

Imogen sniffled and straightened, relieved by the weight lifted from her heart.

Saoirse smiled, large and genuine, and took her by the hand. "Come now. Let's discuss these skaggy wenches, shall we? Been a long time comin'."

16

Tea dribbled from pot to cup, the sound a trickling creek. Saoirse still felt Ma in everything she saw and touched and heard. That house was Ma, or truly, a beautiful duet of Ma and Dadaí, come together again.

"She had a good life," Saoirse said as she eyed the knick-knacks, the crocheted lilac dishtowels, the potted plants lining every surface. "Dadaí, too, for the time he had. Not a moment wasted."

Imogen stirred her tea, the clinking of the spoon musical to Saoirse's ears, a cutlery ballad heard many-a-time at this very kitchen table.

"You okay, little sister?"

Imogen cried.

Saoirse smiled. "That's good. Can't keep it in. Ma would feel slighted if ye didn't wet this table with yer tears after she passed."

Imogen set her cup on its saucer with trembling hands. "I didn't do right by Ma. Or Dadaí."

Saoirse reached across the table and took Imogen's hand. "You didn't do right by yerself."

"I'm sorry, Saoirse."

"Don't be sorry. Be doin' somethin'. And that first somethin' is to talk about these banshees."

"The what?"

Tales from Ramnon had been sitting on the coffee table, waiting for Imogen's eyes. Saoirse said nothing, just led her little sister to the couch, draped her in an afghan, and placed the book in her lap.

"Dadaí's book," Imogen said, her frail fingers tracing the gold-embossed words on the cover.

"Our book now." Saoirse sat beside Imogen and lifted the cover. Imogen gasped at the forbidden lands seen only through Dadaí's lips and never with her own eyes. Saoirse flipped to a bookmarked page, revealing the crooked banshee hunched over the washtub. Imogen reached to touch the page but drew her hand back when the banshee growled and snapped at her like a rabid dog.

"That her?" Saoirse asked.

Imogen shrugged. "Dunno. Maybe one of 'em. There are so many."

The woman's hair floated off the page, tendrils spiraling in the air, licking like black flame at the sisters' faces. Imogen recoiled, her face white and jaw slack. Saoirse put a hand on her back. Instead of pulling away, Imogen cuddled into Saoirse.

"Yeah, no worries, lass," Saoirse said, glaring at the page. "I see 'er too."

"'Tis movin.'"

"Yeah."

"Her hair …"

"Yep."

"Impossible."

"And yet, here it is. Possible."

Saoirse slammed the cover shut, drawing a muffled screech from within the pages. "Enough from you, wench! Shut yer gob!" The book grumbled a complaint, and Saoirse rapped it with her knuckles. "Ain't the first time she's danced fer me, that banshee. She up and walked at me from the page during Dadaí's wake. Screamed to fright' me, she did. Cunt."

"Dadaí's wake?" The look of shock on Imogen's face was like a slap across Saoirse's cheek.

I should have told her sooner. She was not the only one keepin' silent. She was only half the problem.

"Yeah, I shoulda tol' you sooner," Saoirse said. "It's just …"

"You didn't want anyone to think you were crazy."

"I don't give a fuck what anyone thinks. *I* didn't want to believe I was crazy."

"Are we, Saoirse? Crazy?"

"Oh, probably." Saoirse tapped the cover of the book and the pages inside growled. "But for both of us to see and hear them? Mayhaps not."

The sisters sipped their tea while murmurs tried to squeeze out from the pages of the book. Saoirse looked at Imogen, her protruding collarbone, scraggly hair hanging over her face. There was a fresh bruise on her cheek, and her nails were caked with dirt and fuck-knows-what.

"Is that what happened?" Saoirse kept her voice low, steady, like trying not to scare away a canary. "With the drugs?"

Imogen looked into her tea, perhaps to find an answer or a reason to deflect.

❧

Imogen had suffered a particularly rough morning, starting with the bus ride to school. Though the bus was half-empty and the country roads quiet, something banged on the windows the entire journey to the schoolhouse, and the brakes screamed Imogen's name. They were constant now, the voices from nowhere, the impossible sound effects that littered her life. It's hard enough navigating life as a teenaged girl without spectres speaking the tongue of mental illness in your head all day long.

Imogen tried hiding from the noise in the bathroom, the cafeteria, the common room, but quiet was nowhere to be found. Imogen slammed her locker as the bell rang. She'd been skulking around too long, looking for peace. There was no way she'd make it to class on time, which would result in her sixth tardy slip. She'd be sent to the office, and Ma would be called, which would end in a bevy of questions and fretful expressions. Ma was worried about her, she knew. Probably thought she was broken or crazy.

I'm not mad. But I'm not quite right either.

Clutching her books against her chest, Imogen raced on light feet down the hall and up the stairs, hoping to reach her classroom before the teacher could call attendance. And she would have, if it wasn't for the obstacle that placed itself directly in her way.

Placed herself in the way.

A woman in a hooded, white robe was hunched at the end of the empty hall in front of Imogen's classroom. She was combing her long, silver hair, which cascaded onto the floor in great puddles between her feet. Though she was back on, Imogen could tell she was old; her hands were mangled by age and arthritis, her skin waxy and translucent, revealing black veins throbbing beneath.

"Hello?"

When the woman turned her head in Imogen's direction, the sound of joints popping and bones creaking echoed through the hall. While turning, the woman stood up straight, and her robe fell to her shoulders, revealing the horror of her face.

The hag was a mass of wrinkles and peeling skin, with ichor and blood trickling out of her mouth and blossoming on the front of her crisp white robe where her nipples would be. Her eyes were solid red, and her teeth sharp and black, a stark contrast to the pale grey of her flesh. When she smiled, her skin gave way, her cheeks split with an audible squelch, releasing a dam of black blood that trailed to the floor like oily snakes.

When Imogen opened her mouth to scream, the woman opened hers too, and from the hag's mouth came a cough wet with death, a crimson mist that splattered through the air, speckling the lockers, the floor, and Imogen herself. The woman coughed and laughed, laughed and coughed, drenching the hallway in a slick red that tasted like vomit and stank of spoiled meat.

Imogen ran, skating on the fluids, slipping down the stairs. She turned back to look. The woman's arms were extended, flaps of flesh swinging from her biceps as she toddled towards Imogen. Her face was twisted in confusion, as if she couldn't understand why Imogen just wouldn't stop and accept a hug from those bony, rotted limbs.

Imogen didn't look back again. When she reached the first floor, she broke into a sprint, crashed through the double doors to the back rugby fields, and didn't stop until she was hidden behind the old eucalyptus tree at the edge of the school property. Gasping and wiping at her shirt and face, Imogen dared to glance around the massive trunk at the school to see if she had been pursued.

"Hey."

Imogen let out a yelp, but quickly stifled it when she saw it was only Liam, an older boy she'd met once in clubs.

Though she tried to speak with a steady, non-lunatic voice, it came out as deranged and manic. "Hey."

"Runnin' from the law? Or just the chem final?"

Imogen wanted to smile but couldn't. She kicked the dirt and examined her feet, her clothes, her arms, all of which were clean of blood or any other unsightly substance.

Liam sat, far enough away that he couldn't touch her, but close enough to have a whispered conversation. "You look shook."

The old woman approached from a distance, shambling across the field. Though she was far away, her wail was like sirens directly in Imogen's brain. The woman was shaking her head and crossing her arms in an X.

Imogen nodded. "I am."

The woman reached them, panting, her black tongue hanging down between her breasts. Standing overtop Liam, her eyes filled with glowing red blood and sharp claws extended from necrotic fingertips. She slashed at Liam, raking away at his cock and throat, but had little effect. Her mouth opened wide, releasing a wail like shattering glass that poured from her throat along with thick, black bile that drizzled over Liam's head.

"You always look a right mess," Liam said to Imogen, oblivious to the death above. A cringe tightened Liam's face the moment he said it, obviously regretting his choice of words. "What I mean to say is—"

"I do," Imogen interrupted. "I look a mess, and I am one. Always."

Liam looked at the dirt between his own feet. "I can help, you know."

Imogen closed her eyes, imagining Liam in absence of the hag. His honey locks and hazel eyes, that touch of Welsh that clouded his Irish lilt. She had spied on him before, playing football, fooling with his guitar on the corner of campus when he thought no one was watching. He'd once been long and lanky but was now sturdy and thick, a product of hormones.

"You can?"

Liam slid his hand into his denim jacket and pulled out a baggie full of dense greens mashed together in clumps. Imogen saw, processed what she was seeing, then her heart sank into her stomach.

He didn't want to comfort her. He wanted to sell to her.

"It'll help," he said, his voice saccharine sweet. Luring. "Won't charge you this round."

Of course you won't.

But as he rolled a joint for her, a hope blossomed in her belly. A possibility of silence and peace.

❦

"It began that day with Liam and the weed. That worked for a spell, but they came back. Only sounds at first, then I saw them. Hair, eyes—all chattering death and sharp nails."

Saoirse almost couldn't bear to watch her sister, squirming in her seat, recalling the sins of her youth that led to the devastation of her present.

"When did the tar find ye?"

"High school party."

"Did it help?"

Imogen bit her lip. "It did. Until it didn't. By then, I was hooked. Now I'm taking it because my body tells me to. Doesn't banish them, though. Makes them worse, I think."

Saoirse nodded. Took a singular problem and multiplied it to many. "Well, one step at a time. Let's banish the poison, then wage war on the banshees."

Imogen traced the lettering on the book cover. "Is it real, Saoirse? The banshees? Ramnon?"

Saoirse wanted to say yes. To tell her sister they weren't crazy, that fantastical things and places did exist. Magic was easier to accept than reality, and much more beautiful.

"I fear they're not real. But I don't know everything, so perhaps."

"Mental illness?"

"Perhaps."

Imogen put her elbows on the book—which groaned in return—and put her head in her hands. She looked exhausted. Broken.

"Enough mopin'," Saoirse said, wrapping her arm around Imogen and giving her a shake. "One thing at a time. Let's get you locked up."

Imogen's head snapped up, and she looked at Saoirse with tears in her eyes. "What of Ma? Her funeral?"

"Won't be ready for that for a week, and it's unsafe for you to wait. I'll get you a day pass. Or we'll hold the funeral later. Ma's ashes ain't gonna spoil sittin' 'round in a jar."

Imogen scowled.

"Face it, Imogen, we ain't beatin' the beast in yer veins by sittin around and waitin' for it to tame itself. Yer goin to hunker down at Fionnbarra Treatment Facility 'til your veins be free of tha' toxic sludge before we worry about Ma's ash, or banshees, or a broken brain. Whatever the fuck we gots goin' on."

Imogen's eyes widened in fear. "They'll be there, Saoirse. The banshees. In the treatment facility. And I'll be trapped."

"You sure will. But ye won't be the only one there with demons on your shoulders. I bet you won't even take the prize for craziest loon in the room."

Imogen's mouth contorted, a squeak leaking out.

Saoirse gasped. "Was that ... a laugh?"

Imogen fell into Saoirse's arms, and the Ramnon book tumbled to the floor, releasing an "oof". Saoirse kicked it aside with a scolding and held Imogen.

"To bed," Saoirse whispered in her hair. "Rest.'Tis been a long day."

Saoirse guided Imogen down the hall to their old bedroom, lifted the covers, and tucked her into bed, pulling the comforter up to her chin just like Dadaí had always done.

"Read me a story," Imogen said, her eyes fluttering.

Without hesitation, Saoirse fetched *Tales from Ramnon* from the living room and returned to Imogen's bedside.

"Not that," Imogen said, her face scrunching like she'd eaten a rotten capelin.

"Don't be foolish," Saoirse said. "Ye be hearin' the banshees anyways, regardless of where this book is. This is what Dadaí read us at sleep time. Let it work its magic."

Imogen didn't protest.

"Here's a tame one," Saoirse said, opening to the very beginning of the book. "The introduction."

Imogen raised a brow, but Saoirse held up a hand, stifling an argument.

Saoirse began. "Ramnon. What is it? Where is it? Ramnon is the place beyond, gateway to The After. All manner of beast congregate there, shuffling through, staying a while. A safe resting place for the fantastical, if you will.

"Ramnon. A land of gritty gold and muted colours, shifting sands and black waters. Who resides there? Vampyres, werewolves, Sluagh and wendigo. Selke and Vanheks swim the black waters of the lake alongside the likes of Nessie and Ogopogo.

Faeries and dragons occupy the skies, and gorgon and yeti roam the dirt paths. Ghosts come too. Humans who lived tragedy or died by the same come to find peaceful rest in Ramnon's loving arms.

"It's horrible, and beautiful, and forever. A place for misfits, for fantasies, for those who don't belong. The after and always for unfortunate souls."

A snort distracted Saoirse from her reading. She looked up to find Imogen's lips pursed, blowing out soft air as she snored. Saoirse swiped a greasy hair off Imogen's forehead, then kissed her lightly.

"G'night, dear sister. Dream sweet."

17

Imogen was asleep, but Saoirse was far from it. After leaving Imogen's room, she poured up yet another tea and sat at the kitchen table, wondering what she would feed her insomnia to keep it from getting bored. Bored insomnia led to thinking, and thinking led to anxiety.

Fuil Olagón.

The phrase popped in Saoirse's head, snatching her attention. It was the last thing Ma said to her. Her last words ever, in fact. Saoirse didn't know what it meant, but she did know one thing. Though Ma had been disoriented, brain damaged from the stroke, she wanted Saoirse to have something in the trunk at the end of her and Dadaí's bed.

Saoirse glared at *Tales of Ramnon*, which she'd placed on the table after leaving Imogen. "Now listen 'ere. Keep yer gob shut while she be sleepin', or I'll toss ye to the waves."

The book answered with silence. Saoirse nodded, satisfied, but tucked it under the couch cushions just to be safe before heading to the master bedroom. It was like opening a tomb, going into that bedroom, where less than a day before Ma had slept, dressed, lived. Bits of her and Dadaí remained, but to Saoirse, it was an empty cavern full of loss.

The trunk waited at the end of the bed, brighter than the rest of the room. She and Imogen had sat on that trunk lots when they were small, chatting with Ma and Dadaí, watching them go about their adult business. The trunk was more than a piece of furniture, though. From time to time, Saoirse caught her parents dipping in there, Ma retrieving yarn for her crocheting or Dadaí picking at old songbooks. It was a treasure trove forbidden from wee hands and eyes.

But Saoirse was no longer wee, and Dadaí and Ma were no longer around to forbid access. When Saoirse unclasped the lock and lifted the lid, the box exhaled, wafting out a breath scented with old parchment and mothballs. As Saoirse remembered, there were dozens of skeins of yarn on one half, all colours of the rainbow, with glittering beads strung throughout. Saoirse ran her hand over the wool, the colours exploding in her mind, slashes and splatters of indigo and crimson, teal and eggplant. She brought a violet skein to her nose, sniffing in the aroma of her childhood. An unfinished piece was still on the hook, waiting for the toil of Ma's hands to complete its creation.

On the other half of the trunk were stacks of loose papers and photo albums. Saoirse pulled out old song books, tunes Dadaí had written out by hand. He'd pass out the songbooks at Christmas, and the family would sing and sway, whoop and holler until sleep took them so Santa could sneak in. Saoirse flipped through the pages, spying rings from tea mugs and smears of chocolates, remnants of a happy, messy life.

Beneath the songbooks were photo albums, thick and curled,

the fabric covers faded and tattered. Saoirse flipped through the first few, smiling at pictures of her and Imogen as babes, playing naked in the yard and covered in dirt. Ma and Dadaí's wedding photos were in there too, a day full of wine and daisies, laughter and song. Deeper down the pile were Ma and Dadaí's school albums, pictures of them with friends, on sports teams, and posing outside pubs in downtown Dublin.

The next book of photos was much older, childhood photos of Ma and Dadaí and their respective families. These albums were stiff and brittle, the glue beneath plastic photo covers flaking off like dry skin. Some people Saoirse recognized from family gatherings, others she did not. This book delved way back into the toddler years, where Ma and Dadaí were the ones naked in the dirt and playing in the sun.

Saoirse leaned over to retrieve the final bits that lay on the floor of the trunk. Mostly loose papers and photographs, some sentimental cards and postcards. And a bundle of folded fabric tied together with a single string of twine. Embroidered on that fabric were two names.

Saoirse and Imogen.

Saoirse tugged, releasing the knots, and bristles of twine sprinkled over her lap. She unfolded the cloth, peeling it back. Inside was a green velvet box. As Saoirse's fingernail found the seam, a wet growl rumbled from within, jittering the box in her hand. Slowly—to not startle the contents, or get bit, or both—Saoirse lifted the lid.

There were two matching pendants, old and tarnished, each on a green silk cord. The gold was sculpted into an image of three women, mouths open, hair entwining and tangling together into a circle that shaped the pendant. Saoirse pinched one of the pendants between her fingers and lifted it to her face. Then to her ear.

She could hear them, as if far away, their voices lost in a valley. They were whispering to each other, giggling, crying. Saoirse closed her eyes, swearing she could feel a puff of air expelled from their tiny metal lungs as the language of old Ireland rolled off their tongues.

Saoirse placed the pendant back with its sibling and was about the shut the case when she spied a sliver of ivory peeking from beneath the green velvet backdrop. Prying the padding of the case off, she revealed a black-and-white photograph. The image stared back at her with familiar eyes, black as the night.

It was a woman, dressed in a light gown, her dark hair tied in a thick plait that hung down her body. As was typical in older photographs, she was not smiling, but there was a joy on her face, nonetheless. In her lap, she held a small boy no older than a year, his bald head and two teeth gleaming for all to see.

Dadaí.

Even as an infant, he had that mischievous smile and little dimple on his chin.

But that woman. Saoirse didn't recognize her, but she knew her. Perhaps she didn't, not really, but she looked just like the woman she'd seen in her nightmares the night Dadaí died. The one who had attended both his graveside service and his wake. But this woman was very much alive, at least she was in the photograph. Her cheeks were full, her hair tidy, and her outfit snug against a curvaceous frame.

But those eyes. Dark, watching. Saoirse leaned in, her nose almost touching the woman, taunting her to move like the banshee in the Ramnon book. But the image defied her, remaining still and silent.

Saoirse flipped the photograph over. There were brown stains, wrinkles, and an address. And one line scrawled across the bottom.

I love ye, girls.

Saoirse stared at the handwriting, her heart full and breaking at the same time. It was Dadaí's. She was certain. She could hear his voice. And when she touched the ink he'd left for her and Imogen, she could hear him speak.

I love you.

The address stole her attention. She ran her finger over it, as if testing its authenticity. After a moment of consideration, she flipped the picture over and spoke to the woman on the other side.

"All right then, stranger. I'll play this game."

The woman didn't respond. Saoirse tucked the photograph back in the jewelry box and tucked it under her arm. After cleaning up the trunk and sealing it once again, she looked back at the empty bed, imagining that the imprints there were holding hands together somewhere in the great After.

Saoirse whispered as she left the room. "I love ye."

18

Breakfast was Saoirse's favourite meal. Even now, with Ma absent from her own kitchen table, the day was sunny, the food steaming, and the house full of love.

"What will become of the house?" Imogen asked as she stabbed at her eggs, poking little bits into her mouth.

Saoirse was pleased to see her eating. She'd noticed the tremor in Imogen's hands and the wildness in her eyes. She'd have to whisk her little sister away to treatment as soon as possible, before the urges became too great for her frail body to handle.

"Well, it's ours of course," Saoirse said.

"Will you give up your place?"

Saoirse thought of the pride she had when she purchased a house of her own with money she'd saved. She thought of the little town of Ballinspittle, the quaint peace, her autonomy.

"Nah. I'll be keeping my place." Saoirse set her fork down

and folded her hands in front of her. Just like Ma used to do. "You take it, Imogen."

Imogen startled, her gaze snapping up to Saoirse. "No!"

"And just why not?"

"It don't belong to me!"

"It belongs to the family. I dunnah need it. You do."

"I can't."

"You will."

"It ain't right."

Saoirse leaned forward, tapping the table to punctuate her point. "This is part of it, Imogen. Yer new life. Startin' it right."

Imogen opened her mouth, an argument forming, but none came.

Saoirse continued, "This is our family home. Ma and Dadaí would be so happy to have you here. And you can host the next dinner!"

Imogen cocked a brow and nodded down to her withered, jittering body.

"Yeah," Saoirse said. "Maybe I'll take care o' the first few, 'til you's clean and healthy."

They spent the rest of the breakfast picking at food, sipping tea, and gazing in silence at their new normal. Once everything was finished up, Imogen slinked over to the couch and covered herself in one of Ma's afghans, shivering.

"Ye ain't well," Saoirse said.

"I need a hit."

"Like a hole in the head."

Imogen closed her eyes and held her stomach. "It's awful."

"Well, that may very well be, but ye'll have to suffer a short spell. I called the centre, and they'll take ye, but not until three."

Imogen sat up. "You called already?"

Saoirse had expected some backtracking. "Sure did. And you's goin'. For Ma and Dadaí. For yourself."

Imogen's lip quivered. "I'm scared, Saoirse."

"Of course you are." Saoirse brought a pair of sleeping pills to Imogen to help her sleep until her admission. "Here, these'll keep you from runnin' away before we go, even if I gotta carry your sleepin' ass inside."

Imogen nodded. "Of course I'm going."

The smile on Imogen's face put Saoirse at ease. While Imogen rested on the couch, Saoirse cleaned the dishes and pans. Once she heard the soft sputters of Imogen's snores, Saoirse was confident the medication had taken hold. She gathered her coat and purse and quietly slipped out the door.

Sleep tight, m'love. Got a thing to tend to. Won't be but a couple o' hours.

ONCE THE SOUND OF SAOIRSE'S ENGINE FADED INTO THE distance, Imogen sat up, letting Ma's afghan fall from her shoulders. With a quick sweep of her finger, she retrieved the sleeping pills from beneath the couch cushion, then threw them down the sink. Guilt roiled in her belly, but the physical anguish outweighed the shame of deceit.

Her entire body ached, tremors wracking her lungs, nausea churning her guts. She was cold and hot all at once, and her left eye wouldn't quit twitching. With jagged nails, she picked at her skin, at the itchy raw spots that burned like craters below the surface.

One hit. Just one hit and I'll make it there, to the centre, get clean and live happily ever after.

With the first two kitchen drawers searched with fruitless results, Imogen's panic reached a boiling point at the third. She pulled the drawer right off its track, spilling the contents over the floor. Then the next drawer. And the next. Until there was a mountain of playing cards, plug-ins, batteries, dried out pens, and random junk littering the entire kitchen.

Where the fuck are they?

Imogen gnawed at her nails, biting to the quick until her fingers bled as she rushed around the house, scouring every surface, every container. She was about to move to the bedroom when she passed by the back door. The sight niggled a possibility in her mind.

Bursting onto the back porch and hitting the grass at a run, Imogen reached Ma's old pickup in no time. She threw the door open, scrambled into the driver's seat, and fumbled for the ignition. Her fingers wrapped around the key fob and she shuddered with joy. When she fired up the engine, it backfired, and she screamed, both sounds vibrating the core of her bones. She moved her hand to the gear shifter and looked in the rearview mirror. Behind the truck, lingering in a plume of dark exhaust, were a pair of charred hands, reaching, talons dripping blood.

Imogen looked away from the mirror, put the truck in drive, and fishtailed down the driveway until she hit the highway. Her tires screeching, she pinned it until she reached top speed. The road was abandoned, the skies clear, but out of nowhere, a black froth of gossamer whipped the windshield, shrieking as it made contact.

Imogen screamed, her own voice sounding far and distant. "No!"

"No!" the gossamer mimicked back.

Imogen squeezed her eyes closed and whispered under her breath. "No, stop. No stop."

A chorus now, many voices, chanting, mimicking and contorting Imogen's voice. "Nostopnostopnostop."

Imogen screamed. When she opened her eyes, she had to crank the steering wheel to avoid careening into the ditch. Her eyes flickered to the rearview mirror again. The gossamer was not floating behind her, belching from the truck's exhaust pipe. It was inside the cab, solid smoke occupying the back seat.

And three faces, long and pale, hollow black eyes and cavernous mouths closing and opening like fish gulping air. Sounds clattered between them, an indistinguishable dialogue of grunt and mewls. Skeletal fingers curled over the seat, tugging at Imogen's hair, cupping her shoulders, stroking her cheek.

"Nostopstopnostopno," they cackled and cooed.

Imogen forced her eyes to stay forward on the road. The conversation in the back seat intensified, but Imogen hummed a lullaby, determined to drown them out.

Not real. Not real.

The car swerved as nails pieced Imogen's arms and blood rained in fat plips to the center console, but Imogen forced her eyes to stay on the road and increased the volume of her lullaby. The passengers responded in kind, their chatter swelling to wails and mournful songs.

With trembling hands and a throbbing head, Imogen navigated the streets of Cork, narrowly avoiding traffic and people, determined to reach the asylum. She had just about done it when her passengers escalated from pitiful to forceful. A hand coiled into Imogen's hair, yanking her against the head rest as nails—ten or twenty, Imogen couldn't tell—poked into her neck. Imogen let go of the steering wheel to pull them off, and the car struck a fire hydrant, sending a geyser of water straight up into the air.

Imogen blinked, and they were gone. The sounds, the gossamer, the hands. All that was left was a crumpled truck and a surge of water. Imogen stumbled out into the street, blood from her broken nose dripping down the front of her shirt. The water spraying up was roaring, voices trapped in the stream, screaming, begging for attention. Imogen was transfixed by the racket, all notes in every octave, music riding the stream and splashing to the ground like shattering glass.

Our Lady's was peeking over the rooftops, a beacon of relief. Imogen ignored the music of the hydrant and bee-lined for the asylum.

Through the door, down the hall, into the common room. Lifting sleeping bags, kicking off blankets, searching blank faces.

Cait was nowhere to be found. Imogen was prepared to do anything and everything to get that one last hit, but Cait wasn't in the common room, and Imogen had no desire to brave the second floor. Or go anywhere near the third. But desperation irritated like a mosquito, and Imogen could think of no other option. As she was heading across the common area, ready to hit the streets, her foot caught on a ruck sack strewn along the wall. Someone had tucked it under a blanket, but the strap had been liberated and snagged Imogen's toe. She stared a moment, noting the bulging fabric, then dropped to her knees. After only a moment of her hands plunged in the darkness of the bag, she emerged with a baggie of heroin.

Hesitation. A quick search of the floor for eyes that might be watching, knowing.

No time to think.

Imogen shoved the baggie in her pocket and ran for her room.

❦ 19 ❦

Following the prompts on her GPS, Saoirse found herself in a sleepy residential district on the outskirts of Cork city. She had the photograph of the woman and Dadaí set on the console, their eyes watching her as she drove. Halfway expecting the picture to come to life, Saoirse kept her eye on it for most of the drive.

The address on the back of the photo took her to a care facility tucked in amongst the rows of bungalows. The building took up half the city block but blended with its neighbours quite well. Its facade included dark brick walls, windows lined with flower boxes, hydrangea spilling to the ground, and a tidy lawn complete with gnome and gargoyle sculptures. If it wasn't for the bars on the windows and the keycard lock on the front door, the place might pass as a cozy home.

Saoirse tucked the photograph in the breast pocket of her jacket and went to the front door. She eyed the camera before pressing the buzzer. After a few minutes of enjoying the warm breeze and the melodies of birds, a voice crackled over the speaker.

"Welcome to Grace's Gardens! How may we help you?"

"I'm hopin' ye can." Saoirse reached in her pocket, pulled out the photograph, and held it up to the camera. "Ye got this lass in there?"

Without comment, after a brief moment of thick silence, the electronic lock on the door beeped, unlocking. Saoirse pulled the handle and went inside.

Grace's Gardens was dressed to the nines, with lush hardwood, intricate art on the walls, and warm studio lighting. It was the smell that gave away its true nature. A medley of urine, old person musk, and soiled adult diapers dominated the air, despite the incense and potpourri tucked in every corner.

Death lives here. You can slap some perfume on it, but it's still the dirt of graves, not gardens.

A leggy brunette in cartoon scrubs rounded the corner, clipboard in hand. "Hello!" she chimed as she held out her hand. "I'm Una."

Saoirse took her hand, giving it a shake. "Saoirse. Thanks for indulging me."

"It's no trouble. Curious mystery, I'm sure. One easily solved. Come with me."

They snaked their way through a few administrative offices, landing in a tiny one tucked in the back. The nameplate told Saoirse that Una was the head administrator. Una rounded her desk and motioned for Saoirse to take a seat.

"Wasn't difficult to recognize her," Una said. "Or him, for that matter. Those beautiful dark eyes."

"Ye knew him?" Saoirse asked.

"Yeah," Una said, swiping away a tear. "'Twas a good man, Finn."

"Ah, so ye know he's dead."

"Tragic."

The closed file on the desk lingered between them, Una's hands folded atop it, hesitant to relinquish its secrets.

Saoirse waited her out. Finally, she tapped the file with her perfectly manicured fingernail. "He visited once a month, like clockwork. Even though most times she was full of rubbish and mania, he kept on comin', bringing flowers and sweets. Good man."

Dadaí never mentioned this place. Or this woman. Saoirse was unaware he had been coming here, month after month, until his death. She wondered if Ma knew.

"Did ye ever see my Ma?"

"Roison?" Una worried the corner of the file between her fingers. "A few times. Aibell was quite unpleasant, so Finn didn't bring Roison back. Lovely woman, your Ma. Tolerated the vitriol spewed at her and offered only kindness in return."

Saoirse spoke the name quietly, more to herself than to Una. "Aibell."

Una's gaze stayed steady on Saoirse before falling to the file. "You don't know of her, do you?"

Saoirse shook her head.

Una patted the file. "I could show you this, Saoirse, but I think ..." she trailed off, her eyes wide. She nibbled at her lip, scraping off a line of offensively pink gloss. Saoirse recognized anxiety like a sibling.

"May I see her?" Saoirse asked. "I suspect what I want to know is not in that file."

Una stood and led the way out the door. Her hands were trembling ...

Like Imogen.

... her pace quick.

She wants this over with.

Una stopped at a set of locked doors, swiping her key card and peering down the hall.

Terror sits in her heart, put there by this woman.

Una pointed down the hall without looking. "She's in room four-eighty-two, on the left at the end. The door is locked, but security will let you in. When you want to leave, just rap on the window and they'll let you out."

"Should I be worried?"

Una's smile was full of pity. She placed a hand on Saoirse shoulder. "She's very ill, Saoirse. I'm sorry that you didn't meet her when she was well. Dementia has taken its toll, I'm afraid. The nonsense she spews, that she believes, is downright ..."

Saoirse figured Una couldn't find the right word. One that was strong enough for the sights she'd seen and the sounds she'd heard. Saoirse gave her a smile and a nod, then walked away on her own, absolving Una of any further involvement. When Saoirse approached door 482, the security guard, a man the size of a fridge, heaved himself out of his plastic chair.

"So," Saoirse said. "Anythin' I'm to know? Don't feed 'er after midnight or get 'er wet?"

He chuckled, his dimples leaving pocks in the sides of his chubby cheeks. "How's about you don't do nothin' at all. For starters, don't be goin' in there."

"Well, I'm goin', so I get what I get."

He dipped his head and swiped his key card. "Yes, ma'am. Luck be with you."

※

Room 482 was a tomb, dank and dark other than a slip of dusty sunlight seeping through where the curtains parted. When the door clicked shut behind her, Saoirse jumped.

"Wee bit skittish, ye be."

The voice was guttural and lilting and accompanied by an echo of a thousand tiny whispers, all pitches and tones, mimicking each of Aibell's words a moment after she spoke them.

"Ay," Saoirse said, squinting in the darkness.

Aibell laughed, a cackle coated in smoker's tar and old whiskey. The noise was coming from everywhere around the room, consuming the entire space and burrowing in Saoirse's mind.

"Enough nonsense," Saoirse scolded. "Lemme see ya, sags an' all. If yer in your skivvies, that's no mind. I'd prefer it over not havin' my eye on you."

A sigh came from all corners of the room. The dust in the sunlight swirled in a pirouette as a chair groaned, squeaking as the weight came off it and moved across the room. With a click, light poured from a dusty rose floor lamp in the corner.

"Better?" Aibell asked.

Saoirse had seen some wild things in her lifetime. Unbelievable creatures. This woman ranked right up there with the woman at Dadaí's wake. She was old, her skin worn leather, her long wispy hair white and matted. Her bones were mangled like twisted tree roots, knobs and edges protruding everywhere. She stood at least seven feet tall, though it was hard to tell; her spine was crooked and her head cricked so her cheek touched her shoulder.

"So whaddya think of me?" Aibell asked. She blinked twice,

lids squelching over dry, milky white eyes. "Am I what you expected?"

"I's not shocked, if that what ye be askin'."

Another cackle. "You must be Saoirse. Finnegan always told me you were filled to tha brim with sass and spice."

"I was always too old for bullshittin' around."

"Your sister be more sensitive. A gentle petal."

"Ye know us well," Saoirse said, "but we haven't had the pleasure of knowin ye."

The air sucked out of the room as Aibell's mouth drooped, revealing black, toothless gums. "What? He never told you?"

"Nay, he did not. I knows you're Aibell because Una out there tol' me."

Aibell's tongue wriggled, a grey mass marred by seeping warts. She clicked it against the roof of her mouth, tsking as she shook her head. When she spoke, her words turned to music, a woeful tune. "Finnegan, Finnegan, ever the protector, quiet are ye. Ye cannot deny them and who they be."

"Who, Imogen and me?"

"Family tree, thick and hard, chop it all you like, 'twill grow in any yard."

Weary of rhymes and nonsense singsong, Saoirse crossed her arms and ignored the ravings. "Yer my grandmother, I suppose."

"Youthful, am I?"

"Not what I would call ye, but—"

The shriek that bellowed from Aibell was so strong, it ruffled Saoirse's hair. "Must be! For I ain't yer grandmammy, foolish child."

Aibell. The name wasn't familiar. Her Dadaí's Ma was Beatrice, and her Ma's Ma was Alice.

"The fountain of fecking youth am I!" Aibell threw her hands in the air and shuffled around in a pained, crooked dance. "I be Aibell, your *great* grandmammy!"

"Wow. Okay, colour me impressed. But I think mayhap you've confused the ole rusted drinkin' fountain in the common area with the fountain of youth."

Aibell stabbed a mangled finger at Saoirse. "It be coming for you, too, smartass cunt. Time, she finds us all and dances upon us with her jagged toenails and bunions. I's just thankful for each day I avoid the final blow of her heel."

As if floating, Aibell moved across the room, her sheer gown covering the tops of her feet. She came to rest in the corner where she clawed at her face, black fingernails etching delicate lines of crimson in her translucent flesh.

"Why are we not Aibells as well?" Saoirse asked. "Imogen and I. Middle names, at least."

Aibell twitched, her neck cracking as her body jerked with subtle palsy. "Finn. He always wanted the best for you. Easy, comfortable. Normal. His way to disconnect you from your truth, until it was time, I suppose." Her head cracked to the side. "Whaddya want from me? Hugs and kisses and years' worth of Christmas prezzies?"

"Ma jus' passed."

Aibell fell silent, her eyes searching Saoirse. Then her face contorted into a scowl. "Fuck. Goddamn."

"Yeah."

"Ye's orphans now."

"I guess."

"Either o' you skags gots a family o' yer own?"

Saoirse shook her head.

Aibell laughed, yellow phlegm sputtering from the back of

her throat and settling on her black, cracked lips. "If I'm yer only family, yer fucked."

"Imogen and I got each other."

"Huh." Aibell poked a finger in her mouth and gnawed on her black nail. "Ye be the last of the line. Well, Finn, I suppose it's time to tell them."

A shimmer of gold rippled over the milk of Aibell's eyes.

"So, about them banshees," Saoirse said.

Aibell stilled suddenly, and the room erupted with dozens of hushed conversations. "What about 'em?"

"They be real?"

"Sure are!" Aibell squealed and clapped her hands. "Say, don't get sand in yer teeth, wee one, if you land face first!"

Hysterical laughter exploded from the woman, and her gown slid off her shoulders, revealing scaled white skin beneath. Her long breasts jiggled as she giggled, which made her laugh even harder.

"Dadai read us *Tales from Ramnon*."

"Oh, yer Dadaí did like his tales, didn't he?"

Aibell walked over to the dresser and pulled out a large music box. When she lifted the lid, a dancer spun, tinny music piercing the room. It was a distorted version of "Irish Washer Woman." The voices in the room crescendoed in delight and sang along.

When I was at home I was merry and frisky,

My dad kept a pig and my mother sold whisky,

Aibell clawed at the mirror behind the dancer, peeling it away to retrieve a piece of paper.

My uncle was rich, but never would by aisey

Till I was enlisted by Corporal Casey.

Crippled, exposed, with jerking tremors in her legs and arms, Aibell crossed the room to Saoirse in three loping strides.

"Our blood is viscous, tainted, and everlasting as the kiss o' death."

She licked the paper with that yellow goo on her tongue then stuck it to Saoirse's forehead before dancing off and singing, "crowns and gown and sceptres fer ye and yours and me!"

Stifling a gag, Saoirse peeled the paper from her forehead and wiped her face with the sleeve of her jacket. Aibell ripped open her blinds, bathing the room in bright sunlight.

Saoirse looked down at the picture. It was a page torn from a textbook—art history from the look of it. On it was the portrait of a woman, her hair as long as the train on her gown, an intricate crown upon her head. Below the drawing was a caption:

Aibell, the Ua Brian Banshee
Banshee of the O'Brien Clan that ruled over Northern Ireland during the tenth and eleventh centuries. Said to be the original banshee, and queen of all who followed.

Aibell looked on in awe. "Royalty. The Main Bitch, ruler of the rest."

Saoirse pointed at Aibell. "You?"

Again, that laugh, taunting, horrible. "Naw, ye wee idjit! Not me! I's alive, you dumb fuck! But the name has been passed down many generations."

Aibell moved closer, hovering over the picture. Bloody drool from her lower lip spiraled down on the portrait's face, and the painted woman opened her mouth, greedily lapping at the blood with a wild hunger in her eyes.

Saoirse flipped the picture to cease the gore. But there was horror on the back as well, a phrase written in rough cursive.

Fuil Olagón.

"Fuil Olagón," Aibell hissed. "The *Blood Wail*." With a viper's speed and precision, Aibell grabbed Saoirse's crotch. "It is *inside* us, chil'.

Saoirse screamed, and Aibell mimicked her, wailing along at the same rhythm and tempo, and the myriad voices in the room wailed in kind. As if suspended in water, Aibell's hair floated into the air, whorling in with the voices, draping over Saoirse's face until she was choking on both hair and noise.

The security guard came through the door flanked by a pair of nurses, one of them brandishing a syringe.

As she was being hauled away, Aibell slashed Saoirse's arm with her nail, drawing a line of blood. The room screeched into slow motion, all sounds and movements muffled and stunted as if moving through thick fluid. Aibell placed her cheek against Saoirse's and whispered into her ear, the sound of a thousand voices.

"The wailin' blood be in you and yer sister. It's what you are. Leave no one in your wake, and the line ends with you. In Ramnon."

With a snap and a whir, the room returned to real speed. Within a breath, the guard had Aibell's hands wrenched behind her back as the nurse pushed medication into Aibell's vein. Aibell's noise and movement fluttered to nothing more than indistinct chitters and whispers as they lifted her on to the bed, restraining her wrists and ankles before covering her with a blanket.

"Ma'am, are you okay?" the guard asked Saoirse.

Saoirse looked down at her arm, at the stinging line where Aibell's nail had sliced her flesh. There was no blood, only a line of glittering, fine sand that lingered only a moment before blowing away in the breeze from the vents.

"I'm fine." Saoirse stood and brushed the phantom grit off her arm. "I need to go."

"Don't blame you," the nurse with the needle said. "Her flights o' fancy be a bit much."

As Saoirse hurried down the hall towards the exit, a voice chased her, squealing in one ear, then both, coming from the ceiling, the floors, and the walls.

"Fuil Olagón."

20

The pinch of the needle piercing Imogen's flesh was only a brief inconvenience of pain. She pushed the entire hit at once, determined to make peace last until she was safely stowed away at the treatment facility. Flopping on the mattress in her room, she watched the water stains in the ceiling tile swirl and sway while a rush of fluid heat poured over her body. The tremors in her fingers calmed, and her heart slowed, pattering a gentle tempo rather than an aggressive staccato.

The pain was gone. All was quiet. She was warm and healthy and happy.

Lies.

Whispers lured her to a seated position. Euphoria trembled her body, weakening her limbs. In her doorway stood Aisling, lean and naked with the rabbit mask upon her face. Imogen floated, following her down the hall, up the stairs, and onto the third floor. The saloon was empty, except for Mauve, who tended the bar. She set a snifter down, which the young banshee plucked up with slender fingers and poured into Imogen's mouth. The booze was warm, gurgling down her throat and into her belly, heating her body as it entered her.

Be with me. I can give you what you need. The drugs are only death.

Aisling was naked, as was Imogen, the heat from their bodies colliding as they leaned against the bar. Mauve poured up more drink as Aisling put her hands on Imogen's hips, guiding her to a barstool and lifting her on to it. The wood was cool but smooth against Imogen's flesh, and Aisling's touch, warm and soft. Gentle and slow, Aisling pressed her palms on the inside of Imogen's thighs, opening her legs. Cool air chilled the dampness inside Imogen, but it was quickly warmed by a gust of Aisling's breath as she parted Imogen with her tongue, tasting, pressing, teasing.

The drugs. They are liars.

Imogen arched her back, pressing herself into Aisling's mouth, euphoria quivering through her and exploding in a great gush. Aisling gave her a moment, then pulled her to the floor, pressing her shoulders down and continuing until Imogen climaxed again, clenching and releasing in great pulses.

Imogen reached for Aisling's hand, her face, desperate for more. Aisling wasn't there, but the syringe was, cold and sharp in her grasp. Beneath her, the boards moved and screamed, jamming splinters into her back. When she flipped over, thousands of millipedes with multiple heads and sharp tongues writhed beneath her, slicing her skin and lapping up the blood like dehydrated hounds.

"Aisling." Imogen's voice came out on a weak squeal of air, her throat coated with sand and dust.

Imogen was on the third floor, but not in Ramnon. It was the asylum, with its derelict equipment and empty offices. The third floor. Empty carts, dust-covered furniture, and pillaged cupboards.

No wood. No gold. No sand. No Aisling or Mauve.

No Ramnon.

"There is no Ramnon!" Imogen screamed, her voice echoing through the room. "No such thing as banshees!"

Myriad voices wailed, shaking Imogen's bones to the marrow. "*LIES!*"

Though the word had come from everywhere but her, the screech burst the blood vessels in Imogen's eyes, sending crimson trickling down her face in creeks of tears. She ran for the door, bursting through and falling down the stairs, hitting her forearm on the bottom step with a deafening crack. With the heroin wearing off, she felt every bit of pain in every millimetre of that splintered bone. She screamed, but only gold dust coughed out of her throat as she ran for her room. When she flew through the doorway, there was someone on her bed.

"Hello, lass."

It was a man, or at least half of one, his greasy mullet resting on wasted shoulders. His pants were sagging low, revealing a thin line of dandruff-coated pubic hair beneath a concave stomach. On his head, he wore a cap with an IRA badge, and on his face, he wore a cocky smile as his eyes rolled up and down over Imogen's body.

The cool draft on the wetness between her legs reminded her of her nudity. She bent to the floor and picked up her outfit, which was neatly folded, and donned it while the man watched.

"You have something of mine," he said.

"Doubtful," Imogen scoffed, but then she realized.

The hit. The high.

The stolen drugs.

"I ... I'm s-sorry, I didn't mean—"

"You accidentally stole 'em?" He stood, looming over her like a church tower, his voice a gong. "No, you wanted them. You *needed* them. You are a dirty thief and a liar."

"I never said I didn't take them."

"But you did. Take them."

Her hands trembled; her voice caught like a solid mass of hair in her throat. She couldn't speak, so she nodded.

"I see." He hesitated, hovering above her. "Well, I know a need. I've had a few myself. When that tar gets you, it gets you hard. Gets *obsessed* with you."

Imogen's muscles loosened at her relief. "Thank you so much for understanding. You see, I'm heading to treatment this afternoon, and I didn't think I could make it, but I really want to go, I have to go ..."

She noticed the bulge in his sagging jeans, his finger stroking the side of it, coaxing it to attention.

Shit.

"We can work out a payment, little bird."

No.

Her internal voice was joined by a chorus of complaints outside her head, coming from the vents, the hall, within the walls.

"I can see you're weak and frail. I am too. Just give him a lick, a quick suck. Swallow me and we'll call it even."

No!

The voices screamed along with her, rattling inside her skull.

Imogen finally screamed out loud. "No!"

And all the voices screamed with her.

NO!

With a force buried deep within her, Imogen drove the heel of her hand up under his chin, snapping his head back with a crack. He dropped to the floor, his eyes rolled back, leaving only white, his head hitting the concrete with a wet thud. Imogen stood, stunned, as a gleaming pool of blood spread beneath his cracked skull, framing his mulleted, horrid head in a crimson halo.

The room spun, swirling, whirling. Her stomach churned, and she vomited. She braced herself on the wall with a hand that was suddenly too big, swelling like a balloon, just like her eyes, which threatened to burst. She was disoriented, panicked, sweating and freezing, and sick. She scratched at an insatiable itch that crawled with a thousand feet up her arms and over her face.

The heroin. I'm coming down, is all. It's okay. I'm okay.

She plunged her hand into his jeans pocket and grabbed another baggie of drugs.

One more hit. A few more hours. I can make it.

She ran up the stairs and burst onto the third floor.

❧ 21 ❦

Saoirse touched her arm the whole way home, feeling for an incision, for a tacky scab of blood, for the fine grit of glittering sand. But her skin was bare and smooth, save a dusting of freckles. Aibell's voice whispered at her in every click of the car's turn signal, every swoosh of the wipers, every barmp of a passing horn.

Fuil Olagón.

Blood wail.

Though she'd had a change of clothes stashed at Ma's, she hadn't showered since before the hospital. After everything that happened, she wanted to cleanse her mind, and refreshing the body might do the trick. She would pass Ballinspittle on the way to get Imogen, and it would only take a half hour to scrub up. An important day awaited her, and she wanted to be ready for it.

The road was quiet as she approached the little fishing village, its brightly colored buildings a warm welcome for tourists and residents alike. The greens and blues of forest and ocean shimmered against the grey of the rainy sky, gusts of wet wind bolstering their sparkling dance. Saoirse passed through the town, admiring its beauty, tranquility, and the colour of culture splashed over every face and surface.

Life is good.

Red lights blinked, startling her to attention. With a white-knuckled grasp, she steered the car, correcting her hydroplane as she tap-danced on the brakes. When she came to a stop, mere inches from the car in front of her, she saw that there was a line of taillights staring at her, some flashing, others a solid defiance of movement.

"What in the bloody hell?"

Up ahead, just past the town, the famous grotto loomed above the road and the beach, illuminated by electric lights that gave it attention all day at all night. Along the beach, on the opposite side of the road, looky-loos lined the benches to catch a glimpse of the tourist attraction. The barrier at the bottom of the hill was adorned with bright blue lettering, stating I AM THE IMMACULATE CONCEPTION. Above that, tucked in her hidey hole in the grotto, was Our Lady in all her concrete glory.

"Ay, ye up to yer games again," Saoirse muttered. She lowered her window, stuck her head out into the drizzle, and yelled up the hill, "I've no time fer your nonsense today, Mary! Knock it off!"

A horn behind Saoirse beeped a scolding, and the heads in the car in front gave a collective shake. Saoirse flipped a respectful bird—hidden beneath her dash—then inched forwards with the traffic until it moved no more. Ahead, a familiar Garda, Murray Johnson, wandered down the lane of stationary cars, sipping on a steaming beverage.

"Oi! Murray!"

Murray's head snapped in Saoirse's direction, and he walked towards her, a smile peeking out from beneath his plump mustache.

"Saoirse! Here to take a gander, are ya?"

"I'm makin' my way home. Tryin' to, at least." Saoirse pointed up the hill. "What's up that bitch's knickers today?"

Murray crossed himself, then craned his head to look up the hill. "Seems she's up to mischief, so they say. Not much I can see, but you know how those things go."

Our Lady. The concrete statue in the grotto of Ballinspittle. Source of the famous Ballinspittle Phenomenon of 1985, when Mary decided to put on a show, moving and floating and wearing other faces. People came out in droves to see the miracle, despite the fact the Bishop of Cork had dubbed it an illusion of light. To this day, tourists hung around like mosquitos, seeing what they wanted to quench their need for faith.

"I've never seen her so much as fart," Saoirse said, glaring up at the statue. "And this jam up?"

"Tourist with a flat. We'll have 'er cleared shortly."

"Fuckin bugger sake ..."

"Gotta run, Saoirse. Say hi to Roison for me, will ye?"

Saoirse's head bobbed in an automatic nod. Ma's death was surreal still. A mist of rain trickled down the windshield, a calming wash as Saoirse thought about life without both Ma and Dadaí. It was only her and Imogen now, and that thought clenched her heart in fear.

But it was a new start. The beginning of Imogen's journey to wellness.

The drops of rain fell harder now, thicker, each hitting the windshield with the sound of Aibell's voice.

Leave no one in your wake.
The line ends with you.

Saoirse swiped the wipers, and the rubber against the window squealed in Aibell's voice.

The wailin' blood be in ye!

Saoirse shut off her wipers and covered her ears, but the grumble of her engine rose like a roar from a beast's belly.

"RAMNON."

Then all was quiet. Not silent, though.

A soft song rolled down the hill like fog—a melancholy tune sung by a woman, sad and old, her voice trembling with vibrato and tears.

"*Oft, in dreams I wander*
To that cot again,
I feel her arms a huggin' me
As when she held me then."

A gasp from the car behind her. Then a honk from a horn up ahead. People dressed in rain slickers leaped off the benches, standing, pointing as the song got louder, faster, distorted.

"*Too-ra-loo-ra-loo-ral,*
Too-ra-loo-ra-li..."

Saoirse looked up.

The statue of Mary had moved. Her hands were no longer pressed together in prayer and her face no longer turned to the sky. She held her hands out in front of her, grasping an object that was thick and meaty, pumping, blood leaking over Mary's white robe.

A heart.

The statue's face was contorted in sorrow, the mouth moving with the rhythm of the song, its chest heaving as it sobbed and wailed. But the face was not Our Lady. Not Mary.

It was Imogen.

Saoirse gasped, and the statue looked down, directly at her with Imogen's eyes, full of pain and terror. The statue's jaw dropped open, and the rocks on the hill rumbled as its belly bloated out, blasting a wail across the land. The robe opened, revealing a belly split from throat to pubic line. Handfuls of bloated intestines slithered down Imogen's thighs like gluttonous snakes, bile and shit and blood streaming from their sliced bellies. Mounds of millipedes squirmed in place of Imogen's breasts, her areolas rings of gyrating worms. Imogen screamed, blood vomiting out of her too-large mouth as she pointed frantically beyond where Saoirse stood.

Behind Saoirse, the occupants of the car had gotten out and were pointing up the hill.

"Will ye look at that!" the woman said. "I believe she blinked!"

The man shook his head. "Naw, that bulb above her flickered. That's all."

Saoirse looked up and down the line of cars. People saw little bits of something, or thought they did, but obviously not as dramatic as she was seeing. When she looked back up, Imogen still looked down upon her, but the white robe with the blue sash, though black with blood, was closed. She mouthed silent words that Saoirse heard in her head.

Fuil Olagón.

※

A LONG HOUR LATER, SAOIRSE HAD FLOWN IN HER HOUSE LIKE a bat on meth, showered, gathered her things, and was on the road to Ma's. She still had plenty of time to get Imogen up, feed her, clean her up, and get her to the treatment center without having to rush her with a cattle prod. After everything was said and done, and Imogen was safely tucked away in treatment for the coming months, Saoirse would rest. She lost Ma. She was losing Imogen for a spell. And the banshees, those horrible screeching, shifting wenches were all up her craw again, pulling out all the stops.

But why now?

In her heart, Saoirse had known all along. More than once she had wondered if Imogen shared her experiences. Saoirse thought back to her research on banshees, about what they really were.

Not ghosts. Angels of death. Messengers.

When Dadai died.

And Ma.

Who's dyin' now?

Saoirse gasped and pinned the gas pedal to the floor. She was well over the speed limit and pert near in the ditch by the time she swerved into Ma's driveway.

Saoirse left her car door open and bolted inside. There was a pile of blankets on the couch, but no Imogen.

"Imogen!"

Nobody in the kitchen, and no used dishes or clothing draped on chairs. A quick sweep of the bedrooms and bathrooms confirmed the house was empty. As Saoirse leaned on the counter, contemplating the possibilities, the back door clapped against the wall. It had been left ajar, the screen door banging against the house. With each impact, there was a screech. A cry.

"No, Imogen, no, no, please tell me ye didn't."

Saoirse ran into the yard, her eyes following the tracks of Ma's truck tires in the mud.

"Fuck!"

The long grass on the cliffs mimicked her. *Fuck!*

Saoirse stopped running and put her hands on her knees, breathing hard, tears blurring her vision as she looked at the empty space in the barn where Ma's truck used to be.

"Oh, Imogen."

The grass replied, weeping. "*Oh Imogen.*"

Saoirse stood up straight and screamed at the cliffs. "Shut. The fuck. UP!"

The grass swelled and turned dark, floating and rippling like black hair under the ocean, and the wail blasted Saoirse off her feet. "SHUTTHEFUCKUP."

Saoirse flashed both middle fingers at the cliffs as she ran for her car.

22

Floating. The sensation of being neither warm nor cold, hurt nor comfortable.

Imogen sat at the bar, the grit of sand itching her bottom as Mauve poured her a drink.

"'Tisn't real," Imogen said before slugging back the shot.

A trickle of fluid from her inner arm dribbled onto the bar top, forming a pool of blood and heroin. A tiny two-headed snake with tentacles on its body slithered up to the puddle, slurping it up with two forked tongues.

The saloon was full of all sorts of colourful patrons. Wee people with red beards and tall hats, gangly men and women with tongues hanging from elongated snouts, pale shadows with red eyes and blood-stained lips.

"The banshees are gone," Mauve said as she polished a glass. "The ball is over for another year."

"They don't stay?" Imogen asked, her head swaying, her vision blurry with a bitter high.

"Nah. They've got business to attend. People dyin' here and there."

Imogen downed another drink, the alcohol barely staying beneath the surface where it belonged. Her heart seized and loosened, every contraction a chore. Her hands were weak, her neck weaker. She rested her forehead on the bar, and a line of drool connected with the pool of blood and drug like a spider's web.

"What if there's none?" Imogen asked, her words as slurred as her vision.

"None what?"

"Family. The banshees. What do they do if they don't have any family left?"

Hot tears flowed down Imogen's face. Mauve lifted Imogen's head and ran the soiled bar cloth beneath her, wiping up her fluids.

"Then they get to stay, make their life here alongside the rest of folklore."

Imogen reached for her drink, pouring a sip into her mouth, but sat up and scowled at the cool, tasteless liquid.

"This be water."

"Yeah," Mauve said. "You've had plenty."

Imogen nodded, then swayed on the barstool. Mauve reached across and steadied her. "Imogen. Don't go killin' yourself before it's time, ye hear?"

"My sister." Imogen cried, a smile forming, even though it was painful, cracking her dried, chewed lips. "Saoirse. She will save me today."

Imogen closed her eyes and imagined life. Living in Ma's house, having a job, tending to the garden, and hosting dinner for Saoirse every weekend. She'd have a dog, something big and furry that would leave tennis balls and tumbleweeds of fur around the house. And maybe one day she'd meet a woman who'd make her feel the euphoria the drugs did. Better even.

In her daydreaming, Imogen lost her balance and slid off the stool. She hit the floor head first, the impact sloshing her brain inside her skull.

A concussion, she thought. *Must stay awake.*

Her arms were heavy, filled with lead, and her legs were stuck to the floor, adhered by layers of spilled drink and urine. The pain in her head crawled to her stomach, lurching and heaving until all food and drink came erupting into her mouth. The stench of acid and decomposition hit her nostrils before the fluid did, and she snorted the vomit back, trying to breathe.

But her head was a dead weight, refusing to move, to turn to the side, to give the vomit a channel to exit so she could breathe. Her nostrils stung from the regurgitated stomach acid, her chest aching in want of breath. Straining and struggling, the ocean settled in on her chest, the salt water and gentle breeze calming her, cooling her, welcoming her to its icy blue depths.

"It's no matter," Saoirse said with a smug grin on her face. "B'sides, I tol' you so."

Imogen knew her sister was right, but she hated it. Saoirse was always right. It wasn't fair. No, she shouldn't have been playin' on those cliffs in her fancy pantsy emerald princess shoes. Cliffs were made for boots, Dadaí always said. Now she had a great big ole scar marring her prettiness.

"Gives ye character," Saoirse said. "Ye not borin', and this shows it."

Imogen wailed, crossed her arms, and stomped her feet. Dadaí came in, scooped her up, and sat on the bed, holding Imogen in his lap.

"I dunno what her feckin' problem is," Saoirse said. "I's covered in scars 'n shit, and you don't hear me whinin' about it."

Dadaí came to Imogen's defense like he always did.

"Saoirse, Imogen is only five. Things are scary when you're little."

Saoirse stuck out her chin and crossed her arms. "I's never scared."

Dadaí laughed. "Not that you'll admit. But being scared is nothin'. It's heart, it's personality, same as your spunk."

Dadaí patted the bed, and Saoirse cuddled up to him. Imogen twirled her sister's hair in her fingers.

Ma appeared in the doorway with a warm smile for the family. "You've always been the sensitive one, Imogen. Always more affected by scary stores and wee injuries," Ma said on the other side of Saoirse, and she and Dadaí created a circle of hugs that held the whole family tight.

"What we want for both of you," Dadaí said, "is to embrace who you are. Don't try to change it. Accept it, be at peace with it, and see yourself for the gifts ye are."

"Don't be scared," Ma said. "Don't be embarrassed, guilty, apologetic. Just be you."

The family cocoon hugged and rocked on the bed, Dadaí warbling his lullaby as Ma hummed along.

"Too-ra-loo-ra-loo-ral,

Hush, now don't you cry ..."

※

IMOGEN'S HEAD ROCKED, BACK AND FORTH, DADAÍ'S LULLABY singing in her ear.

Too-ra-loo-ra-loo-ral,
Too-ra-loo-ra-li ...

Her tongue was no longer sour with the taste of vomit, but grit crunched between her molars. Her whole body shivered, grinding against the sand and dirt of the saloon floor as she shook back and forth.

Imogen.

Fuil scread chráite.

A dull pain emerged inside her throat. She tried to scream, to breathe, but she could not. Gagging, struggling, she attempted to push the obstruction from her windpipe.

Imogen's head snapped to the side, the sound of a slap echoing in her head.

Imogen.

Fuil Olagón.

Imogen.

Blood wail.

"Imogen!"

Saoirse?

Fighting against the crust of vomit and dried tears, Imogen opened her eyes, blinking away the sand. Saoirse was overtop of her, shaking her by the shoulders.

"Imogen, oh my fuck, Imogen, hold on. Medic's on the way."

Though Saoirse's eyes were wild and red, her cheeks streaked with tear trails, and her chest heaving, she looked relieved. Imogen was lying on her side, Saoirse holding her body in place and head in her lap. She was rocking and singing as Imogen came to her senses.

"Overdose." Imogen's voice was gritty with sand, her mouth just as dry.

"Yeah, lass. But you're gonna make it."

"No." Guilt, shame, anger. Everything rushed up on her, crashing with the pounding of her head and the roiling of her belly.

"Yes, you're sure as hell gonna make it," Saoirse said, her voice breaking. "Cuz I say you is!"

Saoirse pulled Imogen up to her chest, and Imogen wrapped her arms around her and cried.

"I'm scared," Imogen said. "It hurts."

"I know," Saoirse said, as she combed her fingers through Imogen's hair. "But I'm not scared. Not anymore."

Imogen looked up at her, puzzled.

"This is it," Saoirse said. "The rock bottom. The beginning of a new life. Only way ta go is up. We gots a plan, and we got each other. We'll get through this."

Imogen closed her eyes and put her head on Saoirse's chest as Saoirse sang.

"Too-ra-loo-ra-loo-ral,
Hush, now don't you cry."

The world deteriorated to slow motion, the sounds muffled and strained. As if her batteries were dying, Saoirse's voice stretched and distorted into whole notes, dragging. Ramnon dissolved around her, replaced by the sterile, decaying shell of the Asylum's third floor.

From the ceiling, long hair twirled, cascading down and draping over Saoirse's shoulders like a cloak. The owner of the hair, a gangly banshee attached to the ceiling like a spider, reached down, coiling her long nails through Saoirse's hair. She sang along with Saoirse, but out of tune, a melancholy, dissonant version of the lullaby.

Too-ra-loo-ra-loo-ral,

Too-ra-loo-ra-li,

A new voice growled from behind Saoirse.

"You thieving bitch."

It all happened too quick. Too quick for a warning, too quick to heave up and launch Saoirse out of the way. The look of surprise on Saoirse's face was more terrifying than the arm that reached around her, driving the blade of a filthy knife deep between her ribs. Blood blossomed like an Irish rose over Saoirse's blouse, saturating the shimmering fabric and pouring to the floor. Saoirse touched the hilt of the knife, then tipped over on her side.

"Oh, my fuck," the mulleted junkie cried, his shaking hands weaving through his hair, pulling. "I ... what have I done?"

"Murder," Saoirse said, blood spraying from her lips. "They call this 'ere thing murder, you feckin whelp."

"I ..." the Mullet swooned, the colour draining from his face. "She ... took my drugs, and I ... oh, fuck. Fuck!"

His pupils disappeared into his head as he stumbled back a few steps and collapsed on the floor in a heap.

"Good," Saoirse said with a nod. "Ain't breathin' my last listening to that wanker."

"Saoirse!" Imogen pulled herself to her knees and put her hands around the knife.

"Imogen." Saoirse laid back, blood pooling beneath her.

※

"Saoirse."

Aibell stood above the sisters, her eyes both sad and joyful. But it wasn't the demented Aibell, naked and spewing filth from the confines of a care facility. It was the Aibell of old, her regal gown flowing like an indigo river over the Asylum floor.

Only moments ago, Saoirse had been holding her dying sister in her arms. Now the roles were reversed. She lay in Imogen's arms with a fire in her belly and a panic in her mind. Imogen was frozen, words and movements suspended.

Roison's voice called to Saoirse from the back of her memories.

"You need ta look out for your sister. She is young and soft, and we need to give her all the love's been stole from her."

"Saoirse." Aibell's voice brought Saoirse back to the present.

"Am I dead?" Saoirse asked.

Aibell smiled, golden light twinkling in her eyes and sparkling in her mouth. "Soon."

"Ay." Saoirse touched her side, and a jolt of pain seared through her bones. Icy panic and shock threatened to take hold. "Fuck."

Anger shivered through Saoirse's body, replacing the shock. "Damn fecking wretch."

Aibell shook her head. "Do not spend your last moments in anger."

"It ain't fair," Saoirse mumbled, and a thousand voices mumbled with her. "Her damn drugs ended *my* life."

"No good to assign blame for an illness like this."

The love and pity were too great to remain angry with Imogen. As was the worry.

"Who will take care of her?"

"She will take care of herself." Aibell's voice was a song, sweet and reassuring. "You have saved her, Saoirse."

The panic subsided, the pain dulled, and Saoirse's heart lightened. "I'm scared."

Aibell knelt, cupping Saoirse's face, her own a bright, warming sun. "No need. It won't hurt."

"It already feckin hurts!"

"Not for long."

"Great. And what of after?"

The younger, crazier Aibell's words skittered through Saoirse's mind.

"The line ends with you. In Ramnon."

The regal Aibell leaned over Saoirse, her black eyes alive with swirling stars of gold. "You've grander things waiting for you, Saoirse. You always have. As does she. You just get to arrive sooner, is all."

Surreal relief washed over Saoirse, a cool ocean tide carrying with it the scent of Ma's garden.

"All right," Saoirse said. "That be it, then."

She wasn't scared. She wasn't in pain. She was a conglomeration of warmth and beauty and peace. As the world reanimated, Imogen's voice coming into focus, Aibell sifted away into golden sand, blowing away to some great After.

"No ... no, no!" Imogen cried, panicked, her heart clenched, her hand fumbling over Saoirse, searching for a way to stop the blood flow, to fix her sister.

"Lass." Saoirse reached up and cupped Imogen's face. "The medics are on their way for ye."

Imogen puffed out a sigh of relief. "They can help."

Saoirse smiled. "You. They will help *you*. They can't fix this mess."

The blood loss was great, a lake rippling around the sisters on the floor. In the distance, the faint wail of sirens broke through the sounds of city traffic.

Saoirse reached into her coat pocket and drew out the jewelry box, pushing it into Imogen's hand. Imogen took it but did not look. She could not take her eyes off Saoirse, her whiter-than-pale face, her fluttering eyes.

"Imogen, be you. Live your best life. You deserve a moment's peace. And embrace those wailers ..."

Saoirse coughed, and a glob of blood poured out of her mouth and down her shirt. She motioned for Imogen to come closer. Imogen leaned forward and placed her cheek to Saoirse's lips. When Saoirse spoke, a mist of blood wet Imogen's ear.

"We be banshees, too."

Saoirse gasped and clutched her wound. Imogen sat up and took Saoirse's face in her hands.

"I love ye," Imogen cried.

"And I love ye."

With a sputter and a groan, Saoirse's head lolled to the side, dribbles of blood leaking from her mouth and rolling over Imogen's hand.

"Saoirse?"

Imogen shook her, but Saoirse was limp, her eyes fixed, her final breath expelled in a silent note.

Imogen tilted her head, opened her throat, and wailed. It was a sonic blast that rippled the pool of blood beneath them and shook the entire building like an earthquake. With that sound, Imogen expelled years of anguish, of pain, of addiction. Everything she lacked and every pain that festered inside her like infected rot flew away on that scream of anguish.

Imogen continued to wail, joined by all the banshees of their clan—a symphony of keening and mourning. Soon, the stomping of the medic's footsteps provided percussion to the persistent, mournful screams. Even as they pulled her off Saoirse and out of the lake of blood, Imogen kept wailing, all the way to the ambulance, the hospital, only quieting once they had sedated her and strapped her to the hospital bed. Even then, the wails continued in her dreams.

23

Room 482 was noisy with the pinging of monitors and hiss of Aibell's oxygen machine. Imogen sat on a stool beside the bed, the old photograph clutched in her hand, one of the necklaces around her neck. The breeze from the window blew a stray tendril of Aibell's black hair across her face, which Imogen tucked behind her ear with a tender touch. Aibell's eyes fluttered open, and she smiled as her fingertips brushed against the pendent.

"The three guises of the banshee," Aibell croaked. "The young woman, the stately matron, and the raddled old Hag. They are the triple aspects of the Celtic goddess of war and death, namely Badhbh, Macha, and Mor-Rioghain."

Imogen touched the pendent. "That's why I'm here. There are a great many things I do not know."

Aibell smiled in recognition. "Imogen."

"You are Aibell."

"Yes." Aibell tried to sit up, but Imogen put a hand on her shoulder.

"Don't. Save your energy."

Aibell groaned and shook a fist at her body. "Fuckin meat shell. 'Tis failing me, I'm afraid."

Imogen toyed the edge of the photograph with her finger.

"You come to ask me what she did," Aibell said, eyeing the photograph.

Imogen nodded and bit her lip, trying to stave off the tremble that would lead to more sobbing.

Aibell's eyes glistened, and her mouth tightened. "Suppose she be dead if she can't tell ye."

Imogen nodded again, the movement liberating her tears.

Aibell placed her hand on Imogen's. "Ye look well, dear."

Imogen sniffled. "I just completed six months of treatment. I moved into Ma's old house yesterday."

Aibell clapped her hands. "Yes! Atta girl! You do our family proud."

The lavender dress Imogen wore was soft and luxurious, a sundress she'd bought the minute she walked out of the treatment center. She bought it from the shop where Saoirse had bought all her clothes for their visits with Ma. Imogen filled it out now, her thighs gently touching, the soft fabric draping over the curves of her hips and breasts. She was healthier than she'd ever been, but full to the brim with sorrow and guilt.

Aibell stopped her whooping and cheering and patted Imogen's hand. "That melancholy will always be there. But don't let it rule. You are Queen of yourself! Grow, live yer life, don't waste yer luck or yer family's efforts."

Imogen straightened her back, held her head high, and looked into Aibell's black eyes.

"We are banshees," Imogen said.

"Yes."

"I was never crazy."

"Wouldn't go that far." Aibell smirked, and Imogen couldn't help but smile.

"So tell me," Imogen said, settling back in her chair. "Tell me about my family. About being a banshee."

Aibell sat up and patted the bed beside her. "Come. Sit. There's only a short spell before you'll wail for me."

Imogen sat beside Aibell, and Aibell drew a deep breath before starting.

"Once upon a time ..."

For the next few hours, Imogen listened to tales of the mystical race Tuatha Dé Dannan, from which her family had descended. Aibell described the many branches of their family tree, curving this way and that. She spoke of death, of life, of acceptance and love.

After talk of fae and death and family wound to a close, Imogen opened her mouth, finding her voice as Aibell drew her last breath, and released the song of their family.

The Blood Wail.

III
HAPPILY EVER AFTER

Ma's house was the same as it'd always been—cozy and full of love. Vases of Ma's favourite flowers were placed on each piece of furniture, and many lifetimes of photographs cluttered every wall, pictures of the family in all their ages and stages.

"Miss Imogen?"

The bedroom door squealed as it opened a crack.

Imogen cleared her throat. It was getting harder to speak, her throat dry, her mind tired.

"Yes, dear. Please come in."

The nurse entered with a tray of pudding and a glass of Irish whiskey. "Brought ye some of the good stuff. Unless ye want that blessed prune juice."

Imogen coughed out a laugh. "Rosalie, you are the best."

Rosalie set the tray on the bedside table. "How ye feeling, ole gal?"

"Old."

Rosalie laughed. "Well, ye are beautiful and full of life. You don't look even close to your hundred and four years!"

Imogen sighed. "I feel it, though. My time is drawing near."

Imogen looked at the pictures on the dresser. Her graduation photo from nursing school. Pictures of trips she had taken across Europe and Asia. Standing next to an elephant during her stint in the Doctors Without Borders program. Then a panoramic shot of the state-of-the-art addiction treatment center she'd spearheaded on the old grounds of Our Lady's Asylum.

"Are you okay, Imogen?"

"Such a life. I've been so, so lucky."

Rosalie tousled Imogen's hair and pulled her blanket up to her chin, just like Dadaí did when she was a little girl in that very same bed. "Luck isn't the word for it, Imogen. You are a hard worker with a kind heart. You've changed and saved so many lives."

Tears wet Imogen's eyes. When she closed them, she saw Dadaí, Ma, and Saoirse. All smiling.

"Do you want the tele on?" Rosalie asked.

"No thank you, Rosalie. I haven't much time left, and I like the quiet."

With teary eyes, Rosalie left Imogen to her privacy. Imogen sighed, her chest tight, her head heavy. She blinked, slower, slower, until the last breath she drew was not air, but sand, soft and thick. It filled her lungs and pumped through her veins, filling her, becoming her until she sifted away to nothing.

The ground was soft, dirt and sand. Imogen opened her eyes. She was no longer in her bedroom, but outside, the sky a monotone sepia, black trees reaching for her with branches like claws. The air was neither hot nor cold, but perfect. She looked down. Her hair was long and red again, her skin pale and unblemished, her body young and lean and healthy.

A hand cupped her cheek.

She looked up into emerald green eyes, and her heart was full for the first time in forever.

It was Saoirse, radiating beauty and love.

When Saoirse spoke, it was a symphony of peace and happiness.

"Welcome to Ramnon."

The End

AFTERWORD

Though this story is fictional, I based some locations on real buildings and towns in Ireland. I have played with them to fit the story, but the inspiration is very real!

Imogen roosts at the derelict, abandoned Our Lady's Asylum in Cork. This is a real place, though not at all like I describe it in the story. St. Anne's Asylum was once part of Our Lady's Hospital, a four-story building overlooking the River Lee, a short three-kilometer walk from the city of Cork. The site is rumored to be haunted, but is no longer abandoned and derelict. It stood vacant for many years and suffered a terrible fire in 2017. The building was sold in 2018 and restored into apartments--Atkins Hall apartments--which are now available to those not spooked by its history.

Ballinspittle, the town that Saoirse called home in her adult years, is an actual village in County Cork. I was drawn to this village, and wanted to use it in my story specifically because of

AFTERWORD

its picturesque beauty and small-town feel, but also because of the phenomenon of the moving statue. Yes, that was real! In 1985, Ballinspittle gained attention both nationally and internationally for the spontaneously moving and changing Blessed Mary statue tucked up in a hillside grotto. Apparently, she levitated and changed her facial expression, as witnessed by many people. Despite the Bishop of Cork declaring it an illusion of light, pilgrims flocked from all over to see Mary move. She was vandalized by three men in 1985 who destroyed her hands and face, but the original sculptor, Maurice O'Donnell, was able to repair her. To this day, the site receives flocks of tourists who come to catch a glimpse of the phenomenon.

There are several songs used in this story. The song playing in the saloon in Ramnon is *The Irish Washerwoman*, a traditional Irish jig. The song *Too Ra Loo Ra Loo Ral* is an Irish-American lullaby originally written in 1913 by composer James Royce Shannon. Bing Crosby made the song popular in the 1940s, and was a favourite of my father. Dad used to sing it to me and play it on the guitar when I was little.

GUTTED
A RAMNON TALE

JAE MAZER

GUTTED

❦ I ❦

The lights were mesmerizing—turning, spinning, flashing.

The smells were intoxicating—sweet, savoury, sour, earthy.

Belinda liked the way the cotton candy melted on her tongue, granular and sweet, like eating a cloud fat with crystals of rain. She stood under the strings of globe lights ranging across the entire spectrum of the rainbow, the tinny melody of the carousel grinding in the distance.

"Bell!"

Momma called for her, an urgent voice through the crowd. Momma had probably wanted to leave an hour ago, tired of the mass of people and the lateness of the hour. Belinda wasn't tired, though. She could keep going, 'round and 'round the Ferris wheel, hands coated in melted cloud, playing game after game and mounting ride after ride.

"Bell! To me, Bell! Immediately!"

Momma meant business. Belinda knew that she was crusin' for a bruisin' if she evaded departure even one moment longer.

But the lights were so pretty, and the cotton candy so sweet.

Belinda ducked behind a portly man who was clutching a can of cheap beer in his chubby hand. She ducked and dodged her way through the crowd, the smell of fried Oreos pulling her, and body odour repelling her, in every direction. She twisted and turned until her momma's voice was a speck in a sea of white noise, growing ever fainter as her feet padded along the dirt path.

I only need to be invisible for another moment, then she'll go the other way, try to find me by the rollercoaster. As far as the Zipper, even.

Belinda wandered well past the hustle and bustle of the rides and the food and the balloons, and into the mysterious world of the tent vendors: sellers of all things eclectic and bizarre—fortune tellers, soothsayers, vagabonds peddling their wares.

Belinda slowed her step, taking care to stay against the tents so she could remain hidden. The crowd had thinned out this far at the edge of the carnival, and she didn't want her mother to spy her. Belinda's eyes wandered into the tents as she passed, ogling cheap jewelry, patchwork clothing, soaps and powders and grains of every kind. The vendors were crooked and greying, a tooth here and there, scraggly white hair, and long colored braids, dreadlocks, and feathers.

The tent with the sand stopped Belinda in her tracks. She lingered there, under the blue tarp, her eyes twinkling with the reflection of a hundred or more glass vials hanging from nylon cords strung up around the frame of the tent. There were shades of sepia, of black, crimson, shimmering and sparkling like dripping galaxies. She reached out and touched a vial full of dark purple sand, spinning it in the light.

"You like it, dear?"

Belinda startled at the voice, a snarl doused in a wheeze. She pulled her eyes from the purple sand and looked deep into the tent at the vendor. It was a woman, bent and shriveled, skin hanging from her frail frame in sags and stretched rolls. The vendor had nary a tooth in her head, and her smile was tinged with black rot and shimmering with tacky strands of drool, her tongue thick and pressed against the roof of her smiling mouth. And her eyes were solid black and glowing in the night.

"Cat got yer tongue, mah sweet?"

The woman took a step forward, leaning on a dirty ivory cane that creaked under her weight. Belinda stepped back, the twinkling grains of sand in the vials spinning in her peripheral like stars glittering, twisting . . .

"Uh, sorry, ma'am, I's just lookin'."

"An' touchin'," the old crone said, licking her crusted lips with that meaty tongue.

Belinda moved on, quick as she could, offering a nod as she left. She watched her feet, which carried her off in a sprint, and she suddenly regretted leaving the safety of her mother's voice, the comfort of her proximity. Many panting breaths later, Belinda realized she had been so intent on putting space between her and the withered vendor that she had followed the path away from the edge of the carnival and into the outlying woods.

"Momma?" she said, her voice small and sweet like the candy floss hiding in her molars. She knew full well her mother couldn't hear her, but she needed to hear the sound of a voice.

"Momma's not here."

The voice was rough and unfamiliar. It lacked the lilt of the vendor and was punctuated by the sound of clicking teeth.

Belinda turned and saw a figure, large and looming, shoulders broad and hair thick and long.

"Wandered a might out of the way, haven't we?" the man said, adjusting the brim on his shallow bowler. He wore a stained white tank top on his flabby frame, and his fingers pointed, all skeletal and knobby. "The carnival is the other way, my love." He slid his red-lensed glasses down to the tip of his nose and peered at her over the cracked frames. "Nothing out this far but the wolves."

Belinda should have run, but she didn't. She couldn't. In her head, she screamed at her feet to go, to move, to run far, far away and find her mother and never ever come back to that horrible place. But she stood statue-still, staring into the eyes of the man with the fish breath and elongated hands and stains on the front of his trousers . . .

His eyes changed. They dulled, his pupils wide and fixed, and his mouth curled into a silent scream. He stumbled backwards, revealing a third guest on the scene.

The sand vendor was there, hands on her hips, clucking her tongue at the panicked man.

"She's but a girl, you whelp," the vendor sneered. "A *child*."

The vendor looked up to the sky, and the stars looked back at her, twinkling in the solid black between her lids.

Belinda looked away. She didn't know why—she didn't know what was going to happen—she just knew she didn't want to see it. She hid her face behind her hands and squeezed her eyes shut so tight that tears dribbled down her cheeks.

And then it happened, whatever it was. A shift, a rumble. Rough sand whorled around Belinda, licking at the exposed flesh on her calves and caking between her fingers, drawing rivers of sand down the tears on her cheeks.

Something has come to take him away.

Belinda peered into the light leaking through her fingers and saw something wrong. A place that didn't belong.

Golden sand to match the muted sky, the same colours all around. No longer a forest, but a desert, and a one-street town with tumbleweeds and cookie-cutter cabins for homes. And a black lake topped with a yellow sky, and scores of dead trees reaching with broken, charred fingers.

There were things in this place that could not be. A tall bird woman perched in the trees, a severed boy part dangling from her beak. Another woman, this one made of fractured ice, gliding along the lake with a thick, raven plait trailing behind her, her eyes gleaming gold. A pair of redheads who were too long and too tall and too pale, perched on the rocks, wailing a mournful ballad in eerie dissonance.

"Where am I?" Belinda asked as her hands fluttered to her sides.

A clap of hands, and the forest returned. The vendor was standing a few meters away from her, examining a dark stain on the forest floor.

"Predator," the vendor chuckled. "Not no more, though!"

The vendor clucked her tongue then dropped her chin, her eyes finding focus on Belinda's face. Her scowl turned to a grin once she locked eyes with Belinda. Belinda's blood ran cold, and she froze. The woman came to her, her movements jerky and strained. Belinda swore she could hear bones creaking beneath her layers of flesh and blood.

"You," the woman said, tapping Belinda's chest with a bloody finger. Belinda looked down. The woman turned her hand over, opening her palm. "You ain't got enough fear."

"I's plenty scared enough," Belinda said, hands on her hips.

The woman studied Belinda's face. Then her eyes lowered, crawling over Belinda's body, coming to rest on her abdomen. Belinda shivered and crossed her arms over her belly.

"You like the carnival?" the woman asked.

Belinda nodded.

"The people?"

Belinda paused. Thought. "No, not really."

The woman snorted. "Me, either. Filthy lot."

Her eyes were too dark, Belinda thought. Her fingers too long.

"You don't feel quite right, do you?" the woman asked.

Something was wrong. The air was thick soup, and the ground moved beneath Belinda's feet like shifting sand. The trees were no longer trees but creatures that loomed and watched like hungry zombies as tall as the sky.

The woman was looking at her weird. Her eyes were wet, and her lips pinched tight. She shook her head, like she was rattling thoughts inside it. Then she moved her arthritic hands faster than she should have been able, rubbing her palms together, cracking her swollen joints and ticking her long fingernails against each other. A vial on a leather cord materialized in the woman's empty hands, and she held it out for Belinda, letting it swing in front of her face like a pendulum.

"This one, you like?"

The sand in the vial was purple and glittery, granules glinting in the moonlight. Belinda could see the stars in that sand: a multitude of universes, swirling peacefully, cascading like waterfalls . . .

"Want?" the vendor cooed.

"Uh . . ." Belinda did. She really wanted it but knew she

couldn't have it. Her folks could barely afford the Value Village shoes strapped to her feet.

"No charge," the vendor said.

"I—I'm not sure I want it."

"Naw, chil', you want it, you do. But the question rolling about inside your head is *should* you take it."

Belinda nodded, a stray ringlet loosing itself from her matted ponytail and falling down over her freckled nose. The vendor stepped closer still until her breath fluttered that ringlet over Belinda's face.

"Easy answer to your foolish question," the vendor said, closer still, their lips touching as she spoke. "You should. You should always take what you want."

There was power in that sand. Belinda could feel it buzzing through her bones like the hum of a mouth organ.

Belinda grabbed it. She didn't think, didn't hesitate, just swiped the vial from the woman's grasp, turned tail, and sprinted back through the woods, towards the lights and the sounds and the smells of the carnival. She was all of a sudden chilled, but the vial was hot in her hand, practically searing her skin as she scrambled down the path. She held tight, though, as if she was grasping a dying star.

In mere moments, she was out in the open, sprinting past the dark tents and into the light of the carnival proper, rides and screams and tinny music singing at her from every direction. Her brother Danny came into view, and Belinda thanked all the gods, if there were many or one or none, that it wasn't Momma, red-faced and hands on wide hips, foot tapping a crater in the dusty ground.

"Belinda," Danny said as Belinda screeched to a halt. "Where on earth have you been!? Wandering away in a place like this, with the likes of these . . . carny folk."

"I's sorry. It's all just so pretty, and I found this—"

"It's all right, Bell. Just get in the car."

Belinda hung her head and walked to the car. She turned her head a few times but was unable to make out any faces in the crowd while avoiding looking up and seeing Momma's face. She could feel it, somewhere near, angry and judging. Belinda squeezed her already clenched fist even tighter and felt the vial, solid and sure, pressed into her palm. A droplet of blood ran down her pale hand, plipping on the gravel lot as she crawled into the backseat of the old station wagon.

2

Water spiraled down the sink. It was tinted a pretty pink like rose petals. Belinda watched it go, the gross-tasting tap water mixed with fat drops of her blood. It was mesmerizing, watching the red swirl together with that hazy water in the yellowed porcelain sink of the Jack-and-Jill bathroom she shared with her brother Danny. It was morning. Belinda was in a fog, still emerging from her depth of sleep. And she was transfixed by the colourful water.

"Why you gotta do that?" Belinda asked her blood. "Why you comin' out?"

She knew where the blood came from, and why it was coming, but she didn't know how that cut on her hand had got there. She left her hand under the running water, wondering if she kept it there all day long would it wash all the blood from her body? Of course, she knew it wouldn't, but it was a wonder in her mind. Wonders like that passed through her brain all the time, uninvited but not undesired.

But she did want to know where that blood was coming from. Not exactly where it was coming from—she could see the gash on her palm where the blood piddled out into the sink. The question was how the gash had gotten there in the first place. And though she was bleeding, it didn't hurt. Not at all.

Belinda's eyes twitched from the swirling peppermint of blood in the sink to the glass vial sitting on the back of the toilet tank, its purple sand glittering beneath the dirty bathroom bulbs. She hadn't had a chance to truly examine the vial; it had been far too dark crammed in the back of that Buick, and she'd been far too sleepy once they'd arrived at their bungalow out in the country. Besides, her mom was fit to be tied about Belinda absconding into the night amongst the swath of carnies and ne'er-do-wells. There was room for only scoldings, not examination of stolen trinkets. So, Belinda had stowed the vial beneath her pillow and retrieved it the moment her eyes peeled open, coaxed by the rising of the sun. And now here she was, hand draped over the sink, rinsing away the mysterious blood.

I remember, Belinda thought. The cold press of the glass, the sharp sting of a laceration. Everything had moved in slow motion—Danny tugging her toward the car, fat drops of blood splutting in the dirt at her feet, shining in the lights from the carousel.

But here it was, in the light of day, a fully intact vial of sand with nary a grain amiss, far as Belinda could tell. There were no cracks in the glass, no sharp edges, no hooks or jewelry attachments that might have marred her tender flesh.

"So why do I have a gash?"

Belinda's cheeks reddened. She'd overheard Danny talking with his last girlfriend about her gash. Belinda didn't have to listen in much to know that they'd been talking about girl parts.

Why they called it a gash, Belinda didn't quite know, other than it was open like a cut. And sometimes blood came from that gash, so they said, but Belinda didn't believe any of that nonsense. Why would you bleed if you weren't hurt?

The plip of another drop of blood drew Belinda's attention back to the sink. "Why, indeed, if I didn't get hurt . . ."

"Bell!"

Momma's voice was shrill and commanding. It always was first thing in the morning. It wasn't a school day, so there was no need for rushing, but that almost made her mom even more grouchy. The need to get them out and getting on with their day, doing something other than lollygagging in front of the television or the computer or whatnot. Momma'd holler at Danny to do work around the house or tell him he was working too much.

"Bell, breakfast!"

"Coming!" Belinda shouted.

"Now! What are you at up there, running so much water?"

"Coming, Momma! Geez!"

Belinda let the water run over her wound for another few seconds before she swiped a handful of toilet paper off the roll, grasped it in her fist to hold back the blood, and grabbed some bandages from the cupboard. After grabbing the shoebox filled with a bunch of loose and mismatched dollar store bandages, Belinda gave her hand another rinse to wash away toilet paper bits that had stuck to her skin.

"And then how're you gonna dry that so the bandage sticks?"

Belinda jumped, upsetting the shoebox and spilling bandages across the floor.

"Goddammit," Belinda said.

"Big mouth for such a young lady," Danny said. "Momma catches the Lord's name falling out your mouth like that she's likely to burst all the blood vessels in both her eyes screeching at you like a banshee."

"She's not here to hear," Belinda muttered. She looked at her hand, dripping blood and water into the sink, then over at the toilet paper on the roll, then at the paisley towel hanging on the rack.

"Uh uh," Danny said. "Don't even think it. You stain Mom's towels with blood, and she'll force feed them down your gullet and call it breakfast."

Belinda looked at the water in the sink, the pink swirls, and got mesmerized again. She figured she might as well stay and watch all day, caught in the predicament she was.

"Here," Danny said. "Let me help."

Danny popped into his room for a second, then reemerged with an old tattered black T-shirt in his hand.

"Here," he said, "shut that faucet and give me your paw."

Belinda did as she was told. She rarely did that for Momma, but she'd always listen to Danny. Danny wasn't her brother so much as he was her friend.

"Thanks, Danny," she said as her brother patted her hand dry.

His touch was gentle and slow as he examined the wound, pulling it apart ever so slightly.

"Ouch!" Belinda yelped. "What'd you go and do that for?"

"Seeing if you need stitches," Danny said. "Which you don't. I'll wrap it up good and tight, but you'll need to be careful with it."

Fat chance, Belinda thought, imagining the bike ride she'd been waiting for all week long. Carmen—her bestie— and her had been planning to ride down to Bear Creek for weeks, but prairie storms had rolled in and forced them to hold off. The sky had finally cleared yesterday at noon while they were stuck in that stuffy old school, and Mom had paid for carnival tickets after school, so this morning was the first chance Belinda and Carmen had to break free and ride. And no mystery gash (tee hee) was going to keep Belinda puttering around like a feeble old gramma.

"How'd you manage this, anyways?" Danny asked as he sizzled the open skin with peroxide.

"Dunno," Belinda said, trying not to cry. She didn't like to cry in front of Danny, though he always hugged her and rubbed her hair when she did. She wanted to be tough in front of him. She wanted to be like Bill and Jordy and all his guy buddies.

"It's jagged," Danny said. "You catch it on a nail?"

"Dunno."

Danny stopped wrapping the hand and looked into Belinda's eyes.

"You don't know?" he asked. "How do you not know how this happened? This is a pretty big gash."

Tee hee.

"I got it at the carnival, I think," Belinda said with a shrug. "When we were leaving the carnival last night."

"Jesus Fucking Christ," Danny said. "At the carnival? You probably have eighteen different diseases and infections now. Might as well have a bleach bath or you'll sprout extra arms and legs and a head from your left armpit."

He tried to keep a straight face, but Belinda's eye roll set him off laughing.

"You can't grow heads from armpits, butthole," Belinda said, one hand on her hip.

"Oh, yes, you can," Danny said. "That's why you get hair there. It's like grass, and the heads, like plants!"

"With green hair?" Belinda giggled.

"No, girl, c'mon! Is the hair there green? If the grass is brown, the pit head's hair will be, too."

Danny could hardly finish wrapping and taping up Belinda's hand; he was laughing so hard tears were streaming down his face, and Belinda was laughing so hard she couldn't keep still. Danny did the voice of the pit head while Belinda used her good hand to mimic a face tucked under her arm. All was well, good, and happy until Mom's voice blasted up through the floorboards.

"So help me, my Gentle Jesus, if you two brats don't get yourselves down here in the next two minutes—"

Danny didn't react. But then, he never did to Momma's screeches. He slipped out of the bathroom, and Belinda wiped down the counter with his black T-shirt, taking care to get every drop of blood, no matter how faint. She reached for the faucet to give the sink a final rinse and was surprised to find more swirls of pink than there should have been. And it was darker now. Red. The faucet was closed, but the sink was filling, growing darker, the swirls of soft red turning thick, dark, overtaking the water that had now reached the lip of the sink.

Belinda blinked. Hard. Twice, then three times as the water overflowed the sink, gushing over the counter and splashing onto the floor. Belinda looked at her tiny pink feet that were now splattered in water and blood, but she did not panic.

Blink. All I need to do is blink and it'll all go away.

But it didn't go away. The water kept rising, pouring over the counter like a waterfall, and now it was spraying from the bathtub as well. Water gushed from the shower head, which she had not turned on, and from the bathtub faucet, which couldn't be running at the same time the shower was running. But it was running, all three faucets, gushing water that flooded the bathroom, reaching Belinda's ankles in the span of a half-dozen breaths.

"Danny," she called, but her voice trickled out as no more than a whisper.

Don't be a scaredy cat, she scolded herself. *It only makes it worse. Blink. Blink. Blink.*

Warmth trickled down the inside of Belinda's thighs. Heat prickled her cheeks, shame from peeing herself, but when she looked from the bathtub back down to her feet—to the twenty-odd centimeters of water that had accumulated—she didn't see the trademark yellow of urine in the water. It was blood, gushing from her gash, sliding hot and thick down the inside of her thighs. She cupped her hands over her girl parts, trying to hold in the blood, trying to hide it, but the force of it pushed her hands away. All she could think to do was drop to her knees, let the water wash her legs and privates, hide this mess.

Her knees crunched into the linoleum. It was dry, abrasive. The water was gone, replaced by sand, and she was sinking, deeper, sepia sand scraping against her body, peeling away skin as it pulled her down, scratching her jaw, threatening to slit her throat. Her hands plunged into the sand to find her legs, the limbs she could use to stand and walk straight out of that bathroom, but her legs were not there. Below her torso was a tangle of bowels and intestines, thick and clogged with sand. Belinda screamed, but only sand spewed from her mouth. She blinked, blinked, and sand grated her irises, peeling away the blue like jelly in the golden sand.

"Belinda."

She was in Danny's arms. He was rocking her, stroking her hair. The acrid stench of vomit found its way into her nose, and she gagged, tasting vomit on her tongue.

"It's okay, Belinda," Danny said, his voice an ethereal song. "It was another seizure. We are in our bathroom. I have you. You are safe."

Belinda was woozy. Exhausted. A dark figure stood in the doorway, arms crossed, looking on. Momma. Belinda couldn't make out Momma's face. Was she concerned? Scared? Irritated? Angry? Belinda would never know. She never knew. She never saw her Momma's face clear after the seizures. Never heard her voice. Only Danny's, and the melody of his comforting words.

❦ 3 ❦

Belinda stabbed her bacon with her fork and slid it through her scrambled eggs, stretching cheese and gooey white across her plate. Danny made the best eggs ever, and bacon was always delicious, but Belinda's tummy was jumpy. She didn't remember the seizure, only the things her brain had played in front of her eyes like a flickering film. Blood, sand, drowning. It always happened like that during a seizure. While her body twitched and contorted in ways she didn't know and didn't remember, her brain showed her a reel of lies. It had been stronger this time, though. And different. Before, it was just vague shapes on a foreign landscape, a rough palette of muted golds and blacks. But it wasn't scary because it was far away and there was no sound. This time there was sound. And Belinda hadn't been in that faraway land. She'd been home, in her bathroom, staring at her own blood. And there'd been sand. She had felt it. She'd never felt the lies her brain told before.

"You aren't going to touch your eggs?" Danny asked.

He sat beside her, hovering; his chair was facing her, his arms propped on the table, so he was aimed at her.

"I'm okay, butthole."

He nodded. But he wasn't sure, Belinda could tell. She supposed that was okay. Sometimes there were aftershocks after a big seizure.

"I'd love for you to eat," he said as he nibbled the last of his own eggs.

Belinda's mouth popped open, ready for an argument, but this wasn't Momma. This was Danny, and he'd made these eggs, and put cheese in them like Momma never did, and he did it because he knew Belinda liked cheese so much.

Belinda put a mouthful of stretchy, gooey eggs in her mouth.

"Good," Danny said, and his face lit up. "They taste okay?"

"Boss," she said, and her tiny mouthful was followed up by shoveling. She was so hungry. She never knew she was, especially after a seizure, until she started to eat. It was like the seizures reset her body and it needed to be reprogrammed to eat again.

Danny, seemingly satisfied that she was trickling back to normal, stood from the table and carried his empty plate to the sink. He whistled while he scrubbed the stuck and burned bits off the pan; Belinda loved Danny's music because it was a tune he always whistled or hummed while he was working around the house, while he was reading, or while they were driving in the car. When she asked him what it was, he never knew. Just some jingle or shitty radio song or something he'd heard someplace. Sometimes, when Belinda pressed her ear to his bedroom door, or to the locked bathroom door when he was in the shower, she thought he might be singing words, but she couldn't quite tell what they were. She wished she knew so she could sing it herself.

After gobbling up the remainder of her breakfast, Belinda

washed it down with a glass of freshly squeezed orange juice. Danny must have gone to town the day before to stock up on fruits and veggies. She hoped he also grabbed marshmallows to roast over the fire pit. That was her very favorite thing on Saturday nights.

Belinda washed her own plate, then dried all the dishes and tucked them away in the cupboard where they belonged. Stray socks nagged at her from the corners of the living room, so she gathered those up, along with the clothes from hers and Danny's bedrooms, and threw them down the basement stairs. She'd deal with that laundry when she got home from her bike ride.

The kitchen was moderately clean, as was her bedroom, so Belinda figured she had earned her keep and could disappear for the day without much consequence. Danny's voice was murmurs behind his closed bedroom door, so she left him a note telling him she'd be out riding with Carmen on the back trails.

Belinda left the stuffy confines of her house, excited about the day's adventures. The morning air was damp with the chill of moisture, the grass still glistening with the ghosts of fog. It always surprised Belinda how long it took for the sun to burn away that moisture, but she didn't mind the slow process. Sparkly grass was best, both for her eyes and her bare feet. But Mom would kill her if she saw Belinda tearing off on her bike without shoes, so Belinda slipped on a pair of old flip flops that were laying on the front porch and took off into the garage to snag her bike. Soon, her hair was blowing in the breeze, and her face was stretched into a wide grin as she careened across the gravel driveway and to the house down the road. Carmen said she'd be ready by mid-morning, and Belinda had waited quite long enough.

A few minutes later Carmen's driveway crept into view, so

Belinda picked up speed with no care for the impact of the bumps on the wound on her hand. Dust plumed into the air as Belinda ditched her bike in Carmen's driveway, then one, two, three loping strides and Belinda was rapping on Carmen's door with both fists.

"C'mon, Carmen! We're burning daylight here!"

The door creaked open, and Carmen's older sister, Sam, stepped onto the threshold.

Belinda's tummy did a full flip and her legs turned to jelly.

"Hey, Bell. You and Carmen heading out on the trails this morning?"

Belinda couldn't speak. Though she wanted to turn away, she couldn't. It felt like some sort of steel rod had formed over her spine, sprouting a claw at the back of her head, holding it in place so she had to look at Sam.

Sam was horrible.

Is it even Sam?

Sam's eyes were dry sockets full of carpenter ants and millepedes writhing in little balls with thousands of little legs. Her skin was flakey and stiff, and covered with lacerations that seeped thick amber blood. All her skin was like that, from her freshly scalped head to the tips of her way-too-long toes that had fat bloody splinters jammed up beneath each and every nail. Sam was naked, but Belinda wasn't blushing, because Sam wasn't *normal* naked. Her nipples were like knots in wood, her gash like a chop from an axe, and her once-olive skin was now coated in patches of slimy-looking stuff that dripped off her body in great, stinking globs.

"Belinda?"

What is *this not-Sam thing?*

Whatever it was, its breath was rank like rotten mushrooms

and rancid squirrel meat. Belinda's stomach did more acrobatics, and she heaved, her body trying to expel the stench and sight of Sam.

The Sam-thing took a step toward her, and those splinters under her toenails scraped across the porch, popping Sam's toenails off as they stuck in the wood. Sam reached out her hand, which wasn't a hand but an infected stump oozing with more amber goo and covered in bees drowning in Sam's fluids. A single bee wriggled free and shot straight into Belinda's ear, striking her brain with enough force to shock her like a taser.

Belinda hit the deck with a crash.

Sam screamed for Carmen. For Danny.

Belinda blink, blink, blinked. Washed it all away.

Then Sam was there, kneeling over her. And it was Sam, not the Sam-thing. It was Sam with her pretty green eyes, smooth olive skin, and long raven hair.

"Oh, honey, it's okay," Sam said as she stroked Belinda's cheek with her slender fingers. Belinda noted that there was no stump, no bees, only glittering emerald green nail polish. "Danny's on his way."

But Sam's breath. Though it wasn't rancid, like what had billowed from the Sam-thing, it was sickly sweet. More than cotton candy, more than marshmallows. It was so sweet that Belinda could taste it on her tongue and feel it gurgle in her belly. Her mouth watered, and she had an intense urge to sit up and press her lips against Sam's, breathe in the aroma and swallow it whole.

"Carmen," Sam said over her shoulder. "Call him again. Make sure he's coming. Now."

Belinda said no, but only in her mind. Her lips wouldn't quite work, and her voice was stuck in that sweet aroma that coated the inside of her throat.

It's a brain lie, Belinda told herself. She shivered. *No. I never know my brain lies until I'm awake.*

Am I awake?

Belinda didn't want to be. She wanted this all to be some awful dream she could wake from. She wanted to be normal, to go for her bike ride, to feel the branches clawing at her hair and the cool creek wash over her feet. She wanted to hear Carmen's laughter and eat gooey marshmallows off a stick.

Belinda blink, blink, blinked until she forced her eyes to stay closed. The world around her was a whirlwind of noises and sensations: Sam's voice, car tires, the shrieking caw of some sort of super large bird high in the trees. Danny, humming his song, answered by the sounds of wailing off in the distance. The wet morning dew on the deck beneath her shoulder blades and the grit of sand between her teeth and under her eyelids. Nothing belonged together. Only half the things made sense.

Brain lies, Belinda told herself as she floated up into the air, supported by the familiar and comforting embrace of her brother's arms.

❧ 4 ☙

The trees beckoned Belinda; their long branches were extended like arms, mossy fingers curled as if petrified mid-gesture. Belinda longed for the feel of the rough bark against her back, for the tickle of the grass beneath her bare feet. But instead, she was stuck inside, with the hard wooden windowsill threatening to stab splinters into her bum and her forehead pressed against the dusty, discoloured glass of her bedroom window.

"It isn't fair," Belinda moaned, her lip puffed out in a fat pout.

"But Bell," Carmen said as she fiddled with a loose thread on Belinda's bedspread. "Danny's just worried, is all."

"He's overprotective."

"Belinda, that was scary."

"It's always scary." Belinda shot a glare at her friend. "But it's me who should be scared, right? It's my body going wonky, not his."

"What if you get really hurt? Or your brain explodes or something. I heard seizures do that."

Belinda shifted her weight, sitting tall and rotating to face her friend. "It doesn't hurt. Not when it's all over. And I'm not sick."

"I think it's dangerous."

"You don't know."

Carmen's eyes dropped to the bedspread, where she gathered another thread to replace the one she'd snapped. "Have you seen a doctor?"

"Momma doesn't believe in doctors."

"You should be taking medicine."

"That's what the medical establishment wants you to think."

Carmen rolled her eyes. "Now where did you hear that nonsense?"

"Momma told me."

"And just how do you know she's right?"

Belinda had no answer. Instead, she looked back out the window, to the large maples dotted across the lawn. They were stunning against the backdrop of pines and spruce that dominated the forest beyond the yard. Their autumn leaves glowed in the midday sun, handprints of fire against the azure ferocity of the midday sky. She wanted to be out with those trees, not confined to her bedroom. Outdoors, she loved. Indoors, not so much. She wanted to feel the breeze on her face, the earth beneath her feet, the trees and grass and animals at her fingertips.

"Momma wouldn't do something to hurt me," Belinda said. "If she thinks I'm gonna be okay, I'm gonna be okay."

Carmen opened her mouth to say something, but immediately shut it. Belinda wondered what else her friend might have to say. And she needed their conversation to drown out the argument raging from the front of the house. It was clear as day, even with Belinda's door closed. Danny was yelling. He probably thought he was whispering, which he kinda was, but his voice carried, nonetheless. Sam had followed when Danny brought Belinda home in his arms, her legs swinging and kicking his hip as he walked. She had lost her flip flops on the journey; they were strewn on the lawn, several meters away from each other.

That's what Belinda felt every time she had one of her episodes. It seemed like Danny was being pushed farther and farther away from her. Her seizures were thrusting them apart, very much like those poor flip flops on the lawn. Danny was super caring and supportive—Belinda was quite sure he'd move oceans and mountains for her if he could—but she could see it in his eyes. He was tired. Sad. Breaking each and every time he had to deal with her nonsense.

And now he was downstairs, arguing with Sam over her. The arguments were always about her. She was the entire source of this family's stress.

"Man, they're really going at it," Carmen said.

They were. Sam was almost at a full screech, and Danny was scream-whispering back. And Danny was hard to fluster, even in the worst of times.

"Let's go downstairs," Belinda said as she slid from the windowsill.

Carmen jumped at the movement, her face contorted in worry.

"But . . . are you okay? Should you . . ."

Hands on her hips, Belinda faced down her friend.

"Look," Belinda scolded. "I'm not made of glass. I'm not BROKEN!"

Hot tears welled in Belinda's eyes. She didn't want to be different. She wasn't weak, she wasn't frail, she wasn't some terrible thing that didn't belong.

Carmen wrapped her arms around Belinda and pulled her into a tight embrace.

"I know, Bell. I'm sorry. I love you."

Bell didn't dare speak, because speaking might give her tears permission to flow. She hugged her friend and patted her back to tell her everything was okay.

Belinda donned a University of Alberta hoodie she'd stolen from Danny many moons ago, when he had been considered for their medical program. He was good at basketball, too. Would've gotten a scholarship from the Golden Bears if he'd enrolled. But he declined the acceptance to stay and help out the family. With their dad disappearing not long after Belinda's birth, it was hard times around home. The onus fell on Danny to provide, even more since Momma had been spending so much time working away from home to make ends meet.

Belinda shushed Carmen as they left the bedroom. Even though the morning had ended in disaster, Belinda was determined to not spend the remainder of the day in the house. The girls crept down the hall and got down on hands and knees to crawl past the kitchen without being detected. As they approached the kitchen, the argument was in full-swing, loud and clear.

Sam. "It's not okay. She needs a doctor, Danny."

He shook his head. "No. She's fine."

Sam put her hands on her hips. "She's not fine, Danny. You didn't see her."

"I *do* see her. I see it all the time."

Sam's hands moved from her hips, and she crossed her arms in front of her.

"All the time? This happens all the time?"

Danny said nothing.

Sam's lip quivered. "It's awful, Danny. Awful. And where's your mom?"

"Working," he mumbled.

"And what does she think of this?"

Danny shrugged. "She knows best. Belinda is safe."

Sam glared. "It's irresponsible."

"I love Belinda," Danny barked. "I would never let anything happen to her."

Sam's eyes softened. Then something weird happened.

She unfolded her arms. Wrapped them around Danny's neck.

Even weirder? He put his hands on the small of her back. Laced his fingers together. Pulled her body to his until they were pushed together, her boobs squished against his chest.

Belinda grabbed her mouth to stifle a giggle.

"I only want the best for her," Danny said.

Sam nodded, a resignation, then leaned in and pressed her lips against Danny's.

A stew of laughter brewed in Belinda's belly. She didn't want to get caught, but she had to get out of there real fast or her laughter would deceive her and ruin the stealth. Carmen had been in the lead and hadn't seen the smooches in the kitchen. Belinda was delighted at the prospect of spilling the gossip once they got out amongst the trees.

They made it without their siblings detecting their exit. Belinda made it all the way to the scatter of trees in the yard before uncovering her mouth, unleashing gales of laughter to the woods.

A large maple in the center of the sparse grove provided enough cover for Belinda to slide behind in case Danny or Sam happened to peer out the kitchen window or go have a drink on the back patio. Belinda slid down its rough bark until her bum landed with a thud in the dirt, and she convulsed with laugher so pure it squeezed tears from her eyes.

"What's so fricken funny?" Carmen asked, laughing despite not knowing the punchline.

"They were . . ." another fit of laughter, then ". . . KISSING!"

Carmen stopped laughing.

"Who?"

Belinda took a gulp of breath, trying to steady her voice so she could speak. "Danny and Sam!"

"What!?" Carmen screeched, her voice several octaves higher than usual. "What kind of kissing?"

"Like, mouth-on-mouth."

"Was . . . did he have his tongue in her mouth?"

Belinda slapped her friend on the arm. "I don't know, butthole! I don't have X-ray vision!"

Carmen grabbed Belinda's hands. "Ooh, I don't suppose they're doin' it!"

Belinda's laughter slowed. "Doin' it?"

Red flashed on Carmen's cheeks. "You know. Like, the sex."

"The sex?"

"Yeah."

"What's the sex?"

"Has something to do with people who love each other or something. That's what mom says. She wouldn't tell me more, not until I'm older."

Belinda wondered if and when her momma would talk to her about the sex. Her momma had not talked to her about any of the things that adults do and feel and think. Belinda was going in blind and unprepared. And she didn't want to talk to Danny about any of those things. He had a penis, and she did not. It wouldn't be the same, and they'd both be embarrassed.

"Well, they were kissing," Belinda said. "So, they love each other, and are probably doing the sex, whatever that means."

A few moments of silence, of studying each other's faces, then the girls tipped over in fits of giggles and snorts, rolling in the grass and covering their clothes in the stains of nature and joy. Belinda's eyes found the bright blue sky, and the tree branches found her gaze, crackling brown and crimson fissures across her view. Belinda's laughter slowed as she watched the branches swaying in the light breeze, leaves fluttering, wood creaking anguished pleas in her ears. Belinda tried to ignore the voices of the trees, tried to only hear the music of her friend's laughter, but the trees were shouting. *Bellowing*. So loud Belinda thought she might cry or puke or do both at the same time. The ground beneath her heaved, and she knew it was the tree's legs trying to burst forth from the soil. If she didn't move, Belinda thought, the tree would stomp straight down on her and drive its roots through her black, black heart.

"Bell?"

Belinda sat up. Carmen's face was grey with terror. "Is it happening again, Bell? What do I do?"

Belinda shook her head. "No. I'm fine."

"You're not fine." Carmen stood. "You should have seen your face."

Belinda faked a laugh. "I can't look at my own face, you butthole. Not without a mirror."

Carmen was not in a laughing mood, apparently. "No, I'm serious. You looked . . ."

"What?"

Carmen's mouth moved, as if searching for the word.

"Guilty. Terrified. Both."

Belinda laughed for real. "Well, that's pretty specific."

Carmen huffed. "Stop it, Belinda! You need to take this seriously. The people around you are scared to death."

Now Belinda stood, her blood the boiling lava of anger.

"You're scared of me?"

"No-no, I—"

"Am I a fragile, pathetic thing to be feared?"

"No, I—"

"Well, if you're that uncomfortable, maybe we shouldn't hang out for a while. Not until I'm perfect enough for you."

The tears swelling in Carmen's eyes told Belinda she had stung her friend. But she wouldn't apologize. Because Carmen had hurt her, too.

Carmen turned to go but hesitated. Her expression softened. "Is it okay if I go? Leave you alone?"

Belinda threw her hands over her head and, for the first time since they'd met in kindergarten, shouted at her friend. "I'm not a baby! Fuck off!"

Carmen gasped, then furrowed her brows into an angry caterpillar before spinning on her heels and stomping off towards her house. Belinda plunked herself back down in the dirt and slammed her back against the tree. She hadn't realized how exhausted she was until the tears poured from her eyes and sobs belched from her throat. She was tired. So, so tired.

Maybe I am weak.

A baby.

Maybe I'm nothing and no one.

The ground welcomed her as she tipped over and cried into the dirt. She could hear the soil drinking her tears, swallowing her pain as leaves fluttered above, their rustling a soothing melody.

5

Belinda took her time out in the yard. She stayed on their property so Danny wouldn't be too upset, but she didn't go near the house. She played in the dirt, had a swing on the old tire swing hanging from the large tree in the back, and arranged rocks into a little town in the dirt at the edge of the woods. About an hour after Carmen left, Sam left, too. Sam paused and stared at Belinda; Belinda couldn't see the expression on her face—Sam was too far away—but she was pretty sure she knew it was sad. Full of pity. All the things that Belinda was sick and tired of. Sam didn't come over, though, and that was good. Belinda didn't want to smell her or see the Sam-thing again.

Danny didn't come out to get Belinda. His head popped up like a gopher in her bedroom window, then his bedroom window, then in the kitchen, looking out into the yard. She appreciated that he left her alone for a bit.

The wind picked up, coughing clouds that shuddered with

light and rumbled as if their bellies were too full and fat with rain. Belinda's tummy rumbled, too, but not from being too full or too fat. Quite the opposite, she thought as she placed her palm on her tummy, feeling her insides roiling about, complaining of hunger. The last thing that had passed her lips had been the delicious breakfast Danny had cooked before she adventured out to Carmen's doorstep. Where the Sam-thing had been waiting for her.

"Bell! To me, Bell!"

Her momma's voice sliced the air like a blade through flesh. A gulp, a shiver, and Belinda trotted off towards the house with her hand on her belly. She knew she'd be scolded for being outside after an episode, but that was okay. The time out in the fresh air, in amongst the trees, was worth every wicked thing her momma might say or do.

Belinda dragged her feet up the back steps and through the patio door, letting the screen slam behind her to announce her arrival. She stood in the kitchen, arms crossed across her chest, face scrunched into a palette of sassy wrinkles. She waited for someone to come. No one came. She tapped her foot. Still, no one came. She leaned on the counter, expelled a noisy, dramatic sigh, and still no one came.

Surely, they heard the screen door.

Momma just called.

Where's Danny?

Whenever Belinda had an episode, Danny was on high alert. He proved that by popping his melon head and mop of curls into every window to check on her while she played outside. But now . . .

The feral growl from Belinda's stomach reminded her of her hunger. She shrugged off her solitude and marched over to the fridge to grab a snack. Though really, she should make a full meal. Momma would be none too pleased to see her eating pickles and cheese enough to spoil her dinner. But that was precisely what Belinda did. She offered some pepperoni, cheese, and pickles as a sacrifice to her growling tummy to silence its complaints. As she gulped down the food, she debated about calling out to Danny. But then Momma would hear, and she would come, too.

Belinda polished off the entire jar of pickles, half the pepperoni stick, and most of the cheese, but her belly wasn't feeling any fuller, and was certainly no quieter. *Give it time*, Danny always said. *You gotta let your food settle.* But Belinda was impatient and ravenous. She grabbed a bagel and smeared it with cream cheese without taking the time to toast it. After gobbling that down, she popped open the plastic Costco container and ripped a hunk of meat off the rotisserie chicken that was probably intended for tonight's dinner.

Momma's gonna be mad, anyways, Belinda thought as she clawed off another chunk.

Belinda considered going back outdoors. She would have, for sure, but the wind was howling at the moon like a werewolf, brewing a nasty storm with its voice. Belinda thought about the little town she'd made from rocks at the edge of the woods and hoped the fine folks there could weather the onslaught of prairie rain they were about to receive.

Belinda swallowed hard. While she was daydreaming about her pretend town, she'd consumed over half the bird. Now Momma was gonna be mad for real, and for real mad never ended well for anyone.

Belinda shut the fridge door as gentle as she could, as if the soft suction of its closure would alert someone to her presence more than the slam of the screen door had. She looked at the pantry door, and at the cupboards, considering what other snacks she could grab. The chicken hadn't put a dent in her hunger.

"Bell! Here! Now!"

Busted.

Belinda shuffled out of the kitchen and down the hall. Sounded like Momma was in Belinda's bedroom. Belinda made a mental inventory of what she had in there, wondering if there was something she'd brought in that'd make Momma extra-spicy mad. It was good to be prepared for these things. But Belinda could think of nothing.

"Hurry up! What's taking you so long?"

But Belinda did not hurry. She slowed, crossed her arms, prepared for battle. Momma shouldn't be in her room, invading her privacy. And where was Danny?

Belinda stepped into the glow spilling from her doorway, which was only the dim light filtering in from the murky sun shrouded by the approaching storm. The actual light was off, and her room was empty.

"Momma?"

Belinda poked her head in the bathroom, wondering if Momma had stumbled upon a bloody mess that wasn't supposed to be there, that wasn't there, but maybe it actually was. But there was no mess in that bathroom, and no Momma.

Momma would not be in Danny's room. Danny was older than Belinda, and he helped out around more than a brother should, so Momma left him to his privacy. So, Belinda concluded she must be in the master bedroom. Belinda was excited about this. Even when she was in trouble, she was never allowed in the master bedroom, so this would be super cool, even if she was getting yelled at.

The door was closed. Belinda stood in the hall, shifting her weight from foot to foot, debating about knocking, or walking in, or walking away.

"Come in, Belinda."

It was weird, that voice. It wasn't mad. It sounded like Momma. Maybe? Belinda wasn't so sure. The voice was unfamiliar enough that the wee hairs on the back of Belinda's neck rose to attention.

"Come."

Belinda placed her hand on the knob and pushed the door open. As the master bedroom came into view, Belinda was struck with an aroma that nearly brought her to her knees. It was sweet and seductive, like the scent coming off the Samthing. Belinda's mouth watered, and her belly screamed with a hunger so deep Belinda was sure her own insides were going to consume her.

Belinda had been in the master bedroom before. It was plain, with off-white walls, beige carpet, pressboard furniture, and paintings of mountains and chickens hanging on the walls. Boring and traditional. Now, the master bedroom was all wrong. The floors were crooked, rotting wood with nails sticking out here and there. The walls were wood, too, round logs stacked atop each other like a log cabin. Fire burned in an old wood stove in the corner, crackling and snapping with each step Belinda took into the room. The wood squealed out some moisture, and it sounded like pigs at the slaughter. Or like little laughter, hiding beneath the bark.

The bed was the worst. It was large and looming, a four-post monster made of gnarled obsidian, all sorts of beaks and talons and teeth carved into the ebony rock. And lying on the bed was a mass of shiny crimson, gurgling and wiggling and cooing.

"Momma?" Belinda whispered past her tears.

But she knew Momma wasn't there. There was only this thing, reaching for her, curdled in its own fluids.

Belinda didn't want to see. She didn't want to go to it. But she went, floating until she was at the side of the bed. It felt like there was an invisible string in her mouth, resting on her tongue, pulling her down until her face hovered about the bloody mass. The thing on the bed curled in on itself, its head large and round, its tiny fingers flexing, grasping—

Its eyes popped open. They were dark chocolate, just like Belinda's, just like Danny's.

"Momma!"

The voice did not come from Belinda this time. It came from this thing on the bed, the thing that sat in a pile of its own carnage, giggling and babbling and growling.

Run, Belinda screamed in her mind, but her legs would not go. She righted herself so her face was not within reach of the grotesque spawn, but her lower half would not move. She glanced at the door, hoping Danny would rush in and save her, but what she found there was far worse than what was on the bed.

Those are mine, she thought, as she looked at the pants standing in the doorway. They were filled out, as if they contained legs, but the body was severed at the waist, exposing the lower digestive tract, which still churned and pulsated as if still in use.

Those are mine! she screamed at the legs that wore her favourite pants. The pants that had a few super pretty rocks she'd collected in her pockets.

Belinda looked down.

"Those are mine," she said aloud. She, too, had been severed at the waist, but she was the upper half. Her entrails swung beneath her like tattered ribbons, swinging to and fro beneath the air from the ceiling fan as she floated in place beside the bed. The bloody creature on the bed squalled and Belinda screamed, both splattering blood over the white carpet and yellowed bedspread with the tiny yellow roses. Crying and screaming and blood filled the room until everything was red and wet. Out of air, Belinda gulped in a breath to start screaming again, but a blink washed it all away. She was standing at her dresser, in her very own bedroom, the vial of purple sand clutched in her hand.

"Hey, Belinda." Danny strolled through the door, hands in his pockets, eyes on the carpet. "You doing okay, kiddo?"

He didn't know. She wasn't having an episode—not anymore, at least.

Calm down, Belinda thought, willing her heart to quit punching her ribs.

"Belinda?"

Fake it, she told herself. *He can't know you had another episode.*

"Thank you for letting me play outside," Belinda said. "I know I was supposed to stay in bed, but my day was ruined, and I didn't get to go on my bike like I wanted, and—"

Danny raised a hand and smiled. "Hey. I'm not upset."

His smile melted Belinda into a calm she wouldn't have thought possible just moments before.

"No bits of mad at all?"

"Maybe a few little crumbs of frustration, but defs not mad."

Danny stepped forward and wrapped his arms around her. Belinda dissolved into his hug, feeling it and thinking of nothing else.

"I know it's hard, Belinda."

Belinda backed up and sat on the bed. Her eyes flickered to the doorway. She wished she was some sort of sea creature, and her eyes could stretch and curve and see down the hall into the master bedroom.

That was NOT an episode.

"I just want to be normal," she said. Her lip started quivering, and she felt the baby sobs clawing their way up her chest.

Danny sat on the bed and rubbed her back, and Belinda tipped over and rested her head on Danny's chest.

"Normal's not a thing," Danny said. "Nobody is normal because normal isn't real."

"Okay. I wanna be healthy."

"You are healthy. And strong."

"I ain't."

"Grammar."

Belinda sat up. Crossed her arms. "Healthy girls don't have episodes. Healthy, strong girls don't have to miss out on bike rides and miss school and stay home so much."

Danny winced. "Are you uncomfortable? In any pain? Do you feel nauseated, dizzy?"

Belinda shook her head.

"There you go," Danny said. "Not sick."

"Then why I gotta stay home after episodes? I never hurt and never feel pukey!"

Belinda wiped her nose with the back of her hand. She was full-on crying now. She couldn't stop it. All she could think of was her bike sitting all alone in the grass, the trails unexplored, while she was stuck in here with her broken brain and the bloody demon on Momma's bed and all the horrible and wonderful things she saw and smelled that were all lies.

Danny opened his mouth, then closed it, then opened it again, like he couldn't find words. And Belinda didn't want him to. He'd only be trying to comfort her, but he didn't know any better than she did.

"Where's Momma?" Belinda asked.

Danny looked at his feet. "Work, I suppose."

"It ain't fair," Belinda said.

"I know," Danny said.

They sat quietly for the next few moments, holding hands. Belinda could see that there were tears in Danny's eyes, too, but she didn't tell him she saw. She didn't want him to be embarrassed. He looked at her hands and gasped, making Belinda jump and drop the vial of sand.

"What is that?" Danny said as he pointed at the vial like it was a cockroach riding a rat.

"My treasure I got at the carnival."

He kept pointing but didn't pick it up. "Did you steal this?"

Belinda shook her head. "Uh uh! I would never!"

"How did you get it?"

"Some ol' carny gave it to me."

Danny hesitated, then bent over and picked up the vial. It nearly slipped from his hands. Belinda leaned in and looked closer. The sand appeared brown through the sheen of blood on the outside of the glass.

"Belinda, are you bleeding?"

Belinda opened her fists. No blood. Dry and pale and clean, other than the dirt from her rock town.

Before Danny could ask any more questions, Belinda jumped up and ran down the hall to the master bedroom. Without a pause, even though fear slammed her heart against her chest once more, she threw the door open.

The room was right. Normal old pressboard furniture, metal bedframe, clean yellowed blanket with yellow roses embroidered on the fabric.

Danny rushed up beside her. "What?"

Belinda looked at the vial in Danny's hand. It, too, was clean and dry, the purple sand glistening beneath the naked bulb on the ceiling.

Something was off. Danny had secrets, maybe many secrets, judging by the look on his face when he held the vial up for a second examination. He said nothing but tucked the vial in his pocket and forced a giant ol' lie of a smile across his face.

"What a weird day," he said. Belinda noticed a tremor in his voice.

Lies and secrets make you wobble, she thought.

"You must be hungry," Danny said as he turned and left her side. "We have a chicken from Costco if you want . . ."

Belinda didn't hear the rest of what he was saying as he walked down the hall, away from her, away from that bedroom where everything was as it should be, but nothing was quite right.

6

Right from the get-go, school days were horrible days. Everything, from the gross school bus to the bullies to the boring classes, was awful. And this day was particularly bad because Belinda's one and only ally was not speaking with her.

Well, I'm not speaking with her, either, Belinda thought, drooping out her lower lip.

Carmen stayed up on her porch with Sam and did not move until Belinda was in her seat. Their seat, though that's not where Carmen chose to sit. She sat with Millie, the stinky girl with the braces and the greasy yellow hair. No one ever sat with Millie. She had peed her pants in first grade and stank of urine ever since. And her hair was yellow like urine, and her face shiny like it was wet, which was probably pee, too. Super gross, but there Carmen sat, regardless. It was either share a seat with Millie or come to the back of the bus and sit with Belinda. A lump swelled in Belinda's throat at the choice her former bestie had made.

The stench from the diesel bus caused Belinda's stomach to clench, further exasperated by the bumping and heaving as it traversed country roads full of pocked gravel and random trenches. The more Belinda jiggled and bounced on her seat, the lonelier she felt. There was no one beside her to knock elbows with, or to compare snacks with, or to gossip with.

It was worse at the school. The bus pulled up, and the driver ushered them out like bleating cattle, separate little pods of children scattering every which way. Belinda was alone and didn't know which way to go.

"Go on with ya," the bus driver cawed, swiping her salt-and-pepper mane away from her crazy eyes. "Get away from the bus and on to yer business."

Belinda moved away from the safety of the bus's shadow. She didn't want to hang around outside, where cliques and clans of students mingled and chatted, shooting her the occasional glance and giving her the once-over. Belinda became acutely aware of her outfit, her hair, her body, and wondered if they were all noticing those things about her as well.

Usually, she and Carmen would go hang out in the library or by the lockers, but Carmen wasn't talking to her—no, *she* wasn't talking to *Carmen*. Belinda was isolated. Alone. Vulnerable. And she hated it.

She sulked through the front doors, down the halls, feeling the breath of whispers striking her from all sides. There was almost an hour before first period started; that was far too long for Belinda to go sit in class, but not long enough to walk down to the corner store and grab some coke gummies. Because she wanted to keep busy, or at least look busy, Belinda decided to head to the cafeteria and grab some breakfast. Momma loaded her account so she could charge lunches, but never really checked what Belinda was spending it on. Momma'd be fit to be tied if she knew Belinda was wasting their money eating a second breakfast when they had perfectly good toast at home.

The aroma that greeted her when she passed through the cafeteria doors turned on her saliva like a faucet, and Belinda had to swallow so drool didn't fill her mouth and leak out the sides like a gross baby. She was still so hungry, despite having downed a whopping four slices of bread slathered with molasses right before she boarded the bus.

There was no one in line; very few kids ate breakfast at the school. Most were too busy with all their friends and their smiles and laughter and judging to be able to fit food into mouths full of mean words. Belinda shuffled her feet up to the breakfast line and grabbed a tray. The lunch lady was back on, working away at eggs stuck to the wide grill against the wall.

"Hello," Belinda said. Her voice was small and soft but felt booming in the quiet of the cafeteria.

Even so, the lunch lady did not turn. Her body jiggled as she worked the food, and Belinda cringed at the dark stains of dank moisture beneath the woman's arms and where the fabric of her apron tucked between the folds of her back fat.

"May I have some pancakes, please?"

The woman didn't hear Belinda. Or she was ignoring her, Belinda thought, like everyone else always did. Belinda was agitated, by her loneliness and by her hunger, both growing hotter and more ferocious by the second.

Belinda slapped her hand on her plastic tray and pushed her voice to a yell. "May I have something to eat!"

The lunch lady's folds jiggled. Then a gurgle rumbled deep in her hefty body. Her spatula clattered to the floor as she bent over and held her giant girth in both her hands. It took Belinda a moment to realize what the lunch lady was doing.

She's laughing.

The gurgle crescendoed to a cackle, then a roar as laughter blasted from the woman's throat all over the grill, the walls, from one end of the school to the other. Belinda covered her ears, then her eyes, then her entire face. Now, everyone would look at Belinda, this horrid, gravelly laughter drawing their attention like a siren song.

"Please stop," Belinda whispered. "You're embarrassing me."

The woman stopped so suddenly that the quiet caused Belinda to jump. She was surprised the woman had even heard her over her own raucous brays.

"Stop what, m'love? Cookin? Laughin?"

With great effort, it seemed, the woman turned, spinning on her clogs like a crooked, broken dancer in a music box.

Belinda's blood turned to solid ice. "You," she squeaked, hardly believing who she was seeing.

And just like that, Belinda's hunger was gone, replaced by a too-full ache in her belly that threatened to split her in two. All that toast and molasses and juice Belinda had consumed only an hour before threatened to squelch up her throat and out her mouth, giving the entire school something else to laugh about. Belinda swallowed the bulging clot of vomit, hard, and it sank into her belly like a swollen river stone.

The woman was horrible, even worse than Belinda remembered that night at the carnival. It was the same woman, the sand vendor, but she had changed. Her body seemed to be both rotting and growing, like she was decaying and swelling all at once. Her flesh was puffy, her belly and throat bloated, but her skin was thin and crackled, with some patches thin enough to settle around bones that protruded this way and that. Her eyes were the same, wide and black, and her limbs too long and crooked. She smiled, exposing her black cavern of a mouth, with gums coated in thick, dark slime.

"Now let's get to business, my darlin'. You says you's hungry, so let's get you fed."

Belinda shook her head.

"Yes, that's what you said." The woman approached the serving platters set on her side of the glass. "I'll fix you up a nice plate."

"You're the vendor," Belinda squeaked.

The woman scooped a spoonful of scrambled eggs onto a plate, and viscous black pitch dribbled from her seeping gums, spiraling down and pooling on the pile of eggs. "Aye," she said. "I am."

"But you're here."

"Aye. I am."

The pile of eggs became a mound, then a mountain, too tall and perilously close to tipping off the plate.

"No, thanks, I don't want eggs, please."

"It is possible to be two things in a life." The woman cackled and continued scooping eggs, even though the plate had reached its max, and greasy white chunks were rolling off and falling to the floor like thick, yellowed snow.

"You . . . work here . . . and the fair."

Another spoonful of eggs, and half the plateful tipped down the front of the woman's apron, dribbling down her clothes like snot.

"Look," Belinda said, "I really don't want those eggs."

The woman slammed the spoon down on the now-empty

serving platter and reached over the partition to place the plate on Belinda's tray.

"Enjoy your breakfast, little one!"

The woman returned to the grill. Her voice rang through the cafeteria, but it did not belong. It was soft, sweet, melodic, far away—a song familiar deep down in Belinda's memories, but foreign at the same time.

Ang gatas at ang itlog ay pagkain pampalusog
Ang saging at papaya ay pagkain pampaganda

The woman's singing swelled as she worked at the grill, scraping, flipping, greasing.

Ikaw uminom ng gatas at kumain ka ng itlog
Hindi magtatagal at ika'y bibilog
Alagaan mo ang manok bibigyan ka ng itlog.

Every sound the woman made, from the sweet melody of the song to the wet grunts from her diseased, infected mouth, were like blades penetrating Belinda's brain. Belinda wanted to be far away, outside where the harsh chatter of the other children would ring like soft and joyous harps next to the filth belting from this woman's lungs. But Belinda couldn't move. A searing pain in her stomach kept her locked in place. She dropped her tray to clutch her stomach, and her plate smashed on the floor, spraying eggs several meters in every direction. The few kids mingling around the cafeteria stared. Kids appeared from a nearby hallway to point and stare and laugh, but Belinda didn't care. She didn't care about the kids or the eggs or even the lunch lady's gross mouth and weirdo song.

What she did care about was her belly. When she clutched at the pain, her fingers found a bulge beneath her shirt. As her fingers fondled the odd bump, the pain softened until it was but a ghost of a sensation, and all that was left was the pressure of the new thing held against her belly button. Belinda lifted her shirt, and the first thing she noticed was a ribbon tied around her waist. It was beautiful, bold ruby red and royal blue framing an embroidered yellow sun and three tiny glittering stars that decorated the inside of a white triangle. Beneath that ribbon that was tied ever-so-carefully around Belinda was the lump.

Who?

How?

When?

Belinda fumbled at the ribbon with trembling fingers until she unlaced the bow. The lump fell to the floor with a dull crack. Belinda knelt beside the mess.

It was an egg. Not just a plain old breakfast egg, but a real live egg with a chick inside. Belinda stroked the goose-fleshed skin as the half-formed chick writhed and mewled in its half shell. Its head was backwards, its body contorted and broken from the fall, but still it lived, crying and struggling against the egg membrane and a smear of its own blood.

"I'm sorry," Belinda said, and tears dripped from her eyes and down on the pink chick. "I didn't mean to. I didn't know you were there."

The chick creaked its tiny head and fixed its milky eyes on Belinda. When it opened its beak, a caul of membrane sealed the air, but the sound came, nonetheless. Screaming. Wailing. The tortured cry of a human baby but ten times as loud. Belinda scrambled backwards away from the chick, slipping in the cooked eggs she'd dropped over the floor, slipping and sliding to try to get away. The broken chick pulled itself from its shell and slithered towards her. All its orifices were squirting thick blood as it lurched at Belinda, bellowing its hateful, pained cry the whole time.

Belinda couldn't find purchase on the wet floor, and the chick managed to reach her. It crawled up her leg and onto her belly, leaving a trail of mucus and slimy blood in its wake. Paralyzed by both fear and wonder, Belinda watched as the chick's screeches quieted to gentle coos and it nestled itself onto Belinda's belly button. Belinda brought a finger up to stroke its fleshy body, but before she could, the chick lifted its head, then pecked down and penetrated Belinda with a wet squelch. It buried its beak into the soft flesh above Belinda's bellybutton, then squirmed and wriggled its way through the puncture like a worm. Belinda screamed and screamed and ripped at the opening, but the chick was quick and strong, and in the blink of an eye, Belinda watched the last talon on the chick's tiny foot disappear below the surface of her body, and the wound seal and disappear like it had never been there at all.

"What are ya at down there?"

The lunch lady was standing overtop of Belinda, staring down with those black eyes and rotting smile. And behind her, circled in a half moon, was an entire horde of children, pointing, laughing, and whispering.

Belinda groped her belly. Dry and clean. Surveyed the surrounding floor—broken plate, a whole mess of cooked eggs, no eggshell, no ribbon, no chick. There was a smear of blood, however—on the front of her shirt and down the seam of her pants.

"I fell," Belinda said.

But she did not get up. She cried. She didn't care who was watching. Didn't care who was looking, laughing, hating. She pretended she was sitting in her yard, in the little town she'd made from rocks and sticks and moss, where she would dissolve into sand, and no one would ever find her ever again.

7

The nurse's office was gross. Not gross like the cafeteria with the gruesome lunch lady and the slimy eggs, but its own kind of gross. It reeked worse than the cafeteria, with the stench of sanitizer, bleach, boogers, and sick farts all mixed together. Belinda fought the urge to gag, though her stomach felt like a bottomless pit, empty and growing deeper by the minute.

"Belinda?"

And it was far too bright. Mostly everything was white—white walls, white tile floors, white bedding on the white bed. To break up the overwhelming whiteness, the room was splattered with neon animals and emojis and a twinkling, blinking sign above the nurse's desk that screamed LIVE LAUGH LOVE.

"Belinda, do you understand?"

Belinda squeezed the soft wrapper in her hand. It squished like foam and was soft and smooth like a flower petal.

"This goes in my vagina?" Belinda asked, turning the pad over and holding it in her open palm.

"Sweetie, no. I mean—there is a product called a tampon that women put inside their vagina, but at your age, I think you'll find a pad is more comfortable. Open it up, have a look."

Belinda peeled the small piece of tape and unfolded the pad in her lap.

"What do I do with this?"

"See the sticky side?" the nurse said. "That sticks to your panties."

Belinda crinkled her nose. "Like a diaper?"

"Well, no, but . . . I suppose. A little."

"The blood comes from my butt? Or from where I pee?"

The nurse sighed. "Neither. Has your mother not talked to you about this?"

She hadn't. But Belinda's momma hadn't spoken to her about much in a great while.

"But won't people see the bulge?" Belinda said, steering the conversation away from emotions she didn't want to feel. "I wear a lot of tights. Cool ones with animals on them. I know people aren't supposed to be lookin' at my privates, but I bet they do."

"People won't notice, sweetie. Many women wear these."

"Are you wearing one?"

The nurse flushed a red as neon as the offensive decals on the walls. "That's private, Belinda."

"But you tol' me a period is nothing to be ashamed of."

"It isn't, but it's private."

"Why's it private? If most women got one, why's it such a big secret?"

"Well, it just is. Not a secret, I mean. But private."

"Seems silly."

The nurse stood and picked a set of spare clothes off her desk, and handed them to Belinda, along with a plastic grocery bag for her dirty clothes. "Why don't you use the bathroom here to clean yourself up and change. Stick the pad on your panties. You shouldn't have any trouble."

Belinda gave the pad the stink eye. "I don't want this bulgy thing touching my girl bits."

"You'll get used to it," the nurse said.

Belinda doubted that very much, but she was tired of talking to the nurse. The office was so bright and stinky, Belinda thought her eyes might burst out of her head. She took the clothes from the nurse and locked herself in the single bathroom adjacent to the nurse's office. The lights were bright in there, too, but there was no neon, so that was good. The smell of sick poops and vomit was in there, though, so Belinda hurried. She took off all her clothes and threw them in the plastic bag, then evaluated herself in the mirror.

There was blood smeared across her belly and abdomen. Belinda squatted down and checked between her legs. There was no blood on her bits or on her thighs. She took her panties from the bag and inspected them. No blood there, either. And she would know if there was any blood on them. They were light yellow with ugly pink flowers. Danny had bought them for her at Sears when she tore her last pair trying to get them on. She outgrew stuff fast, and Momma seemed to pay no mind. So, Danny had done the shopping, and Belinda ended up with these lame-o flowered granny-panties.

Belinda swiped a hand between her legs and held it to her face. Nothing. No blood. She conducted a more thorough exploration and got the same result.

She was not relieved. She wanted it to be her time to period.

At least then there'd be an explanation for the blood. She wanted to be like the other girls, with their puberty and their tampons and their lumpy diaper slabs. But here she was, with weirdo chicken blood on her clothes from a chicken that wasn't there. A demon chicken, or a ghost chicken, or a crazy chicken that was only in her brain.

Belinda wrapped the pad in toilet paper so the nurse wouldn't know she didn't use it and tucked it deep into the garbage can. She washed her hands and pulled on the clothes the nurse had given her. They were from the lost and found, and they were two sizes too big. Belinda almost cried.

Just another thing for everyone to tease me about.

Belinda sulked out of the bathroom with the plastic grocery bag clutched against her tummy.

"All better?" the nurse asked, her voice an annoying cheese grater.

Belinda nodded. She was on the verge of crying and didn't want to say anything because that would let loose the tears. And she didn't want anyone to see her crying. She was already horrified enough by the scene in the cafeteria and the terrible Fresh Prince clothing. But the nurse could tell something was wrong; Belinda could see it all over her peachy face and in the way her pink-glossed mouth curled down into a frown. That mouth opened, about to start another conversation Belinda didn't want to have, but a ruckus from outside the door provided a distraction.

"What on earth?" the nurse said.

She walked out of the office to the school reception area with Belinda close on her heels. The lunch lady was there, and she was fit to be tied.

"Rude!" the lunch lady said, stabbing her thick finger at the woman behind the desk who was cowering in her chair. The lunch lady's face was crunched up into angry wrinkles like an old bulldog.

The office staff shambled out from behind closed doors to see the commotion. The principal, in her blocky heels and too-tight pantsuit, walked around the counter to confront the lunch lady.

"What's the problem here?"

The lunch lady turned her black gaze to the principal, but caught sight of Belinda, who was hiding behind the nurse. The lunch lady's scowl smoothed into joy, and she reached her hand out. A warmth enveloped Belinda, wrapping around her like a shawl, and her tight anxiety loosened as if someone had pulled a binding thread free.

"Oh, there you are, child. Are you okay?"

Belinda nodded. She should have been upset, or scared, or grossed out. This woman was super gross, after all. But Belinda felt none of that. Not like she had felt before, at the carnival, in the cafeteria. Now she felt safe, comfortable, calm.

The lunch lady kept her eyes on Belinda but addressed the principal. "I was just checking on the young woman. She had quite the upset in the cafeteria." The lunch lady faced the receptionist again, and her expression contorted back into feral rage. "And this harpy wouldn't tell me anything! Wouldn't let me back to see her!"

The receptionist opened her mouth to answer but the principal cut her off. "Belinda, do you know this woman?"

All eyes turned to Belinda. She nodded.

"You do? Who is she?"

The lunch lady hissed, and the principal jumped. Everybody jumped at that sharp, wet sound.

"Ask *me*!" the lunch lady said. "I'm right fucking here, you stingy, proper twat!"

"Okay," the principal said. "That's enough, ma'am. You need to leave."

No!

Belinda's bad feelings tickled her insides again. Sensations of unease, embarrassment, the haunting reminder that she was a weirdo. Even stranger? Belinda felt a surge of protectiveness growling just below her surface.

Belinda stepped forward. "Um, she's the . . . uh, she works in the cafeteria. Cooking."

Glances were exchanged between the staff gathered at reception.

"No," the principal said. "No, she doesn't. Mrs. Barber has been our lunch lady for years."

Belinda stared at the lunch lady, vendor, old woman, whoever she was. "I know, but she was cooking, and she gave me eggs in the breakfast line."

All eyes shifted to the woman. The principal looked her up and down. So did Belinda. Her apron was covered in oil, eggs, and the black muck from her mouth. She had pus-filled burns on her knuckles and forearms, just like Carmen's uncle who had worked as a line cook at the Smitty's.

"She was cooking?" the principal said, her voice shrill and rising with each syllable.

Belinda nodded.

"That's it," the principal said. "Sharon, call the RCMP."

The old woman clucked her tongue and coughed out a raspy giggle. "Don't get your knickers in a twist. I'll be on my way."

The principal ignored her. She hopped on the intercom and called the gym teachers to the front.

The old woman burst out into forceful laughter. "Madame, you'll need more than a pair of sweaty try-hards in short shorts to deal with me. But I don't wish to cause you any more angst, so out I go."

With a hard shove, the old woman opened the double doors to make her exit. She paused and looked back, directly into Belinda's eyes. Her eyes grew too wide, pert near covering her chubby cheeks, and her smile split her face ear to ear, releasing dribbles of sludge down her mottled flesh. Through the bustle of the school staff shouting and arguing and moving to and fro, Belinda heard the old woman's voice as she stood meters away from her in that doorway. It was not coming from her lips, or anywhere else. It was as if it had sprouted right inside Belinda's ears, wet and thick like wax.

"It's okay, m'love. Come when you're ready."

And with that, the woman made her exit, the bright morning sun swallowing her whole. The commotion inside had slowed to a blur and a dull roar—there was lots of noise, lots of movement, but it was distorted and slow. Belinda knew people were talking, but she couldn't understand what they were saying; it was as if they were speaking to her underwater. Their movements were the same, fluid and murky and all muddled together. Above that, clear as a bell, Belinda could hear other sounds. Birds cawing. The banging of wooden doors. A keening, sweet and dichromatic and haunting all at once.

A hand on her shoulder.

"Belinda?"

Carmen.

The world came back into focus. It was still chaos, but proper chaos. Staff were hustling around, gossiping about the old woman, moving and speaking as they ought to in the real world.

"Are you okay?" Carmen asked.

There was no anger in her tone.

"Yeah, I guess."

"The kids said you peed yourself with blood."

Belinda shrugged.

"It's just your period, right?" Carmen asked.

"You know what a period is?"

"My mom told me. She had to. When Sam gets hers, she's a giant bitch. And she eats all my school snacks and yells at everyone for existing."

"Geez. Glad I don't have a big sister."

"Well, Mom says boys are just as bad. They get something called boners that they hide in their pants. They stick out everywhere and they spit stuff all over the place."

Belinda gasped. "Gross!"

The girls laughed, and for a second, it was like all was right in the world.

Carmen's laughter faded, and she examined her shoelaces, maybe looking for words.

"Hey," Belinda said. "I was a bit of a jerk the other day. I'm sorry. I guess that's just my periods, right?"

Carmen smiled and Belinda's whole body relaxed.

"Yeah!" Carmen said, her mouth blooming into a smile. "I hope I don't get my periods. It sounds bloody awful."

Laughter exploded from the girls, which drew the attention of the principal.

"Enough!" she scolded. "Now Belinda, if you have everything sorted out, you two need to scurry on to class."

"Yes, ma'am," the girls chimed in unison.

They walked back to class, hand-in-hand. Belinda would have

been overjoyed if it weren't for the impossible sounds still echoing in her mind like music buried in sand.

8

On the bus ride home, things had returned to normal. The seat next to pee-pee Millie was empty, and the seat next to Belinda was occupied by her bestie. The familiar knock of their elbows together as the rickety old bus bounced over pits and potholes made Belinda's soul smile, but something lingered there, just below her surface. She couldn't quit thinking about the lunch lady. The vendor. And about the chicken, the ribbon, the blood. And even as she tried to focus on Carmen's snorts and laughter as she tried to time her farts with the bumps on the road, Belinda could still hear noise in the background. Not the crunching of bus tires on gravel, not the shrieks and squeals of the other children on the bus. It was something far away, behind a veil. Chittering, cackling, snapping.

"Butthole!" Carmen shouted and gave Belinda a shot on the arm. Belinda feigned a smile, but Carmen clearly wasn't buying it. "What's wrong?" Carmen asked, then dropped her voice into a whisper. "Is it your periods?"

"No!" Belinda snapped, then pulled her knapsack over her lap like there was actually a giant girl-diaper there she was trying to hide. "Not everything's about that, you know."

Carmen quickly nodded. "Sorry. I know, but . . . I don't know."

Belinda pulled another smile, forcing it into place. "I guess maybe I'm grumpy, yeah."

Carmen hugged her and Belinda rested her head on her friend's shoulder.

"I'm sorry I'm such a sensitive potato," Belinda mumbled.

"Baked or fried?" Carmen asked with a giggle.

Belinda thought of French fries and her tummy warbled. Then thoughts of meaty gravy and thick cheese curds poured atop those fries turned that warble into a loud and ravenous growl. Belinda pulled her knapsack tight against her tummy to muffle the beast, but Carmen noticed anyway.

"You hungry?"

"Yeah."

Carmen dug in the front pouch of her knapsack and hauled out a peanut butter granola bar. Belinda loved those, but Momma would never buy them. Belinda tore it open and bit half the bar, filling her cheeks like a chipmunk and chewing with exaggeration to maneuver the large hunk of bar around her mouth.

Pain exploded in Belinda like a hand twisting her stomach, then a violent nausea sent the bus into spins. Belinda heaved, and the gooey, half-chewed bar fell from her mouth and slopped to the floor in a lump.

"Ew!" Carmen said. "Gross! Belinda, what's wrong?"

Belinda used the sleeve of her borrowed jumper to wipe the vile taste off her tongue.

"Gross," Belinda said. "It's rancid!"

"What?" Carmen said, looking at the wrapper that had fluttered from Belinda's hand onto the seat between them.

"That bar! It's gone bad. How long has it been in your knapsack? Since kindergarten?"

Carmen rolled her eyes. "No, jerk face, since this morning."

While Belinda continued to cleanse her tongue on the sleeve of the ugly jumper, Carmen plucked the wrapper off the seat and examined it.

"See," Carmen said, pointing. "Doesn't expire 'til next year. There's nothing wrong with it."

"You try, then, if you think it's so tasty."

Both girls looked at the slimy lump on the floor, and then got the giggles. But Belinda's were only on the surface. It wasn't a spoiled bar. Belinda knew that. *She* was what was spoiled. There was something very, very wrong. As if to voice its agreement, her belly roared, vibrating every centimeter of her flesh.

The bus rolled to a stop on the country lane at the end of Carmen's driveway. The plume of dust caught up, shrouding the girls as they hopped off towards Carmen's house. The driver waited until Carmen opened the door to pull away.

"Sam!" Carmen shouted. "We're home!"

Fear like weird fingers tickled the hairs on the back of Belinda's neck. Crooked fingers, with yellowed nails, and as much as Belinda tried to convince herself that it was only the wind rustling those pesky hairs at her hairline that wouldn't catch up to growing as long as the rest of her hair, she couldn't help but envision the old crone reaching for her, touching her, feeling her right deep down to the inside of her belly.

"Hey, girls! How was your day?"

Sam's footsteps were light and graceful down the hall, but

still too loud for Belinda's ears. She didn't want to look at Sam. Would she be Sam, or some rotting, spoiled thing that had taken Sam and replaced her, mimicking her, all the while digesting her?

"It was okay," Carmen said, looking at Belinda.

"What?" Belinda asked.

"Are you okay, Belinda?" Sam asked. "Did you . . .did something happen at school?"

Belinda's shoes had six lace holes on each side. Belinda counted them, one at a time, rather than look up at Sam.

"I didn't have an episode, if that's what you mean," Belinda mumbled.

"I think you should just tell her," Carmen said. "I mean, she's got one, too."

"Got what?" Sam asked. Now Sam was standing in front of them. Belinda allowed her eyes to move off her own laces and on to the *Exorcist*-puke-green polish on Sam's toes.

"I, uh . . ." Belinda pulled her knapsack in front of her body and hugged it close, as if Sam was going to immediately be able to see through her clothes and stare at her girl parts and know she was lying. "I got my period."

Sam came closer. Put her hands on Belinda's shoulders.

"Damn! Oh, my god, you're growing up so fast!"

Before she knew it, Sam was leading her to the couch. Belinda refused to look up at her. She hoped Sam thought it was because she was embarrassed about her period.

"Did blood soak through your pants?" Sam asked. "Is that why you're wearing that . . . outfit?" A snicker.

"Uh . . ." *There was no blood gushing out of my privates. It was from my tummy, from where the greasy chicken burrowed into me.* "Yeah. I did."

Sam waved a hand. Belinda saw the movement in her periphery. She still refused to look.

"That's no mind," Sam said. "That pretty much happens to everyone, even if it's not their first period. You never know when that shithead is gonna arrive. Did anyone see?"

Belinda shrugged.

"Well, it's a part of life, honey. And it sucks, but we deal. I'm gonna get you some hot chocolate. And a doughnut. Oh, my god, you can't imagine how good those things taste when you're on your rag."

Sam flitted off into the kitchen as Carmen sat next to Belinda on the couch.

"You okay?" Carmen asked.

"I feel fine," Belinda lied. She was so hungry it felt like her stomach had turned into an ugly troll that was eating her from the inside out. Saliva pooled beneath her tongue at the thought of devouring a doughnut. Maybe six.

"Don't be embarrassed," Carmen said. "Just think. You're basically an adult now."

Belinda wanted to be happy. If it was her period, that would mean she was normal. That she was like Momma, and Sam, and probably even the crone who kept popping up everywhere. But it wasn't her period, and she wasn't normal.

"Here you go!" Sam chimed as she pranced back into the room with a tray full of goodies.

Don't come near me, Belinda thought, but wondered why that thought had manifested in her brain. She'd always liked Sam.

Sam didn't listen to the words in Belinda's mind. She invaded Belinda's space, reaching across her to place the tray on the coffee table in front of her. Sam's arm brushed against Belinda's jumper. Belinda wanted to close her eyes, to turn her head, but she couldn't. She was frozen, staring at the thick jagged splinters of wood Sam had for fingernails. Belinda's eyes crawled up the crooked branches of Sam's arms, to the bare knots growing on Sam's chest like breasts. Those knotty nipples were seeping dark sap that dripped and dribbled on Belinda's pants like viscous, clotting period blood. When Sam spoke, Belinda was drawn to the sound, and was unable to avoid looking directly into Sam's face.

"Are you feeling sick? Headache? Tummy pain?"

Mountain pine beetles flowed from Sam's mouth as she spoke, chittering and gnawing at each other as they writhed and clawed their way back up into Sam through her nose, her ears, her eyes, her mouth. Her hair was thick moss tacky with bloody sap that flowed down the striations in her bark-flesh like creeks of molasses.

"Do you have a tight, puffy tummy? That's just bloating. I can give you some Midol if Danny says it's okay."

Belinda shook her head. "No, I don't want Danny to know."

Sam was sitting so, so close. The outside of their thighs touched, and Belinda tried to pull away, but the sap stuck them together like glue.

"I get it," Sam said, releasing a fresh onslaught of insects as she spoke. The beetles moved in droves, climbing over Belinda's thighs and into the cracks of the chesterfield. "But Danny will understand. I mean, he won't *understand*, but he knows about periods."

Sam smelled so good. Heat radiated from her body, wafting into Belinda's nose, carrying with it the taste of fresh baked goods and savory perogies. Belinda took a deep breath to consume whatever was coming off Sam's body, out of her mouth, from every hole and surface that Sam had. It was like every tasty treat ever merged into one glorious aroma.

"Momma never told me," Belinda whispered, then swallowed hard to keep drool from pouring out of her mouth.

Sam was quiet for a moment, then she took Belinda's hand. Her skin was rough, not pleasant like her scent. Belinda fought the urge to pull away for fear she would end up with a palm full of splinters.

"Your Momma is wrong," Sam said. "In so many ways."

Shocked as she was by the Sam-thing beside her, Belinda felt a tickle of warmth at the acknowledgment that maybe Momma wasn't always right after all.

Belinda looked up into the hollow caverns that were Sam's eyes.

"What?" Belinda asked.

"Your momma should have told you. About all of this. And she should be around more. Or at least some. I mean, Belinda, you haven't been well, and it's all perfectly normal, but you might need medical attention."

These were things Belinda knew to be true. But hearing them said out loud brought forth a wave of sadness and madness. She wanted to lean into Sam, hug her, and be hugged in return, like a proper mother and daughter. But those gross bugs and scratchy bark . . .

"Hey," Carmen said. "So, you get your period?"

The Sam-thing looked at Carmen. Carmen didn't flinch, didn't make a face. She looked completely calm and composed.

I'm the only one that sees.

Belinda took care to relax her shoulders. She was hallucinating. She needed a doctor. She would tell Danny, and he would take care of her, and it would all be okay.

"Of course, I do," Sam said.

"Are you . . . having the sex?"

Sam gulped a swallow of air. "Well. Yes, I've had sex."

Belinda and Carmen gasped in unison.

"Oh, stop," Sam said. "That's as normal as a period. Do you even know what sex is?"

Carmen giggled. Belinda had so many questions, and the uncomfortable humour was a relief.

"With Danny?" Belinda asked.

The Sam-thing's seeping mouth crackled into a wide smile with a sound like splitting wood. She shrugged, and Carmen let out a round of whoops and hollers.

"Holy shit, you're doing the sex with Danny!! Belinda, you'll be my niece!"

The Sam-thing groaned and stood up. "You two are a circus. Belinda, I'll let Danny have *the talk* with you."

Sam. Danny. Belinda didn't know how to feel about that. She loved Sam like a sister. Maybe even like a mother. But something wasn't quite right. She couldn't put a finger on it.

As Carmen followed her sister into the kitchen, pelting her with all the questions, Belinda listened to the skittering of thousands of tiny feet ticking, following the girls into the kitchen as swarms of insects dropped from Sam like diseased acorns. But Belinda wasn't scared. Well, she was less scared. Because she knew there was nothing wrong with Sam. It was her. Her brain, her body. And she would talk to Danny about it, tell him everything, and he would make the world right again.

9

The giant tree was rough but solid against Belinda's back, and the rustle of its leaves in the gentle breeze was a comforting lullaby. A book lay open on Belinda's lap, but she couldn't focus to read. And besides, the brightness of the day had descended into the warm ombre of pinks and purples that would soon devolve into navy, leaving her little light but the moon and the stars. Certainly not enough light to read by. But the weight of the book on her legs was comforting, and the tree made her feel solid. Grounded.

In contrast to the sole porch light lit on Belinda's home, Carmen's house was a beacon; every window was aglow with the light of lamps. Carmen's parents had arrived home as they always did, shortly before supper. They'd invited Belinda to stay for perogies and sausage, but Belinda had declined. Not because she wasn't hungry, but because she couldn't imagine sitting across from the Sam-thing and having to swallow food. Instead, they had gone home, and Danny had made her favourite—Kraft

Dinner with a splash of hot sauce. Even though it was her favourite, it tasted ugly, and that made Belinda sad. She did her best to finish it, but she had to fight it down, macaroni by macaroni.

They chatted though dinner, Belinda doing her best to hide her displeasure with the food, then Danny popped over to see Sam for a bit. Belinda had wondered if Sam was still beautiful to him, or if he also saw a tree. She supposed Danny wouldn't be having the sex with a tree.

Now, as Belinda's house stood dark and lonely, and she sat alone against the tree in her back yard, Carmen's house was full of life. Belinda watched the silhouettes of Carmen's parents hustling and bustling around the kitchen, and Carmen's head moving about her bedroom. It looked like she was dancing, probably to that new Harry Styles song, which Belinda would be sure to tease her about later. That guy wore skirts and looked prettier than the both of them combined. It wasn't fair.

But Belinda's focus was on Danny. And Sam. Danny and Sam, their faces so close in the upstairs window, so close, then touching, and touching again.

Is that the sex? Belinda wondered, but she'd heard that they should be laying down for that.

Danny wasn't with Sam for long. He said he'd only be there a short while, and Danny always did what he said. Danny was the one person Belinda could always count on. And sure enough, Danny and Sam's heads pulled apart one last time, then Danny's form disappeared from the upstairs window and reappeared out the front door. He spotted Belinda in the yard, yelled one last goodbye into Carmen's house, then headed towards the tree. When he reached Belinda, he didn't tell her to get up and come inside. He usually did, because it was getting dark, and the creatures of the night would soon be waking. But tonight, Danny settled on the ground and rested his head against the tree.

"You could've stayed," Belinda said.

Danny tilted his head down to look at her. "What?"

"With Sam. I'm fine. You could have stayed and hung out with her."

Even in the dark, Belinda could see his wide, glowing smile.

"Bell, I wanted to hang out with you. Sam and I see each other lots."

An awkward silence, fat with suppressed giggles, swelled between them.

"You know—" Danny started, before Belinda burst out an interruption.

"You and Sam are having the sex. She told."

Danny groaned. "Oh, lord."

"But you are, aren't you?"

Danny smiled again. "Yeah."

More silence, then Danny asked, "Do you know what that is?"

NOPE.

"Don't wanna know."

Danny laughed. "Good. Because explaining that mess is not on my want-to-do list. But Belinda, I will explain it. Whenever you're ready."

"I . . ." Belinda kinda wanted to know, but she wasn't sure she wanted to be talking about penises and stuff with her brother. "Why doesn't Momma tell me? She's supposed to, isn't she?"

Danny's smile faded, and he looked to the sky, gazing at the leaves overhead. "Yeah. There are a lot of things that'd be better for Momma to tell you. But you're stuck with me, while Momma's busy."

Belinda crossed her arms in a hug over her chest. "Why?"

Danny's head tilted down, his eyes pulled from the leaves above their head. "Why are you stuck with me? Because you're too young to be stuck by yourself, kiddo."

"No. Why is Momma so busy?"

"She has to work, Belinda. Living's expensive. Since Dad left . . ."

Danny's eyes glistened with tears and his mouth shut into a tight line.

"Why?" Belinda whispered.

Danny looked at her but did not speak. She figured he couldn't. She knew that feeling, where the tears were there, and they came out on your voice if you talked, so you kept quiet so the tears would stay in your head where they belonged.

"I mean, why did Daddy leave? I don't remember him."

Danny drew a deep breath in through his nose and exhaled slowly. Despite what looked like his best effort, a tear escaped and trailed down the stubble on his cheek. He swiped it, and Belinda pretended not to see.

"Daddy had a hard time," Danny said. "He's a good man, he just couldn't . . . and Momma's good, too. She does the best she can."

"She never tells me stuff. I never, ever get to see her."

"I know." Danny looked back up at the canopy of branches, as if he might find answers hanging in place of the leaves.

It's okay, Belinda thought. *I have Danny if Momma doesn't want to be around.*

"Sam told me stuff, too," Danny said.

"Told you what?"

"You started your period today."

Oh, my god.

"Danny, gross."

"Ha," he said. "It really isn't. Just a pain in the ass. But all girls get 'em."

She nodded. "That what the nurse said. Sam, too."

"Listen, I know I'm a dude, but I know things. If you want to talk about it—"

"I really don't."

"Okay. Well, would you like me to pick you up some pads?"

"Diapers?"

"Well, you are my baby sister, but no. Pads. You could try tampons if you prefer. I'll pick up both and you can try what you like."

"Ugh, Danny, stop!"

Danny laughed. "Hey. It ain't easy for you. Least I can do is help you out however I can. Sam suggested chocolate and drugs."

Danny warmed her heart. He would do anything for her, but the mention of Sam drew Belinda's attention to the tree pressed against her back, and the memory of the Sam-thing that was more bark than flesh.

"Danny. There's something I want to tell you."

Danny went very still. Tense. Belinda could sense it in his stiffness, the way his breathing quieted.

"There's something wrong with my brain. I think I have the mental illness."

"What?" Danny said.

He moved away from the tree to sit in front of Belinda. He took her hand, and Belinda's own eyes moistened. It wasn't sadness, though. Not really. It was almost anger. Frustration. And a touch of relief that she was finally going to get this off her chest.

"My episodes," Belinda said. "I . . . see things."

Danny was quiet, his voice level and calm. Eerie. "What kind of things?"

"Sand. Lots of sand, like up in the bathroom. It was bleeding from me like blood. And there's lots of actual blood, too. I can smell it so bad, and I taste it on my tongue."

Danny nodded but said nothing.

"And in Momma's room. On the bed. There was a . . . I think it . . . it was a dead baby on the bed. But it wasn't dead, it was moving, but it was all blood, like a giant clot. And it was making noises."

Danny grimaced, but still he did not speak. His eyes were focused on Belinda's face, and her eyes on him. She was getting it all out—there was no stopping it now. She had to see Danny's reaction. Whether he was disgusted by her, or hated her, or was afraid of her. That was a worse nightmare than all the blood and sand and chickens in the world.

"And in the cafeteria. It wasn't my period, Danny. It isn't my period, I mean. There was blood, but it wasn't mine. Well, it *was* mine, but it wasn't from, you know, down *there*."

Danny cocked his head and looked down at Belinda's stomach. "What? Bell, are you hurt?"

"No, no. Nothing like that. Actually, no, not now, but at the time . . . it's really hard to explain."

Danny was looking at her face again. "But there was blood."

Belinda nodded. "Yes."

"Was it your blood?"

"Um, yes, but also, there was . . ." *I'm going to sound crazy. Because I am crazy. But it's okay. Danny will help, and he will still love me, and everything is going to be okay.* "There was a baby chicken. It came from an egg that was tied to my belly with this red and green ribbon, and I dropped the egg, but the chick came after me and, I know this is gonna sound crazy, but the chicken pecked into my belly and went inside . . ."

All the colour had escaped from Danny's face, leaving him whiter than virgin snow. His eyes were wide, but his lips were smiling. Belinda knew it was a fake smile.

Danny squeezed Belinda's hand. "It's okay, Belinda."

"And the kids, they saw blood. And they thought . . . it was on my pants, and the nurse gave me a diaper—"

"Pad."

"Whatever. Point is, there was blood, but it wasn't from down *there*, and I'm obviously crazy, but am I?"

Belinda was sobbing now. Sucking in great gulps of air that sat like a lump on top of her belly. "What's wrong with me, Danny?"

Danny pulled Belinda's hands and brought her into his lap. She rested her head on his chest and cried as he rocked back and forth, stroking her hair.

"Nothing," Danny said. "There's nothing wrong with you."

"I'm not normal!"

"You are exactly who you are supposed to be. So that's normal."

But Danny was shaking. His colour hadn't returned. And he had this weird look on his face and tears in his eyes.

"Are you scared, Danny?"

A hesitation, then, "I'm okay, just a bit sad, maybe. I don't like it when you're uncomfortable or hurting. But everything is going to be just fine."

"I think I need a doctor, Danny."

He shook his head. "Why do you think that?"

"Where's the blood from, Danny?" Belinda jumped to her

feet, and Danny startled and almost fell backward. Belinda lifted her shirt to show her blemish-free abdomen. "There's no cut, no hole. But there was blood on my clothes! Maybe it was never there, and I don't know what to do!"

Belinda crumpled to the ground, and Danny gathered her in his arms again. He was trembling just like the leaves over their heads.

"Okay. I'll take you to see someone," Danny said.

"Doesn't Momma have to take me?"

Belinda could hear Danny's teeth grinding before he spoke. "Momma's busy. I'll take you."

Belinda had no desire to argue. She preferred Danny, anyways. Danny cared. He was there when Momma wasn't.

"Look. Let's head on in and I'll make you some hot chocolate."

Belinda nodded. "And a snack? I'm so hungry."

"You didn't finish your Mac and Cheese. Why don't you eat that?"

Because it tasted like rat poop.

Belinda shrugged. "Dunno. Don't really like it."

Danny sighed. "I'll see what else I can find."

Danny stood and pulled Belinda off the ground. He started walking toward the house, but Belinda paused. Turned towards the edge of the woods. There was a sound. A scratching. Knocking on wood. The tinkle of music.

"Coming?" Danny asked.

"In a minute," Belinda said, her eyes focused on the contorted, misshapen shadows of the forest. "Just gonna stroll while you make the hot chocolate."

"You sure? You okay?"

"Uh huh."

Belinda could tell that Danny wasn't sure, but he always respected her space. After contemplating something for several moments, Danny slowly made his way to the house. Once he was inside, Belinda followed the odd sounds coming from the woods. Once she was within four meters of the tree line, she realized the weird noises weren't coming from the woods at all, but from the edge of their yard.

The little town she'd constructed from rocks and dirt and sticks had come to life. Hints of candlelight shone in windows, shadows of things moved to and fro, coming in and out of cabins and lodges. Water in a central fountain trickled down, shimmering in the moonlight. All sorts of sounds emanated from every structure—cackling, hissing, cawing, wailing. And music from a little building with a double set of swinging doors. An Irish jig plunked out from a player piano. All impossible things that Belinda had not created but were eerily familiar.

Belinda reached out and poked the saloon doors with her pinky finger, and they swung open with a tiny squeak. All the lights in the impossible town extinguished and the sounds fell silent. A blink, and it became an arrangement of rocks and sticks and mud, just like Belinda had made, and nothing more.

But a new sound appeared in the distance. A slow pulse, throbbing. The beat of a deep drum. Belinda looked towards the sound, towards Carmen's house. The sound was coming from there, speeding up, growing louder with each thrum. The lights in the upstairs window rippled with each beat, and Belinda wondered if the sound was causing the light to flicker, or the flickering light was causing the sound. She stood and walked towards Carmen's house, and the sound intensified; the tempo went from a steady canter to a roaring sprint, and the volume increased from a muted pulse to an ear-shattering decibel.

Thump.
Thump.
Thump.

Belinda covered her ears and retreated. When she turned back to her own house, she found Danny's head blocking the kitchen light as he prepared hot chocolate beside the sink. She focused on Danny's form, moving to it, focused on nothing else but the shape of Danny, which led her to the quiet safety of home.

10

The bed clothes were sandpaper against Belinda's skin. She shed them as she slid out of bed. She was awake but hadn't woken. Not really. Her bedroom was fog, her body floating, wispy gossamer moving like warm fluid. To the window she went, beckoned by the beauty of the moonlight and the enchanting siren song of the thumping from the house next door. Her vision tunneled as she gazed longingly out the window at the dark house standing there like a specter, inviting her with warm arms like a mother. The house gyrated in rhythm with the pleasant thumping that pulsed the night air, thrumming the stars.

Belinda's legs were gone. She'd left them standing beside her bed, pajama bottoms tied up with a neat little bow around the waist. Her toes still wiggled, her glittered polish sparkling even in the dark. Belinda must have detached from her legs when she'd stood from her slumber. It didn't hurt, but it should. She was calm, though she knew she shouldn't be. But she was.

The window wasn't open, nor was it there. The glass was just gone, leaving a gaping opportunity in its absence. Belinda floated outside like a cloud, sailing over the yard and the trees below. Even from way up high, Belinda's eyes were sharp, piercing through the slithering black of night to see the bustle of the wee town below. Her rocks had become cottages, her sticks a saloon. Laughter and the clinks of glasses reached all the way up to her ears, drawing a smile across her face.

The thumping demanded Belinda's attention. She soared away from her house, away from the impossible town, away from the comfort of the tree in her yard, towards the droning pulse of the house next door. Tender fingers tickled the place where Belinda's legs used to be. She looked down as she glided across the sky, and found not fingers, but the bulge of her intestines trailing behind her like ribbons on a gown, leaking blood and bile and feces to earth like viscous clots of rain.

But still, she was calm. Even as she placed her hand upon her belly and wrapped her fingers around exposed organs at work, digesting, converting, expelling, Belinda knew, deep down, this was right. Things were as they should be.

Belinda perched atop the house next door. Her innards trailed down the shingles, resting there, gleaming and oozing trails of slime. She pressed her body against the roof and the pulse vibrated through her skin, filling her muscles, and sent a gentle percussion through the marrow of her bones. The sound heated and aroused the growling beast in her belly and forced her mouth to moisten. An ache radiated in her mouth and neck; it was as if someone was pulling her tongue from her throat, but with pleasure, like physically coaxing a cobra from its den.

The aroma was intoxicating. Sweet and savoury all at once. Belinda needed that scent to solidify so she could feel it in her mouth, fill her cheeks with it and gulp it down into her belly. Her tongue flickered, teasing the corner of a shingle, the pleasure of the grit drawing more tongue from her throat until it was impossibly long.

Blink.

Belinda was in the bedroom. Or her tongue was. It had pierced the roof and was exploring the ceiling. There was something below on the bed. It was the source of the sweet intoxication that was dominating Belinda's mind and body. The tongue reached out, tasting the air overtop the figure, feeling the deep breaths that the form on the bed expelled in hot, wet vapour. Manipulating her tongue like a thick finger, Belinda pulled back the comforter, exposing what lay beneath.

It was a gorgeous woman, hair black and shiny as a raven, skin smooth and taut. A sheen of sweat made the woman's nudeness gleam, and the chill from the removed comforter caused her nipples to swell into dark mountains, heaving as she breathed. Belinda licked the woman's throat with the tip of her tongue, then traced a line between her full breasts, down her abdomen, coming to rest on the soft patch of skin below the woman's belly button. Belinda lingered there, her tongue drawing circles as saliva pooled on the woman's pale flesh. A narrow proboscis birthed itself through the end of Belinda's tongue, releasing a dribble of thick white fluid. Both proboscis and tongue swirled in the milky wet on the woman's abdomen before the proboscis drew back and stabbed into the woman. She moaned, a sound somewhere between pleasure and pain. Belinda explored inside the woman, tasting, sampling, pushing through walls of flesh, the thick casing of the womb membrane. Belinda's body tremoured in euphoria as she finally drank, drawing meat and blood through her new tongue appendage while the woman pushed her hips up, thrusting against Belinda's hunger.

They stayed locked like that, Belinda and the woman, until both were panting and spent. Belinda withdrew her tongue, which sealed the proboscis within again, then pulled the covers over the woman's moist, shivering body. There was no blood. The woman was not contorted in pain. Belinda was full, and all was well.

※

Belinda screamed. Sat up in bed. Threw her covers on the floor. She lifted her pajama shirt, ran her hands over her belly.

Danny ran into the room, breathless. "Bell?"

Belinda wiggled her toes. They were attached to her feet, which were attached to her legs, which were attached to her body.

"Bell, what happened? Are you okay?"

Belinda jammed her fingers in her mouth, felt her tongue, pulled on it.

"Bell, talk to me!"

Belinda tried to speak, but her throat was dry and rough. She swallowed, then swallowed again, trying to force down what felt like clumps of sand. Danny grabbed the glass of water off Belinda's bedside table and put it to her lips.

"Drink," he said.

Belinda obeyed. The water was cool as it poured over her tongue, and it soothed the raw pain in her throat. Her ears ached as she swallowed, and pain prickled through her body.

"Growing pains," Danny said. His voice was soft. Eyes were wet.

Belinda still couldn't speak. Her tongue was foreign meat in her mouth, dry and thick.

"A bad nightmare," he said.

Perhaps it was, Belinda thought, but it seemed as real as the pain in her mouth and anguish in her soul. The sweet nectar of that woman still sloshed in her belly. Her hunger had disappeared completely, leaving a feeling of satisfaction.

Nonsense, Belinda tried to convince herself as she rolled her tongue around her mouth, searching for that tube, that other thing buried within. But her tongue was lumpy and gross and normal. Nothing there that shouldn't be.

"You want me to leave the light on?" Danny asked.

Belinda nodded. But she didn't just want the light on. She wanted Danny to stay. To watch her. To hold her legs if her body lifted off into the air. To grab her trailing intestines like Maypole garland and pull her back down to the earth and hold her until she was happy and safe.

Belinda never had to ask. She still hadn't spoken a word when Danny came back in her room with a fresh glass a water, and a sleeping bag and pillow tucked beneath his arm. She drank as he rolled his makeshift bed out on the floor right beside her bed.

"It'll be okay, Belinda."

She gulped another mouthful of water. Each time the cool liquid funneled down to her belly, it washed away the taste of the dream. That delicious aroma and taste from the dream was a vanishing memory, one that might not have been there at all.

"Yes, it will be okay, Belinda." Danny paused. Sat on the edge of her bed and put his arm around her. He inhaled through his nose, and his exhale shuddered, bringing with it creeks of tears that streamed down his face. "I'm going to take you to see someone. We can't hide from this anymore."

Hide from what?

Danny wasn't looking at her. He was looking out her window, down to the yard below. His eyes moved back and forth. He was watching the leaves of their giant tree do their witching hour dance in the nocturnal breeze. Belinda leaned her head against Danny's chest. The thumping there reminded her of that same pulse from the neighbour's house. Carmen's house. Sam's house.

It was a dream.

Was that Sam?

Heat rose in Belinda's cheeks as she thought of the naked woman moaning and thrusting and gleaming on the bed.

"It's okay, Bell. It's all going to be okay."

It sounded like Danny was trying to convince himself. But that was okay. At least he was there. At least he didn't run away like Daddy or avoid her like Momma.

Belinda was exhausted. She didn't know if she could sleep with the nightmare so fresh in her mind and on her body. Would it happen again? Would slumber carry her away, out of her house, and into the night?

If she decided to get up and leave her legs again, they'd be right on top of Danny. He'd know and he'd help, and everything would be quite all right.

Danny's eyes were wide and glowing with moonlight as he stared off into the night. Belinda focused on the light in those eyes and took deep, slow breaths as her eyelids grew heavy, until she fell into a dark sleep.

11

Danny let Belinda stay home from school the next day. Normally, she wouldn't want to. Staying home was boring, especially because if she was home and not in school, it meant that she was sick, and she was confined to her bed, doomed to watch *The Price is Right* and munch on plain old toast. But this was different. It had been a restless night, and both Belinda and Danny were tired. She was pretty sure Danny hadn't even laid down and caught a wink of sleep. She felt guilty but appreciated the safety of having him stand guard.

The school assumed it was her periods, and that was fine. Danny didn't correct them. And what would he say, anyway? That she flew out of her legs last night and needed to recover? That she had a scary dream like a little baby? No. She'd made quite the scene yesterday with the "period" in the cafeteria, so nobody needed to be told anything. They assumed, and for once, that was okay.

"Are we going to the doctor?" Belinda asked.

"We'll see someone, yeah," Danny said.

He stood at the stove, flipping fluffy pancakes and gulping coffee. He looked terrible.

"I'm not hungry," Belinda said softly. She didn't want to offend him. He was trying so hard, she didn't want him to think she wasn't grateful. "I just . . . my tummy's a little upset."

But it wasn't upset. It was absolutely perfect. No hunger, no cramps, no grumbles. Physically, she felt better than she had in a long time.

"You haven't eaten much lately, Bell. You okay?"

She nodded. "I'm not doing the anorexia, if that's what you're worried about. Just listening to my guts."

Danny laughed. It was a magical sound, especially since he'd looked so haunted and exhausted lately because of her.

"When are we going?" Belinda asked.

"Later," Danny said.

"Shouldn't we go right when they open? Do we need an appointment?"

Danny slid the pancakes onto a plate in a stack and set the pan and spatula in the sink.

"Later," he repeated.

Belinda watched his face. It was strained. Exhausted. Mad?

"Danny, are you upset with me? I'm sorry about last night."

Danny finally looked over at Belinda, then slid a chair up next to hers.

"No, Bell. Not at all."

"What are you then?"

"I'm worried."

"Worried that I'm sick?"

"Worried that you don't feel well."

"Which means I'm sick."

Danny shook his head. "Not necessarily."

"If people don't feel good, they're sick."

"Or maybe you're growing. That's all. Puberty."

"Puberty? Like I'm gonna get boobs and stuff?"

"Maybe," he said.

"Maybe I'll get boobs?"

"Bell, no. You will get . . . look. Everything is perfectly normal. You are fine. But I'm going to take you to see someone to put your mind at ease. And mine."

"So, you *do* think there's something wrong?"

Danny groaned, then returned to the sink to scrub up the dishes.

"If you aren't going to eat," he said, "why don't you go outside and play for a while? I'll come get you when it's time to go."

Belinda didn't argue with that. She loved to play outside, and Danny wasn't making her stay inside like he normally would if she stayed home sick from school. After pulling a jumper over her head and Logans on her feet, Belinda bounded outside. The mid-morning sun burned hot, gilding the edges of the leaves and blades of grass in gold. Belinda skipped out into the yard, relishing the tingle of heat against her face. It was a beautiful day. If she had more time, she might head into the woods, down the path, and to the little hidden creek where she and Carmen had made a dam weeks ago. But she didn't want to stray too far from home in case Danny called for her. Belinda really wanted to go to the doctor to get fixed up.

After deciding that staying in her yard was the best option, Belinda moseyed over to her little rock and twig town. Her steps slowed as she approached. She half expected it to have come to life with voices and movements, actual structures with doors and windows and candlelight. But it was just a mishmash of forest debris arranged in Belinda's crude interpretation of a town. She shook her head at how ridiculous she was being.

It was a dream.

Who believes their dreams?

Babies, that's who.

Like a bird, Belinda started gathering rocks and sticks and moss to continue construction of her little town. She added a few buildings and used a wider branch to dig a lake on the outskirts of town. Later, when she and Danny were back from the doctor, she'd fill that hole with some water so she could have an actual lake.

"Everyone in my town will be nice to me. No one will point, no one will laugh, and no one will whisper about me behind my back. I won't have *episodes*, and there will be no blood and chickens and tree people. I'll be normal. And Momma will be there, and she'll want to be with me, and we'll live in a cabin together, and everyone will be happy."

The tree in their yard rustled, startling Belinda. There was no wind, but the tree acted like there was, its branches creaking and swaying and leaves flapping as if they were being assaulted by a violent gale. Belinda's hair hung loose beside her cheeks, only moving in response to the gentle air of her breath. She squinted her eyes, trying to spot a creature in the tree, but spied something else instead. Something on the ground, standing a few meters from the tree, staring up at its movement.

"Sam?"

Sam stood there, face turned to the sky, hair draped down her back. She was in a nightgown that brushed the tops of her feet, and it, too, was blowing in a breeze that was not there.

"Sam?" Belinda stood, but Sam took no notice. She was so

focused on the tree that she didn't react to Belinda's approach. She just stood there, staring up, her body wavering like a willow.

When Belinda was within a few meters of Sam, she stopped. Sam was odd, the way she was moving, the way her eyes were so dark, staring up into the nothingness of the old tree. Then it occurred to Belinda.

She's Sam.

Sam had smooth skin, plump lips, and shiny dark hair free of moss or sap. There were no bugs spilling out of her open mouth, and nothing crawling out of her ears, eyes, or nose. Belinda wasn't very close, but she couldn't smell anything at all. Maybe the slightest whiff of shampoo, but no delicious aroma like she'd noticed before.

"Hi," Sam said.

Belinda jumped and let out a yelp at the sound of Sam's voice. But Sam's voice was normal, albeit a bit weird.

In slow motion, Sam let her head loll to the side so she could face Belinda. With what seemed like great effort, the rest of her body followed suit, until they were fully facing each other. Sam's eyes were dark—had they always been that dark?—and her skin was so smooth. She looked quite lovely.

"Are you okay, Sam?"

The slightest movement, and Sam's brow furrowed, creasing a line between her eyes. Her mouth opened and closed like a fish gasping for water, then her mouth moved around, forming words.

"Sam," she said. "Yes. I'm okay."

"Sam, why are you acting so weird?"

"Weird. No, just some fresh air. You?"

Sam had no facial expression. Her brow had unfurled, leaving her skin a smooth palate, with no hint of smile lines or curve of her lips in any direction.

"I . . . I'm just getting ready to go to the doctor."

Sam looked up and down Belinda's body, then down at her own.

"You sure you're okay, Sam?"

Sam nodded, then stared up at the tree again. Belinda didn't know what to say, what to do, so she backed away. She was just about to run to her house when Danny came out the back door.

"Bell! Ready to go?"

Belinda looked at Sam, then at Danny, who was also looking at Sam.

"Hey!" Danny said as a smile spread across his face.

He jogged down the porch steps, heading towards them, towards Sam, and a lump formed in Belinda's throat.

There's something wrong with her, Danny.

But was there? Belinda wasn't sure.

"Hey, Sam," Danny said as he arrived.

He walked right to Sam and pressed his lips against her cheek, pausing there for an uncomfortable moment before pulling away. After a few seconds with no response, Sam's head did the slow, sideways loll thing, her body creaking and turning until she faced Danny.

"Sam," she said, and smiled widely.

Danny's smile faded.

"Sam, what's wrong?" He put his hands on her shoulders. "What happened?"

Sam shrugged. "Nothing," she said with a smirk.

"Danny," Belinda said, weeping. A deep terror had rooted itself in her guts, and she didn't know why.

"Danny," Sam said, almost under her breath. "Yes, Danny. Bell said you're going to the doctor."

Danny nodded.

"Everything okay?" Sam asked, a slight inflection in her tone. More normal than minutes before.

"Yes, well, I think so," Danny said. "Had a bad night. I think she needs to see someone."

"Good choice," Sam said. "Quite a very good choice. It's about time."

Danny looked stung. He winced, crossed his arms, and took a step away from Sam.

"I'm doing the best I can, you know," he said. There were tears in his tone.

"I know, sweetheart," Sam said. "I'm sorry."

Danny hesitated, then stepped back to Sam and pulled her into a hug. Sam put her hands on his face and pulled him in for a loud, wet kiss. Danny's eyes, wide, found Belinda, and his face turned red.

"Sam," he laughed, pulling away.

"It's okay," Belinda said. "I know you guys do the sex."

Danny laughed out loud. It was a nervous sound, made worse by Sam's lack of laughter. But she was smiling. At least there was that.

"I'll let you two go," she said.

And with that, she spun, her hair pirouetting around her, and walked back to her house, slow and steady and awkward.

Danny watched her go the entire way, not peeling his eyes off her until she disappeared inside.

"She's acting weird," Belinda said, her voice wavering.

"Nothing for you to worry about," Danny said. "You have

enough to think about. Now, how's about we stop for some lunch first?"

Belinda crossed her arms.

"Do we have an appointment, Danny? Cuz we shouldn't wait until the end of the day if we're gonna just walk in."

"We don't need an appointment."

Belinda scowled, and Danny bent down until his face was in front of hers. "Trust me."

Belinda wanted to. She really did. But Danny was being weird, too. Not weird like Sam, but not normal Danny. Deciding there was nothing she could do about any of that, Belinda agreed to lunch, and she and Danny headed off in the old station wagon. As they passed Carmen's house, Belinda looked in the bay window at the front and saw Sam standing there. Sam's head was tilted and resting on her shoulder, and her arms were out to the side. She looked like a cross, and her face like a screaming Jesus—mouth wide open and eyes full of pain and terror.

12

The road was bumpy, and Belinda's tummy roiled with nausea. She hadn't had anything to eat that morning, but her belly felt full and sloshy.

I ate.

"No, I didn't!"

Danny looked over the console of the car. "What?"

"Nothing," Belinda murmured.

The station wagon rolled down the road at an easy pace, throwing very little dust to obscure the acres of canola that shimmered bright as the sun. Belinda's eyes caressed the fields, and she saw every flutter of each and every petal, every flight of everything winged and iridescent. The clarity was breathtaking, and the stench repulsive. It made Belinda's tummy churn even worse.

"You okay, kiddo?"

"Where are we going? Town's the other way."

"We're not going to town."

"How come? That's where the doctor is."

"You think there's only one doctor?"

Belinda thought of her doctor, with his white, candy-floss hair and wide teeth and super cold stethoscope. He was a beast of a man, towered over Momma, but was gentle as a cub.

"Dr. Patterson's our doctor," Belinda argued. She looked over her shoulder to the road behind, searching the weak plumes of dust for signs of life. Direction.

"He's not the only one," Danny said.

"But he's our doctor."

"Oh, yeah?" Danny sounded aggravated now. "When's the last time you saw him, huh?"

Belinda couldn't remember. She remembered checkups, standing on a scale, pressing her back against the wall and trying to stretch out her spine as long and tall as she could against the height chart. But she didn't remember when that had all ended. When had they stopped measuring her height? Surely, they measured her weight, but she couldn't for the life of her declare how much she weighed at this moment.

"When *was* the last time I saw him?" Belinda wondered out loud to herself, but also seeking info from Danny.

"I don't know."

"Momma took me."

Danny didn't respond. His eyes were very firmly planted on the road ahead, his mouth sealed.

"Momma should be taking me now."

Danny said nothing.

"I'm not your problem," Belinda said, rage moistening her eyes. "I'm her kid, not yours."

Danny blinked, long and hard, and guided the truck onto the shoulder. Once they were stopped, he finally looked at Belinda.

"You are not a problem," he said. His face was much more relaxed, but there were tears in his eyes. "And you are my sister. I love you, and I would do anything for you."

Warmth tingled Belinda's body. Happiness. She reached across the console and gave Danny a forceful hug.

"I love you too, butthole," she said.

Danny hugged back, hard. When he pulled away, there were some sneaky tears streaming down his face.

"Look," he said as he cranked the truck into drive, "we're burning daylight. We best get going unless you're planning on being out until the witching hour."

"Geez," Belinda said, peeking up at the sun watching them, high in the sky. "How far is this place?"

"We'll get there when we get there."

"Is it a hospital?"

"No."

"A loony bin?"

"Belinda! Have a nap or something."

She wasn't going to push any more buttons. She was super curious, but not worried. She did trust Danny. He loved her, and he would take care of her. She kinda wished they were going to Doctor Patterson, but maybe this was for the best. Maybe this was a specialist that worked with brains and stuff.

Belinda rested her head against the window as the fields rushed by, gold turning to green as the truck was enveloped by the forest. The rhythmic rocking of the vehicle and monotone drone of the tires on the blacktop lulled Belinda into heavy blinking, then light slumber. Every so often, a pothole would jar her awake, but not fully awake. She knew she was still sleeping because of the things outside the window, lining the ditch. Some were tall—too tall—and some were real short, like dwarves or trolls. Some had feathers, some had fur, and some had scales that shone silver and gold in the speckles of sun filtering through the trees. Some had blood smeared across their faces; some had meat grasped in their talons, body parts dangling from beaks and eyeballs pierced on antlers.

Dreaming.

Just like before.

Belinda placed her hand on her stomach and found it was intact. She closed her eyes to make the monsters disappear, and she heard their conversations. Growls, cackles, caws, wails. The seat beneath her bottom crunched as she wriggled to get more comfortable, and the rough grit of sand itched through her leggings. It was everywhere—on her seat, in her clothes, filling her mouth and scratching behind her eyelids. Belinda gasped, convinced her lungs were full of sand, and she came to full consciousness.

"You okay, kiddo?"

Nothing. No beasts lining the road, no sand in the car.

"Fine," she said, even though she was sure she sounded anything but.

"Bad dream?"

"Guess so."

"We're just about there."

"We are?"

They were in the middle of nowhere. There was thick tree cover on either side of the road and not a car coming or going in either lane. Belinda didn't recognize the place, but Danny seemed confident he knew where they were and where they were going. Suddenly, through the trees, Belinda caught a gleam of metal.

"Is that it?"

Danny didn't answer. The forest opened up into a yawn, exposing a gravel parking lot and massive archway covered in fading, flaking, colourful lights.

Oh, my god.

"Danny, what the hell?"

"Hey!" he said as he pulled the truck up in the closest spot and put it in park. "Watch your language!"

"I think it's called for! Why are we here?"

Danny didn't answer. He shut the truck off and pulled the key out of the ignition, but he didn't move.

"I want to see a doctor," Belinda said.

"You don't need to see a doctor," Danny said. His voice was quiet. He was acting guilty, or like he felt bad, but Belinda didn't know why. Because this wasn't the doctor?

"What do I need, then?"

Danny took a long breath and gazed up at the colourful arches.

"I think you need to speak to someone. Someone who . . . understands."

Danny exited the car, came around to Belinda's side, and gently opened her door.

"C'mon, butthole," he said as he extended his hand. "Trust me."

It wasn't that Belinda didn't trust him. She'd follow Danny pert near anywhere. But this made zero sense.

Belinda took Danny's hand, and together they left the empty parking lot behind and walked beneath the entryway arches to the carnival.

13

The carnival was sound asleep. Belinda had never seen a carnival in the light of day. Though the shadows, the noise, and the assault of flashing lights were scary in their own way, the quiet stillness of the rides and attractions in the daytime was more ominous than anything she'd seen in the dark. A carnival was supposed to be loud and alive. The lights were supposed to shine, the games were supposed to make noise, and the people were supposed to be dirty and grungy and half-hidden by shadows and shame. Now, the booths were a ghost town—animatronics hanging unpowered, lemonade machines not spinning, not frozen, rides still and empty. There was a heavy stench of urine and vomit that wasn't overpowered by the smell of corn dogs, grease, and candy floss floating through the air.

And there were no people. There were no customers, which wasn't surprising; the park didn't open until dusk, but Belinda didn't realize that there would be nobody anywhere. No security, no maintenance people, no cleaners. If she'd wanted to, if she wasn't so concerned about where Danny might be taking her, she could have snatched a shimmering unicorn or giant stuffy from the wall of the balloon pop game.

"Hey, where are we going?"

"It's okay," Danny said.

"That's not what I asked."

But Danny said no more.

They walked through the games area, past the funhouse. Ravens watched from their perches in the trees, their black eyes gleaming, following Belinda and Danny as they passed out of the carnival proper and into the shanty vendor village beyond. Belinda's entire body tensed as she thought of the vendor. The lunch lady. Whatever she was, her tent was back here, in this grubby area that was dark even in the daytime.

"What are we doing here, Danny?"

"Don't worry," Danny said. "You're safe."

Belinda really tried to believe that, but her fear was loud and obnoxious, yelling in her ear and making her heart flutter. But the farther they walked, the calmer she got. Just like the food stalls and game booths, the vendor area was abandoned during the day. As they approached the end of the path, and the final few tents, Belinda was satisfied that she and Danny were alone inside the perimeter; there was no movement and no sound other than the rustling of the trees beyond the forest's edge. But then, a crack. A creak. A cackle.

"Why are we here?" Belinda asked. Maybe she was talking to Danny, maybe to herself, maybe sending the question out into the ether. Whoever she asked, no one answered.

The cackle belonged to the vendor. Belinda recognized the

wet sputum dancing on that husky laugh, the throaty bray booming from that belly. But then a second sound joined in, creating a dissonant duet. It was musical, lilting—a song of a laugh.

"Danny, what's going on?"

The final tent was occupied. It was the vendor, her crooked form hunched over a tiny table laced with a plate of food and a dented copper tea set. She wasn't alone. Her companion sat across from her, back on to Belinda, her shoulders heaving as she laughed the beautiful aria from her throat. This woman was tall and long, but heavy-set, with bold auburn hair swirled into a messy bun balanced on her head. Her velvety emerald dress swept the ground like a train, resting atop bare feet that were paler than white and spidered with a roadmap of indigo veins.

Danny's feet came to a halt at the edge of their tent, his toes just shy of crossing the invisible line between the tables. His mouth opened, but he did not speak. Instead, he reached for Belinda's hand and drew her to his side. His hand was shaking, which made Belinda's tummy do a little flip. She thought she might cry.

The women continued chortling until the vendor took a swig of her tea, and her eyes trailed over her cup to Belinda and Danny. She paused, but resumed her sip, slowly drawing liquid, swishing it around her mouth, then swallowing hard and loud.

"Welcome," she said. She brushed the crumbs off the front of her sari wrap and heaved herself to her feet. She was hunched and crooked, as if her spine was a twisted root, and her movements were jarring and disjointed.

"Danny, what are we doing here?" Belinda asked. Danny did not answer. He was transfixed by the vendor as well, but maybe not afraid. It was something else.

"My dear," the woman said as she approached, and Belinda winced, anticipating the rough callus of the woman's palms set upon her cheeks. But the woman was not speaking to her.

"Hi," Danny said. His voice trembled as bad as his hand.

The woman cupped his cheek, and he leaned into her touch. Closed his eyes. His mouth was a tight line, like it was when he was sealing in big emotions like sadness or madness.

"It must be very hard, you coming here," the vendor said.

Danny opened his eyes and tears poured out. His words remained contained behind his sealed lips.

"But you came, so it must be time."

His crying intensified. It came out in coughs, and the vendor embraced him, and there they stood, swaying in that hug, Danny's tears soaking the vendor's silk sari.

When they finally pulled apart, the vendor turned a kind eye to Belinda.

"Sweetheart," she said, "I'm taking a minute with your brother. I'll be with you shortly."

"No!" Belinda yelped, and latched onto Danny, her arms around his waist and her fingers digging into his sides.

"It's okay, Bell. I'm not leaving. We'll be a minute, and then . . . when it's your turn to talk with her, I'll be here. Waiting."

"Danny, no—"

Danny got down on one knee in front of her and took her hands in his. He pulled her close, spoke to her heart.

"You are safe, Belinda. This is what you need. Trust me."

And she did. She really did trust Danny. This was awful, and she was frustrated, and oh so confused; but Danny knew what was happening, so it must be okay. Or it was gonna be okay. But it sure didn't feel like it as Danny and the vendor walked away from the tent, her arm threaded through his, leaning into each other with uncomfortable familiarity.

"Sit," the other woman in the tent said.

Belinda had completely forgotten there was someone else there. The woman didn't turn, so Belinda couldn't see her face, but her voice was lovely—not rough and scary like the vendor's. Making a wide berth, Belinda moved into the tent, around the woman, and took a seat in the vendor's chair.

The woman was pale—so pale she was almost clear. And her hair shimmered like fire against her alabaster flesh. Her fingers were long, her lips black, and her eyes emeralds sunken into her gaunt face. She was both beautiful and ugly, ethereal and terrifying.

"What's yer story, lass?"

The accent was unfamiliar. Something from overseas. Whatever it was, it was heavy, and her voice more song than speech.

"What's tha matter wit ya? Dumb?"

Belinda shook her head.

"Well, ye ain't deaf, that's for sure. So ye can speak, and ye can hear, but ye say nothin'."

Belinda did, in fact, say nothing. Instead, she lifted the teacup to her lips and took a sip. It was amazing. Heat rolled over her tongue, dribbling to her belly, filling her more than it should have.

"Well, you're a stubborn arse, then."

The woman took a draw of her own tea, plucked a snack off the tray, and popped it into her mouth. Now that Belinda was closer, she could see that upon the tray wasn't any kind of snacks she would be interested in. The tray was covered in piles of roaches, decapitated mice, obese slugs, and meaty sparrow bodies, not even plucked of their feathers. The woman picked a sparrow up by the foot, stuffed it in her mouth, and sucked off both meat and feathers in one fluid motion. She dropped the bones on the tray with a clatter and gnawed up her mouthful of bird with squishes and rips and cracks.

Belinda should have wanted to puke. To run.

"Try a rat," the woman said over a tongue covered in feathers. "Juicier. Don't gotta fuck with the feathers."

Belinda gasped.

The woman sneered. "Oh, please. Go on wit ya. A lass the likes of ye certainly heard your share of the devil's tongue."

Belinda scrunched her face. "The likes of me?"

The woman went still. Her eyes darkened and focused on Belinda's face. Then she released a huff of air and slumped back in her chair as if that breath had deflated her entire body.

"Oh, my gentle fucking word, lass. Ye don't know," she said, and massaged her temples with those long fingers, blackened nails scraping along her flesh.

Under her breath, she muttered a string of nasty sounding words—Belinda didn't know for sure, because she didn't recognize the language.

"Is that French?" Belinda asked.

The woman clasped her chest. "Fuck no!"

Belinda gasped again. The woman spat on the ground.

"Fucking Francophones, baguette sucking motherfuckers. No, girl! 'Tis Gaelic."

Belinda was confused.

The woman slid forward in her chair and extended her hand across the dead critter tray.

"Aye, lass. I'm Saoirse."

Belinda took the woman's hand. It was warm and soft, just like her voice.

"Belinda," Belinda said.

"Please ta meet ya."

Belinda took her hand back. "What did you mean when you said I don't know? What don't I know?"

Saoirse smiled. "A great many things, you tiny pup. You've yet to live."

"I got my periods," Belinda blurted. "I'm old enough to know stuff."

Saoirse laughed. "No, you didn't. And no, yer not."

"My periods? Yes, I did."

"Did not."

The heat of anger and embarrassment rose in Belinda's chest. "You don't know me!"

Saoirse picked up her teacup, dropped in a couple maggots like sugar cubes, and settled back in her chair.

"You be right. I don't know ye. But if you're here, I know what you're about. Whatever you be, you's not so different as you think."

Belinda studied Saoirse's face, then looked around the tent. Hundreds of vials of sand twirled and glittered in the waning sunlight. Bones and feathers hung, too, twirling like wind chimes with each breath the wind exhaled. Marking the perimeter of the tent were bookcases full of leather-bound tomes that appeared old and well-loved. And fluttering at the back of the tent was a flag hanging from a crooked pole. When Belinda saw it, her bowels clenched, and anxiety wrapped its claws around her windpipe. Saoirse must have noticed, because her face wrinkled in worry as she followed the path of Belinda's gaze.

"What's wrong with ya?" Saoirse asked.

Belinda pointed at the flag.

"It's a flag, ye wee idiot."

Belinda stabbed the air with her finger, pointing at the flag, mouthing words that she hadn't the air to voice. The horizontal flag had a royal blue stripe on the top, a crimson red stripe on the bottom, and a white equilateral triangle at the hoist. In the center of the white triangle was a golden sun with eight rays, and a yellow star on each of the three vertices.

Saoirse stood, glided over to the flag, studied it, and yanked it down from where it hung. She came back to the table and handed it to Belinda.

"'Tis the flag of the Philippines."

The flag was silky in Belinda's hands. It flowed through her fingers like water, and she imagined its softness, cool and smooth across her belly.

"That's where she's from," Saoirse said.

"Where who's from?" Belinda asked.

Saoirse took her seat again. "Tita."

"Who?" Belinda asked.

A scrape and shuffle caught Belinda's attention. The vendor had walked up right behind her, hovered over her, startling her.

"Someone walked over my grave," the vendor said.

Belinda looked up into her dark eyes. "Tita?"

"Yes, I heard you gossiping about me."

Now it was Tita's turn to extend her hand to Belinda. "Pleased to formally make your acquaintance," Tita said. "I am Tita."

"Belinda," Belinda whispered.

"I know," Tita said, and offered a gentle smile.

"How do you know?"

"Hag," Saoirse muttered.

"Pardon me?" Tita said, scowling at Saoirse.

"You fecking heard me, ye ol' cunny," Saoirse snapped.

"Keeping these youngsters in the lurch while you fiddle-fucked around, keepin' secrets like some old goddamn gatekeeper."

"You think you know better?" Tita screeched.

"Aye. I fucking knows I do."

"Oh, really."

"*Yes*, really, you half-eaten spaghetti squash."

"Please," Belinda whispered. "What's going on?"

The women quit bickering, and both softened as they looked at Belinda, who was shaking in her chair. Saoirse stared at her for a long moment before rising from her seat.

"I best be going so as you two can start at it," Saoirse said. "Lots to discuss."

As she gathered her shawl and glided out of the tent, she placed a hand on Tita's shoulder.

"Go easy and slow, Tita. It ain't easy. I wish my sister'd known much sooner than she had. Makes life easier, knowing what ye are."

Saoirse floated down the path, her gown trailing behind her, humming a lullaby that was the most beautiful thing Belinda had ever heard.

"She's a good friend," Tita said.

"You don't seem to like each other," Belinda noted.

"We love each other. And that's how love is sometimes. Rough and harsh and steeped in truth."

The carnival beyond the vendor's tent came alive with a burst of air. Frightened, Belinda looked in time to see a tornado of feathers raining down upon the games and rides, shading the sun and twirling to the ground in a macabre ballet. But then they were gone like smoke the instant they hit the dirt.

"Saoirse knows nothing subtle," Tita chuckled.

Belinda could not tear her eyes from the sky. It was blue but hazy. Belinda blinked, then blinked again. Against the backdrop of azure, the clouds were gritty piles of crystal sand. Then they weren't so white anymore; yellowed stains spread across the clouds like a disease, turning white sand to gold, then muting it to sepia.

"Come, child," Tita said, taking Belinda's chin and tilting it from the sky. "Like Saoirse said, we have much to discuss."

14

Belinda and Tita sat across from each other, each holding a teacup. Nothing was right. Nothing was wrong, exactly, but nothing was as it should be. Belinda feared looking up at the sky, which was sand, or down at her feet, beneath which was more of the same.

Tita's voice was also sand—gritty, flowing, both sharp and soft at once.

"Do you know what she is? Saoirse?" Tita asked.

"What's in this tea?" Belinda asked. *This tea must be tainted*, she thought. Saoirse had left the tea there, watched her take a sip, and it had drugs in it, and now she was high, and Danny would be upset. But Danny'd brought her here, and Belinda didn't figure Danny would have anything to do with drugs. Danny was a good boy and a good man and a good brother.

"It's blood," Tita said.

Belinda looked into the cup. It was sand, glistening, glittering, crimson. She took another sip.

"Saoirse is a banshee," Tita said.

Another sip, then Belinda asked, "A what?"

"Banshee. Harbinger of death."

"Like a doctor?"

"No, child."

Belinda focused on her tea, stirring her spoon through the red sand, drinking up the sweet, savoury aroma.

"This isn't real," Belinda said. "You drugged me."

Tita shook her head. "I fed you."

"I was so hungry."

"I know you were, child."

Belinda stopped stirring and set her cup down on its saucer by the tray of dead things. She let her eyes come to rest on Tita's eyes rather than the crimson whatever was in her teacup. Tita's eyes were pools, deep and gold, the colour always moving.

"Why am I hungry?" Belinda asked.

"Because you need to feed."

"Eat?"

"No."

Nothing made sense. Though there were itches of panic nibbling at Belinda's guts, she felt calm, safe. She was still in the tent, still in her clothes, the forest still stood tall and stoic outside, but it was as if she was in a trance. A fog that made everything just a little off.

"What's wrong with me?" Belinda asked.

Sadness creased Tita's face. She said nothing, only waited.

"Well?" Belinda said.

Nothing.

Belinda crossed her arms across her chest. "Danny was supposed to take me to a doctor."

Tita scoffed. "Doctor would do you no good."

Belinda narrowed her eyes. "But I'm unwell."

"How so?"

"I don't feel good."

"Ah, that's precise."

Frustration tightened Belinda's muscles. "Something's not . . . right."

Tita smiled. "Or perhaps it wasn't right before. You felt wrong before, and now you feel right, and you aren't used to that."

It was useless. Belinda figured she'd be better off firing her questions at the tree in her back yard.

"You are not a doctor," Belinda grumbled.

"No."

"Then what are you?"

The whirling pools of gold that were Tita's eyes stilled, her pupils dilating, focusing on Belinda as she leaned back in her chair. Fine hairs of fear rose on Belinda's body as Tita pointed two fingers at Belinda. Those fingers were long and boney things, tipped with jagged black nails like chipped and fractured claws. She took those two fingers and stretched them across the table with the dead snack, pulled up Belinda's shirt, and, without breaking eye contact, scratched a horizontal line across her stomach right below her belly button.

Belinda tugged her shirt down and pushed Tita's hand away. She didn't want to think about any of this anymore, and she didn't want to be around Tita or Saoirse or anyone weird. She wanted to go home with Danny and forget all of this.

"You are magical, Belinda. Just like me, just like Saoirse."

Belinda swallowed. Hard. "I'm a . . . banshee?"

Tita laughed. "Thank goodness, no."

"Then what am I?"

Tita clapped, the sound of cymbals crashing, and leapt to her feet.

"Aha!" Tita squealed. "Finally, you ask the correct question!"

Belinda, scared by Tita's outburst, answered in a meek and trembling voice. "What?"

"You have been asking what is wrong with you, when you should be asking what is right with you. Yes. What are you? That is the question that's been a long time coming, now, isn't it?"

Tita went to her shelves of many books and scratched a fingernail over the spines. The sound was obnoxious in Belinda's ears, like someone raking a talon up the Devil's backbone. Finally, after what seemed an impossibly long time, the scratching became a tapping as Tita's finger settled on a wide tome. She clasped the book in both hands and pulled it from the shelf. The surrounding books collapsed in as if that particular tome, the one in Tita's hand, was the strongest on the shelf. The keystone holding everything else together. As Tita brought it closer, its beauty was revealed.

It was massive, with a thick spine. The cover was a warm, glorious brown, somewhere between cinnamon and carob, and ornate designs of rose gold were etched in the leather. The edges of the pages were all colours of the rainbow—emeralds, rubies, citrines, amethysts—and they shone and twinkled like the sands in the vials. When Tita set it on Belinda's lap, Belinda sucked in a deep breath. The book was ripe with the aroma of wood fire, cedar, and the taste of warm copper. Belinda opened her eyes to the calligraphic script etched across the front:

Tales From Ramnon

That was it. No author, no other words.

"What's Ramnon?" Belinda asked.

"A place."

Belinda was too entranced to even roll her eyes. "Yes, but where?"

"Everywhere and nowhere. It's after life and before afterlife."

Belinda stroked the spine. Her finger tingled, as if the book was feeling her back.

"So, it's not real," Belinda said.

"It's very real. A haven for misfits. For *The Other*. A corner of purgatory, a nook of a home for those with no other."

"After we die?"

The vendor shrugged. "For some."

It was all too cryptic for Belinda's taste. She pinched the cover to pull it back, but Tita rested a soft hand upon the title, stopping her.

"Are you ready to know?"

Belinda looked into the woman's eyes again. They were no longer whirlpools but windows to a faraway place. In them, Belinda saw her little town come to life: a saloon, creatures wandering the dirt streets, cabins made of logs. The swinging squeal of saloon doors radiated from Tita's ears, and all manner of cackle, wail, snarl seeped from her throat.

"Ramnon," Belinda said, and her belly gurgled in response.

"Yes," Tita answered.

When Tita spoke, her voice was wet. Belinda dared to look at her lips. They were dribbling blood, the thick plasma coating both her teeth and her tongue. But it wasn't a tongue. It was a snake, a tube that wriggled like a worm, licking the blood off Tita's yellowed, chipped teeth. Belinda followed the trail of a spool of blood that dangled off Tita's lip, spiraling down until it came to rest between her heaving breasts.

And farther still, Belinda's eyes dropped to Tita's abdomen. Tita's clothing was soaked in blood in a line straight across her midsection. Belinda watched in horror, transfixed, as Tita lifted her shirt, exposing her stomach. And Belinda saw the whole of Tita's stomach, churning and working, exposed through a wide gash that not only spanned from one side of Tita's body to the other, but clear around, too. Belinda could see the back of Tita's chair below the top half of her body and above her lower half. And, just like Belinda in her own dream, Tita's organs kept on working, grinding and churning and oozing, despite being exposed to the world.

Tita came off her chair, and her entrails fluttered behind her like meat ribbons, draping over the table as she came nose to nose with Belinda. In her mind, Belinda was screaming, but not even a puff of air could escape her horror-stricken throat. Tita's smile widened, and the worm within extended out—long, thin, gyrating—until its mouth reached the book on Belinda's lap. It licked the cover, smearing blood across the glimmering words and worn leather, then tap, tap, tapped it three times before raveling back up into Tita's mouth.

Tita took Belinda's face in her hands and spoke, her breath hot with the rank stench of old blood.

"*Aswang.*"

"Belinda?"

Danny's voice washed it all away. Belinda wasn't even sure she blinked, but she must have, because Tita was back sitting in her chair, all in one piece. The fog had lifted. Everything was clear and as it should be—no more sand clouds in the sky, no movement within Tita's eyes, no crimson in the teacup. But in Belinda's lap lay the massive tome with a glistening streak of red across the cover.

"Belinda, are you okay?"

Aswang.

Tita said nothing as Danny stepped over the threshold of the tent.

"Thank you for your time," Danny said. He seemed irritated. He and Tita stared at each other for two moments too long before Danny looked down at the book in Belinda's lap.

Tita said nothing as Danny led Belinda away. He kept glancing down at the book Belinda held tight against her chest. When they reached the car, he asked her to put it in the back seat and cover it with her extra jumper. She listened. That book scared her as much as it appeared to scare him. Then he hugged Belinda, long and warm and hard, before they drove off into the twilight. As Belinda drifted off to sleep with her head against the window, a voice whispered inside her ear, licking her mind like a tongue.

Aswang.

15

Belinda wasn't mad, but she didn't want to talk to Danny. He had said nothing to her since the carnival. Albeit Belinda had been sound asleep the whole way, and mostly asleep as Danny carried her into the house and put her in her bed; but she'd been awake for two whole hours this morning, and he hadn't come to talk to her. And he must have heard that she was awake. She made sure to make lots of noise, hoping he would come see her, but he didn't.

Belinda got dressed and dragged herself down the stairs. Danny had cooked bacon and sunny-side-up eggs. Belinda's old favourite. Not anymore. Now it smelled like spoiled bologna cooked on a car radiator.

"Were you gonna wake me up?" Belinda asked as she plunked herself down in a kitchen chair.

Danny gave a weak smile. "I knew you were awake. I could hear you slamming around up there."

Belinda huffed. "Where's my book?"

Danny stared at the eggs, perhaps hoping they'd answer.

"I put it in Momma's room," he answered.

"Why?"

"To keep it safe."

"From what?"

"Just to have it where we could find it."

"What is it, Danny?"

"I don't know, but it looks expensive and old."

"Why did you take me to the carnival, Danny?"

What was real? What wasn't?

"That's a . . . friend of Mom's."

"Tita?"

Danny nodded.

"I don't remember her."

"Last time you saw her, you were little."

"Huh. Well, I know why I don't know her, then. Because she's Momma's friend, and Momma's NEVER AROUND!"

Danny sighed, set his spatula down, and turned the gas off. "I know."

"She needs to be here!"

Danny sat at the table. "I know."

"Then why isn't she here? I'm not okay, Danny! Why doesn't she love me?"

The words were like a slap across Danny's face. His mouth dropped open, and his eyes had the sting of pain in them. He stood abruptly and knelt beside Belinda's chair. When he took her hands, it wasn't gentle. It was firm and serious.

"Belinda. Momma loves you very much. So much. You have no idea. She would do anything for you, just to make sure you're okay."

Belinda yanked her hands out of Danny's.

"Not true," she spat.

Danny stood and took a step back.

"If she cared so much," Belinda said, salt in her tone, "she'd be around more. At all, actually!"

"There's a good reason—"

"Yes, yes, I know," Belinda said, mocking her brother. "She's working. Life is expensive, Belinda."

Danny glared. Belinda was silenced. She thought this might be the first time her brother had ever glared at her. The thought of him being upset at her put a lump in her throat, tears in her eyes, and a rock in her belly. But enough was enough. She couldn't go on like this and he wasn't being fair.

"Sorry, Danny, but it's not fair."

He considered her words, then returned to the stove. He didn't look at her.

"I'm sorry, too, Bell."

She watched him carefully. "Sorry for what?"

He flipped the eggs and bacon onto two plates, set one in front of her, and took his plate out to the porch. He didn't slam the door, but he might as well have. The sound of it closing was like an axe through Belinda's heart. He'd never not had breakfast with her before.

Belinda tried her best, but she couldn't swallow any of the food. She would have thought there was something seriously wrong with it, but she could see Danny eating his out on the porch. He wasn't making faces, or spitting it out, but Belinda's food tasted rotten and dirty. She couldn't eat it, but she didn't want Danny's feelings even more hurt, so she threw it in the trash and hid it under some balled-up paper towels.

Belinda glanced at the clock. Fifteen more minutes before the school bus came, but Danny was still sitting on the porch, staring out into the yard. Belinda slid open the doors and stepped outside.

"Bus'll be here soon," she said.

"I think you should maybe stay home today," he said, his eyes focused on the woods.

"Why? I don't feel sick."

"I know," Danny said. "But maybe you just need some time. You've been feeling off."

Belinda considered it. She'd love to go to school, to hang out with Carmen and pretend everything was okay. But what would happen at the school? Would Tita be there? Would she get her periods, or her chickens, or whatever the heck happened?

"But what about your work?" Belinda asked.

Danny finally looked over at her and smiled. "I don't give you enough credit, Bell. And I'm sorry for that. You are old enough and certainly mature enough to be by yourself for a day. You know what to do in case there's an emergency?"

Belinda beamed. "Yes! Call you at work."

Danny raised an eyebrow. "A real emergency?"

"Oh, yes, well, 9-1-1."

He nodded. "Yep. And you can always run next door. Sam's off today."

No, thank you, Belinda thought, imagining Sam being a weirdo out in the yard the day before.

"I'll be fine," Belinda said. "And I promise I'll rest."

"Doubt that," Danny said with a smile.

He brought his dishes inside and grabbed his coat while Belinda watched. She was nervous. She had been on her own plenty of times before. Never for a full day, though. But they were out in the country, and Belinda wanted some time to herself. More importantly, time to snoop in Momma's room. Maybe flip through *Tales from Ramnon*.

"I love you, Belinda."

"Love you too, butthole."

Danny hugged Belinda, kissed her on the forehead, and opened the door. He hesitated, but then went to the truck without turning back. Belinda caught him staring in the rearview mirror as he drove away.

He's worried about me, she thought. *But I'm a big girl now. And practically an adult, since Momma's quit Momma-ing.*

Belinda was anxious to creep through Momma's room, and see the book again, so she dillydallied. She picked at some toys, flipped through a Sweet Valley High book, even dusted the furniture to help Danny out. She was on the verge of chickening out, but then she thought about sand. About the sand pouring from her wound, the clouds of sand at the carnival. She thought about her little village of rocks and twigs and mud that came to life. She thought about her episodes, and her periods, and about chickens and eggs and banshees. And Belinda got angry. Angry that Momma was not there to help her, to guide her through whatever this was, to give her answers and take her to get some real help.

With fresh fire in her belly, Belinda stomped down the hall to Momma's room and threw the door open with such force she thought it might fly right off its hinges. Once the room was exposed, Belinda's bravado shriveled. The bed was there, dominating the space, reminding Belinda of the bloody mass she'd seen upon it during her episode.

Aswang.

Belinda blinked. Ignored the voice in her head.

Of course, there was nothing on the bed but sheets and a

duvet. It was tidy, freshly made. Belinda sat, and the mattress squeaked a complaint. Belinda buried her face in the pillows. She could not smell Momma. She thought, hard, but could not remember if Momma even had a smell. But on those pillows, there was nothing. Fabric softener and dust.

Guilt prickled at Belinda as she began her search. Every time she opened a drawer, the sound startled her. The wind outside caused her to hold her breath when the forest creaked, and she just about jumped clear out of her skin when the house settled with the regular pop-bang of an old structure.

Belinda decided she should not feel guilty even if Danny or Momma showed up and caught her rifling around this bedroom. She had a right to look around. She lived here, after all, and Momma wasn't around, and Belinda wanted . . .

What do I want?

Belinda wanted her momma.

The scent of the leather cover on *Tales from Ramnon* wafted into Belinda's nose. She spied the book sitting on Momma's nightside table. Belinda had yet to open that cover to expose the secrets within. And she still wasn't ready for that. Not just yet.

Next stop was the closet. Not quite a walk-in, but not small, either. Belinda marveled at all the stuff. Shelves heaped with clothing—sweaters and pants and shoes. One half of the closet contained menswear—a few suits, collared shirts, and an Edmonton Eskimos jersey. Belinda pulled the jersey off the hanger and hugged it. Smelled it. There was a faint trace of men's shampoo.

The other part of the closet was Momma's. Flowing dresses, some pantsuits, blouses, and slacks. Belinda ran her fingers across the fabric, pretending it was Momma's soft arms. Though Belinda's feet were much smaller, she poked them into Momma's high heels and wobbled in and out of the closet, trying to keep her balance. She made it a good ten steps back and forth before the heel tipped to the side and Belinda toppled to the floor. She laughed, and the sound ringing in the empty house was unnerving. Belinda looked over her shoulder, expecting to see the Sam-thing, or Saoirse, or Tita, but found only the empty bed and the open door.

The empty hallway was threatening. There was nothing there but space, but in Belinda's mind, that space had teeth. The hallway was a throat ready to swallow her. As she stared at the open door, she felt utterly and completely exposed. The hallway beyond was dark, and the house so quiet, but maybe too quiet. What was lying in wait for her outside the light and safety of this room?

Belinda jumped to her feet, ran over, and slammed the door. Locked it. Put her back against the wall and slid down to the floor. She watched for movement beneath the door, but the darkness stayed perfectly undisturbed. Belinda scolded herself for such foolishness and was about to get up off the floor again, but she spied a cardboard box tucked beneath the dresser. She crawled over and pulled it out.

It was a shoebox coated in a thick skin of dust. Belinda wiped it with her sleeve, then carefully lifted off the lid. The box was full to the top with all sorts of stuff—papers, photographs, cards. A card near the top was a get well soon card with a sad looking bluebird holding a bouquet of lilies in his beak. Inside, the message was pretty generic.

Feel better soon!

Belinda found another card, this one funny, with a golden retriever dressed as a nurse on the front.

Heard you're feeling ruff! Get well!

And another one, this one with mice in straw hats cuddling each other.

Thinking of you.

And another, and another. Some were addressed to Momma, some to the whole family.

Was Momma sick? Belinda wondered.

Setting aside the cards, Belinda grabbed some of the papers and started reading.

Oh, no.

Treatment plans.

Pre-op instructions.

Prescription information pamphlets.

Momma?

In a panic, Belinda dumped the box, searching for answers that might spill out right in front of her. Papers and cards splayed out across the floor, along with a few empty prescription bottles and a hospital wristband.

The tension in Belinda's body uncoiled and softened, the snake of her anxiety turning docile.

Thank goodness, Belinda thought as she picked up a wristband. It was way too small to be Momma's.

Belinda's brow crinkled as she read the name printed on the band.

Belinda Meredith Parker

But Belinda couldn't remember being sick. Not sick enough to have a hospital band. She tried to think back, to Doctor Patterson, to all her check-ups. But it was covered in a fog . . .

Sand

. . . like gossamer draped across her past. The wristband had been cut, but Belinda sized it around her wrist. It was a perfect fit, which was even more confusing. She couldn't have been much younger when she'd had the wristband, or it'd be too small. Unless they fasten them real big. She honestly didn't know.

As she pondered the band and her health, something on the floor with the pile of papers caught her attention.

The wristband slipped from Belinda's fingers and dropped to the floor. And there it was, laying right next to a silky ribbon. A red, white, and green ribbon speckled with yellow stars and a yellow sun.

Aswang.

Belinda picked up the ribbon. Slid it through her fingers. It felt like the flag at Tita's tent, but it wasn't the right shape. It was the Filipino flag in colour, but it was a true ribbon. Like the one that'd been around her waist in the school cafeteria.

There was no more time for thinking. For considering. Belinda was going to drive herself mad. She stuffed everything back in the shoebox, except for the ribbon, which she wrapped and tied around her wrist, then she tucked the shoebox under her arm and marched out the door. After donning a jumper and her runners, Belinda took the shoebox and all its mysteries and left the house.

❧ 16 ❧

The road was dusty, the wind nippy, and Belinda's legs were aching. She thought the walk into town would be easy-breezy, but she realized her error once she was halfway there. She switched the shoebox to her other hip, then back again, fussing at herself for not thinking to stuff the whole thing in her backpack and carry it that way. But Belinda was determined. If she had to struggle with the thing the whole way, and walk for days, she would. She wanted answers, and she'd been waiting long enough.

After another twenty minutes—though Belinda was pretty sure it had been twenty days—a truck pulled onto the shoulder just in front of her. Belinda slowed down. Danny had warned her about stranger danger, and Belinda didn't recognize this truck. When she reached the passenger window, it rolled down, and to Belinda's profound relief, a familiar face came into view.

"Belinda, sweetheart! What are you doing out here on your own? Shouldn't you be in school?"

It was Olive, the woman who ran the bookstore on Main Street. Momma used to go to a book club there the first Thursday of every month. Belinda would get to hunker down in the kids' section on the rainbow beanbag chair and read all the books her heart desired. Miss Olive made the best chocolate chip cookies, and in the winter, she'd give Belinda hot chocolate with cut-up marshmallows in it. And not gross marshmallows like those little lame things that came in the hot chocolate packages. *Actual* marshmallows that were soft and squishy and would melt in her mouth.

Belinda missed the bookstore and the rainbow bean bag chair and the real marshmallows. She couldn't remember the last time Momma had taken her.

"I, uh, am off today," Belinda said. "But I gotta run into town for some errands."

Olive looked puzzled but didn't press. "Would you like a ride? Town is an awful long way for your little legs."

Belinda was overjoyed. She set the shoebox on the floor of the truck and hoisted herself into the seat.

"Thank you so much, Miss Olive," Belinda said as she buckled her seatbelt.

The truck started off down the road, kicking up dust and rumbling like a beast.

"What kind of errands does your momma have you running?"

Olive was concerned. And Belinda didn't want Olive to be concerned because she'd heard stories about Child Services and orphanages where they fed you gruel and made you wear burlap sacks over your head. She didn't want Olive so concerned she phoned the authorities.

"Oh, well, I decided to run them myself. To surprise Momma."

Olive gave her a sideways glance. "Would your momma approve of you heading out on your own like this?"

"I've done it before," Belinda lied. "She and Danny, they practiced with me."

Olive nodded. But she didn't look convinced. Regardless, she asked no more questions about the oddness of Belinda's quest.

"So how have you been? I haven't seen your momma in ages."

Belinda wondered when Momma stopped going to book club.

"We've been really busy. Momma especially. Working lots since Daddy left."

Olive's jaw dropped. "What?"

"She's gotta work a couple jobs, but don't worry, Danny takes care of me—"

"Phillip left?"

Belinda looked over at Olive, the woman who had been friends with her momma for an entire lifetime.

"Um, yeah," Belinda said. "But we're doing okay. I mean, I don't really remember him well. Danny does, but he's doing good, too."

Olive was shaken. Belinda could see her trying to figure things out, process all the information as the kilometers rolled by. Neither of them spoke, even when they passed the town sign into Picton. Finally, Olive parallel parked the truck in front of the market and killed the engine.

"I'm so sorry about your daddy," Olive said. She was wringing her hands in her lap. "I...I had no idea. Is your momma okay?"

"She's okay," Belinda said with a shrug. "I'll be sure to tell her I saw you. Maybe we'll try to come back to book club sometime."

Olive nodded. "That would be lovely. I miss your momma."

"Me, too," Belinda said.

She grabbed the shoebox and hurried off before Olive could ask more questions.

When did Daddy leave? Why did he leave?

Belinda was very small. She must have been. She couldn't remember.

There's so much I don't remember.

Belinda's thoughts were a billiard ball, bouncing around her head, trying to find a pocket of memory. Everything was a fog, a shroud of vague hints of her past. The one thing she could remember, quite clearly, was where she was going. Down Main Street, take a right at the coffee shop, down to the end of that lane, and to the small office building on the left. As she passed through the door, a little bell tinkled, proclaiming her arrival. The receptionist looked up from her screen and offered Belinda a smile with her ruby red lips. After a moment of consideration, and a glance at the door, the woman looked over the top of her glasses and studied Belinda.

"Good afternoon," the receptionist said. "Can I help you?"

"I'm here to see Doctor Patterson," Belinda said with confidence.

"Do you have an appointment?"

"I do not. But I need to see him."

Again, the receptionist glanced behind Belinda at the front door.

"Are you here with your parents?"

Belinda shook her head. "No, but he knows them. And me. He's our doctor."

"Oh, okay. Can I get your name?"

"Belinda Meredith Parker."

The receptionist ticked her nails on the keyboard, then, "Yes, here you are. We haven't seen you in a while. We don't take walk-ins, but I'd be happy to schedule you for tomorrow. Or maybe he could squeeze you in at the end of the day. Is this urgent?"

If Belinda waited until the end of the day, Danny would know she snuck out. But he'd probably know, anyway, because Belinda planned to get home on the school bus with Carmen.

"I can wait, if he'll see me at the end of the day."

The receptionist smiled. "Yes, I will check with him. What will he be seeing you for today?"

"Um, uh . . ." Belinda looked at the shoebox in her arms. "It's my periods."

"Oh, okay. No problem. Just let me . . . I think we might need your mother here—"

"I just want to talk. No exam."

The receptionist nodded. "Let me check with him. Hold on."

Belinda looked around the waiting room while the woman disappeared down the hall. The bead toy in the corner was still there; it had been there since forever. Belinda could remember sitting on her legs, running the beads back and forth on their track. Red was her favourite. And she liked looking at all the old magazines stacked up, especially the ones with the celebrities in their fancy clothes.

"Belinda?" A deep voice, chocked full of surprise. "Belinda Meredith, is that you?"

Doctor Patterson strolled into the room, his white coat hanging off his outstretched arms. He was emotional, which Belinda found weird. His eyes were all wet, but his smile was very wide, showing off all his great big teeth.

"It's me!" Belinda said, and walked up to the man, allowing him to wrap his arms around her in a hug. He did not let go. His chest was jittery, and Belinda realized he was crying. When they pulled apart, he wiped away tears and put a hand over his mouth.

"Well, I'll be damned," he said. Belinda gasped, and he laughed. "Sorry for the language, dear. Please. Come on back."

Doctor Patterson led Belinda back into an exam room and patted the table.

"Oh, I don't . . ."

Belinda was going to argue against an exam. But she was sick. This was what she wanted, wasn't it? A checkup? For the doctor to give her some pills to fix her right up?

Belinda crawled up on the table and sat, crossing her ankles and letting her legs swing against the metal. She set the shoebox down beside her and kept her hand on it. Doctor Patterson looked at the shoebox with his eyebrow cocked but didn't address it.

"May I?" Doctor Patterson asked, motioning to his stethoscope.

Belinda nodded.

Doctor Patterson placed the stethoscope on Belinda's chest, on her back, told her to take a few deep breaths. Then he looked in her ears, her eyes, her mouth and throat. He took her blood pressure, then he had her lie down and tapped all over her tummy, which made her giggle.

Once the exam was complete, Doctor Patterson sat on his stool and stared up at Belinda with wide-eyed amazement.

"Am I healthy?" Belinda asked.

"So far as I can tell!" he said, clapping his hands together.

"I was sick, wasn't I?"

The happiness waned a bit. "Yes. Quite ill, actually."

"The flu?"

He shook his head and laughed. "No, sweet girl. Not the flu."

Doctor Patterson leaned forward and clasped his hands together. They were about to have a serious discussion.

"I have evidence," Belinda said, thrusting the shoebox at him, "so you have to tell me." Belinda flipped off the lid and handed over the medical bracelet, and then the cards, the prescriptions, the treatment plans. "I have all of this," Belinda said, "and no one is telling me what's going on, and Momma's always working, and I don't feel sick, but . . ."

Doctor Patterson straightened the papers and placed them back in the shoebox beside Belinda.

"Are you feeling sick again, Belinda?"

She nodded. The tears were there, waiting, so she didn't dare speak.

"Can you describe to me how you feel sick?"

"I . . . have episodes."

"Episodes?"

"Like, I black out. But not really. I see stuff. Danny said it's like a seizure, like I'm somewhere else, and sometimes I fall down."

Doctor Patterson's joy had turned to concern. He started jotting down notes on his computer.

"Good, good. I like that you are keeping track of your symptoms. You are seeing things?"

"Am I crazy?"

"Perhaps."

Belinda's tummy clenched. Now she really wanted to cry.

"But, Belinda, my dear. If you are, that's fine. It's not an easy road, but there are treatments for any number of mental illnesses. But I think we are jumping way, way ahead of ourselves. We need to rule out all the possibilities before we consider the presence of mental illness."

"Was that how I was sick before?" Belinda asked. "Mental illness?"

Doctor Patterson finished up typing and looked at Belinda. His face wasn't scared. Maybe a little sad, but pretty peaceful. "No, honey. You had cancer."

What?

"No, I didn't."

"You have been through a lot. And the body and the mind are not exclusive entities, you know. When the body is sick, the mind suffers along with it. A good deal of cancer patients have difficulties with cognition for many reasons. Healing, procedures, medication. The body gets tired, and the mind does, too. Memory issues are not uncommon."

The treatment plans. The prescriptions. The hospital wristband.

"But . . . I remember *none* of it. Doesn't cancer make you super sick?"

Doctor Patterson nodded. "Sure does. And you were super sick, kiddo. We discovered a malignant tumor in your brain. It couldn't be operated on due to the proximity to your brainstem and spinal cord, so we hit it with everything short of nuclear weapons. I thought we were losing the fight, but . . ."

Belinda looked down at her body.

"I got better."

"It would seem so," he said with a smile.

"Seem so?" Belinda was confused. Perhaps more than when she came in. "You didn't know I got better? Did you think I died?"

Did I die?

"I knew you didn't die. I would have heard through the coroner. This is a small town. No, your mother got frustrated with all the treatments. Nothing was working, and you were wasting away. We had exhausted most of our options. She wanted to explore alternative methods, so we discussed a list of homeopaths and new age practices that gave her some hope. I figured it would at least bring her some comfort until it was your time, but it seems your time never came."

Alternative methods.

"I just got better?"

"Doubtful," Doctor Patterson said. "In fact, practically impossible. I've seen some pretty miraculous science in my time, but brain cancer is no joke. Your mother must have found some sort of miracle worker."

Tita.

Aswang.

"And my checkups have been normal?"

"Well, my girl, I haven't seen you since! Your mother popped in, months after the last time I saw you, and she was positively beaming. She said you were on the mend. She told me she was going to bring you by—had an appointment, actually—but the two of you never showed up."

"You . . . shouldn't I have had check-ups?"

"Yes, well . . ."

Though he was still smiling, it wasn't as wide, and had lost some of its warmth.

"I'm not saying you should have . . . I feel fine."

She didn't feel fine, but he looked so guilty.

"Suppose I should have checked, but your mother said she was worried about your immune system . . ."

"No, no. It's okay," Belinda said. But it wasn't.

Doctor Patterson clapped his hands, as if to startle away all guilt and doubt. "You are here now, and you are well! And that makes me so, so happy. But . . . you did come in. The nurse said you started menstruating?"

"Ugh."

"It's perfectly natural," he said.

"So I've been told. A lot."

He laughed. It was genuine. The warmth had returned. "I'm guessing you're having some tummy trouble? Pain? There are medicines for all sorts of symptoms. I can give you some samples, you can try them out, see what works best. And you have a new doctor?"

Belinda shrugged.

"Okay," he said, his bushy white eyebrow rising into an exaggerated arc. "Well, you can go see the new doctor, or I'd be happy to see you, but eventually, you will need to come in for a full physical. A Pap smear. Has your mother talked to you about that?"

Belinda shook her head. So much Momma never bothered to tell her.

"There's time to decide," he said, sketching a note down on a piece of paper. "I'm just pleased to see you looking so, so well."

Belinda didn't know what to do. She had more knowledge, which is what she had come for, but now she didn't know what to do with that knowledge. So, she had been sick, Momma had taken her to see Tita, and Tita did . . . what?

"Thank you for your time," Belinda said, and slid off the table to her feet.

Doctor Patterson followed her lead and stood. "Again, I can't tell you how happy I am to see you. And healthy at that! A miracle."

They strolled down the hall and to the front desk, where Doctor Patterson pulled out his bin of toys and stickers for

Belinda to choose from. She wasn't a baby anymore, so that made her a bit grumpy, but she did like toys and stickers, so it was okay.

"Say hi to your folks for me," he said. "And Danny. How's he doing? Must be off to college by now."

Belinda shook her head. Doctor Patterson got that ice in his smile again.

"He was going to study medicine, I thought. That boy had a spectacular brain for science. Fascinated with medicine. I remember what a chatterbox he was during exams—"

"I gotta go," Belinda said. "Sorry."

Doctor Patterson waved a hand. "No worries, my child. You're probably due back to class. Do you need a note?"

Belinda nodded. She didn't want a note, didn't want to wait around there anymore. But it was no good to tell him that she hadn't gone to school, anyway. That she missed a lot of school. But what did it matter? She must have missed a lot while she was infected with the cancer, too. Not that she remembered any of that.

"Oh!" Doctor Patterson exclaimed as he scrawled a note. "I plum forgot to ask. How's your baby sister? I never did get a chance to meet her."

Belinda blinked. Swallowed, hard.

"Baby sister?"

"Yes! She must be up and walking by now. Makes for a busy house, I would guess."

Sweat bloomed on Belinda's skin like dew on petals, cold and shimmering, but coated in sand that itched every millimeter of her body. Her temperature plummeted, then rose, then plummeted again, fluctuating each time her heart rattled in her chest.

"I don't—"

Now the smile was gone. Neither Doctor Patterson nor his receptionist had any happy left on their faces. It was replaced by horror and pity in equal measure.

"Oh no," Doctor Patterson said as he brought a trembling hand to his face. "I just assumed everything was all right. Mom and babe were both healthy the last time I saw them, when she came in to tell me you were all better—"

"Babe?" Belinda squeaked. "Momma?"

The doctor expelled a long, trembling sigh. "Belinda, when I saw your mother that last time, she was eight months pregnant. I did the ultrasound myself. I didn't realize something had happened. I am so, so sorry."

Belinda grabbed a glow-in-the-dark ring from the toy box, dipped into an awkward curtsy, then bolted for the door. She heard their voices, following behind the closed door, then louder when it opened. They were calling after her as she ran outside, down the street, around the corner.

No.

I have no sister.

I never did.

But then again, she hadn't remembered being sick, either.

She didn't know what to do, where to go. She had to talk to Danny. And he *had* to talk back. She knew about her sickness now, so he'd have to tell her everything. And she'd have to see Tita again, see what miracle or witchcraft the old crone had done to make Belinda all better again.

The world was spinning, and Belinda thought she might be in real danger of flying off the planet if she didn't calm down, slow down, take one step at a time, like Danny always told her to.

It was almost four o'clock. She would go to the school, get on the bus with Carmen, go home.

Belinda had a plan, but she felt awful. Nothing made sense. She didn't trust anyone, least of all herself.

What's happening?
Who am I?
What did Momma do?
What am I?

Belinda pulled her hood over her head and sobbed, snot and tears soaking the fur on her hood as she trotted off towards the school.

17

"Where were you today?" Carmen asked as the bus bounced down the road.

Belinda rested her head against the window. "Doctor."

"Why?" Carmen asked.

"My periods."

"You gotta go to the doctor for that? What do they do about it?"

"I dunno, some pills and stuff."

"Huh."

Belinda stayed pretty quiet most of the way home. Anger brewed in her belly. What would she say to Danny? And more importantly, how would she say it? She was mad, but was she mad at him? Yeah. He was hiding stuff and lying. And that wasn't fair.

Mostly, though, she was mad at Momma. Momma wasn't there. After everything Belinda had supposedly gone through,

Momma wasn't around. And Daddy left, probably because of Momma and because Belinda had been sick. Maybe Daddy was living a new life with a new family. A family that wasn't broken. Or maybe Momma had left with him, and they had a pretty little baby girl that didn't have cancer and didn't have episodes and was perfect in every which way.

Belinda stomped her foot on the floor of the bus, and Carmen jumped.

"What's wrong with you?" Carmen said.

"Periods." That seemed to be a good go-to excuse for everything. And people didn't want to talk about periods, so they left Belinda well enough alone when she even said the word.

What's so scary about blood?

Belinda's mouth watered at the thought. She was terribly hungry again. Which should have been no surprise. It'd been days since she'd actually had a proper meal.

Much to the chagrin of the motley old bus driver, Belinda was on her feet before the bus rolled to a stop at the end of Carmen's drive. Belinda was feeling sick. The diesel fumes from the orange beast combined with the rage swelling inside her made for a grumbly, heaving tummy. As soon as the door opened, Belinda hit the ground running. The fresh air smelled great, and the cool air calmed her nerves. She sprinted towards her house faster than she'd ever run before. For a moment, it was like her feet weren't touching the ground, but she was instead striding upon the billows of dust from the country road. She was a bird, soaring, screaming through the air faster than any girl could.

When she reached her front porch, she wasn't out of breath. No sweat had formed anywhere—not under her nose, not in her pits beneath her cozy, thick hoodie. Her heart was a soft patter peacefully existing in the cage of her ribs.

Belinda was terrified.

What is happening to me?

Am I a vampire?

A quick swipe of the pad of her thumb over her top teeth confirmed that no fangs had sprouted there. But this didn't put Belinda's mind at ease. She stomped into her house and went straight to the fridge. There was a pack of ground beef there thawing from the night before. Danny must have intended to make spaghetti to get her to eat. Spaghetti was her favourite. Belinda tore into the package and shoved a fistful of raw meat into her face. She chewed on it, sucked, swallowed a thick clump of the copper-tasting chuck. She looked at the Styrofoam tray and the smear of blood across the white. Like a cat, she lapped the blood up, savouring the gritty texture and sharp taste on her tongue.

Do vampires have to eat human blood? Is that what I need?

Belinda spit into the sink, then rinsed her mouth with lemon juice. Though the meat was fresh, it tasted spoiled. Tainted. Wrong.

Enough, she told herself. *Be brave, Belinda.*

The words were hers, but also not. Tita's voice chirped in her head, and behind it, the call of a myriad sounds. Creatures, cooing, scratching, ticking, cawing, howling.

Belinda went to Momma's room. The contents of the closet meant something very different now. The baby clothes, all yellow and lavender. Belinda assumed they were hers, but they weren't boxed up, weren't stored away somewhere deep. They were front and center, waiting to be used. Many still had tags on them.

Belinda was crying, and her tears were both angry and sad. Momma didn't want her anymore. Momma had a new little girl now, and they'd gone someplace else, somewhere far away from Belinda and whatever horrible monster she had become.

Tales from Ramnon growled from its spot on the bedside table.

The bed creaked as Belinda lowered herself onto it. She crawled into the middle and pulled the book into her lap. It was soft and warm, like the leather cover was skin, and the pages within were made of muscle, bone, and blood. She breathed, and the book breathed, too, its pages swelling, exhaling with a shudder. Belinda traced the golden letters on the front, and she felt a finger push back, following her movements. When she finally opened the cover, she yelped. She didn't know why. But she had imagined something lunging out at her, a mass of feathers and claws and fangs and talons jumping from within the prison of their cover and feeding on her body.

But there was none of that. Only words printed on onionskin paper that smelled like the woods. It was a medley of pine, the cool freshness of lake water, the aroma of old, musty wood and forest loam. As Belinda flipped the first page, the music of nature ignited, all those beastly sounds harmonizing like a choir, accentuated by the percussion of wooden doors, footsteps, and wind through trees.

There was a table of contents. Belinda allowed her finger to slide down the list, pausing at each name. And each time her finger stopped, the corresponding soloist sang out.

Sluagh.

Wendigo.

Banshee.

Troll.

Vandheks.

Melusine.

Creatures. Some Belinda had read about, or saw on television or in the movies, and others she had never heard of. Her finger kept sliding down the list until she found what she was looking for.

Aswang. Page 482.

As all the other sounds fell silent, one sound remained. A slurping. A loud, glugging swallow. The churning of wet meat being stirred in a plastic bowl.

Belinda turned to page 482 and screamed.

A girl hovered there, in the air on the page, a specter hanging in the night sky. She was gorgeous, with black eyes shining like the sea, dark hair draped over her slender body, entwining with her entrails that floated behind her. On the ground below, next to an obsidian lake, stood the girl's legs, detached from her body at the waist.

Belinda forced her eyes away from the girl, but the girl on the page floated down to the words, pointing an elongated, skeletal finger to the text. As Belinda read, the page girl followed along with that horrible boney finger.

"Aswang. From the annals of Filipino folklore from the sixteenth century, the Aswang is considered a shape-shifting evil spirit. She is ghoul, she is witch, she is vampire."

The page girl's finger moved along the words, her jaw opening and closing as if reading Belinda a bedtime story. Behind the girl, leaking from her severed midsection, was a trail of bile and feces and blood that slithered across the page like a snake.

"Daywalkers. Sun does not hurt the aswang. They feed at night, though, because the gods do not watch at night. When she comes, she uses her music—the *Wak-Wak* sound the aswang makes is like feet walking backwards, so people think she's retreating rather than coming. Sometimes, even, her feet *are* backwards to confuse her prey."

Belinda looked down at her feet. They were not backwards. This was somewhat of a relief. Her eyes returned to the page., which was crinkling under the weight of the illustrated girl.

"Both human and monster, weak during the day, eyes bloodshot from lack of sleep. They love, they hurt, they form deep friendships. They are quiet, shy, kind."

Not so bad, Belinda thought. But as she kept reading, the horror reignited in her guts, swirling like diarrhea and vomit ready to explode.

"... bloodthirsty animals at night, when they need to feed. They attack through rooftops, using a proboscis that extends from their tongue..."

Belinda's trembles turned to violent tremors. The illustrated girl paused, her black eyes finding Belinda's. She gave a smile, exposing sharp, black teeth and a flickering narrow proboscis poking from the tip of her tongue. Belinda redirected her eyes to the words at the end of the bony finger and continued reading.

"... babies. The meat of the unborn. The proboscis pierces the womb, sucking out the fetus..."

The bony finger moved faster, the words flooding Belinda's mind, crashing together like white-water rapids.

"So as not to be discovered, the feeding of the aswang does not immediately kill the victim. Feeding on the fetus causes the mother to shift. The aswang takes the soul with her when she feeds, and the mother is replaced by a shell. A doppelgänger. This replacement will quickly deteriorate, taking their final form as flora or tree."

Sam.

No.

It's not possible.

Belinda looked at her feet again. They were not backwards.

Not backwards, she screamed in her mind as she rolled her ankles around, wiggled her toes. The illustrated girl slapped a rope of intestines on the page, drawing Belinda's attention back to the text.

"During the day, the aswang walks among the humans undetected. Unless you are close enough to see your reflection in her eyes. You will appear, in the eyes of the aswang, to be upside down…"

Belinda thought if she read one more word, she might die of fear. She flipped the page to see how much more information there was on the aswang. The illustrated girl followed, sliding over the page as it turned, settling on the top paragraph of the next page. The movements of her joints—the twist of her wrists and the cock of her head—was accompanied by that *Wak Wak* sound the book had talked about. There were a few more pages of info, which were more pages than Belinda could stomach. Her eyes grazed the pictures instead. Precise, careful drawings, labelled in another language—Filipino, Belinda figured.

An egg, with the silhouette of a chick inside.

A ribbon tied around a woman's belly, below her belly button and above her mound of private hair.

A tube filled with liquid and chunks of solid.

Belinda screamed.

"Belinda?"

With a crash, Belinda slammed the book closed, and when she did, the *Wak Wak* sound intensified, combined with a feral screech of pain.

I crushed her, the illustrated girl.

Good.

Carmen was standing in the doorway, backpack still on her shoulders, eyes wide.

"Belinda, are you okay?"

Belinda shook her head.

"I . . ." Carmen looked at the book, then up at Belinda's face. "You left the bus so quick. Miss Terry was super mad you stood up while she was still moving. You know how she is about it, so she'll probably phone your momma—"

"No, she won't," Belinda said. "She'll call Danny because Momma's never here. She left because I'm a monster."

Belinda threw *Tales from Ramnon* against the wall. The pages fluttered, roared like a steam train, then fell silent and still on the carpet.

"Oh, Belinda." Carmen dropped her backpack on the floor, crawled up on the bed, and hugged Belinda. Belinda let her. "Your momma isn't gone. She's just gone . . . lots."

Belinda sniffled. She knew it was true. Daddy left, but Momma did, too. But Danny wouldn't leave. He would never leave her.

Unless . . .

Belinda pulled back from Carmen and looked her right in the eyes.

"What do you see?" Belinda asked.

"Um, what?"

"What do you see?" Belinda demanded. "In my eyes."

"I . . ."

Carmen took a deep breath, then looked into Belinda's eyes. Stared. Studied.

"What do you see?" Belinda asked, barely a whisper now. She opened her eyes wide, held very still.

"I see, uh, your eyes are dark brown, super bloodshot . . ."

Belinda waited.

"They . . . your lashes are beautiful, Belinda. So long—"

"Not that. In my eyes. *On* them. Do you see yourself?"

"Oh. Yeah, I do. I . . ."

Carmen's brow furrowed.

No.

Belinda knew. It was almost as if she could see through her best friend's eyes.

"Yeah, my reflection, but it's super weird. It's upside down. Is it . . . I've never noticed that before. Is it supposed to be like that?"

Belinda closed her eyes and got off the bed. She was a freak.

An aswang.

"Can we go play at your house?" Belinda asked.

Carmen just stared at her.

"I'd like to go play at your house, please."

Carmen nodded, slowly. "Okay. Yeah, of course, but . . . you're acting real weird, Belinda."

"I don't feel so good."

"Is it your—"

"Periods, yeah. Can we go?"

Carmen slid off the bed, swiped her backpack off the floor, and went out into the hall. She walked all the way down the hall, through the kitchen, and out the front door with her head cranked backwards so she could watch Belinda.

She's afraid of me.

She should be.

I'm a monster.

18

Guilt stung every centimeter of Belinda's skin. Carmen was sobbing. She was terrified and shocked at the sight of her sister, who had obviously changed significantly since Carmen had last seen her that morning before school.

Sam was sitting on the chesterfield with knitting needles in her hands and a half-finished shawl draped across her lap. Belinda stood in the doorway, staring at Sam's eyes. Once hazel, they were now the colour of spoiled milk.

"Sam?" Belinda said.

Sam's jaw shifted, her head tilted, and strands of greasy hair slid off her shoulder and swung beside her shining, oily face.

Click, clack, click, went the knitting needles, back and forth, up and down. But there was no pull through, no loops, no knots. Sam was going through the motions, conducting an opera with the batons in her fingers, but the shawl remained the same: limp, lifeless, and unchanging in Sam's lap.

"Sam?" Carmen parroted as she sat on the chesterfield beside her big sister.

But she's not fat, Belinda thought. She examined Sam's midsection, trying to decide if a real whole baby could have been in there, but it was hard to tell with the shawl blocking the view.

"Sam," Sam said, mimicking Carmen. Then her head jerked to face Carmen and Carmen nearly slid off the cushion.

"Sam?" Carmen repeated, leaning away from her sister.

Sam did not smile that creepy smile like she had out in Belinda's back yard. So that was good, at least. But she was still acting like a weirdo. Her face was expressionless, her lips moving as her mouth spoke silent words. With the yarn and shawl tangled in her lap, Sam looked at her sister while she knit the air.

Click, click, clack.

Belinda took a step forward, knelt, and put her hand on Sam's leg just below the hem of her shorts. She was going to ask Sam a question that only Sam would know the answer to, to see if she was an imposter or not, but Belinda never said a word. As soon as her hand made contact with Sam's skin, Belinda felt the wriggling beneath. The skin on Sam's leg sloughed at the mere touch of Belinda's palm, and when Belinda pulled her hand away, Sam's skin stuck like sap to Belinda's own flesh. Belinda stood and backed away, pulling a large patch of Sam's skin with her as she went. And below that flesh was not blood or muscle, pus or bone. It was sap, viscous and thick, and swimming in that sap were pine beetles writhing, choking, drowning in the tree fluids.

"Go get Danny," Belinda said to Carmen.

But Carmen didn't hear. She was screaming. She grabbed her sister's arms and tried to pull her to her feet, but Sam's arms peeled away like sausage casings, leaving exposed tree branches in their place. Carmen screeched and hollered, and Sam mimicked her, making almost the identical noises as Carmen screamed and screamed until her eyes flipped, rolled to solid white, and Carmen collapsed to the floor.

"Danny!" Belinda cried even though she knew Danny wasn't home.

Sam stood, suddenly, and held her arms, her *branches* out to Belinda. Belinda took a step back and Sam took a step forward, and all her clothes fell off, torn by the sharp branches jutting from her flesh. She was screaming now, but they were no longer imitations of Carmen's screams. She was wailing out her own pain, her own horror. She followed Belinda, reaching for her, pleas for help dripping from her lips like bloody sap.

"Hel—," Sam said. "Ge . . . help!"

Belinda kept backing up. Sam started gagging, then belching, and her branch arms went to her throat as thick vomit poured down the front of her body. But it wasn't vomit. It was insects—maggots, beetles, millepedes, ants, all congealed in the amber fluid coming out of all of Sam's holes. They didn't stay out, though. The bugs that spewed from her mouth and nose rode in dribbles and droplets of the thick goo before scrambling for purchase and crawling over her body and back into her nose, mouth, and up her girl parts.

Sam was choking on her sap and all those insects. Belinda knew she should help, but she didn't want to touch Sam. As they moved through the kitchen, Sam forward and Belinda in reverse, Sam kept bumping into walls and furniture, and when she did, she shed patches of skin, revealing the tree bark and bugs beneath.

Back, back they went, until Belinda bumped into the patio door. She fumbled with the lock for a moment—she didn't want to take her eyes off Sam—but finally got it, and their slow, awkward procession continued to the yard. Belinda backed down the patio steps onto the cool grass. Sam followed, but her feet remained on the top step; they cracked off from her legs at the ankle, and her skin started falling off her bones, dripping off like rotting meat with every step. One breast hung low, then swung as Sam took a step. When it fell from her body and struck the ground, it exploded like a water balloon and showered Belinda with bugs and fluids.

She could taste Sam in her mouth. But it wasn't meat and blood. It wasn't death. It was life. Fresh and crisp—the taste of pine and wood and river water.

They had made it halfway through the yard when Sam started having a seizure. Or at least, that's what it looked like to Belinda. She jerked and twisted this way and that, the stumps of her legs sprouting jagged bones like roots that stabbed down deep into the earth. The sounds coming out of Sam were agonizing. Mewls, pleas for it to stop, bargains for death. The horror was further exemplified by the illumination from oncoming headlights.

Danny!

Belinda ran, making a wide berth around Sam, screaming Danny's name. The truck had barely rolled to a stop when Danny's door flew open, and he came running.

"Belinda!"

"Danny!"

She leapt into his arms, and he lifted her off the ground. Held her tight.

Over his shoulder, she saw the passenger door of the truck swing open.

"Belinda," Danny said as he set her on the ground. "What's happened? Are you all right?"

Belinda could find no words. Warmth blossomed in her pants between her legs as her bladder let go. Her body was a violent tremor, the words flying from her mouth barely intelligible through her screams.

"Danny, don't hate me, I'm sorry, I did that . . . but it will be okay, right? But oh my God, can you help? Help me, Danny! Help! Help Sam!"

At the sound of Sam's name, Danny got a puzzled look on his face. He started towards Sam's house, but Belinda grabbed his arm.

"Belinda, what's happening?" Danny asked. "What's going on?"

Tita stepped up beside Belinda and Danny. But she wasn't looking at the panicked tangle of brother and sister. She was looking past them, into the yard. And her face was a collage of sorrow.

"Oh," Tita said. "Oh."

Danny looked from Tita to Belinda, then out to the yard.

"What?" he demanded. His voice was all high and squeaky, which made Belinda cry even harder.

"I didn't mean to, Danny! I didn't! Don't hate me!"

Danny looked confused, but only for a moment more. Then his confusion turned to something ugly. Something more horrifying than Sam. It was rage Belinda saw on her brother's face, and a pain the likes of which she'd never seen. Danny glared at Tita, then lunged at her. The old woman closed her eyes and stayed still, accepting the impending blow. But Danny stopped just short of striking Tita with a white-knuckled fist. He spit on her face, instead, then walked out to the center of the yard.

Belinda grew very quiet. She listened. She watched. She followed Danny out to Sam, but Sam was no longer Sam. In the place where Sam had stood, suffering and changing only moments before, was a tree. It was slightly taller than Sam had been, but even in the purple light of dusk, Belinda could see that the tree was growing taller as they watched. The insects upon its bark were calm, the sap solidifying, and new green shoots of leaves were sprouting on the ends of Sam's hundreds of new fingers.

Danny touched the tree. Caressed the bark. Smelled the leaves.

Tita had followed but stood back. Danny would not take his eyes off the tree. Now it was his lips that were moving, just like Sam's, moving but making no sound for Belinda's ears to hear.

"Danny?" Belinda had never felt so upset in all her life. He would surely hate her now. Not only did Momma and Daddy run away because she was a monster, but she killed Danny's girlfriend and he would leave, too.

Danny stuttered. "Is this . . ." he shuffled his feet so he could face Tita. "She was . . . Sam was . . ."

"I'm so sorry, my boy," Tita said.

"Sam was pregnant?" Danny asked.

Tita's nod was slight, but Danny saw, nonetheless.

The feral bray that exploded from Danny's throat made Belinda scream as well. He sobbed, he choked on his tears, he vomited on the grass at the new tree's feet. Tita stood by, silent and stoic, while Belinda watched her brother's pain blasting from his soul. He sat, crossed-legged on the ground in front of the tree, and rocked. Words came from his mouth, rapid and manic, but Belinda could not understand a single one.

She couldn't take it anymore.

"I wish I had died!" Belinda screamed.

Both Tita and Danny looked at Belinda. Danny's face was swollen and red with sorrow, but his eyes were wide with surprise.

"Don't worry, Danny," Belinda cried. "I hate me, too! I wish the cancer would have ate me right up, put everyone out of the misery of having to have me around."

Belinda started slapping her own face. Ripping at her own hair. When Danny stood and tried to stop her, to embrace her in a hug, Belinda wrenched away, and bit chunks out of her own arms. She was furious with herself—*hated* herself—and wanted this all to end. For everyone's sake, especially Danny's.

A strong hand grabbed Belinda by the ear.

"Come," Tita said.

It wasn't a question. Tita hauled Belinda across the grass by her ear. Belinda fought, and when her ear started to tear away from her head, Tita grabbed a fistful of her hair. Belinda struggled, punched, kicked, bit. Finally, Tita'd had enough, and dropped Belinda on the grass. Belinda was about to scramble up and run away into her house where she would drink every bit of bleach she could find, but Tita was not done. Tita was going to get Belinda to wherever she intended her to go. With a ripping squelch, Tita's body separated in two. Her legs remained standing on the grass as her upper half swooped down like a raven and plucked Belinda off the ground. Tita hoisted Belinda up into the air and flew, her entrails streaming behind, dripping gore over the grass as they passed over Sam's yard, then Belinda's, until they came to rest along the edge of the woods, where Tita threw Belinda on the ground.

"Ouch!" Belinda yelped.

"Settle yourself, child," Tita scolded. "Wait here. Your

brother needs a talking to. You both do, but someone else can manage you."

"But—"

Before Belinda could argue, Tita pulled a vial of sand out of her pocket. Belinda recognized it straight away. It was her vial, full of purple, glittering sand. Tita popped out the cork and threw the sand in Belinda's face. It was excruciating. Sand scraped Belinda's eyes, coated her tongue, filled all her organs. She was choking, screaming, coughing sand into the air. She dropped to the ground, clawed at her face, spit out endless lumps of sand. Finally, the scratchiness subsided, and Belinda drew a deep, clean breath. She put her palms on the ground, pressed herself up. The ground moved beneath her. It was soft sand. She blink, blink, blinked. Opened her eyes. It was no longer purple dusk. The world around her was washed out in muted sepia, and she was surrounded by buildings—cozy log cabins. The air smelled of wood stoves and tasted of ash. And the sounds of a myriad foreign tongues spoke all around her. She was too scared to look, but she spied snippets. A feather here, scales there. A little man, smaller than her hand, wearing a black bowler cap, skittered by like a cockroach. In the trees, which were lifeless and black as charred flesh, sat birds bigger than the tallest men she had ever seen.

A few meters from where Belinda lay in the sand, saloon doors on a wooden building swung opening, emitting a squeal like claws on bone. Belinda stood. Walked forward. Went inside.

Saoirse was sitting at the bar with a tall drink in her hand, engaged in a lively discussion with the barkeep. The barkeep was beautiful, with dark chocolate skin and super big boobs squeezed into a lavender corset. Another woman sat beside Saoirse. This woman was also quite pretty, but in a subtle way, with short hair and a peach smile. When the saloon doors swung shut, their wood clapping together, all three women looked her way.

"Aye," Saoirse said. "There she be."

The bartender winked at Saoirse, and Saoirse slid off her seat.

"Well, I'll let you kids be," Saoirse said.

Belinda barely knew her, but she wanted Saoirse to stay. She was the only one in this strange place that Belinda recognized.

"Please, stay!" Belinda cried.

"Na!" Saoirse squawked. "I'm too Christing old to be talkin' about fetuses and goddarn chickens."

The short-haired woman at the bar slapped Saoirse on the arm, and Saoirse muttered something nasty under her breath before she sidled off into some other room deeper in the saloon.

Belinda was terrified. She didn't move. The short-haired woman was the only person left in the saloon. She didn't look dangerous, or like some sort of foul creature, but she was a stranger, and Danny said never to talk to strangers.

The thought of Danny crawled up Belinda's throat like a boulder, wedging there and forcing out tears.

"Come now," the woman said. Her voice was gentle, warm, and inviting. "Sit."

The woman left the bar and took a seat at a lower table. She pulled a chair out and patted it. Belinda was tired. So tired. She sat.

"May I touch your hand, Belinda?"

Belinda nodded. She had nothing left. If this woman wanted to eat her, so be it. She'd be better off ate and shat out than being Belinda anymore. Belinda was a monster.

The woman's hands were warm and soft. She held Belinda's hand in one of her own and stroked it with the other.

"It's okay, Belinda. You'll be okay."

"Who are you?" Belinda asked as tears leaked from her eyes. "Where am I?" Belinda asked, even though she already knew.

"I'm Nell," the woman said. "Welcome to Ramnon."

19

Belinda and Nell sat quietly together at the table in the saloon. They had been talking forever—at least, that's what it felt like to Belinda. Nell had offered her something to eat and drink several times, but Belinda had declined. Food was disgusting.

"Belinda," Nell said in a voice sweet as honey. "We have your kind of food here. In a glass, or a bowl, or something that will help you feel less sad or scared."

Belinda didn't want to drink blood. To eat people meat. It was gross, and it was cruel, and she didn't want to be this vampire ghoul thing. Nell had explained it all to her—all the same stuff Belinda had read in the Ramnon book, only in more detail.

"So, I'm stuck here," Belinda said. "In Ramnon."

Nell took a moment, then answered, "No. It's a safe space for you, though, while you find yourself. We can all come and go as we please, but this is home."

Belinda thought about it. About Tita in the vendor tent at the carnival, in her school cafeteria, about Saoirse cussing over tea.

"You can all come and go? All the creatures?"

Nell nodded.

"But how?"

"We learn," Nell said.

"But why?"

"Many reasons."

"Are they alive, the other creatures?"

"Yes and no."

Belinda studied Nell's face. Her skin was smooth, her smile quiet, her hair a fluff atop her head. Simple beauty.

"What are you?" Belinda asked.

Nell was quiet. She sipped a steaming cup. It smelled like flowers.

"I am just a woman," Nell said. "But I died. I was saved by coming here. I go back to the before-life during the day. I was a nurse, and I continue to help people . . . medically."

Belinda was confused. Her face must have showed it because Nell continued.

"I suppose I'm a ghost," Nell said. "I have more good to offer the world, and this place allows me to do that. To return."

"As a ghost."

"I suppose so. I have a connection to Ramnon. To the beasts here. My husband was a wendigo."

"What?"

Nell smiled. "That's a story for another time."

"So . . ." Belinda looked around the saloon. She tried to see out the windows, but they were yellowed and dark, just like the world outside. "Am I . . . am I dead now, too?"

Nell shook her head. "No, honey."

"But I live here now?"

Nell considered this, took another sip. "It's a safe place for you, Belinda."

"But my home. My school. Carmen." Pain flared in Belinda's chest. A swelling, unbearable sorrow. "Danny."

Nell reached across the table and put her hand on Belinda's. "Belinda, you are aswang. And you are so very young. Do you think you could still live there, like you are?"

Belinda looked down at her belly. Ran her hands across it, wondering precisely where she detaches from her legs.

"How did this happen?"

"In your case? It was a ritual," Nell said. "Tita is Filipino. Also, she's an aswang. She serves the before-life—your world—as a healer. Your mother came to her seeking help when you were sick."

"Cancer," Belinda mumbled.

"Yes. Stage four. There was no hope, not in your world. But Tita knew a way. She tied a fertilized chicken egg around your belly with a ribbon. When the chicken passed from the egg to inside you, you became aswang."

The ribbon. The chick. The cafeteria. Belinda hadn't been seeing things. She'd been *remembering* them.

"I killed my brother's baby," Belinda said. "I . . . ate it out of Sam."

Nell's voice was quiet. Soft. Sad. "I know."

Belinda cried. She didn't think it was possible to have any more tears left in her body, but they flowed like rivers dirty with murdered baby blood.

"So . . . what? I grow up here?"

"You won't grow up, Belinda. You are what you will always be."

Belinda wanted to die. To rot to dust, like the bodies in the cemetery. How wonderful, that finality. But she was stuck being a gross vampire thing.

"Aswang often live there, in the real world," Nell said. "But they are experienced and wise. They know to feed far from home to avoid suspicion. An aswang could live in the before life if they had someone to guide them—"

"I can't kill babies and people."

"I know."

Nell was quiet. Belinda was, too. She thought about her room and all her stuff. The books she liked to read, the books she would never get to read. She thought about her ambition to have a farm and all the animals. She remembered Danny cooking her breakfast. Though periods sounded just awful, she never even got to have one, or do the sex.

Belinda wept. Nell moved her chair next to Belinda and hugged her.

"Do you miss your home?" Belinda asked.

"No," Nell said, without hesitation. "I am lonely here sometimes, but I might meet someone to share my life with here, in a way. I like this home better. My home wasn't good."

"Mine is good," Belinda said. "*Was* good. Now Danny hates me, and I have nothing left, and I wish I could just die and have it all over with."

The thought of Danny hating her was too much to handle. Belinda pushed back from the table and yanked away from Nell. Nell didn't resist. Belinda raged around the saloon, crying, howling, cursing her life, her death, her everything. Belinda couldn't breathe, couldn't think clearly. She wanted out, away from the saloon, away from Ramnon. She burst out of the swinging doors and ran down the street, dodging humans with wolf faces, beasts with racks the size of oak trees, women flying, hair and tails floating behind them. She ran by a fountain with a stone woman with snakes for hair and bloody water pouring out of her vagina into a marble pool below. Belinda ran and ran until a ticking sound approached, growing louder, closer, until it was a loud WAKWAKWAK in her ears and head and bones. Tita swooped down, her intestines drooping down and dragging bloody lines in the sand as she plucked Belinda off her feet and into the sky.

20

Belinda woke at the base of the tree in her yard. The scent of Ramnon was fresh in her nose, its taste pungent on her tongue. Someone was holding her hand.

Nell?

Tita?

It wasn't Nell. Or Tita. The hand was larger, stronger, achingly familiar.

"Danny."

He was holding her. She didn't dare look up at him. She didn't want to see the hatred in his eyes.

"Danny, I'm sorry."

Danny held her tighter.

"I love you, butthole," he said.

He was crying, but he didn't sound mad. Belinda sat up, rolled onto her knees, and looked into Danny's eyes. Lots of sad, but no mad.

"Do you hate me?" Belinda asked.

He laughed, then a sob escaped. "Never. I would never hate you."

"But I . . ." Belinda looked towards the neighbouring yard at the new tree rooted in the ground. It was still night, and the moonlight shone silver off Sam's leaves.

Danny did not look over. He was too upset still, Belinda supposed.

"You are too young," Danny said. "It's all too much. No one can blame you for what you didn't know. Didn't understand."

Belinda struggled to find the words because she could barely believe them herself.

"Danny, I'm an aswang."

"I know."

"Did you know all along?"

He nodded. "You were sick, Bell. So sick. Momma and Daddy were devastated, but Momma . . . She adored you, Bell. She was prepared to do anything for you."

Belinda ran a finger over her belly, imagined the ribbon tied there.

"Nell told me. 'Bout Momma making the deal."

Danny scratched the dirt with a stick, doodling out his emotions.

"She thought it was best," he said.

"You know about Ramnon?"

Danny nodded.

"Have you been?"

Danny looked up at her. Cocked his head. "People don't just go there. Not unless they're dead, or . . . something else."

Belinda looked down at her hands. They were girl hands, pink and soft, with glittery nail polish at the end of her slender fingers. "Something like me. A monster."

Danny set the stick down and took Belinda's hand. "You aren't a monster, Belinda."

"I killed Sam."

Danny choked. A sob, maybe something angrier, but he composed himself quick. "Yeah. But you didn't mean to. It's not like that."

"I wish you'd told me . . . no, that's not right. *Momma* should have told me. She made me the monster, so she's the one who shoulda told me about it." Belinda stood and balled her small girl hands into fists, willing them to become a monster's talons. "How dare she? How *dare* she do this to me?"

"Belinda, she saved you."

"And then what? She didn't like what I became? So, she took Daddy, and they ran away with their perfect, not-sick, not-monster baby?"

Danny's eyes grew wide. His mouth dropped open.

Belinda's chest was heaving, racked with sobs and screams and sadness and anger. "Yeah, I know, Danny. Doctor Patterson told me. I changed, and Momma was pregnant, and they ran away, and I hate her!"

Danny shook his head.

"I do!" Belinda screeched. "I do hate her!"

"No," Danny said.

"Yes!" Belinda screamed but stilled at the sight of Danny's face. It wasn't shocked, like it usually was when Belinda shouted, which was not very often. It was sad. So very sad. "Danny, what?"

Danny's head kept shaking. His words spilled out, cotton whispers. "Momma never left."

Belinda let his words spin round and round her head before they settled. They made no sense, those words. Momma was gone. How long had it been since Belinda had seen her? She didn't remember being sick, and she didn't remember Momma's big belly...

No.

Belinda looked across the yard at the Sam tree. Its baby buds were bursting out of the branches. In contrast, the wide leaves above Belinda's head rustled like voices. *A* voice.

NO.

Belinda took a step. Then another, until she was pressed up against the tree. She closed her eyes. Pressed her cheek into the bark. Breathed in, and smelled the wood and the sap, but also Momma's honey lotion and lavender shampoo.

Belinda remembered.

Momma on her bed, eyes moving back and forth beneath eyelids soft and pink as petals.

Belinda on the roof, proboscis pierced through shingle and wood and womb, drinking her sister.

Momma, jagged and disjointed, creaking out into the back yard.

"Belinda," Danny said.

He was on his feet now. His hands were on Belinda's shoulders, holding firm, keeping her from collapsing.

"Momma?" Belinda cried.

She yanked away from Danny and looked up at the sky. The giant tree was there, watching, her leaves rustling out a lullaby into the starry night. How many times had Belinda leaned against that tree, reading a book, telling her secrets to its wood? How safe she had felt there. Calm and warm and wanted.

"Momma knew what could happen," Danny said. "It was worth it. *You* were worth it, Belinda."

"I killed her!"

Danny gulped a deep breath. "You *changed* her. Just like you changed Sam. And you couldn't help it. You didn't know, and it was instinct—"

"I'll never grow up, Danny! I am cursed to be here, stuck in this little baby body. I'll never get my periods, never have the sex. Carmen is gonna grow old and get married and have old lady bridge parties, and I can't even buy alcohol!"

Danny was crying now. Though there was no wind, the tree above rustled violently, swaying with emotion.

"I never, ever got to live!" Belinda said. "This was all for nothing! All of it! And what do I have left, Danny? You're gonna grow old, and I'm gonna be a monster, and I'm gonna be all alone!"

"She was too young." Tita sidled up to the tree. "And you're right, young sprite. Perhaps we should have told you. But that was so much trauma for your young mind. I suppose there wasn't a right answer. Only a mother's soul-deep love and need to protect her cub."

Belinda screamed. Fell to her knees.

Tita and Danny locked eyes. Belinda watched some sort of conversation transpire between them in that gaze. Words that had been said already, now repeated by each other's eyes.

"There is no wrong choice," Tita said to Danny, then she dipped her head and walked away.

Belinda curled up into the fetal position. She rocked, she hummed Momma's lullaby, but no amount of distraction could take away her anxiety. Her life was gone.

Danny's hands felt lovely on her shoulders. She cried, knowing she wouldn't feel those hands forever. Knowing she would have to move on to Ramnon, or stay here, but she had lost her life. No point in school, in friendship, in anything.

Danny pressed on Belinda, rolling her onto her back. She

looked up at his face. It was calm, peaceful, a beacon of hope in a storm of death. The trees overtop danced and shimmied behind him as he leaned over Belinda, pressing into her for what felt like a final hug.

Maybe he'll kill me.

Maybe he can end this, and it will all be over forever.

"I love you," Danny whispered into Belinda's ear. His voice was wet and sweet and safe.

He pulled back, looked into her eyes. It was creepy, the way he hovered over her face like he was going to plant a kiss on her.

And then he did.

With gentle force, Danny sealed his lips around Belinda's. She was too startled to react. They stayed locked that way for several moments, with Danny taking deep breaths and returning powerful exhales in and out of Belinda until a rock formed in Belinda's guts. That lump wriggled and wretched, and pain shot through every fiber of Belinda's being. The lump slithered, swelled, moved upwards until Belinda couldn't breathe because it was lodged in her throat. She tried to pull away from Danny, to gasp for air, but he put his hands on her face and held her in place. The lump birthed from her throat into her mouth, allowing air to pass into her lungs. She felt the lump, soft and squishy, writhing and squirming in her mouth. She could feel Danny's tongue, too. It was rough and thick and gross. And he was poking at the lump, stroking at it like she was. The softness was wet and stringy and tasted of blood, and finally, Belinda realized what it was.

The chick gave a wet chirp as it passed from Belinda's mouth to Danny's. Danny let go of Belinda's face and sat back with his hands pressed over his mouth, holding the chick in. He closed his eyes. Took a loud breath in through his nose. Swallowed.

The chick moved down Danny's throat in a pulsing lump, and he panicked, gulping for air that would not pass. It was over quickly, though, and Danny shuddered a sigh of release.

"What did you do?" Belinda screamed. "What did you do?!"

Danny's eyes fluttered and he sank against the tree, and his head lolled to the side, his feather-coated tongue hanging from his mouth.

Their mother's leaves above rustled a lullaby as Belinda crawled into Danny's arms and held him as he'd held her for all her life.

21

The stick in Belinda's hand was hard and cold, and it shook as she etched a line through her little town of dirt and rocks and branches until she came to a stop at the saloon. With the tip of her stick, she tapped the little door once, twice, three times, hoping someone would materialize, come out of that tiny tavern, and swell to real-life size and help her out of this mess.

"I love you, butthole," Danny said.

Belinda wanted to tell him that she loved him, too. But her throat was a solid clump of tears.

It was dark outside. Belinda loved dark nights, when the sky was clear, and the moon was shining silver cascades of light onto the navy lawn. Belinda would have loved this night if it were any other night, but it wasn't. This was the night her brother traded his life for hers.

"It doesn't hurt," he said.

She didn't believe him. He shifted, his hands squeezing his body, touching his own stomach.

"You hungry yet?" Belinda asked.

Danny shook his head.

Another lie.

"Why'd you do it, Danny?"

He leaned forward and wrapped his arm around her.

"Because I promised," Danny said. "I promised you I'd always keep you safe."

"But how will you—"

"It will take some getting used to," Danny said. "But I have more control than you. I know what I am, and what I . . . need."

Belinda's tummy flipped. "You can't, Danny."

"Can't what?"

"Eat people. It's wrong."

He nodded. "Yeah. It is. But there's a way."

Belinda's head snapped up. "No murder, Danny!"

He smiled, but it was weak. Unsure. "No murder. I promise."

"Then how—"

"It'll be fine—"

"Who's gonna take care of me, Danny?" Belinda's body convulsed with sobs, her voice crescendoing to a sharp pitch. "What am I gonna do when you're flying around with your legs in your bedroom and your body . . ."

"Stop," Danny said. "Look. I will take care of you until you are old enough to take care of yourself. You will grow up, and have a career, and rule the world, okay?"

Belinda wasn't convinced. She didn't understand how any of this was gonna work.

"I can stay here," Danny said. "I will have . . . help."

Belinda looked over at Carmen's house. The police were there, asking questions about Sam, Belinda supposed. After Carmen had woken up, she called her parents, who rushed home. Carmen remembered Sam acting strangely, then she was gone, and that was that. A missing person. Belinda felt awful about that, and she could tell Danny felt worse. He'd probably have some trouble to deal with—he was her boyfriend, after all. But no one would ever really know what happened. No one but her, and Danny, and Ramnon.

"Who's gonna help us, Danny?"

Danny's head tilted as he looked down at the little model of Ramnon. Belinda looked, too, and in her mind's eye she saw the saloon door swing open, and a woman standing there, watching, listening.

"You will be just fine, Belinda. You will grow up, and be normal and happy and healthy, just like we always wanted. And I'll be right here with you until the end and beyond."

22
EPILOGUE

It was the fourth appointment of the week. It was a small town, but it served all the outlying areas, so it maintained a steady business.

Nell washed her hands. Donned her surgical gear. Went in.

She spoke to the young woman. Calmed her, supported her.

The anesthesiologist administered medication to help her to sleep.

This one was further along; Nell opted for dilation and curettage rather than suction-aspiration to avoid any medical complications.

Nell performed her work with precision and care for the woman beneath her instruments. The fetus, placenta, and membranes were set on a stainless-steel tray beside the woman. Nell tended to the woman swiftly, ensuring she was healthy and ready to wake.

"Give me a moment to dispose of this before you bring her around," Nell said to the anesthesiologist.

Nell put the remains in a medical waste bag. Carried it out of the operating room, down the hall, and into a small office at the back of the house.

Danny waited there, floating near the top of her bookcase, his long, black fingers scraping over the spines of her volumes of books.

"You're welcome to borrow any of them you like," Nell said.

Danny smiled, his black lips parting from ear to ear, revealing sharp teeth and a proboscis tongue. Nell handed him the medical waste bag. Though hungry, he was careful to be polite and tidy; he drank his meal with the utmost care, not splashing a single drop outside the bag. Nell took the bag from him and nodded. He would need no more until next week.

Nell returned to the woman. The woman was roused awake. The woman cried while Nell held her hand, and they talked about life and death. The woman had a great support system. Nell wasn't worried. Not all were as lucky as this one.

⁂

BELINDA WAITED ON THE PORCH. IT HAD BEEN A LONG DAY and her bones were tired. Squeals of laughter surrounded Momma Tree as Belinda's grandchildren raced and frolicked, playing some sort of game with wands and swords and glorious magic. Belinda's daughter and son-in-law were huddled next to the fire pit, foreheads pert near touching, whispering sweet nothings to each other.

The wind picked up. Belinda could smell sweet sugar and the sharp tang of copper on the breeze.

"Danny."

He appeared at the side of the house with Timbits and coffees in his arms.

Belinda smiled. They embraced. In contrast to Danny's eternal youth, his glow, his muscle and height, Belinda was bent and bowed, a wisp of the woman she'd once been.

"Hey, Bell. How is everyone?"

Belinda motioned to the yard. Sparks from the fire floated in the air like faeries, and the children squealed like fae themselves. "Magical," she said.

Danny smiled.

They sat on the porch together, and he handed Belinda her coffee.

"How was work today?" Belinda asked.

"Busy."

Belinda said no more. He was full and satisfied, and that was good. Though he never got to go to medical school in his before life, because of her, he was able to fulfill that dream in his own way. In his afterlife.

Danny held Belinda's hand, and she held his. She wished to visit Ramnon, see the place that he and Nell called home. He told her tales of a log cabin with a fire that was always burning. A place where he had many friends, and nights full of singing and dancing and drinking.

Danny smiled. They both looked up at the leaves on the giant tree that shaded her great-grandchildren below. In the distance, Belinda could hear the sounds of merriment—caws, growls, chitters, wails. They no longer scared her. They welcomed her.

Life beyond life.

Ramnon.

ABOUT THE AUTHOR

Jae Mazer is a Canadian who was born in Victoria, British Columbia, and grew up in the prairies of Northern Alberta. After spending the majority of her life battling sasquatches in the Great White North, she migrated south to Texas to have a go at the armadillos. She is a connoisseur and creator of gothic horror, splatterfolk, splatterotica, and folk horror. She's degreed, won awards, been in anthologies, owns a couple of breweries, has chameleon hair and lots of skin ink, and enjoys mustard and alcohol.

ALSO BY JAE MAZER

Novels

- Landing in Eden
- Delivery
- Pal Tailor
- Gahl's Door
- Chrysalis and Clan
- Notch (written as J.M. Adler)
- Crone: A Witch's Tale
- Beautiful Beasts: A Collection of Visceral Horror
- Ripples of Silence (co-authored with Gerry Mazer)
- Tales from the Den (co-authored with Jessica Raney)
- The Sisters Three
- The Tales from Ramnon Novellas: The Feathered, The Consumed, The Wailed, The Gutted
- Mister Picket Blackmaw

Inclusion in Magazines and Anthologies:

- *The Wish* in Sicklit Magazine
- *Flight of the Crow* in Eclectically Heroic by Inklings Publishing
- *The Waif and the Witch* in Hair-Raising Tales of Villainous Confessions by Madgirl Publishing
- *Hurt* in Hair-Raising Tales of Villainous Confessions by Madgirl Publishing

- *The Ballad of Big Sammy Purdue* In Monster Party
- *Death Served* in Books of Horror Volume 1
- *Of Your Own Creation* in Books of Horror Volume 2
- *Mozart in the Flames* in Books of Horror Volume 3, Part One
- *Blubber Murray* in Twisted Legends by Crimson Pinnacle Press
- *I Didn't Hate This Goodbye,* in Dead Heat by Crimson Pinnacle Press
- *Aisle Four, in Trapped: A Dark Dozen Anthology*
- *Behold, Death Arrives, a Duet of Ash and Fang*, in These Lingering Shadows, A Last Waltz Anthology.

www.ingramcontent.com/pod-product-compliance
Lightning Source LLC
LaVergne TN
LVHW031604060526
838201LV00063B/4723